W9-CEM-284

THE CONTRARIANS

Also by Gary Sernovitz

Great American Plain

THE
CONTRARIANS

a novel

Gary Sernovitz

PICADOR

HENRY HOLT AND COMPANY

NEW YORK

THE CONTRARIANS. Copyright © 2002 by Gary Sernovitz. All rights reserved. Printed in the United States of America. No part of this book may be used or reproduced in any manner whatsoever without written permission except in the case of brief quotations embodied in critical articles or reviews. For information, address Picador, 175 Fifth Avenue, New York, N.Y. 10010.

www.picadorusa.com

Picador® is a U.S. registered trademark and is used by Henry Holt and Company under license from Pan Books Limited.

For information on Picador Reading Group Guides, as well as ordering, please contact the Trade Marketing department at St. Martin's Press.
Phone: 1-800-221-7945 extension 763
Fax: 212-677-7456
E-mail: trademarketing@stmartins.com

Design by Kelly S. Too

Library of Congress Cataloging-in-Publication Data

Sernovitz, Gary.
    The contrarians : a novel / Gary Sernovitz
       p. cm.
    ISBN 0-312-42183-4
    1. Stockbrokers—Fiction. I. Title.

    PS3619.E76 C66 2002
    813'.6—dc21   2002017202

First published in the United States by Henry Holt and Company, LLC

First Picador Edition: September 2003

10 9 8 7 6 5 4 3 2 1

To Rick Greenberg, Liam Garland,
Brian Eyster, and Alex Krulic,
friends and influences

BOOK ONE

· 1 ·

They argued there, from the first. The men who had built that institution had perfected their disputation in the alcoves of city colleges where sectarian rages bloomed, where truth and beauty and wit were weapons, and woe to those who compromised—they did not take their integrity seriously. The men had learned their disputation from their fathers and grandfathers, on Delancey, in Brownsville, who had argued about God and, later, God knows what. Freshler Feld had turned gray and agnostic and important in the eighty years since it was founded. The arguments, the arguers had become less shrill, the sport overtaking the subject (good-bye beauty), and the wavy coal-colored hair had passed through a polyglot prism; all hairs and skins and sexes filled the institution now. Yet a fume of the old spirit remained, hazed into inhabitant by inhabitant, an air that was a stone to sharpen your knife.

Or maybe it was just science, atomic mechanics. Fill a room with punchers and hoodlums, and eventually you'll have a fistfight. Fill a cafeteria with straight-A'ers and valedictorians, self-assured whiz kids and unsecured strivers, and eventually, always, uninterruptedly, you'll produce an argument.

The basement cafeteria of the previous headquarters had further and unintentionally encouraged the contrarians: its fluorescent ceiling, famously low, dampened most sounds. You could hear a colleague accuse you of delusion from across the table, but you couldn't hear the same dart ten feet away. When the company moved four years ago to its new headquarters, halfway between the Exchange and one of its main rivals, the new cafeteria produced the same end from different architecture. A proud advance over the rest of Broad Street's cream stone and aquatint glass, Freshler Feld's new headquarters was enskinned and stuffed in international high-tech. In the cafeteria (floors four and five), across from the outside windows, thirty televisions silently broadcast market reports and business news. Two screens each were embedded between fifteen tapered buttresses that formed the wall side of a series of thin triumphal arches and half-shielded one table from the next. A lucite walkway, midnight blue and bulb-speckled, ran through the center of the cafeteria and scored the footsteps into a human ticker tape.

Three were sitting at one of the little-prized tables, on the television side. Nathanson insisted—he only knew how to insist—that it had to have been Kelch, but David Kim refused to accept it. Nathanson drew in his lips, glared, and reached for his spoon. He flipped his necktie, bought that season, aggressive orange with navy dots, over his shoulder to protect his investment from the soup. Kim and Einstadt watched him steadily spoon in the soup and clearly heard his message: shrimp bisque (even from the cafeteria) supplies a better conversation than you two. Nathanson forgave Einstadt: he had been at Freshler for only two months. And, granted, Kim was Kim and had been Kim since they had started at the firm together six years ago—a jungle herbivore, an amiable bystander, often a butt, whose soul had never absorbed the need for unconditional surrender. Nathanson finished his spoonful. "Now, Kim, act rationally for once and don't, *don't* start an argument for the sake of arguing."

Above a sandwich entering his mouth, Einstadt's blue eyes, incongruous with his skin's sandy coloring, smiled. Nathanson, who did not notice this, decided, exasperated by Kim, to cellophane-wrap his half sandwich and finish it at his desk. He ate there more and more these days, with his and Torvil's and Kelch's and Kim's schedules never synchronized, all of them on the road a fifth of the year. Even when they were all in town, their lunchtime discussions tended toward the pale and bloodless, not like those old battles when their faces seemed colored by warpaint shadows cast by a cafeteria arch. But except for himself, Nathanson mourned, all the decent warriors were gone: gone to lesser rivals for on-the-cheap promotions, gone to upstart foreign banks for double the salary, to asset managers or private equity firms for a better lifestyle, to London or Hong Kong for an acceleration, two years of rocket fuel, on their ascent through Equity Strategy and Research. And in the last two years, as the boom turned exponential, a few of his peers had gone to technology firms, most of them Freshler clients, for the indiscriminately ladled options. Even the ones who stayed told Nathanson, You don't owe Freshler anything. If anyone offers you a dollar more, take it and go. And so most of his friends, his *work* friends, had left the Broad Street nursery, and he was stuck arguing the obvious with David Kim. He would have claimed his ribbon of victory already, but the current issue was important. "Kim, did you even read the article?" Late last night, Nathanson had called Kim at home and ordered him to buy the magazine and read it. And no, it couldn't wait until tomorrow.

"We all read it, okay," Kim answered, looking to Einstadt, who didn't catch the shift in Kim's eyes. Kim then turned his entire head to Einstadt, and Nathanson followed. Einstadt, good-mannered, flickered his finger between chin and nose. *I read it.* But my mouth's full.

"If you read it"—Nathanson spoke louder, his rising volume not slowed by his clenched teeth—"how can you then possibly, *possibly* believe it's not him?"

"Come on. Can you really see *Kelch* talking to some guy that long?"

It was a good point, Nathanson allowed, to himself. He picked at the meat in his sandwich and sneered. "That's completely irrelevant."

"I just didn't see it, Nathanson."

"Then you didn't read it closely enough."

"I read it as closely as you did." Kim had circled the *I* and *you* in a field of emphasis, and separation.

"You didn't. Trust me."

"What do you want me to say?" Kim leaned nearer the table, his mouth open, willing to receive Nathanson's sermon, its sustaining truth. Abruptly, he sat at attention—the man approaching said, "Mr. Kim"—and nodded his head. Nathanson turned, looked, and received "Mr. Nathanson." Once the greeter had passed through three arches, Nathanson turned to the others. In a singsong mock: "Mr. Asshole."

As Kim—and Nathanson—chuckled, Einstadt asked, "Who was that?"

"This guy in Institutional Sales, Lumquist or Humquist—"

"Holmquist," Kim corrected by routine. Nathanson would forget his own mother's name if it served a moment's purpose.

"Yes, yes, yes. *Holm*quist. Anyway, this asshole comes out of business school last year, and like the rest of these morons, no offense"— Einstadt: none taken—"he can barely wrap his puny mind around such difficult concepts as the P/E ratio. The guy must have majored in power networking because he comes up to Torvil out of the blue and asks him out to dinner and tells him to invite some other 'rising star' analysts. So Kim, Torvil, Kelch, and I go—"

"To Padison's," Kim contributed.

"Right, *Padi*son's," Nathanson drew the cliché out of the first syllable. "This guy turns out to be the European grand champion of ass kissing. He was laying it on so thick that I was almost incapable of eating my food. Grade-A crap like 'The part of my job that I'm most excited about is becoming close to the young superstars of the firm.' And what was it? Oh, yes: 'I really think that absorbing fundamental research will be my strength as a salesman.' He said that, 'absorbing,' like he's a roll of fucking paper towels. And then this schmuck asks us for ideas, and after I give him my best one at the time, TLB—I'll never forget this—he responds in this completely ingratiating Euro-accent, 'Great, great but too long-term.' Again and again, with Kelch and Torvil, the same line, 'Great, great but too long-term.' Eventually, he interrupts 'Mr.' Kim so he can recite his private theory on the New Economy, which he probably read in *Sports Illustrated* or on a box of Raisin Bran." Kim continued to nod enthusiastically. "He was making absolutely no sense, but that didn't stop him from babbling on. And the sum total of this dissertation was some pig with a cockamamie ticker, BQFD, BQ . . ."

"BQQD."

"Yes, yes, BQQD—two Q's, mind you—which is now down, by the way, about eighty percent."

Einstadt's mouth joined his eyes in a reasonable, shallow smile, but he didn't laugh, which surprised Nathanson. Nathanson had told the Holmquist story a half dozen times before, usually in a much longer version, with his clown-Nazi accent for the Swede becoming more excitable and wild with each subsequent *great, great but too long-term*. Nathanson's storytelling posture had rubberized his arms and legs, but now, as he looked across to Kim, who had heard the story four of the six times, he regrouped in a taped-tight package. He cupped the styrofoam bowl of soup with more force than the bowl could, in the long term, take. "I have to go upstairs," he addressed Kim. "Unlike you, I don't eat lunch for a living. So just for my own peace of mind, so I can salvage any bit of respect for your obviously limited intellectual capabilities"—Kim sighed at the length of the needless lead-in—"tell me you were kidding before."

"I wasn't. It could have been about a lot of people on the Street."

"You're incredible. They might as well have written in big tabloid six-inch letters above the article K-E-L-C-H." Kelch, yesterday, had been out of the office. However innocent the reason, it hadn't helped his case.

"I just don't see it."

As always, Nathanson slammed his honor on the table. "I guarantee that it was him."

Kim let his honor drop and dally, featherlike, and didn't mind as it slid, hidden, under his lunch tray. "I guarantee that it wasn't."

"What's your collateral, Kim, Num-bah Two Sister?" Three years ago, Kim's co-workers had met his sisters. The three girls, through meat and milk and vitamins beyond the reach of their parents' Korean childhoods, had grown tall, narrow, stunning, their skin like fine-sanded pine. David, who was the youngest child, had not. Although all of his colleagues, even Nathanson, were speechless when they first met Kim's sisters, their tongues rejoined their minds after the girls left. They had never since abandoned the bottomless well of comedy. Kim now bobbed his head, acclimated, and waited for the latest to pass. Nathanson's voice tightened: "It's absolutely beyond me why you can't see the truth here."

"Leave me alone, okay," Kim tried to end the discussion. But then he offered, "Maybe I'm not claiming that it's him or it's not him. Maybe I'm just saying that I would need more—you know, you're sure, I'm not sure—information."

"What is the big, big thing Blue said to us when we got promoted? Come on . . . the big theme of his speech. . . . Time's up. 'Anyone can find information, anyone is able to process information, but—' *But.* Come on, Kimmy."

Kim finished it, mopey and parodic: "To succeed requires three things: maximum clarity"—he rolled his hand, fast-forwarding— "acting forcefully with incomplete information, and understanding how your competitors and clients will do the same."

"See, Joel, we got ourselves a real bona fide company boy here." Einstadt would have expected Kim to be able to recite the gospel, but Nathanson, to Einstadt's surprise, knew it too. Einstadt had heard it for the first time seven weeks ago in Freshler Feld's twenty-fifth-floor auditorium, a half-clam room with a video monitor in each seat, where Harold "Blue" Padaway had delivered one of his famous introductory convocations to Einstadt's group of new associates. *I have no interest in working for an ordinary firm, and you, the people in this room, are going to make sure that that never happens.* Blue was the CEO of Freshler Feld with a divine glow, a common touch, and a reign of immemorial bountiful harvests. (It was actually only eight years.) *Why is it so hard to get a job at Freshler Feld? Because it's the greatest job in the world.* Blue would deliver some version of this truth, never contested, in his annual talks and chatty firmwide conference calls and monthly visits to the cafeteria, where the undisguised sovereign would choose a table at random and solicit his fellow citizens' opinion on the kingdom's direction. Einstadt had been more impressed by Blue than he had planned to be.

Kim asked, for his own defense, "Why do you want it to be Kelch so much?"

"What does that mean?"

"I thought he was your friend."

Sure, Nathanson thought, he was his friend because he worked in this glass box. Kelch and Nathanson (and Kim) had spent three years together as junior analysts working until ten, eleven every night, when shared trench suffering led to comradeship sealed by complaints about the officers, the food, the hours, the pay. But Nathanson's parents hadn't spent twenty thousand dollars a year since he was in the first grade, hadn't clogged him full of classical music and test tutors and museum visits so he could be friends with a midwestern boiled potato like Kelch. Okay, Kelch was laid-back and free of pretense—and he listened to you when you explained things—but that was hardly enough to deny the truth that was screamingly obvious by that article's second paragraph. "This has nothing to do with him being my friend or not."

Kim shot up in his chair, steel-spined, as if a holy spirit had descended from the ceiling and overtaken his body. Nathanson understood that Kim was mocking him and had reached for the rest of his sandwich to take it to his desk. Then the spirit sat down.

"Hey, Joel," Kelch said, getting adjusted. He had met Einstadt twice, briefly, the first time when Nathanson had introduced them a month ago. Kelch nudged the pickle on his plate to a safe uncontaminating distance away from his sandwich.

He held in his breath.

Nathanson offered, friendly, "I thought you were in Boston suckering innocent clients into your overvalued pigs."

"Um, I took the shuttle back last night. Tee-Fog's reporting this afternoon."

"What's that?" Einstadt asked the table. He felt caught behind, running with untied shoes, for Nathanson had defied the laws of emotional inertia: a mood in motion should not be able to spontaneously reverse. Einstadt had been lightly acquainted with Nathanson through friends of friends for most of his life—they had gone to schools on opposite sides of the park—but it was only in the past two months that Einstadt had studied him up close.

"Ticker T-F-double-G," Nathanson answered for Kelch. "Known affectionately by the traders as Tee-Fog, and, not incidentally, Kelch's big 'Focus Buy' stock and road to research analyst glory. Right, Christopher?"

As he removed his pickle from the foam china plate altogether, Kelch, untouched by Nathanson's question, asked Kim with clumsy urgency, "What are you eating?"

Kim mumbled through his bite, "Tuna salad."

Kelch stared at the sandwich as though it were a personal enemy. He hated the smell of its construction, the canned brine and rot, the curdling mayonnaise, the relish's remote dill. When his mother would open a can of tuna in the kitchen back in Rockford, it would pollute the whole house. She would be smoking of course while she made the salad—it was her only claim to the kitchen—and the smoke particles, which had already formed a constant coating on Kelch's sweaters, hair, youth, would deliver on their backs, up the warped stairs, the tuna smell to his room. Even a towel under the door wouldn't help. Kelch couldn't understand why he couldn't smell Kim's tuna now; the sandwich was only three feet away. And he couldn't understand why he couldn't smell his own grilled chicken or that aftershavy crap that Nathanson wore. "*That's* tuna salad?" He then added, flatly, "Huh."

"Kimchi rikes it"—Nathanson winked at Einstadt—"because it remind him of Numbah Tree Sister." No one at the table laughed, and Nathanson quickly pressed on, "Who, by the way, has agreed to be my sex slave for the weekend."

"She had," Kim said, "until she found out that you had a little Jewish prick." Torvil and Nathanson could spend hours volleying racial cracks. Shot: it's tough being an oppressed minority in this firm. Return: I don't know how you got a job here at all; did you fake a circumcision on your résumé? But Kim, still eager and oddly appreciative (after six years) to be a tagalong, rarely ventured a return. Only when Nathanson or Torvil pushed, and usually only when he was drunk. It didn't take much alcohol for his eyes to narrow further, to buttonholes, and he would yell with sluggish-tongue consonants, "Stop talking about my sisters or I'll kill you." Everyone would then laugh even louder. At those times, Kelch suspected that he alone felt any sympathy for Kim, and he would feel relieved too, also curious and jealous. For no one seemed to remember, if anyone even knew, that he had a sister too, back in Rockford. They didn't know her name, they didn't joke about her, they didn't ask about her. The guys at Freshler probably had no way to even conceive of her, Kelch thought: thirty-one with three kids, bulk-bought food, car troubles, and a husband home by five-thirty every night.

After six years, Kelch had ceased the dead-end repetition of *back in Rockford*, the contrasting, resolving *back in Rockford*. He had long ago decided that it, Rockford, constituted a thin wafer of his identity, like Kim's sisters were of Kim's.

Nathanson was not offended by Kim or untrained to respond, but he would not allow Kim to keep Kelch from the center light. He wanted to see how Kelch was handling it. "Kelch, you just missed your best friend, Holmquist."

"Oh yeah." Kelch looked distractedly under his sandwich's hood. "He's a good guy." Nathanson cocked an eyebrow to Kim and Einstadt, but before he could continue, Kelch asked Einstadt, "How are things going so far?"

Einstadt nodded, one imperial gentleman to another, and declared, "It has actually been surprisingly fun." Kelch began to laugh. Kim and Nathanson, of course, knew his laugh, although they couldn't account for its appearance at the moment. Einstadt had never heard it before. It combined a baritone laugh, lower than Kelch's speaking voice, with a softer timbre, fluty and giggling. There was a switching point to its two measures—there had to have been because there were two measures—even if one could not precisely isolate the point. Kelch would be the first to admit that he wasn't funny like Nathanson or Wessex, but his laugh made a joke funny, pumped the joker with confidence. He was good at laughing. The current laugh was indisputably Kelch's, but there was a kink. It ended too abruptly. Kelch swallowed, and his head came down from its skyward delivery. He noticed Einstadt staring at him.

Nathanson and Kim watched Kelch watch Einstadt, and Nathanson, clinching the argument, cocked his eyebrow again. Kelch then looked at an uneaten quarter of Kim's sandwich sagging on the plate, resigned to the trash can. Leaning in, Kelch opened it and, with his pointer finger, scooped up a thimbleful of tuna. Blankly, dreamishly, he brought the speckled glob under his nose and inhaled. His face turned sour and shivered; he was the health inspector declaring Kim's good tuna bad, the fishery bad, the factory bad—everything must close. But it was bad because it didn't smell bad, didn't reek like all of Rockford when his mother was in the kitchen. It didn't smell like anything. Kelch scraped his fingertip across the beveled edge of the tabletop, leaving the dollop to its own gravity. He picked up a napkin and wiped his finger, a pool cue in chalk.

Nathanson rose with his now wrapped sandwich. "After that . . ." He left, and Kim left, and Einstadt left, and Kelch figured that he would eat in his office after all.

· 2 ·

Listen: two things are true, Kelch thought as he sat in his office, his palm mating with the mouse's plastic hump. Two things are true: A: nothing is happening, and B: it wasn't me, really me in the article. Because if something was happening, or if it was really him, Kelch would not have been able to breathe clear-lunged now, to think ordered thoughts. A body vise of absurdity would have clamped him shut, and off. Nothing was happening, and he wouldn't allow it to happen—Kelch was an intimate of an unabsurd world—but as he reinforced the two truths, the inarguable deductive corollaries, the C and the D, did not come. Yes, Kelch thought, it largely follows that I have nothing to worry about, or there will be no repercussions, or no one will find out, but those conclusions *largely* followed. They were fixed on the base truths with sloppy mortarwork; they were not Incan miracles stacked perfect without cement.

For his first three years at Freshler Feld, Kelch had worked for Veena Gupta. (He would have called her his mentor if she hadn't once said that only idiots needed mentors.) In the hiring interview, she had lectured that the key to security analysis, and by extension human thought, was a relentless pursuit of bits. "Do you *know* what bits are?" Um, yeah, sure, Kelch nodded, doglike. Veena continued, laying down four pillars of wisdom. One, the equity market is obviously not a binary system of yeses and nos. Two, nonetheless, all information is composed of smaller pieces of information. Three, apropos of the smallest available pieces of information, the *bits*, one can largely determine whether they are true or false, a one or a zero. So, four, obviously, our fundamental mission as security analysts is to relentlessly pursue the bits. Example: stock valuation is based on assumptions of future financial performance. Revenues are the top line of that performance. Revenues are determined by price times volume. The price and volume of each good or service can be isolated within the limits of public information. Price is determined by supply, demand, competition. Laws apply. The price environment is either strong or weak, true or false, one or zero. "Does that make sense to you?" she asked Kelch, who froze, his mouth agape. His eyes, embarrassed and side-cast throughout the sermon, had superseded his efforts to look into her cold onyx beads. Kelch had failed to heed the most crucial advice of the career office in Evanston. *Ninety percent of interviewees who fail to make sufficient eye contact* . . . He nodded again, wobblingly, waiting for the trick to be revealed, her accusation of the crippling limitation of his mind. And he waited for her umber hands, the left one protected by a hawkish diamond ring, to pick him up by his shirt collar and throw him out of the office.

But the logic, her logic, wasn't a trick, as her return silence indicated then and his experience confirmed over the next six years. He was repeatedly startled by how many other analysts didn't pursue the bits as deeply as Veena, pshawed at Veena's to-the-ends-of-the-possible data models, miniaturist's portraits, listing every possible division of a company, backed-in gross margins, variable depreciation, corrective "z-factors" for quirks in effective tax rates. His models were just as detailed when he was on his own, and Kelch came to believe—to know—that the bits in his models were the only islands fixed to the seafloor of the market of driftwood rumors and jellyfish hunches. Some of the older analysts in the research department grandstanded about their stock sense, about a gut understanding of how the market worked, behaviorally. They would claim feels and access to the market's collective intuition. Nathanson was with these dinosaurs in temperament, if not in practice. (A young analyst could not afford to be otherwise.) Yet Kelch, following Veena, was as distant from the dinosaurs in principle as he was by temper: all his feels were rooted firmly in his cortex. His models, his *process*, as Veena called it, ensured that when he analyzed companies, his in-brain crossing guards and stop signs were not disobeyed.

It had taken a while for these neural pathways to harden in Kelch, and they coalesced in a flash, gestalt moment: his graduation ceremony was an almost whispered suggestion to Veena on the possibility of modeling interest payments for a company she covered, a possibility she had not seen. She looked at his reflection in her office's inside glass wall. (He was standing above and behind her.) Her face seemed to regret its incapacity to smile as she declared, "You have a very democratic mind." Kelch originally took this for an insult, a fascistic argument about the weakness of mass man. But as he later discovered, courtesy of two hints over the next week, a democratic mind in Veena's universe was a complimentary nod to democracies at war, democracies jumbled and flat-footed after a Dunkirk or a Schlieffen plan—Veena's metaphoric pathways were all British—but, once organized, unstoppable. This compliment would join a once-monthly "Good job, Christopher," a quarterly "Very good job, indeed," and an infrequent acknowledgment (her eyes sparking) of, "I see you listened." Kelch did listen, had listened, and he was content, around her, most of the time, to be listening. Veena had never tried to butter him with a gloppy coat of personality. She didn't even recognize, it seemed, his right to a personality inside Freshler Feld.

By relentlessly pursuing bits, Kelch had become a recent vice president without even needing an MBA, was now the authority at Freshler on his own industry sector, and was ranked an up-and-comer two years in a row and only thirty points from being voted into the top three on the Street. (He was currently number five.) And so he no longer had to think about pursuing the bits, recite

Veena's exigent like some grade-school mnemonic. He did it, and in this situation—the situation he had improbably found himself in, or near—the bits were clear: A: nothing is happening, and B: it wasn't *me*. Sure, at lunch, Nathanson had looked at him oddly, but Nathanson was a schemer, a cynic; his looks always encompassed triple meanings, hidden agendas. (That didn't mean he wasn't a good friend.) But *nothing is happening* was as objectively true as any bit, and *it wasn't me* was also true, existentially speaking. Articles are just words. What troubled him, his sinking stomach again recognized, was that the deductive pyramid upward was stalled. The implications were not at the tip of his tongue; they were in the back of his throat, unreachable and itching. For the whole situation seemed to require a different language of a different country, where *'tis nobler this* or *'tis fairer that* were greetings on the street, where treachery and dishonor were currencies with no giggles on the coin face. The language of Kelch's country was plainspoken, it was hard work, and so he repeated again *his* two true bits to ensure their foundational solidity: nothing is happening, and, net-net, it wasn't me.

His lower lip began to tremble, an underground land shift of warning, and he bit it still in three increasingly harder offensives. His eyes closed on the third, and his heart adventured into his forehead. He felt chilled, and alone. And he felt like a day-old, half-formed blister, which didn't hurt if you didn't move, if you didn't touch it, if you pretended it wasn't there. Worse, one that you *had* to pretend wasn't there. Since last night, he had been looking forward to now, to Tee-Fog, because he was sure that, once he was occupied with it, the pretending would come easy. It was his highest-profile stock, his greatest responsibility.

Kelch checked the stock quotes on his computer screen: Tee-Fog was up a dollar and change on intimations of the coming numbers, the sun's calm, elbowed light before a shower. Most day traders passed over Kelch's universe of stocks, the stocks he was responsible for advising brokers and clients of Freshler Feld to buy or sell or hold, but there was thankfully some interest from the hot money

and real interest from serious institutions. It was better to suffer from
the whiplash of excess volatility than to be relegated to covering
stocks like Nathanson's, all old-economy granddads guilty of this
market's unforgivable sin: boredom. No, Tee-Fog filled a strong
niche, mid-to-high profile, and was a good steady grower—twenty-
one percent compound annual growth in earnings since Freshler Feld
took it public four years ago, the share price up nearly one hundred
and seventy-five percent. Kelch called the Freshler block trader, sitting seven stories above him on Freshler's trading floor, to remind
him of the three o'clock reporting time. He checked his e-mail for
any unlikely recent messages from Mike Maggiore, Tee-Fog's manager of investor relations. The last message was still the last, hastily
dispatched in revived telegram-speak: *We'll talk after the call. A complicated issue.* Nathanson or Torvil would have tried to read clues in
the message, either sinister (Nathanson) or winking (Torvil). Yet
Kelch knew that Maggiore, who was an accountant by training and
biology, was just a stickler about selective disclosure—most of the
time, anyway.

The six pages of Kelch's model, self-proud as a completed puzzle,
were crammed with numbers to a half inch of paper's edge, wee
little gnats marching in quarterly columns, spreadsheet declinations
to earnings per share. It was a top-tier piece of work. This morning,
with consuming concentration, Kelch had highlighted the crucial
numbers in neon spring colors: yellow for the ones that Tee-Fog
would report today and pink for the ones he could back into later
with Maggiore's help. The model pages were the only visible papers
in Kelch's office, aside from Tee-Fog's new annual report.

The office was Kelch's first, although now that he had become
a vice president, Weller had promised him a street-facing glory hole
as soon as one became available. His current window, floor to ceiling, its corners curved to match the cafeteria's arcs, had a nice view
of a cubicle's back wall. The office's design was descended, Kelch
had once been told, from the concept of transparency, and the office
was transparent: anyone walking by could—and usually did—

glance in. Had he ever wanted to hide, Kelch could have, just barely, stretched out on the floor perpendicular to the desk, although the desk's supporting dorsal fin would have made it uncomfortable. A flat-screen monitor, no deeper than a hand length, and a detached mouse and keyboard, both of their wires secreted away, alluded to the computer stowed inside the desk and the mighty Freshler network beyond. The chair, a fusion of leather and molded plastic, was an original for the building. Ever since Kelch had adjusted the eight levers and knobs, the chair cupped his spine like a perfect cast. A telephone touchpad was built into the desk, Kelch usually used a hands-free headset, and when he was fully plugged in, the integration of man and technology and room, blood and electrons—"a revolution for a financial institution," the architects had hurrahed—was distinctly mutant: chair as wings, a space bar grown permanently onto his opposable thumbs.

Belatedly absorbing the two knocks, Kelch looked up and saw Johann, his junior analyst, the boy-man he was supposed to mold (as Veena had fire-forged and beat-beat-beat him) into a full professional. Kelch couldn't stand Johann, not for any isolatable reason but for a whole series of misdemeanors: affectations, hiccupy gestures, odd long words here and there. During his initial interview of Johann, Kelch had known that Johann was not his kind of guy, was in fact barely tolerable, but he had hired him anyway. Kelch had been too busy, in principle and in general, to interview any more candidates, and he liked the idea of an assistant from a college that had been to him, in high school, above—and outside—the possible. Kelch had assumed responsibility for all of Veena's financial modeling after three months on the job, but after nine months he still did not trust Johann to have access to his files. Johann couldn't seem to stop himself from "improving," voluntarily, Kelch's models. Kelch suspected that he was also developing his own picks in Kelch's universe of stocks—the deadliest sin for a junior analyst—and sharing his apostasy with two equally suspect cronies, whom Kelch often caught conspiring around Johann's cubicle.

Johann slinked, overly familiar, into one of Kelch's two guest chairs. "I am sure that the Tee-Fog numbers at worst will be within consensus." Almost since the first day of their relationship, Kelch had suffered a layer of nasal condescension in Johann's voice, in its cocktail-party nonchalance. Johann always used complete sentences dripping with clauses, either because he found this amusing to himself or he needed, somehow, to counteract his parents' German birth. He also opened his whole mouth when he spoke and never said "between you and I." Kelch had not discussed Tee-Fog with Johann since last week—they did not sit around and chew over the subtleties of Kelch's stock recommendations—and Johann on his own must have read Kelch's "1Q Preview," reprinted on the network for all of Freshler's salespeople and clients. Well, the kid had to work with what he had. "They are going to report at three, if I am not mistaken," Johann half-asked.

"Who?"

"I was talking about Tee-Fog."

"Well, Johann, Tee-Fog is an 'it.' You and your girlfriend—or cat—are a 'they.'" It had taken Kelch three years to incorporate Veena's favorite nitpick, and he still needed to think about it sometimes before he spoke.

Johann opened up his notebook and jotted something on a clean page. Then, as if to the notebook: "Yes, pronouns are a difficult thing."

"Huh?" Kelch asked, as his eyes were glued to the inbox of his computer, his heart ba-booming, beginning to anticipate the faster minutes that would come after Tee-Fog reported its earnings. In those minutes, he wouldn't have to think about anything else.

"I said, Pronouns are a difficult thing."

"Yeah, right. Pronouns are a difficult thing." Kelch tried to measure the precise depth of Johann's snottiness, but in the moment it took to complete the assessment, Tee-Fog's earnings arrived. "It's here," Kelch announced, and Johann rose to move to Kelch's side of the desk. Kelch did not read the opened file of the earnings report left to right, then down. Hebrew reading and Chinese reading joined

new language reading, diagonal and swirling reading, as Kelch tried
to reconcile the revenue numbers, sentence fragments, excuses, divisional breakdown. This was his job: to process these five pages first
and better and faster for the relevant investing world. But as he
stared at the swelling puzzle, inconceivable and compounding and
wrong, he sensed Johann scanning over his shoulder. He could also
feel, he was certain, Johann's sex, a magnetic field emitted by
Johann's suit-covered sex, panting it seemed, wanting to be noticed.
Kelch swiveled his chair abruptly, forcing Johann two steps back.
"Listen: I can't work with you standing there. I'll forward it to you,
okay, and we'll talk about it later." The words had come out too
desperately, Kelch worried. Then, more clearly, he ordered Johann
out.

His heart turned off, in silent-suspended time; his stomach gur-
gled briefly, spitting. They cannot put this out today—his thoughts
bumped into each other, incoherent—because I can't deal with this
today. Because this isn't right.

The phone rang a double, internal ring as Johann left. Kelch
stumbled on the headset and read the name on the telephone's display: Thomas Mullin, Freshler's market maker for Tee-Fog and most
of Kelch's stocks. Kelch began, or supposed that he was about to
begin, to tell Mullin that he was just calling him on the other line.
The analyst should call the trader with news. But Mullin's "Are these
fucking numbers"—*numbihs*—"for real?" beat out Kelch's stalling
"Hey, Tommy."

Kelch stared at the earnings report, but his eyes lost focus. "I'm
going through them now. I'm not sure. There's something funny—"
He heard Mullin shouting across the trading desk, his accent only
one generation from the Brooklyn docks or a beat in the Bronx.
Mullin kept his sleeves rolled up, his porterhouse forearms exposed;
one suspected that he would have preferred to go without sleeves
altogether. Behind Mullin's voice, Kelch could hear the clatter of
rings and shouts and orders of Freshler's double-story trading floor.

Forty-five was a tight-quartered bunkhouse of block traders and sales traders and options traders, institutional salespeople and arbitrageurs. Forty-six was a circumferential mezzanine, from which equities management could observe the shopfloor. "I'm talking to the fucking kid now. Yeah, *now*. You there? This is fucking bad news, right?"

Kelch cleared his throat to answer, but out of it only staggered an *um* and a *probably*.

"One fucking answer: bad, very bad, disaster."

"It's not that simp—"

Mullin was speaking outside the phone again—"Tell 'em I'm coming . . . in one *fuck*ing second, okay"—and he returned to Kelch. "Hit me, Chris."

Kelch swallowed. "Just—" His mouth tightened; he knew that a second to Mullin was a sprinter's spread from first to last. Yet Mullin, the knot in Kelch's stomach tightened to convey, was going to ruin everything by reducing the clarity of information to a slice of its tip. Mullin was not interested in bits, immovable in their truth; he was an engine of vectors, movement that was its own reward. And the opinion, the vector, that Mullin was about to set in motion, market-moving motion, was a slander of Kelch, a mapmaker's flat projection of the globe. *Freshler Feld declares Tee-Fog 1Q* . . . "Bad," Kelch said, resigned, the word popping out of his sternum. He continued, "But listen: maybe if you fucking understood the first thing about the market and realized that I'm not playing some game here but am trying to analyze the future earnings stream of a real company, then *maybe* your stupid brain would be able to comprehend that the situation may require more than one fucking word." But Mullin had hung up after Kelch had delivered his verdict, and Kelch spoke, he was sure, into empty space. He had heard Mullin's click.

But the dial tone was absent. Kelch could hear only the charged silence of a canyon floor. He threw a pebble. "Uh, hello?"

Nothing.

Kelch typed the results into the message board for all the sales-people and traders at the firm. TFGG 1Q: FIRST LOOK, NOT GREAT. I WILL GET BACK TO YOU W/ FULL ANALYSIS AFTER CONFERENCE CALL—STARTS IN TWENTY MINUTES. The gallery was immediately heard. PLEASE DO.

The black-background screen listed forty tickers and their real-time price, the leftmost column the eight stocks in Kelch's universe. Fif-teen minutes after Tee-Fog reported, Kelch looked for the thirtieth time at its quote, a married couple of integer and fraction, the frac-tion now flittering, resonating, agitated. Kelch held his head at his hair, and as he stared into the screen, he caught the reflected outline of his face. What were the words that that prick had used, Kelch asked himself abstractedly. He couldn't remember, chose perhaps to disremember. He had not read the magazine closely enough last night to itemize its features, but deep-buried snippets, the turns of the phrases, not the phrases themselves, could still be tasted, as in a hangover's cottony mouth.

The magazine's cover celebrated springtime. There was some-thing droll and knowing in the picture of flowers and showers.

And on the inside: *good looking like local weathermen are good looking, boyish athletes with defined chins, clear skin, and smiles that make their mothers proud.* And on the inside: *his good looking is a totally unre-markable good looking.*

Kelch continued to watch Tee-Fog twitter. He appreciated that the market was a logical force—not perfect, but logical. (Veena, her admirers all declared, had mastered the market by being the most logical animal in the zoo.) The facts: Tee-Fog's earnings shortfall was due to understandable, marginal issues. So Tee-Fog's stock price should react proportionately—moderately—negative. But the four and some points that Tee-Fog had fallen was not proportionate, not moderate. It was a hysterical reaction, out of a fever dream. The hot-money idiots had dumped the stock in minutes, as if the company had just announced bankruptcy, but it reported only two cents per share short of consensus (and Kelch's own estimate), and two cents due to a shortfall in its European operations. Who the hell cared about the European operations? Kelch hardly modeled them. They were a mysterious plug, chugging along every quarter at twelve to fourteen million in operating profit; they were a goofy little research center in Belgium, a distribution center in Manchester (or was it Birmingham? no, Manchester), and a gaggle of sales offices, in-country stations manned by ten lonely Americans, about whom no one in the investing world, the world that mattered, had ever heard a peep out of in the four public years of Tee-Fog's existence. It was inexcusable, Kelch ruled, severe, that this immaterial backwater (and some glitchy change in the U.S. tax rate) could force the stock to clutch desperately to a cliff-wall branch, after already tumbling over the edge. It was obvious to Kelch that *they*, the myopes, knew that this wasn't real, knew that there was no reason to flee for the exits for two cents. Sure, the moronic, vindictive, spiteful—disloyal—traders could claim that Tee-Fog had lost its momentum, but that didn't really matter over the long term. Kelch exhaled twice, hard puffs, as if the air were being let out of him in measured, disciplined stages. It was all personal that day: he had avoided (at lunch) being hit, in one lane, by a highway-speeding car only to jump into another lane and—crack, crash, topple over the hood. *Who is the analyst who fucked up on Tee-Fog?* You know, the guy who used to work for Veena, Kelch. *That's the*— Yeah, same guy. *Whoa, tough week.* And people would laugh at him even though they knew that it wasn't *him*, it was just a name or—was that it?—a symbol, like this price for Tee-Fog.

Kelch listed, again, the truth. A: it wasn't me in the article. So forget it. And this time, B: there is no way I could have known about two cents, and C: net-net, Tee-Fog is still compelling, and D: so don't blame me that my Focus Buy stock is down fifteen percent. Don't blame me that your portfolio will suffer because I wasn't aware of some stupid tax thing and some stupid European division's stupid problems. He revised his list, drilled further into the molar for the carious truth. E: It's not worth it. Four hundred and fifty thousand dollars last year—yes, even four hundred and fifty thousand dollars at twenty-eight, maybe seven hundred this year—was not worth getting accused and smeared and insulted by Tommy Goombah Mullin and the rest of these assholes because why? Because the market was filled with will-o'-the-wisps uninterested in the truth, people who didn't really believe in the market as a tool for global, efficient capital distribution, as the manifestation of unlocked shareholder value. If Tee-Fog's earnings were two cents short, and Tee-Fog was a highflier with a forty-one P/E ratio, then the price should move in step with earnings. Forty-one times two equals eighty-two cents, not—now what?—five and one-sixteenth. Five and one-sixteenth just wasn't real.

Kelch wanted more bits, more letters, more thoughts. He didn't want to stop thinking because the next mind, he knew, an empty mind, was a trigger for an implosion: all his hindsight, all his impotence before the market, clawing him into the center—and a heartache through his skin. This wasn't just business.

Kelch had been head-struck by falling shares, seriously, three times before. Yet he could never get used to it, as Vivitz had. Vivitz shamelessly shrugged off responsibility for a downed stock: the market was a fickle and merciless mistress, and what exactly was supposed to be his fault? Kelch, to the contrary, felt, in his kidneys, Tee-Fog's tumbling integers, and in his windpipe, felt small hyperventilatory shudders, felt the green queasy confusion of seasickness, of reaching for a handrail only to remember that the handrail was part of the boat too. He could very well have thrown up. It was more than the stock falling—stocks went up, stocks went down—that sickened Kelch; it was the public embarrassment to come; it was the uncoordination of his mind reflected in the missed estimate; it was recalling that every day for the last three months, he could have averted the disaster (become, alas, a hero) by simply down-grading the stock. It seemed, thickly, to Kelch, at that moment, to be the worst thing that had ever happened to him. For if he was wrong about Tee-Fog—but he wasn't wrong, he was two pennies off—but if he was wrong about Tee-Fog, then he was wrong about everything. He had been that sure. The market was logical, and he pursued the bits; the market was efficient, and he worked long into the small hours; the market was demanding, and he checked his arithmetic; the market was booming, and he was admired by all.

Kelch squeezed his eyes, muscle-conscious, until he felt his eyes' squeeze pull at his chest, which whimpered for mercy. There was no one to turn to in this situation, for restitution, for comfort. He peeked open his eyes one at a time and tried to comfort himself with the simple truth: Tee-Fog will heal one way or another. After a month or two, it will either rebound and the dip today will seem like nothing more than charming frilliness on the stock chart's unended ascent, or it will drift down into inconsequence, as had happened with MJBB, Kelch's menarche, two and a half years ago, which had collapsed only two months after he had initiated coverage of the sector.

And then there was the other thing, Kelch thought too deliber-ately, perhaps just to be thinking. He glued his forehead to both heels of his hands. Although he was staring straight at the triple shine of his knotless desk, he was more alert to the periphery.

Sometimes, in bed at night with Kersten—when he couldn't sleep, when a damp chill anticipated the uncertainty of the market's next-morning bell—he would study her breathing. If it snagged, his heart would beat anxiously, worrying that she would discover that he wasn't asleep. She had told him, a few times, that she really liked how he slept.

She had shared other assumed wonders of his existence. *You know what I really like about you?* Thinking: yes, as a matter of fact I do. *I wrote it down in my journal, let me read it to you.* Still thinking: haven't you given that up yet? *Here it is: "He's softly confident and quietly strong."* Desperate to be said aloud: are you in the seventh grade? Kelch had often enough heard people reminisce about a world that was happy-peaceful-perfect when they were twelve, but only Kersten seemed to have constructed a plan to do something about it. He sometimes sensed that he had been kidnapped for the sidecar. Occasionally, Kersten would say how lucky she was to have found him, but she hadn't found him, she had baked him: she had mixed him and rolled him and scored him with an heirloom tin, and put him fresh-frosted on a special Christmas plate. (Kelch's family bought butter cookies at the drugstore.) Kelch would admit that he had allowed Kersten to form him into nice and quiet and midwestern, some romantic son, sum, of the prairies, a farm boy risen fully formed from a wheat field, in overalls, minus a shirt. He would admit more: in the beginning, he had encouraged her. He had wanted Kersten to believe in the hayseed exotic because it worked, and she, at that party that night, seemed eager to be worked. *Oh, you're not from New York? Me? No. I'm from Rockford, Illinois. Is that part of Chicago?* No, Rockford is country. And the first note of country had been drawled with a grin. But it was a lie—he had felt a muted, exhilarating alarm at marching in deeper—because though Rockford was embanked around a flowing river and though the low rolls and endless flats of the green summer prairie and lion-colored harvest mingled into the edge of the town, the real Rockford wasn't landscape-painted and rural. It was like Kenosha or Flint, the Quad Cities or Fort Wayne, belts tangled in belts, corn woven with rust, a third of a million people, the best off, middle class.

Finally, Kelch released his forehead from his handwall and sniffed at his fingertips, which had been resting in his hair. The fingers didn't smell of his shampoo nor of Kersten's French stuff that sometimes leaped on him through the morning and stuck around for days. They didn't smell of anything. He reached to his tie, royal blue dots on an agreeable navy field, and looped the end toward his nose.

Johann walked into the office. Kelch's face, as his tie uncoiled lizard-tongue back to his belt, was impassive. He was often still when Johann spoke, to set in perspective Johann's questions, snivels, requests. "Anticipating that you have been busy," Johann began, "I've dialed into the conference call on your second line. We can listen to it here together if you prefer or—" Kelch was unable to think or even instinct a reaction to Johann's presence, and Johann, unaware or too aware of Kelch's immobility, welcomed himself to a guest chair, reached across the desk, and activated the speakerphone. The tinny reproduction of the hold music lingered over the speaker, unable to fill even Kelch's tight office. Johann opened his notebook. His small kitteny nose often failed to support the silver-dollar-sized lenses of his glasses. His face was doughy but not fat, and his loose-fitting blond hair flopped over his forehead, which looked as if it had been inching larger by the year. "May I ask your opinion of the Tee-Fog quarter?"

" 'May?' "

"What is your opinion of—"

"What do you think my opinion is, Joe-Hann?" Kelch rhymed *Johann* with *no pan*. "I think it was about two cents too short." He stared at him, this time with purpose.

"Well, I can see how we"—Johann tugged at the *we* to measure the depths of its roots—"may have misunderstood the problems in the European division. Looking at the long view, however, there may have been certain—"

"It's good to see your mind is always busy working, Johann, but keep the theories to yourself, okay."

"What I was trying to say is that I"—there was no ambivalence in his *I*—"was calculating certain—"

The music snapped off, and a female voice, bland and perky-professional, declared that the conference call was about to begin. "Hey, what do you know"—Kelch smiled a faker—"the conference call is about to begin." Kelch set his hands on the keyboard, ready to take notes or broadcast any updates over the Freshler network. Johann, strangely, had settled him down. Peggy Oswald, the CFO of Tee-Fog, Hoder Leary, its CEO, and Mike Maggiore introduced themselves, and Maggiore read, verbatim and drowsy, the low news from the company's press release. "Before we open up the call for questions," Hoder Leary finished the prepared remarks, "we wanted to say that we know that many of the investors and analysts on this call are disappointed by the results. Trust us: we are more disappointed. However, nothing central to the growth story we have been telling over the last two years, as far as we are concerned, is at risk. We are excited about the opportunities this company has to continue to deliver growth and create value for our shareholders. Operator, please open the line up for questions."

Kelch laughed, not his choral laugh but a three-hack sign of disdain. The oh-sorry speech, even in this minor key, didn't sound like Hoder Leary; Maggiore's fingerprints were smudged all over it. Like Blue Padaway, Hoder was his company personified, but unlike Blue, who ruled as a spirit, an air, and an ethos that floated as a halo over everything that the firm did, Hoder was the very palpable Papa of Tee-Fog, a dozen-tentacled baron. He was benevolent and crushing, protective and imperious. He would give an immigrant janitor ten thousand dollars for a family emergency, then purge, an hour later, without explanation, the marketing department. The analysts on the Street all happily swallowed the Papa myth, became Hoder's nieces and nephews, and referred to him as a legend even though no one particularly wrote legends about companies like his.

On the call, Gene Tennenberg asked the first question. Kelch rolled his eyes, deep to the sockets' back, at the announcement of Tennenberg's name. Now the number-one-rated analyst in the sector, Tennenberg had been, by universal judgment, a nobody when he used to compete against Veena. His firm then shifted his responsibility to Kelch's sector, deciding to concentrate on the banking business there. How Tennenberg subsequently became number one was an insoluble mystery and no mystery at all. Kelch had seen his reports, platitudinous summaries of company press releases, sweeping optimistic truisms on the sector's up-up-and-away future, and ago-

nizingly blatant kiss-ups to every company in the sector except for
OPLL, which was Tennenberg's perennial kicking bag to prove that
he was as objective and as hard on these companies as the next
analyst. Sure, Tennenberg also produced his quarterly "Customer
Action Survey," for which his two dog-faced associates, ugly creepy
mutts whom the other analysts rarely saw on the circuit of meetings
and conferences, called purchasing managers at the sector's clients
and obtained a "qualitative/quantitative feel" for trends in the industry. But no one had ever proved, to Kelch at least, that the Survey,
net-net, was accurate, properly designed, or capable of providing
anything material for a thoughtful investor. Nonetheless, Tennenberg's clients, who were also Kelch's clients, took the Survey for
real research, took it for "value-added content" in their investing
decisions, and kept its martyred-forest heft on their desks as an
epistemological paperweight, holding down any worries about how
patchy was their knowledge of the shares they owned. Tennenberg
also chummed up to the management of all the companies. He was
aided in this by his age: at forty-seven, the mustached, frumpy Tennenberg was a dozen years older than his average competitor, and
thus reliable. At meetings, he received big shoulder slaps from CEOs,
got asked about his wife. He, in return, would remember—had
learned—where the CFOs' twin daughters went to college. This act
fooled no one, Kelch figured, except for Tennenberg's fan club of
junior portfolio managers at billion-dollar general growth funds in
Portland or Indianapolis, which held forty thousand shares of Tee-
Fog and Allencor combined. Kelch didn't know where Tennenberg
found the time, but he must have made forty or fifty calls every day
to those B-listers, messages whose only purpose was "maintaining"
the relationships. Sure, Kelch made twenty calls a day himself—not
all of them of great national importance nor to world-shaking
clients—but he always had something to say. Trying to be moderate
and sensible with your clients' time, however, only made sure that
you were number five. When the magazine or research firm polled
clients on the best analyst, a hundred or so had heard in the

last two or three weeks from Chris Kelch, while two hundred and fifty had received a call that week from Perennially Number-One-Rated Analyst Gene Tennenberg, who was Close to Management, Surprisingly Accessible, and A Good Guy.

Kelch figured that he would be a good guy too if he made two million dollars a year.

Tennenberg pitched two softballs, one of course to Hoder Leary and one to "Peggy or Mike," presenting the trio with the opportunity to sing, in turn, of the wonderful progress of the growth plan outlined at the last analyst meeting. Tennenberg signed off with "That's what I thought. Great stuff. Thanks, Peggy. Thanks, Hoder. Thanks, Mike."

Johann said privately to Kelch, "He's an acting genius." (One had to press the pound key and be selected by the operator to be heard on the call.)

"Huh?" Kelch asked; he had not heard Johann.

"I said that Gene Tennenberg is an acting genius. He must be horribly upset. He had the high number on the Street." Did he? wondered Kelch, who hadn't checked the varying estimates lately. Johann then told Kelch that ten analysts had estimated thirty cents for the quarter's EPS, and three analysts had estimated thirty-one. (Mike Maggiore had ensured the confluence of independent minds; he had almost certainly told all the analysts, as he had told Kelch three weeks earlier, "Your number seems within range." No one would have dared estimate twenty-eight cents without permission.) Tennenberg's thirty-one, Kelch figured, hadn't been rooted in any additional information or better modeling—no one modeled earnings as deeply, as thoroughly, as globally as Kelch. Tennenberg broadcast thirty-one because he was a booster, and a penny was a small token for his optimistic shine.

Johann tried to fit in, in the gutter. "It is incredible to me how much of a fucker Tennenberg is."

"Well, Johann, the last time I checked he was number one."

The conference call operator announced Arnold Vi, and Johann, unharmed, revived a grin. "Oh, what a surprise. It's Arnold the Sixth." Kelch had related to Johann the story of the Allencor cocktail party when a tipsy executive vice president, reading the all-upper-case ARNOLD VI on a nametag, had called Arnold "Arnold the Sixth." Johann had since erased the difference between firsthand and sec-ondhand experience and would display Arnold the Sixth as one of his dozen pocketed jewels of insiders' color, as if Kelch was not the source of them all. Arnold began pecking away immediately at his latest idée fixe. He was the anti-Tennenberg, a gadfly, a journeyman who had circumnavigated the Street because all the companies he covered despised him and all the investment bankers at the firm he was then working for, knowing this, didn't want him around. (Or Arnold quit, claiming an insult to his integrity.) He was an obsessive, a needler who looked the part, with a pipe cleaner of a nose and two snaky, permanently purple veins on his forehead. He was pro-fessionally a failure with no chance to change this state; he was already fifty years old. But he knew the sector, and for banks des-perate for coverage after someone quit or was hired away, Arnold the Sixth would suffice, temporarily. Six months ago, Arnold had rotated his obsession from a campaign against the amortization of marketing expenses to a crusade against abuses in option grants. On every call of every company, he asked a variation of the same ques-tion. Now his rapid, dentist-drill voice challenged, "With your stock down significantly today, if you don't reprice your options or rebal-ance your compensation with more cash, don't you risk losing key employees to your competitors?"

Now, there's a question, thought Kelch. Arnold the Sixth was a lot of things, but he wasn't stupid.

To dismiss the buzzing Arnold, Hoder didn't even wave his arm; he just flicked one fingertip. "Arnold, it is laughably premature to discuss this after our share price is down one afternoon." He paused. "Furthermore, as we have talked about, our compensation policy is set by the board of directors." That board of directors line was a cop-out, Kelch knew—Hoder owned the board of directors. He was surprised that Hoder would have gone to the beach in such immodest trunks.

As Arnold followed up, Johann leaned over the desk on both elbows and asked Kelch to check how TFGG was doing. With an echo of Hoder Leary in his voice, Kelch declined: "I'm trying to listen to the damned call." A moment later, hoping that Johann wouldn't notice, Kelch quietly pressed the keys to activate the quote screen. The stock was now down six points.

When the operator announced, "Kathy Guizeta," Kelch's head turned, as if slapped, toward the touchpad. His cheeks were without muscle, past slack, and he cried out, "What the fuck am I doing with my life." Johann sat up in his chair but didn't, it appeared, understand Kelch. Kathy Guizeta covered Kelch's sector at Freshler Feld's third-largest mutual fund client. Thirteen months ago, he had spent two and a half hours in Kathy's office detailing Tee-Fog, guiding her though its history and divisions, sharing the four public pages of his six-page model so she could work with the numbers herself. He ruminated on Hoder's management style, pop-psychologized his personality. And since then, twice monthly, Kathy and Kelch talked about Tee-Fog. The structure of their talks was always clear: Kelch was the teacher, Kathy the student, Kelch was being paid well by Freshler Feld to deliver to Kathy news on and interpretations of developments at Tee-Fog. The Freshler salesperson—the broker—assigned to Kathy had twice e-mailed Kelch to thank him for doing an outstanding job in the relationship. Kelch figured, as Kathy and the Tee-Fog management exchanged hello-hellos, that he must have spent fifteen or twenty hours all told with Kathy on Tee-Fog, and now this bitch was circumventing him, asking questions to Hoder and Peggy Oswald directly, making it perfectly clear—*see if I return your calls anymore*—that she thought that Kelch's ability to keep her up-to-date on Tee-Fog was inadequate and done. She had just declared him an incompetent.

When Paul Galicia had interviewed Kelch, Kelch had brought up

Kathy, bragged about Kathy—at the least, implied Kathy. Now everything was a fucking lie. His stomach was a hurtling elevator, without a floor, without an end, stretching its walls as it free-fell down. God, why can't we wake up tomorrow in the better world to come? Kelch stared at the phone, unable to admit Johann's eyes.

Kathy asked her question clearly, unhesitatingly, with force. "If I recall correctly, you book earnings in Europe from European divisions of multinational companies. A lot of earnings, I think. So I was just wondering, what portion of the European shortfall was due to a slowdown from these multinational customers?"

Two punches hit Kelch simultaneously, one high, one low. First, Kathy's question was important. Second, every other analyst on the call, even Johann, realized it too. Steadying himself, Kelch rushed his hand to the telephone and pressed the pound key, the I-want-to-ask-a-question key. *Why didn't I just ask Maggiore that in my e-mail Monday instead of a dumb question about depreciation?* I could have made, goddamnit, the downgrade of the year.

Kelch heard papers shuffling and could feel the impatience, intolerance, that must have been firing Hoder's nostrils. Hoder—suddenly cowardly?—let Peggy answer Kathy's question, and Peggy confirmed Kathy's point, part of the way. Yes, Peggy said, some of the shortfall was due to multinationals, but they weren't too worried, as much of this was due to the purchasing cycle. The first quarter, as everyone knows, was their slowest. When Kathy followed up, asking in which specific division this shortfall came from, Peggy answered after a long silence (probably a scratch-paper consultation with Hoder) that it was in the core business. Although Kelch couldn't imagine Kathy satisfied with that answer—there had been an invigorating, tangible connection between Kelch and Kathy since their first meeting; she was insatiable, beautiful in pursuit of the bits—Kathy thanked Peggy, yielding.

After two innocuous, maddening questions by small, irrelevant analysts, the operator announced, "The next participant is JoAnne

Housing"—Johann Hausen—"from Freshler Feld." Asshole, Kelch mumbled as he glared at Johann, who had registered for the call under his own name.

Into the speakerphone, Kelch blurted, "Hey, guys." He bit into his lower lip, in preparation. "It's actually Chris Kelch here from Freshler Feld." Kelch counted only two "Hi, Chris"s in return; Hoder Leary had said nothing. When Freshler Feld had taken Tee-Fog public, Kelch and Veena had worked on the deal together, Kelch the deeply junior partner. The department had assigned the stock to him when he received his own universe. After Hoder had learned of this, he raised a holy stink—Joe Tedeschi, the department's global director, implied that the threats had reached Blue himself—but Veena had no interest in a mid-cap like Tee-Fog. She had plenty of high-profile stocks to recommend, plenty of IPOs to flog, and was content to let Kelch take the work. To Hoder, then, Kelch was Freshler's betrayal incarnate, and as much as Hoder was civil to him in meetings, on calls, he always spoke to Kelch in a tone distinct from the one used for Gene Tennenberg or even Arnold the Sixth; he addressed Kelch as a teenager in a controlled voice, delivering, Kelch was certain, the message that Kelch was a lightweight, in over his head, unworthy of being the analyst at one of the country's top investment banks on an inimitable capitalist miracle like Tee-Fog. At an analyst meeting two years ago, Hoder had taken his only explicit vengeful swipe yet and was rewarded with the biggest laugh of that afternoon. "Mr. Kelch," he said, "I think that if you use your fine analytical skills and turn to the first page of the annual report, you will find the information you are looking for," although Kelch had not asked for *that* information and Hoder had misinterpreted the question, deliberately no doubt, by miles. But Kelch had proved (to himself) that he was the better person by not letting that exchange interfere with his analyst's duty to consider only material information. Tee-Fog had still been a great investment.

Kelch cleared his throat and ordered himself to be friendly and balanced and matter-of-fact—this was *his* Focus Buy stock—in front of clients, many of whom, like Kathy, he had encouraged to accumulate the stock. "I just wanted to follow up on Kathy Guizeta's question a few questions back. If the core business is slowing from multinational customers in Europe, is it also slowing from those same customers in the U.S.?"

Peggy Oswald responded quickly; everyone had known that this question was coming. The two previous questions had seemed like plants, delays for dramatic effect. "I think that wouldn't be a fair characterization . . ." Hoder rumbled in the background. "Tell them *what?*" she asked him. "Right. . . ." She enunciated more clearly. "It would *not* be a fair characterization. Our core business in the U.S. is still quite strong, and although there are some seasonal issues in the U.S. with some large customers, especially considering some of their problems in Asia, we are still seeing overall revenues and earnings at levels consistent with our growth plan."

Self-consciously reining in any antagonism, Kelch pushed: "Yeah, but that would imply that there are some other revenues in the U.S. compensating for the shortfall from those customers?"

"Um, it's complicated."

"How so?"

"Mr. Kelch." The other voice came on, the voice that always called him, exclusively, *Mr.* Kelch, the voice that was compact with the conviction that Kelch had not earned the right to believe anything other than that Tee-Fog was the greatest investment available on the market today. "What Peggy is trying to say is that our orders from our large clients are complex and vary due to a number of factors: the purchasing cycle, as she said; area of operation; their inventories, et cetera. And what she also is trying to say is that it is dangerous to stare at a number in isolation. It will hurt your eyes. Like staring at the sun." Mike Maggiore laughed, respectfully.

"Okay, that's true, but can we expect a slowdown in the *growth rate* in the U.S.—in the core business—like in Europe? That is something I think we all need to know."

Hoder answered again. "You have nothing to worry about in our core business, Mr. Kelch." And this was the sign for the good-boy analyst, the analyst who wanted to be among the first to hear from Tee-Fog on important news, the analyst who wanted Mike Maggiore to continue providing him tacit approval for his derived bits, the analyst who knew that Freshler Feld was still in the lead to manage any secondary Tee-Fog offerings as long as the firm continued to demonstrate its commitment to the company—this was the sign for that analyst to shut up.

Kelch's voice climbed higher than its natural pitch, to precariously younger. "Can you please just quantify what percentage of the core business—"

"What are you asking now?"

"Could you please quantify—"

"Quantify what now?"

"Could you please quantify what percentage of your core business is—"

There was some hushed rattling on the Tee-Fog end of the call, and then Maggiore broke in, a referee. "Chris, I think if we continue this conversation off-line, we—"

All the participants on the call, including Kelch, then heard an even younger voice, straining through clenched teeth, say, "Oh fuck it, I give up," and it took all the participants, including Kelch, only a few seconds to realize that it was Chris Kelch who had just done that.

· 3 ·

"Mark, it's Chris Kelch at Freshler Feld. Just wanted to leave a quick message on three points re: Tee-Fog. A: I am not doing anything with my rating just yet. B: I am going to run the new numbers through my model to see to what degree my estimates will necessarily be lowered. And C: I am inclined, preliminarily, to believe that with the fundamentals intact and the stock already down today, net-net the valuation here might—emphasis on the might—be attractive, especially relative to OPLL, for instance. Anyway, I will be in the office tonight and most of the day tomorrow. Please give me a call if you have any questions."

"Marian, it's Chris Kelch at Freshler Feld. Just wanted to leave a quick message on three points re: Tee-Fog. A: I am not . . ."

"Sanjat."

Jeff.

Miko.

Rob.

From five-thirty to six-thirty that night, Kelch left two-by-eight, miter-cut messages for thirty-seven clients at thirty-seven interchangeable institutions in thirty-seven electronic boxes prefaced by thirty-seven begrudging greetings, thirty-seven receptacles simultaneously being filled with messages from Gene Tennenberg, Arnold Vi, and Kelch's other competitors. Kelch could have left messages for a hundred more clients probably, messages that, in normal circumstances, faced a fifty-fifty chance of deletion at "it's Chris Kelch." Kelch read the text of the message from his computer screen. He had learned to work his messages before he began: talking into the machines, into those dark aural holes, tricked the mind after twenty iterations. The assembly-line repetition of action collided with the myth of conversation. "And B: tonight—where was I—oh, sorry, here we go, I am going to . . ." Only for so long could his brain use the brain mass itself to push a button again and again instead of ordering around, as usual, his fingers and toes. Nathanson, even David Kim, had laughed at Kelch when he had admitted to typing out his messages first. It was a private need.

Kelch slogged through most of the messages with only a few falls into the ditch and laughed, fatigued, all in his shoulders, at the strange twist: most of the people would listen to this message because they would want to know if he was calling to apologize, explain, rant, confess. About "giving up," about everything. In six years of conference calls, Kelch had never once heard a *fuck*, had never once heard a silence as leaden, as eardrum-deep as the one that had followed his surrender. Hoder had finally said, "Operator, put on the next caller. We don't have all year." The other analysts had then picked up Kelch's fumble.

That morning, on the subway, Kelch had tried to fix his brain aggressively to the coming Tee-Fog earnings report, and the jostling of the train had seemed to help. The other commuters had encased him, protecting him from Paul Galicia, from consequences and betrayal, from having to panic about abstractions, about eventualities. About the worst thing, perhaps, that had ever happened to him. But now, the absurdity of *I give up*—what could have made him say that?—seemed to invite its cousins of the absurd. If his behavior on the call was absurd, if he could really be such a self-destructive oddball, an Arnold the Sixth the Second, then—this he thought almost explicitly—the earth's sky had lost one tile panel of meaning. If *fuck* could happen, then anything could happen and this really was happening and the market was air. A dry ice quivered behind his breastbone in a constipation of sweat. The only solution was to skate on the sheer surface of the aware.

Because *I give up* could ruin his career. Because *I give up* could, in its six words, cancel six years. Like Tee-Fog itself, one dumb blow could topple months of accretion of eighths and sixteenths. Kelch couldn't—he refused—lose his clients' trust, couldn't lose his job, couldn't let himself wallow in depression. This was all he had, and he wasn't going to give up, go back to Rockford. But why couldn't he just take it back, take everything back, because it was everything lately, his whole life, that was perhaps the worst thing that had ever happened to him. He looked at his list of calls to be made and began dialing one more client, but *I give up* came back again. He removed his headset.

All the recipients of Kelch's voice mail message could translate every word with a trained, reflexive decoder. *I am not doing anything with my rating just yet.* Meaning: concentrate on "just yet" and don't be surprised if I lower my recommendation tomorrow or next week, take Tee-Fog off the Focus Buy list. *I am going to run the new numbers tonight through my model.* Meaning: I will put the new data in my model like every other analyst, but no alchemic insights will result. On the call—you heard—Mike Maggiore told everyone to lower their numbers by four cents per share for the year, and I will take my number down those commanded four, five if I'm being conservative. Anyway, you and I know that for the next few weeks, maybe months, Tee-Fog will wriggle on the ground epileptically and any estimates of future earnings will be ignored by the traders whipsawing the stock, on hunches, for sport. *The valuation here might—emphasis on the might—be attractive.* Meaning: Kelch had no idea what to do because this was the rub, the paradox at the core of the emptiness, the core of the pounding fear of his heart, climbing up a staircase in his chest. The paradox gloated as it whispered its doubt and dread into the ear of every analyst, of every investor. Kelch had told people, loudly, to buy Tee-Fog when it was six dollars more a share, and the stock was even more attractive now, at least on its current year P/E. But Kelch had been wrong, six bitter dollars wrong, this morning. So why should anyone believe him now?

The glue of the global economy was not capital or trade; it was a feeling, a fear, a shared condition of Kelch and Hoder Leary and everyone in between. The businessmen's silver sheets could not quell the insomniac truth that the pyramid was topside down, resting on a dime, the dime standing on its edge. Who was to say that Tee-Fog couldn't fall by ten more points tomorrow? Who was to say that one's competitors, right now, weren't planning to slash prices by half? Who was to say that one's customers would not finally decide, this year, that they no longer needed a new candy bar, a new car, another action movie, the next microchip?

The knot of the paradox grew, a gestating baby kicking, and

Kelch breathed harder, hoping to dislodge it, but he knew that this knot would never become loose until the market vindicated him or censured him, proved him gloriously right when Tee-Fog rose fifteen dollars or proved him wrong when it went down, and wronger when it went downer. This was one more problem he didn't need. The one good aspect about voice mail, Kelch recognized, was that only the ghosts in the machines answered back. For an hour and a half after the conference call, Kelch had talked to a few clients in rare I-speak-you-speak. Those clients were all relatively at ease, resigned to the new share price, knowing that this is what happened in this market, in this kind of sector. (It was a self-selecting group; the only people who called Kelch were the ones who still wanted to talk to him.) The Freshler salespeople, to the contrary, were personally wounded by Tee-Fog's fall as if its dip and failure and surprise was unconscionable, as if they were not paid thousands—millions—in commissions to disseminate news on dips and failures and surprises. *Don't you dare tell me to tell my client to buy more of this pig when he bought a fuckload a month ago on your recommendation.* (Kelch had never talked to that client, but he clamped his tongue.) The salespeople could file the lesson of Tee-Fog (also April 20 and Kelch, Chris) instantly because Freshler Feld hired only the best, quickest, most tunnely minds. It was a lesson they had learned a thousand times: idiot analyst tells clients to stand firm because he can't admit a mistake; or maybe, idiot analyst, caught with his pants down, tentatively tells clients to stand firm, until he has a chance to cover his ass.

A few of the senior salespeople, one bastard in Boston, a conference-called quartet in London, where every child groomed for the City grows up as a bully, had taken the opportunity to remind Kelch that he was not good at his job. *How can you be off two cents on your Focus Buy stock?* Nothing. *Don't you do research?* Do I do research? Kelch wanted to shout back. Listen: I relentlessly track down every number, read as much I can, keep my ear to the ground. But it's a black box. How the hell can anyone independently count revenues from sixteen European offices? How am I supposed to figure out, from the outside, more than the company knows about itself? Mike Maggiore tells me that thirty cents sounds right three weeks ago. Mike Maggiore has no reason to mislead me. He has a hell of a lot of reasons *not* to mislead me. So what was I supposed to do? Call Tee-Fog's accountants and demand an independent audit?

The salespeople all took it out on Kelch because he was young; they couldn't scold Veena (when, rarely, she was wrong). They also took it out on him because of the rules of the Street, where nothing was personal, no matter how hard the punches personally hurt. Everyone would be friends when Kelch picked a winner again.

Kelch had left the office only once since the conference call, to use the bathroom. There, he had turned a faucet on high, let its sound flood his thoughts, and tried to wash the grease of *I give up* off his pink and gray, steak-color face. On his return he detoured into Johann's cubicle, where Johann was leaning far back in his chair and bobbing lightly, low-rider style. He was plotting into the phone. Kelch approached closer—Johann had still not noticed—and asked, "What are you doing right now?"

Johann set his headset down but did not hang up the phone. It was obviously one of his cronies on the line. Perhaps as future material, he said, "I was just placing my dinner order with a colleague. I am assuming that it will be a long night, as we have not yet written the Tee-Fog note."

"Excuse me if *I* haven't written the note yet, Johann"—the note that, the next morning, would contain Freshler Feld's official judgment of Tee-Fog's first quarter earnings and include any lowering of rating from buy to (humiliatingly) hold or (scandalously) sell— "but I've been kind of busy." Johann didn't respond, and Kelch, beaten, exhaled rather than spoke his words: "Have you finished the OPLL and Allencor stuff for tomorrow?"

"Practically so." The ice wall declined to melt. "I would esti-mate that it would be another fifteen minutes before I finish that assignment."

"Just once, don't talk back to me, okay." Kelch returned to his office and began to assemble the scraps of paper on which he had jotted the names of people he was ordered to call, sorted his own database of contacts for holders of (or those with interest in) Tee-Fog. This was the only thing he could worry about now. He reviewed his typed message one last time and dialed the first number. "Mark, it's Chris Kelch . . ."

At seven o'clock, Nathanson walked into Kelch's office and shut the door proprietarily behind him. "Why does Johann Sebastian Cock have such a goofy smile on his face?"

It was Kelch's duty to respond with something homoerotic, ide-ally involving Nathanson, but he had been thinking about Kersten, about explaining or hiding. He had also been thinking about, or had been feeling still, the greasy spread of *I give up*. An exhaustion imprisoned him—even his ankles felt tired—and it seemed like he couldn't remember the time before now. He said finally, "I'm—I, um, I don't know, why?"

Nathanson's eyebrows gestured as he sat down. On top of his five-foot-eight, hundred-and-thirty-pound package, Nathanson let his deep-waved hair grow to a half inch short of flamboyance. In high school, for college, he had been a cross-country runner, and the mini-marathons had distilled the fat from his face, leaving only hard, penned outlines. His face was an extravaganza of features—that is what you saw, features—mud-brown caterpillarlike eye-brows, prominent cheekbones, a down-curved beakish nose. In cer-tain shadowy lights, this abundance of features made him look grotesque, but in other lights, his small face on his slight frame seemed more sculpted, more handsome, stronger than Kelch's, which was officially more handsome but was a desert of features, too symmetrical and right, except for his overlapping teeth on the bottom front. Nathanson was the first and last person Kelch wanted to see now, because if anyone knew, Nathanson knew, and if anyone knew, Nathanson knew. "What do you want, Adam?" It wearied Kelch to even ask that.

"I came for the eighteen hundred dollars you owe me."

Kelch shuffled in his front pocket for change—he had none—then took out his wallet, pinched a dollar, and attempted to toss it across the desk. It landed sorrily in front of him, and he rushed, "I'll get you the other seventeen hundred and ninety-nine tomorrow," but by that time the joke—or the disgust—was five seconds past the approach to funny. Nathanson, who never laughed out of courtesy (at least with his friends), watched the joke surrender on the desk. A realization grabbed Kelch. "I thought you owned five hundred shares of the pig."

"I sold two hundred last month."

"You didn't tell me that."

"Well, you were riding the bubble, my friend. I didn't want to hurt your feelings."

"Hurt my feelings?"

"Come on, Chrissy, geniuses like you and Torvil ride your bubble stocks up to glory and when they pop, you start whining. Me"—Nathanson slapped his palm to his chest—"I subscribe to a simple, honest theory that the man who lives by the bubble, dies by the bubble." The bubble speech was a lazy Sunday sermon preached a million times. (Nathanson, for sure, wasn't opposed to owning high-fliers in his personal account.) The bubble at Freshler Feld was like global warming: a joked-about, expected, accepted threat to existence, but not something people actively worried about, even on the hottest days. On half of the occasions of the bubble speech, Nathanson admitted his own jealousy. His current job—his out-of-favor sector—was perfect for a happy, family-man bureaucrat whose ambition stopped at a million a year, but Nathanson, Kelch knew, had started life too high to end a quarter-mile farther along as an anonymous cog in Freshler Feld. He would have to claw his way, impress his way, fame his way into an outside gear or he would leave the firm.

Did Tee-Fog happen, Kelch wondered. Couldn't the number—those pixels—on the quote screen simply be restored? What had he ever done to anyone?

He asked Nathanson sluggishly, "Would you downgrade?"

"Well, Christy, in my humble sector, no one would sneeze twice about two cents. But you're living in a wonderful new world. I guess—if you're going to make me do your job for you—I would have to know what's the downside risk to your estimate?"

"None," Kelch answered, suddenly eager. This was the line he had been taking in his own thoughts.

"But what about the momentum? That's what your fucking idiot clients care about, isn't it?" Both Nathanson and Kelch knew the answer, but this recitation of a conversation could prove helpful: a dialectical flip-flop down to the reigning cliché. Yes, the stock might be a good value here, but people wouldn't get back into it until they could see with their own cataract-clouded eyes that the upward revisions of earnings estimates would start again. That would take a quarter or two. And then everyone would buy it. And then everyone would recommend it. And then it would be too late for Kelch to make a great call. But no one was going to listen to his call now, because he had already eaten dirt. (Granted, Tennenberg and most of the others had eaten it too.) Downgrade and wait for the momentum to return was the smart way—the safe way—to play it, Kelch understood. Or used to understand.

"Fuck," Kelch dribbled, slumping. "I don't know, I don't know, I don't know."

"What does your asexual Indian guru say about this?"

"I'm not going to beg her for advice."

Nathanson paused, pulled taut his pants at the knees, examined, a touch effeminately, his fingernails, and announced, "But that's not what I came here to talk about." The sentence dangled, in the air, inside a humid calm.

A throb in Kelch's forehead seemed to tug at his lips. He didn't want to do this. "Well, what?"

"Jesus, Kelch, calm down."

"Calm down. My marquee stock blows up, you're acting like a goddamn CIA agent, and I'm supposed to calm down."

Nothing.

"Come on, jackass, what is it you're here to confront me about?"

"Who said anything about confronting you?"

"I don't know, who?"

"Kelch, why are you acting so—"

"Listen: I don't need any more shit today." Kelch wasn't going to allow this to begin, because once it began, it was over. But, maybe, once it was over, he would feel the way he had yesterday morning, before it began: content and bullish and in control.

"Is there anything *you* want to talk about?" Nathanson smiled, near to panting, it seemed, over the delicious possible answers to his question.

To Kelch, there was nothing to say: words, an acid, corrode protection.

"Really. Anything you want to tell your old Uncle Adam?"

"Up yours."

" 'Up yours'? Now there is a Rockford, Illinois–ism if I ever heard one."

"I don't have time for this."

"Okay, I just wanted to ask you . . ." Again letting a pause hang by a spider thread, Nathanson looked over Kelch's shoulder, but then his eyes turned serious, eyes that in a different generation would have shamed a fellow conspirator for losing courage for the murder that would ignite the revolution. "If you wanted to eat with Einstadt and me. We're going to have Chinese in the conference room upstairs."

Bull-fucking-shit, you goddamned piece of shit. Kelch muttered, "I'm eating late with Kersten."

"There are worse punishments in the world."

"Huh?"

"I said there—"

"How's Einstadt doing?"

"What?" Nathanson asked—unactingly, it appeared.

"How's Einstadt doing?" Kelch couldn't understand why, now, he was as interested in that question as any in his whole life.

"He's doing okay, considering that he has to sit in an office next to that humorless bitch Naomi Williamson." Naomi was a perennial target for Nathanson; her dusk-black, heavy-breasted presence anywhere nearby automatically muzzled him from telling three-quarters of his jokes, not that all of them (or even a minority of them) were directed at blacks or women, but they were almost always directed at some human target, and he assumed that they would horrify prim Naomi. Her nearness pushed Nathanson into a crabby mood, and he replied by calling her "the humorless bitch" at every opportunity. This marked an improvement over "Negress," which had been popular for two months until he had abandoned it after an anxious scene, a possible overhearing.

"Hmm," Kelch said. It couldn't have been possible for him to care any less about Einstadt now. His phone rang, and the panel identified the caller. "That's my mother."

"How cute."

After putting on his headset, Kelch asked his mother to hold on. Nathanson stood up and brushed down his pants. There were enough nights backfloating in the collective memory of Nathanson and Kelch, drunken midnights of arguments and "discussions," and even more drunken, even later nights when, sardonicism suspended by the liquor, one would admit, You're a great friend, man, and the other would respond, It really makes all this crap tolerable, and there were enough other late-dinner-in-a-conference-room nights (it was either eat at work or eat takeout alone at home) as recent graduates still dreaming their way up Freshler Feld, and enough interminable days counting the firm's debt to them because the firm, like the engine of every army, ran on the blood of its recruits, and there were enough other bonding glues of six years of communal sufferings and promotions and once-a-year strip-club visits and disposable income that Kelch thought that maybe Nathanson didn't know about the article or didn't care about it or, maybe, would even help him somehow by adding one more voice of denial shouting against the cosmos. Kelch's tone captured all this: "Really, is that all you wanted to ask *me*?"

Nathanson answered similarly, "No, is that all you wanted to ask *me*?"

"Is that all you wanted to ask me?"

"No, me."

"Me."

"*Meeeeee*," Nathanson squealed, and Kelch laughed true and full for the first time that day, and Nathanson, who had once admitted to Kelch that he was minorly addicted to the laugh, gave a lazy sailor's salute and left. Maybe Nathanson didn't know. Maybe it just didn't matter.

Kelch's attention returned to the phone. "Hi."

"Is this a bad time to call? I waited until late." Since moving to New York, Kelch heard his mother's voice more distinctly, as a birdsong, chirpy and guileless, her *t*'s and *d*'s mashed together, her other consonants drenched in vowels.

"Well, it's not been the quietest day." Kelch's exhaustion returned then, perhaps in hypochondriacal sympathy with what could be happening now.

"Oh, yes." His mother paused to consider, and to consider, she exhaled. Cigarettes had given her voice a scratch, not a rasp. "I bet it's not been a quiet day."

"Huh?"

"I understand why it's not been the quietest day."

"What?"

"I understand."

"What—what are you getting at?" Maybe it was not exhaustion that returned, but a dread, eluding and present, a mouse scurrying in a dark room inches from his toes.

Her tone altered. "I'm not sure what you mean."

"What exactly do you 'understand' about my day?"

"Christopher, I saw about Tee-Fog on the computer."

Kelch laughed in a burst of release. But the release was a loop-de-loop, not a reversal, for though the track that had been carrying the article had actually been carrying stupid Tee-Fog, both tracks led on his conscience's rails in the same direction. "How much did you lose?"

"No, no, this isn't about us." As she often did, she swamped her smoker's cough in a clearing of her throat. She was probably, Kelch guessed, holding her cigarette against her temple, transferring nervous little pimples of lipstick from the filter to her brow. "I talked to Bill"—Kelch's stepfather for nine years—"and he said we are still very much up and should hold on to the shares for the long term, and you will never make any money if you start to panic every time the stock market bottoms." Kelch smiled, uneasy. Bottoms? For the long-term? *Shares*? His mother hadn't spoken like this, no one in Rockford had spoken like this, when he was growing up. Well, Bill's counsel, in this case, wasn't horrible, only a little crude. Ann continued, "No, I called because I, um, have to ask you a question for Father Graham—"

"Who?"

"Father Graham. I'm pretty sure you know him."

"Okay."

"It's about the Wulle Trust."

"The what?"

"The Wulle Trust, Christopher. It's very prominent locally."

Kelch would have bet a thousand dollars that his mother had never heard of the Wulle Trust two years ago. But he settled into his chair's snug cast, and his chest, though still tangled, seemed to begin to unknot. "I'm not following you."

"Father Graham, you know, is responsible for some Tee-Fog."

"Jesus Christ, Mom. Why in the world would he own Tee-Fog?"

"I'm pretty sure you remember. Two months ago when I asked you for advice for him." Kelch did remember his half-engaged responses. Formally: *Chris, Father Graham has been named a trustee of the Wulle Trust. How would you advise him to invest it?* Advise him? Tell him to buy some bonds—I don't know. *Oh yes, they already have, let me see here, a "very conservative investment strategy."* (At work and at home, Ann always kept close the relevant stenographer's pad. Both were smothered in fastidious, cross-referenced, cramped handwriting and contained every thought and task that might ever be needed again.) *But he worries that they will not keep up with inflation if they don't balance this with more aggressive instruments. This is what he heard the other day on television from a, oh, what is it here, a someone Arnberg at W. L. Floris. Do you know him?* W. L. Who? *It's a big investment firm in New York like Freshler Feld.* It's not like the Freshler Feld that I work for. *Well, okay, but Father Graham would like to do his part and bring some good "ideas" to the Wulle Trust.* What the hell, Mom. This isn't what I do. . . . *Christopher, it would be so helpful.* I don't know, tell him to buy Tee-Fog. *I knew you were going to say that. I just knew it.* She and Bill had owned Tee-Fog for three years; it was like another grandchild.

Kelch anticipated the punchline: "Did he buy a lot of it?"

"Oh God, I'm not sure."

"What did you tell him to do with it?" He was mainly curious.

"Well, Bill told me to tell him to hold on. It has good, you know, fundamentals, and it was a good investment when it was up six dollars, so it would be an even stronger—"

"And what the hell does Bill know about Tee-Fog?"

The facts: "I'm pretty sure he thinks it's still a very compelling investment."

Kelch began to laugh again. He could hear his mother stare at him through the phone, waiting for him to explain. All this was making him feel better—it was enlarging his belief that the world no longer made sense. For how could his mother so dexterously baton-twirl *compelling*, the Street's private word, its universal term for strong, conclusive, urgent, worthwhile, outstanding, right, good, great? Kelch could imagine the trustee meeting of this Wulle Trust, five upstanding Rockford Catholics convening quarterly to discuss with full solemnity the investment strategy for a million dollars, an amount Veena probably made every three months. Father Graham, head bowed, would place his faith in Tee-Fog, for which an outstanding young parishioner (well, stepson of a longtime parishioner) had vouched. *What are the parishioner's qualifications, Father?* He's a research analyst at Freshler Feld. And the craziness was that the other trustees, Kelch figured, would know what that means. *Then that's a sure thing.*

At Evanston, Kelch was an economics major; he consumed business school electives on investing strategy; he was serious about capital and growth, his and the market's; he was never going back to Rockford. He luckily fell in with the right kind of people at school, guys who knew where the money was. But for his first two and a half years of college, he was barely aware of Freshler Feld. Back then—*then* was only eight, nine years ago, Kelch would think, shaking his head, incredulous—Father Graham and these Rockford Catholics would have evinced nothing but envious, hateful distrust for Wall Street, for those inside traders and junk-bond rascals, unrepentant New York Jews (weren't they all?) closing factories to pile more silver onto their altars to Mammon. And snorting cocaine in limousines. But that was eight years ago, and the eight-year wake of the bull had swayed or seduced everyone with a positive net worth. The bull had held its head down humbly as the citizenry approached with its garlands and applauded, in patriotic fervor, the benevolence of the United Stockmarkets of America: wealth for all. From the storm's eye, Kelch had watched it all happen, bemused, speechless; the metamorphosis had passed, ice age to hot age, in forty-eight months, like a dizzying movietone newsreel of a totalitarian parade. First had come the old investors, people once content to keep their money in mutual funds and blue chips, all gently appreciated for their service. Then came the gamblers, tired of Las Vegas and tribe-land bingo, who swarmed to the new addictive deep-discount commissions, the bigger, better craps table in stocks. Then came the Ann Arnells, soft lambs who had never paid much attention, who had operated for fifty years under the assumption that the stock market was something for other people, a little bit of a racket, and it was best to just leave it all alone. Now, they ordered their 401(k) administrators to dee-versify their accounts: one-third in the index, one-third in the growth, one-third in that there aggressive growth fund. And finally, came the poor, tired, huddled masses yearning for the dream—paying for groceries on the credit card, buying shares with cash. Kelch didn't have to be a virologist to diagnose how the mountain-sized bacterium of optimism and market love had gaily, unstoppably spread. Cable television with too much time and too many stations to fill white-noised every minute with the same theme: which stock were you *really* stupid not to own. Then the computer networks came to diffuse hope and false intelligence. The Bill Arnells now had a chance to access Wall Street recommendations, make their own stock charts, be their own broker, and reach their own conclusions, which were usually What goes down always comes up.

Even if his mother and Bill hadn't sought to pay attention, attention would have found them. Fifteen years ago, a Blue Padaway might have appeared in the Rockford newspaper once a year, more frequently only if he was indicted, but now Joe Tedeschi—or, in his media persona, I. Joseph Tedeschi—appeared on national nightly news programs at least twice a month. And thus Ann *knew* the great Joe Tedeschi, would occasionally ask Kelch, "How's Joe doing?" and later advise her friends that Joe—"They call him Joe there"—was telling everyone to hold tight. And her friends, Kelch had heard with his own astonished ears, would all nod their heads in dim recognition. Granted, Tedeschi was a red dwarf to them, a stellar presence shining significantly less light into their lives than the blinding supernovas on film, in sitcoms, but Ann's friends—her new friends—would nevertheless possess a constant inkling of who he was, however small: he would not totally evacuate their consciousness when the television was shut off, a privilege not awarded to the chairman of the Joint Chiefs of Staff or the president of China. Joe Tedeschi, Blue Padaway, Freshler Feld, even Chris Kelch were *the* story of the last five years, the one song—with its high notes, the New Economy Revolution—that had played through five years of tragicomic scandals, Christmas-card peace, and narrow goodwill: a culture adrift down the big, lazy river, whistling, sunning, and reaching for another beer.

Kelch had witnessed it, seen Rockford, a certificate-of-deposit town, a union town, a farmers' savings bank town, become a clamoring outpost of market love. Six years ago: what 'xactly you doing in New York there, Chris? *I work at an investment bank.* What are you, like a teller or something?

Now: hey, Chris, got any tips for me from Freshler?

And they were all right and they were all wrong, and the bills had never come due. For the bull had forgiven all sins. People *had* become rich and satisfied, and they now scoffed at their scared, silly earlier selves. This was easy, the stock market: look at the money I've earned—*earned.* Sell at your target price. Buy for the long term. Never hold a stock more than a day. Or an hour. Buy what you know. Buy IPOs. Or ride the mo' like the pros. Growth at a fair price. Growth at a reasonable price. Growth at any price. And why not? Appreciation had become a commodity; everything went up, and even when stocks went down, it was just to catch their breath before another climb. Or even if you did, somehow, take a bath in ABCD, the bad apple in the barrel—it was in there to keep you honest—you were more than compensated with a triple in EFGH. But Kelch knew that these new investors were drunk on the evidence of their own gains. The game was still rigged for the professionals, even if his mother liked using *compelling*.

Ann was a fanatic as a mother, not fanatically protective or fanatically ambitious for her children. Her monomania was fanatical interest—she was interested in everything her children did, interested in listening and questioning and sharing the wondrous experiences that faced them every day of their lives. She would press her interest without letting up, and she would question Kelch the same way she smoked—the same way she ate—in nervous, rabbity snatches, as if the cigarette—or the chicken—would be taken away at any time. For Heather, Kelch's sister, Ann's interest meant greedy interest in her three children; she was greedy to baby-sit or attend parent-teacher conferences, greedy to hoard more loot into her secret stores of data about Kyle's ear infection or Brandon's third-grade teacher. It had become mortifying lately—Kelch had been there once—when Ann got together with Dan's parents, Heather's in-laws, and interrogated them about a weekend that they had spent with the grandchildren, not just asking if baby Samantha had spoken yet, but grilling them if Brandon had worked hard on his project on the states and if he was still having trouble spelling Minnesota. On Kelch, his mother did not implant her interest in his personal life. She asked after Kersten, but she never, in that area, revealed her typical, unquenchable thirst. She seemed more interested in his job.

Kelch's laugh trickled away. His mother went on, "Bill also said to tell Father Graham that Tee-Fog is a real company with real earnings, not like some others."

"Tell Bill he has a very sophisticated view of fundamental analysis."

"What is that now? A 'very sophisticated . . .' "

"That was a joke, Mom." It was cheering him up, on the margins, to remember from whence he came.

"Oh, okay, I knew that." He heard a scratching of a pen across a pad.

"I have to get going. I have a lot of stuff to do tonight." This was habit: while Kelch, at five o'clock, could talk to Nathanson for an hour about a stock, with long sidetracks on sports and Nathanson's tragic loves, at seven-fifteen, a call from his mother was usually a suffocating torture, an inexcusable robbery of his little time not owned by Blue Padaway. Strangely now, however, Kelch suspected that he might be able to stay on the phone—wanted to stay on the phone—forever.

"Oh, okay."

Lazily typing tickers into his quote screen again, he spoke extra slowly, on purpose. "I don't know what you want me to do here." When he was growing up, Ann had unfailingly clipped coupons on Sundays, and they ate whatever brand of cereal was on sale that week. Kelch, then, used to dream of a world where his private cupboards were a store's aisle, swollen with so many boxes filled with sugar and prizes that they would need to be library-displayed, spine out. Now he was too busy to keep food in the house. And Ann, after Bill, was part of the investing class.

"I'm not sure what point the Wulle Trust got into the stock. I'm pretty sure I told Father Graham what you always say, that you can't hardly be cautious enough in the stock market and that it is very difficult for amateurs to make money, and he knows all that. But he is a little upset, and I do feel responsible, you know, to tell him something."

"Listen, Mom. Tell him A: to hold on, and B: that I can't worry full-time about his stupid personal portfolio when I got half of Freshler Feld breathing down my neck about this thing too. People are probably trying to call right now." As he spoke, Kelch was tickled by the thought of a Freshler Feld salesperson even thinking about the market after seven o'clock.

"He doesn't have a personal portfolio. This is for the Wulle Trust."

Yeah, right. Kelch heard his thought addressed in Nathanson's voice, perhaps unfairly assigning the cynicism to an ultimate if not immediate source. "Well, then tell him to be more careful with it next time."

For his first two years at Freshler, as far as his mother was concerned, Kelch might as well have been a translator of Sanskrit texts. Then, when the world began to change, Ann accepted the change (it seemed to Kelch) as if it had been orchestrated solely so that she could better understand her son. Some evidence for her suspicion: the meat of the boom began precisely when Kelch joined Freshler Feld. And it had happened before. When Kelch was a second-string shooting guard on his high school's junior varsity basketball team, no mother in the stands had more hungrily assembled a list of vocabulary words than Ann. She thus had a head start on other bandwagoneers when Kelch went to Evanston and Chicago became the seat of the crown of the basketball world. Basketball was Kelch's sport—it was as simple as that—and he thus had no immunity from the fever that overtook Chicago when he was there, a fever of localized intensity twenty impossible degrees hotter than the stock market disorder of the country now (at least during the playoffs). It amused Kelch to be able to discuss the team with dear old Mom in Rockford. It was clear that she had not digested a real sense of the game, but she had, admirably, kept enough facts near at hand to engage Kelch in a conversation, which was really all that she cared to do anyway. The same gap between knowledge and understanding in her command of basketball that allowed her then to make wild but folk-wise claims about invincibility and perfection—Kelch found them exhausting but repeatedly funny—allowed her now, Bulls to bull, to have an abiding allegiance to the comparative valuation of P/E ratios.

"Yes." Ann's *yes* declared that a grand coincidence had finally trumped her flitter of agitation. "That's *exactly* what Bill told me to tell him. That he has to be more careful."

"Then why are you even asking me? Just ask Bill next time."

"I did talk to him first, you know." Kelch liked Bill with a relaxed, enough-for-everyone like. When Bill married his mother, he was a sixty-year-old bachelor, eating dinner with his own nursing-homed mother four times a week, a mother who still had hopes, the story went, in her son joining the priesthood. An account-ant for small businesses—photo labs and dry cleaners—Bill was one of the great, gentle, measured pillars of civilization that would never be rocked, split, or even shaken by earthquake or social revolution. He was also, proudly, a Civil War buff. (At least it made it easy to buy him presents.) Bill was a relief for Kelch; he would always be there, in Rockford, for Ann. He wasn't like the Ghost, as Kelch and Heather referred to their real father, who had been, for twenty-three years, only background radiation in their lives.

Kelch checked his watch again. "Does anyone else have any investing problems? Do you know, uh, like a monk or something who wants to diversify out of energy stocks?"

"I don't think so. I'm not— Chris, I understand that it is, you know, a very high-stressful life you live out there, and I don't want you—"

"What?"

"I don't know. Sometimes I just worry about you alone there in New York."

Tee-Fog could only hide the article for so long, Kelch realized then, acutely, with fright. Sure, his mother, when it happened, would take his side, understanding that it wasn't him. She would rock him to sleep, humming a tune, of an old world, of how he was wronged. But his mother, now, couldn't stop it from happening. His not thinking about it now could not stop it from happening. It not happening now could not stop him from thinking. And on top of it all, it was unbearable that it couldn't be lunchtime again, in the cafeteria, when Tee-Fog was whole. Kelch hoped, he supposed, to communicate all this—the scraping, choking hole widening underneath—without having to drag in all the messiness of facts and defenses and narrative reconstructions. But he only mumbled, "I worry about myself too."

"What are you going to have?" she asked, the *you* girlish and cornering. Kelch had let the story drift away, a log adrift in the cast. Kersten didn't seem to notice the difference between him talking and not—the difference between him today and before—and added, "I think I'm going to have the sea bass— Oh, but I always get fish."

"Don't you even care what I was talking about?"

She continued to concentrate on the menu with a museumgoer's gaze and pursed her lips, half act, half doorknob sign—do not disturb—and then let her lower lip fall as her eyes glided across the choices again, searching, Kelch knew, for a perfect dinner: delicious, healthy, and light enough to permit chocolate at its end. "Of course I care. Let me just make up my mind first. I'm famished." Restaurants were one of her enthusiasms.

Of the four times in the past three months that Kersten and Kelch had been to this dark-wood restaurant—it was a flat, francophone sea of butcher-paper tablecloths and tin-bucket buoys of bread—he had ordered the steak twice. He noted this ledgerlike. He decided now, however, with disproportionate resolve on the chicken, feeling as if he had fifty extra pounds saddlebagged onto each side. After ten months, this thing with Kersten, his longest yet in New York, had reached a startlingly calm plateau, and his muscles had sagged, perhaps in response, become water-filled balloons rather than imagined steel. Looking for something pasta-y to decelerate his bulking, he sighed at the prices. Kelch had long ago discarded imagine-that-then moments about prices and tips and the daily economic screws in New York. Those were supposed to be ephemera in his new universe; to discard was the reward. Anyway, one stock he owned in his personal account, a Torvil tip, had jumped seventeen percent on good earnings last week. And though last week now seemed like last century—a golden age of eternal sunlight—worrying about a hundred-dollar tab when one made four thousand dollars on one stock in one week would indicate a nasty divorce from the reality of money. (Unless you heavily discounted future earnings.) Kelch had done the math: on last year's salary, after tax, he could spend six hundred and seventy-eight dollars each and every day. (This year, he counted on his bonus increasing the figure to over a thousand a day.) He would drive himself mad in this city, whose architecture was inflation, inflation of stories, inflation of people, inflation of appetites up skyscrapers' sixty floors, if he started to pay too much attention to prices and costs, if his memory became not a hard drive of facts but a pestering conscience, if every time he went out to a restaurant like this, he had to recall the scandal of Heather's wedding. Sixty dollars a person, his mother had repeated—her lips barely moving, swearing Kelch to secrecy—after she hung up with the catering hall. Sixty dollars a person, she said again and again, shell-shocked, caught in a cyclotron of words. *Sixty dollars a person.* Even with a cash bar.

The restaurant's rhythm—it was a quiet place, a suspended place, unaccountably slow for its category—had begun to scab over the Tee-Fog call and the Buchalter call and everything else. Nothing, officially, had happened today. And if it hadn't happened yet, it was less likely to happen. And Kelch wasn't, on principle, going to get depressed. He garbled, "I'm going to get the steak o'poi-ver."

Eyes still fastened to the menu: "*Au poivre.*" Travel was one of her enthusiasms.

Kelch, swallowing, spoke to himself. "It was a joke."

"What?"

"O'poi-ver." His face drooped, unhandsome.

She didn't seem to register the second iteration and when she looked at him finally, she smiled, apparently in congratulations. "Oh, the steak really does sound good, but I couldn't get *that*, could I?"

Kelch looked down, toward his belt. "How would I know?" He was too tired to try to convince her of anything, even in play.

"Well, I think I'm definitely going to have the sea bass," she said, sitting up, neck straight, shoulders level, back erect. "And five pieces of the flourless cake for dessert." Directed across the table, her beam, Kelch reckoned, was meant as a cherry of a celebration of sitting in this adorable restaurant in the capital of the world at the fantastically early time of eight forty-five on a Tuesday night. Kelch smiled back, recognizing with exhaustion (as always before a true cliché) that she really was compelling. For his first three years in New York, Freshler Feld was a dehydrator jerkying the days of his youth. It had allowed him no girlfriends (so the boys agreed on the excuse), and only when he was freed from Veena's yoke did he begin to invest dates in what turned out to be a series of underperforming laggards, low-immunity women susceptible to every insecurity that the city carried above its sidewalk, women who fretted over being too career-minded, usually, or not career-minded enough. But Kersten was not like that. She had a clearer idea of what she wanted out of life than any person he had ever met. Kelch had even joked once, to her, that that's what happened when your life had been perfect. She had deflected his comment with a "No, you're perfect," kissing him wetly on the cheek.

Kersten was always attractive—even (or especially) on Saturday mornings in his button-down and basketball shorts—but she had added, Kelch noticed, something tonight. Her hair seemed thick with investment, commitment; her skirt's fabric hugged her in the right places (particularly noticeably, for midweek). She seemed— fresh, and it only made him feel heavier and uglier and more alone. Kersten was a daisy-heart blonde, and though she believed she possessed the other half of the Aryan twin set, her eyes were more overcast than blue. The guys at Freshler sometimes complimented Kelch on her figure, but her stomach was a murmur, soft and indistinct and gentle, and her moderate breasts, like two lazy eyes, pointed in opposite directions.

Kelch had not acknowledged her dessert joke, and Kersten

moved on, stating evenly, "Will"—her oldest brother—"called me today about Tee-Fog." She didn't need to pause to handle the ticker's nickname.

"What did he want, an apology?"

She opened her face: pleasant surprise. "Don't be silly. He *likes* you, a lot. He just wanted me to call him tomorrow after I spoke to you about it." Her brothers, both doctors, were six and eight years older than her. When Kelch met the assembled family, it had seemed like she had a father three times over.

Kelch groaned, "If you remember, I was just talking to you about Tee-Fog. Like when you weren't listening."

Her eyebrows folded in, and she disproved him, nonjudgmentally: "It must have been the worst thing for you to have to call all those clients when it wasn't even your fault."

How do you know what's my fault, Kelch thought. What does it even have to do with my *fault*? My life is coming the fuck apart. I don't have a boo-boo. "Well, it wasn't fun."

The waiter returned to their table, and the temporary crumple in Kersten's forehead disappeared as she excitedly engaged him as if he were performing a unique public service in taking their over-priced order. That was Kersten: nice and super-gracious—genuine—to waiters and cab drivers and children and blacks and Puerto Ricans and everyone else in this horrible town.

Kelch ordered the chicken. If they couldn't call steak with pepper on it a steak with pepper on it, he wasn't going to cough up twenty-four bucks.

After the waiter left, Kersten prompted, "So you were telling me about downgrading Tee-Fog . . ."

Kersten wasn't supposed to know anything about finance.

"Sweetie . . ."

"Okay, but just listen, okay," Kelch said, almost pleading. "I was saying that this banker, um, very smoothly, like he was just asking me to fax him something, said, 'I don't imagine you want to do anything to jeopardize our relationship with the company.' " Kelch had already told her the first half of the story, abridged and admittedly difficult to follow. Storytelling wasn't his strongest suit. He had explained that he had written half of his note detailing the reasons for downgrading Tee-Fog off the Focus Buy list. He hadn't told her about *I give up*, but he had told her that he had not held back on the Tee-Fog conference call, that he had really challenged Hoder Leary—heroically, he implied. He had told her that at seventhirty he had gotten a call from Robert Buchalter, the managing director second in charge of the Freshler investment banking group assigned to Kelch's universe of companies.

But now, before he could complete the story, just, in fact, as he was about to narrate every word exchanged between him and Buchalter, the words tasted wrong in his mouth, bitter and leafy. His mouth quit, and he shut his eyes. The images of what he needed to tell her were there for him to seize, but the words for the images, the words that could communicate his victimization by the conversation—by the article, by humanity—were inside his tongue, not lining up ready atop it. The images came as a collage, melding with each other, burst on burst. Robert Buchalter: heir apparent to the head of the group, who was heir apparent to the head of the investment banking division, who would have been heir apparent to Blue if Blue weren't an immortal. Hoder Leary: calling Buchalter after the conference call (no one had to tell Kelch that Hoder had done that) to tattle and warn Buchalter about the risk to the long, profitable relationship between Freshler Feld and Tee-Fog. Chris Kelch: nodding, controlling his face to look deeply concerned (embarrassingly aware that Buchalter could not see him through the phone), agreeing that the Tee-Fog relationship must not be jeopardized, and stating that Yes, he understood, and Yes, he understood, and Yes, he understood.

"Are you okay?"

Chris Kelch: deleting the note downgrading Tee-Fog from the

Focus Buy list. Chris Kelch: telling Johann it was his lucky day. The magazine: Paul Galicia, haunting, gasping, choked. The magazine: it didn't exist, he had thrown it away.

"Is there something in your eye?" she asked, as if a drop bottle in her purse could cure the whole world.

Johann Hausen: dumbfounded, then serious, then a hint of a smirk. Chris Kelch: instructing Johann to copy the last quarter's note on Tee-Fog and update the numbers. Chris Kelch: no change in recommendation.

"Sweetie?"

Kelch opened his eyes, and he heard the film's tail end slapping the projector's reels. He should be able to share everything with his girlfriend. "What?"

"Um, are you okay?"

He wanted to warn her then, he wanted to crawl under the table then, he wanted something from her, from himself, from his experience on earth. This wasn't it. "I just got like a head rush. You know, like um . . . when you eat ice cream that's too cold." Was that true, he wondered. Was that even close to what happened?

"Oh." Her brows knitted again, and she snuck a look, not wholly furtive, at another table. "That sounds awful," she said differently, less committedly than before.

Kelch opened his mouth, to nothing, and Kersten looked down at her lap guiltily—or, Kelch understood, projecting guilt. A silent gaseous collision of animus, of agitation hung over their table. The silence was at first discomforting, and then it became staring. Eventually their eyes diverted.

Neither of them had wished this to happen. They both knew, and Kersten cared, Kelch was sure, that they should have a bundle of topics to unwrap now, sixty hours of experiences to gift each other with—the lovers' minutiae of daily existence. The last day that they had seen each other, last Saturday, had been particularly indulgent and lazy and childish, spent on a command-post couch with basketball playoffs and glossy magazines, Kersten-made bacon,

Kersten-made eggs, and Kersten-mixed berries with cream. She was impeccable, professional, about these days—cooking was one of her enthusiasms—and she presented the styled plates with an eager, auditioning smile. Nathanson had once explained to Kelch, with typical Nathanson authority, that love worked top-down. You fall in love with a girl, almost immediately, and all the other details, at least perceptually, step into line. Yet Kelch had decided that he had come to love Kersten bottoms-up—the direction that wasn't supposed to work—adding up the bits. At the party where they met, although he had wound up wooing her, he had doubted her sincerity. His experience, in New York at least, had prepared him for no other reaction. *You're like a real midwestern kind of guy, aren't you?* What does that mean? Their first date had been awkward. She probed, excessively it felt, for common ground, sowing hints of mutual likes and shared cultural touchstones. *That's one of my favorite movies too!* Brothers versus sisters. Dogs and cats. But on the second date, which inertially happened, she decided on him, it seemed, pretending or believing or, just maybe, appreciating that MJBB's strengths or PKW's aggressive accounting were interesting enough to constitute a life's concerns. There was more, of course. A: she was irresistibly innocent in the way she asked him questions and made him talk even if he didn't want to. And B: she was cute, not in her looks—there she was more—but in her person, in her brightness, in her attachment to dried leaves and wildflowers and new shoes, to her enthusiasms, to him. And C: they dreamed in the same direction, as she said, quoting someone. He had an unsullied record about recognizing that it was too early to allow in any thoughts about marriage, but he was content now—at least had been in the Eden of last week—for her to pull his dreams along. Before her, he had been too busy to dream.

So he must have loved her, and he knew that he something-ed her, and when he told her that he loved her, he was proud that he had done it first. She had made him dinner—it was a midweek night—a surprise of panfried chicken with roasted potatoes, a replica of a meal that he missed from a diner in Evanston. Hers was even better than the diner's. As he dumped the perfection into his stomach, mewing with ecstatic approval, she said, "I've been looking for this recipe for months," and he said, in the same instant, "Wow, I really love you." Her cheeks dawned in blush, and she stared at him—stopped—her mouth molding around an O. "What did you say?" He coughed, nervous. "I said, I love you." *Really?* "Yeah, I do. I mean, I love you. I mean, why wouldn't I? You're great." She brought her napkin off her lap, set it next to her plate, and she walked to his side of the table. (She never fully unbent her knees, and her head, slapstick, barely gained altitude from its sitting height.) Her lips nuzzled in his neck; her arms secured around him like a stuffed carnival prize. "That's the nicest thing anyone has said to me in such a long time." Her arms felt to him like a sea lion's fins: damp and wide and as impermeable as rubber.

In the restaurant, Kersten's lower lip protruded, ready to tremble sympathetically, it seemed, if Kelch's horrors demanded it. But he only smiled sad-eyed, tilting his head playfully ten degrees. It was permission, and Kersten opened like a fan, the hand-painted watercolor unfurled for admiration. "I can't tell you how hungry I am."

"Huh."

The fan folded, and Kersten readjusted herself in the chair.

Barely intelligible: "I'm sorry."

"There's nothing to be sorry about," she granted a reprieve. "I don't know why that word gets me all upset." She did know: she had told him. "Huh" made a person seem dumb. There was nothing she hated more than seeming dumb.

Silence interrupted them again, and this time Kelch welcomed it. Every exchange seemed accretive to his misery, to his discomfort, to his bad luck. To the vacuum in his chest, pulling his face down into nausea.

Then from the silence it came, with a muffled bang, like death: Kersten said, "Remember that guy at Marigold's dinner, Paul Galicia . . ."

No.

"At the restaurant with Marigold and her friends ..."

No.

"He was wearing those thick frames, you made some joke—"

"I don't remember anything like that."

"Sweetie, I *know* you remember him. There's no way you couldn't—"

"Okay, fine. I got it: Paul Galicia." And so it was over. But how could she be so calm and cute and herself while she ground him to a pebbled end?

"Are you feeling okay?"

"Am I feeling okay?" He stared at her, a stranger. He wanted to turn his face then into a hateful howl and press *her* face straight into how, precisely, he was feeling. He wanted to crush her in it if he could, screw her if he could, crashing the dishes to the floor. He wanted to do something, something physical, forgettable and consuming. He just didn't— He said, "I just don't want to talk all the time." If he didn't talk about it, maybe it wouldn't come any nearer; it was a magic spell, summoned only by words.

"What?"

"That's all I ever do anymore is talk. Talk, talk, talk. Like a parrot."

"You. Talk. Right."

Her smile said it was only a tease. But her tease didn't match his expression, or his words, which had barreled on. "It's like— You can't even *imagine* it. Listen: I'm in my office for the whole day, and I'm on the phone most of that time, and sitting in this chair that's so comfortable that I don't even have to wiggle around or anything to get comfortable, and then all I do from morning to night, if I'm not entering something into a fucking computer"—she fidgeted at the obscenity—"is talk into a phone. I don't even have to hold it up." Watching her, for reaction, he held up his hands as explanations. She could have been a flash card, for a child, of a compassionate face. But it seemed out of the stockroom. "It's like my whole life takes place between here"—he chopped one hand horizontally, uncharacteristically, under his nose—"and here." His other hand chopped mid-chin. He stopped and decided, to himself, that he was more fish than parrot: ninety percent of his armless, legless, noseless life happened inside his mouth. It was a life of glug and glug and glug.

"It's going to be okay, Chris."

"It's not going to be okay." This was true, he was certain. "Listen: I—I don't want to talk about it anymore. I don't want to *talk* anymore."

Kersten leaned in. Her voice had been carved by German cars and a vacation home and two flawless parents; it couldn't help but be soothing, confirming that a life's potential was a direct function of its expectations. "I know, Chris, that sometimes East Coast people"—she held up her palm to shoulder level—"you know, us, me, *guilty*. We're very open and very, you know, talkative, and sometimes I know this stresses you out. But that's what I love about you, your 'taciturn midwestern' thing. It's wonderful."

"Listen: you're one hundred percent incorrect in your assessment. This has nothing to do with the Midwest. So you can drop that speech right now."

"But it does," she corrected gently.

"No. It has to do with one thing: with talking all the time. It has to do with my whole life being nothing but glug, glug, glug."

"But you talk less than any person I've ever met."

If he had had the magazine now, he would have ripped open the bodice of the covers at the staple and stuffed her spoiled nose into its pages, made her smell the filth on the pages, made her see what happened when he talked less than any person she had ever met. Violence thrills, and the violence thrilled, and he loved her, because what else did he fucking have? He said, "Forget it."

"What can I do, sweetie?" Kersten swallowed, and bit over her lower lip. (Kelch did that too, an "amazing" coincidence that they had discovered long ago.) "When you're upset, I'm upset. But talking

is good. Talking"—she paused, apparently, to let this all sink in—
"is the way we communicate."

"Okay, then, let's communicate." He twisted his napkin into a
rope, accepting the challenge. A thought pushed into him. He
acknowledged it. "Do you believe in God?"

"What?" She spat the *t* hard, leaving her mouth ajar.

"Come on. We're communicating. Let's communicate."

Her arms were limp by her sides. Don't hit me, I'm only a girl.
"Why—why are you asking me that?"

"I don't know, Kersten, maybe it's because I don't know anything
about you."

"What does *that* mean?"

"I think it's pretty damn clear what it means."

"Who are you today?" A watery film fogged her eyes.

"Listen," he began lightly, comic-strip upbeat, "I just want to
know more about you. We've been going out for a long time, right?
And the goal of our relationship here is to know everything there
is to possibly know about each other, right? To be able to finish
each other's thoughts and that kind of crap. And I don't know, for
instance, whether or not you believe in God." His delivery became
calm, arrogant, also hypnotic and possessed. Kelch didn't behave
this way; his and Kersten's arguments never nicked arteries. They
were her "suggestions," his resistance, her smiles, his good-natured
capitulations. "I'm waiting."

"You really want me to answer that question?"

"Yes." He broke a sentence into pellets, feeding the baby pigeons:
"Do. You. Kersten. Henry. Believe. In. God?"

She bit her lower lip, and her eyes consulted her glass. She
inhaled, in two stumbling draws, and held her breath in. Looking
up, unsettlingly calm, she asked, "Have I ever done anything but try
to make you happy?"

"No"—his head blew back, feigning shock—"not at all." Not
only had she not ever done anything but try to make him happy,
he hardly had to do anything to make her the same. Neither of

them, Kelch knew, deserved this. "I'm just asking a question for, you know, communication purposes. I don't think that it's crazy of me to want to know if the girl I've been dating for nine months—"

"*Ten* months."

"—ten months, believes in God?"

"Do *you?*"

"I asked you first." He claimed his rights, rigid.

"Of course I do."

He leaned over his plate. "Well, that was fucking easy, wasn't it?"

"Stop treating me like an idiot in front of all these people. Just stop it. Stop it. Stop it." Her repetition, rising, was less an ordering than a threat of tantrumlike permanence.

"No one can hear us. And I'm not treating you like an idiot. You've told me a thousand times that you can't stand it when people treat you like an idiot." Kelch wanted to take a knife then and cut out his tongue. He looked to it, considering the effort. But he couldn't allow any more silences now, for in the silences, his mind stopped running, and everything caught up.

The candlelight duplicated itself, bashfully, in her eyes as she looked to the right, to a table at which another couple was smiling, posing, it seemed, for a commercial for a summery white wine. "You know what, Chris? Tonight is so funny. No, it's not funny, it's *ironic* or surreal or something because I was telling Jen at work that I was so excited—almost giddy—because finally, one time in like months, we were going to be able to have a full night together like normal people instead of you calling me at ten-thirty and saying, 'I'm too tired to do anything.' "

"Yeah?" Kelch was curious.

She half-giggled. "Of course, *yeah.*"

"I'm sorry," he said, sorry, and recognized the confluence of word and temper.

"Why are you so interested in God all of the sudden?"

"I don't know."

"Chris, you can't get all hot and bothered and then just return to being Mr. I Keep My Emotions All Bottled Up. We really have to talk about these things."

He laughed and it begat her laugh, and she reached across the table and put her hand over his; their hands maneuvered on their own until they were palm on palm, and hers drew down to play his fingers as a guitarist, the frets. It then curled into his, and his fingers, pulling soft pressure, were unable to squeeze away the space that leaked through. He would be happy, he would be perfect, if he could keep the oxidizing stench out of their interlocked C's, together an S, if their hands could become a two-dimensional plane that kept out words, Kelch's words, the other's words, and kept out Tee-Fog, a half-million dollars, their dream-quick fight. He didn't want her to know. That should count for everything.

The waiter arrived with the first course, a fancy-lettuce salad for Kersten and beef carpaccio for Kelch. They released their hands to allow the waiter to set down the plates. Kersten turned her face up to the waiter in full-frontal gratitude. "Thanks so much."

She chewed her first bite of salad, wiped her mouth, leaving a pleasant, Alzheimery smile. "How's yours?" she invited him to exchange.

"It's okay. Try it," Kelch said, suddenly exhausted, pushing the plate closer to her. And he wondered then, What do you even see in me? He worried for a moment that he had said it aloud. I now know, he thought, what the rest of the world will think I am if (when) they figure it out, and I know what Hoder Leary thinks of me and what Paul Galicia has to *say* about me. I just lucked into a job—I'm just a representative Wall Street man. Is that what you see in me? Stick me in your model and all the right requirements— humble, quiet, responsible—match up. Is that it, Kersten? Am I just a nice guy who makes a lot of money, and it's a rare combination because, blah, blah, blah, nice guys finish last. Well, I deserve every penny I make. I've worked harder than you ever have.

Kelch reached over to take a forkful of her salad and stuffed too much of it into his mouth. His thoughts then screamed, You must know me, right? So who in the hell do you think I am? Someone, my God, has to tell me. Kelch's mouth dropped open, and a bit of lettuce, unaware, formed a web between his lower lip and over-lapping bottom teeth. Kersten coiled up her face, amused, and pointed theatrically to her own lip. Kelch wiped his mouth and looked in the napkin at the masticated green.

He wanted to release it, the sea reigning through the body. He needed that smell, that occasional deep, wrong smell of wood docks and sawdust, often too rank to consider, too summoning of the unapproachable that lay beneath the folds, and his fingers dug fur-ther, rabbit ears clenching and twisting and penetrating for the but-ton inside. Push here to release. He assumed that that deep smell was the baseline, and he didn't know how she got rid of it most of the time—all of the time—how she covered it with oils or waters or tips from magazines, how she made it into a faint salmon, sweet salmon, a mouthful of wine with salmon. Sometimes a bread bakery on the seashore. Kelch needed her to release it, to him, and two of his fingers plunged deeper—he curled them in—as he continued to peck offstage. Up top, around the headquarters he was frankly not concerned with, her mouth purred and panted, light and encour-aging. But, This is not *the smell*, his nose cried on its own, in a nose language of sniffs and twitches and a stiff cilial chorus. It batted away the fingers as it tried to bury itself inside awkwardly, until the back of his head became a parturient growth. His nose surrounded itself, fidgeting, trying futilely to go deeper, and with his mouth closed, he drew in a gusting inhale that shook the rest of his body, lying straight on its stomach. His shoulders echoed the squall of the inhale as he did it again. "Sweetie"—she propped herself lightly on her elbows, sweating and near and curious—"what . . . oh . . . are you doing?" His left hand waved her off: this has nothing to do with you. On its way back, it joined his other one, and they positioned themselves under her and raised her hips off the bed; she wiggled to assist him, to fuse him with her legs' fork. His hands curled into her nectarine hard-soft gluteal flesh, and as he pressed himself closer, his tongue rose up and displaced his nose and lapped and kissed. I want the smell, his nose cried again, obsessed, too hungry. Her purrs became grunts and then a biplane motor, and her face turned into the pillow. She bit the pillowcase, but the smell never came. Finished, proud, disappointed, disoriented, Kelch flopped himself over and spread his arms across the crucifix. He looked up to the ceiling. Huh.

Leaning on her side, Kersten played with his hair. They had not spoken since their panting calmed. She asked him if he was feeling any better now. He mumbled something in response, but he *was* content, for the moment; the silence and the lingering warmth had emptied his brain of thoughts, of worries, of demands on Kersten to explain whatever he was, whenever that was, before.

She had made her declaration of love almost a month after his. Her back had been against the armrest of his couch; he was leaning into her chest. As they watched a movie, she swaddled him in her crossed arms, lazily drawing on his T-shirted chest with her moisturized, just-manicured, hands. She caressed his hair, patting it down, and kissed him on the top of the head. "I love you," she whispered— his eyelids were sinkered, drifting to river bottom; he wondered if it was just an echo of the movie—but she whispered it the next week and later again in the same position. Kelch couldn't figure out why, but she always seemed to say it into his hair too, as if, he once suspected, it was the hair she was addressing. She always said that he had nice hair.

Monday through Thursday, Kelch and Kersten usually only saw each other one night, for two hours, vertical. Another horizontal half hour or so, which sixty:forty happened, meant that Kelch would get only five hours of sleep and be tired and underperforming (on a relative basis) the next day. In the machine-pressed candies that were their weekends, however, they were inseparable—except when he worked, and he often worked. Weekends meant a birthday party, an engagement party; they meant dinner with two other couples, they meant a movie with friends, they meant some musical she dragged him to (she didn't care if they were for tourists). They were brunch, brunch, an unending parade of brunch, maybe with her parents, who would come down from Connecticut, or maybe with Marigold, whom Kersten preferred to see that way.

A third asleep, in a delicious sleep, Kelch listened to Kersten's fingers drizzle across his pinkish, mostly bald chest. He noted nebulously the silence. It was a rich field for unspoken appreciations, imperceptible brushstrokes, nighttime calm, a field on which a different kind of love could hypothetically grow.

The phone rang. Kelch opened his eyes, a reawakened dead, and looked to Kersten. A late call was psychoanalysis for the penniless, summoning all the great dreads, the most perverse wishes. For a second, the repertory fears appeared: Heather's kids hurt, his mother killed, Dan broke. But that night, special guests appeared: Veena, Joe Tedeschi, Blue himself calling to insist on his appearance tomorrow. On the third ring, Kelch stood up and reached for the cordless phone. Still naked, he walked into his apartment's other room. He disaggregated his love-crusted appendages and pushed the button: talk.

"Chris?" The voice, even over the phone, had a breathy sneak-up quality, a tiptoe timbre, and like the devil of cartoons, it spoke directly into your ear.

"Jesus. Do you know what time— Where are you?" Don't say in town.

"Sorry, guess I wasn't thinking. Must be eleven there," he said casually, as if he had last spoken to Kelch last night, not four months ago.

"What do you want?"

The voice stalled. "Did I wake you?"

"No."

"Well, we're talking, so we might as well talk, right?"

"Hold on." Kelch returned through the open bedroom door and found a pair of briefs on the ground. He put them over his straight frame—his earlier, active life still defined his lines—and indicated to Kersten, with a single finger, that it would be a single minute. He closed the door, not all the way, and returned to the living room. Moving toward the window, he muted his breathing to delay the resumption of the conversation, which he grudgingly allowed was happening. He gazed out of his tenth-floor window and listened to the empty street and the brownstones on the other side of his door-manned tower. Then he looked at the plant, the violet, that Kersten had bought. She had explained that it was the state plant of Illinois. *When the guy described it to me, I thought, That's just like you.* Doesn't like the heat. Does better in shade. A reliable perennial. Kelch had smiled out of politeness and put it on the windowsill.

"Are you still there?" the voice asked.

Kelch exhaled loudly. "What do you want?"

"I just wanted to ask you something."

"Then ask. I have to go to bed. I have a job."

"If this is a bad time, buddy, I can call back later."

"Whatever."

"Seriously, I'll call back tomorrow."

"I don't want to talk tomorrow."

"Well, it's kind of embarrassing now that you're making it into a whole big deal, buddy, when I just wanted to talk."

In every one of these calls, Kelch at some point would resolve to fire a *buddy* back, but a hard-*d* buddy, a popping, dismissive-*b* *buddy*, not the other's gentle, almost lullaby *buddy*. "Just tell me already."

"I just called to ask if you're Scott?"

"What?"

"If you're Scott from this article?" The Ghost was not only a supernatural spirit who could disappear, reappear, travel through walls. Now, as his question bared, he possessed supernatural powers, insight, also clarity. It was unforgivable.

"Why—why are you asking me that?" Kelch sputtered. It was impossible that that question could have occurred to the Ghost. The one time he had come to New York, Kelch had met him at a restaurant. Father and son, standing two feet apart, were both self-conscious for their frozen torsos and arms. It had been four years. Finally, after a few small spastic jerks forward, more on the Ghost's part, they shook hands. The scene was repeated, going as coming.

"I was just reading this, and it kind of, if you know you, made it—"

Kelch attacked the end of his sentence. "Don't call me again." He felt hand-slapped; his right ear filled with stars and a throbbing swell.

"What are you talking about, buddy?"

"What don't you understand? Don't ever call me here again."

The Ghost had no temper; he had no personality, no face. "Hey, *calm* down, buddy"—he dragged out *calm* like a tongue-depressed *ah*—"I just wanted to have a little chat between fath—"

"Between what? What?"

Nothing.

"Right, I think we understand each other. Listen: do yourself a favor. Stop calling me and wasting my time."

"Hey, I'm just trying to—"

Kelch hung up the phone.

BOOK TWO

· 1 ·

With a word, he can destroy millions. Even a tone, a temperance of zeal, can wring millions, sometimes billions, of dollars from a company's stock market value. Yet he is not famous on Wall Street or Main Street. He does not control any capital himself. And even though he earns a salary that makes one blush, he is not by American standards rich. None of this is inexplicable. He works in the equity strategy and research department of one of the country's most prestigious investment banks. His power is magnified by his firm. What surprises you when you meet him, then, is not that so much power rests in someone so anonymous, but that so much power rests in someone so average. He is twenty-eight years old, and his name is Scott.

Or at least that is what I'll call him to protect his identity. Scott and I engaged in a series of unusually candid discussions about himself, his work, his ambitions, and the culture of today's Wall Street . . .

. . .

It was before, it was the first Friday in February, and as they walked into the restaurant, Kelch pleaded with Kersten, double-wrapped in a scarf, not to abandon him at the table. If he wanted to eat dinner with strangers, he told her, he would go to a random restaurant and eat dinner with strangers. That week, Kelch had become a banker's bitch, as they called it in research, advising—leading—the bankers in constructing the marketing story for TFRW's secondary offering. The conference calls, the incessant drafts of presentation slides, the always delayed, habitually interrupted meetings had accumulated, like paste in his lungs, and he could never find the oxygen for a full breath. He just wanted to sleep now, for two weeks straight, not subject himself to being an outcast because he had nothing to say to Marigold's friends. Kersten, he knew, didn't want to be here any more than he did. Over the last two days, she had given him three separate opportunities to lie for them both—*if you have something you have to do, we don't have to go.* She had faultlessly if not convincingly stressed the condition all three times. As they entered the restaurant, Kersten reached for his hand and interlaced her fingers in his. With her other hand, she rubbed his as a talisman for good luck—and quick service.

Kersten found Marigold at the bar and, thus activated, pealed with popped-bottle joy. She raved with unimpeachable sincerity about Marigold's new hairstyle, which to Kelch looked the same as the old. Kelch, moving in to greet Marigold, avoided her waxy lip print with an awkwardly aimed *mmwwt*, his cheek parallel to hers. Marigold was an off-priced copy of her first cousin; in Marigold, Kersten's murmuring stomach was a grumble; on Marigold, Kersten's fair complexion tended to the blotchy and wine-stained; on Marigold, Kersten's sun hair was tawnier, a pencil skin. Although Marigold, to her advantage, had convincing blue eyes. She also, unlike Kersten, had a degree from their grandfather's, their fathers', and Kersten's brothers' college. The older Henrys still went down there occasionally for football games. They also insisted on singing the alma mater at weddings. Kersten, even as a legacy, didn't get in.

Marigold introduced Kelch and Kersten to the four others of the party, all darkly clad in league with the room. The faces of the first couple, whom Kelch had met before, seemed strained; a reluctance about them alluded to an earlier, unresolved fight. Kelch bumped his tongue over his bottom teeth, giving him a tobacco dipper's pooch, as he and Kersten shook hands with the second couple, a guy named Elezandro or Alejandro—*cool it on the accent for a second*—and his girlfriend, whose name was a traffic jam of vowels. After a brief polite exchange, Kersten repositioned herself to talk to Marigold exclusively. Kelch knew that Kersten had a talent for the geometry of a party, of stances and location; when she was the center of the room—the prettiest, the nicest, the most generous laugher, the only woman—she would literally be in the center of the room. In situations like this one, however, when she was apprehensive, she would buttonhole an ally on the side. The others, not seeming to notice Marigold and Kersten drift down the bar, returned to their conversation, which, their posture argued, Kelch had interrupted all by himself. When Kelch was introduced, each had slow-bounced his or her eyes up and down over Kelch's clothes, just once. Marigold's friends—Kelch understood the process—needed only one bounce to place Kelch in a disposable chamber pot of necktied or khaki-panted organization men. Undisturbed in his solitude, which was better than the alternative, Kelch scanned the bar and sneaked a look into the restaurant proper. The lighting was dim and off-centered, the noise explosive, the waiters un-American, and the tables and chairs borrowed from a future past of clunky blond wood. Kelch had asked Nathanson about the place and had rolled his eyes when Nathanson began, "Hipster central . . ." Nathanson had also said that the place wasn't cheap. So where do these people get the money for this shit? Kelch was the only one there, it seemed to him, who looked like he had a job.

This restaurant wasn't in Kelch's New York, he understood; here he was a tourist, or maybe the advance guard. It was in a New York where the streets' sounds were gossip about photographers' assistants or graphic designers and anecdotes about occupational brushes with people quite famous, it was implied, in their fields. There were other New Yorks, Kelch knew—at least he knew, in theory, about other Manhattans—the fabulous New York over which those famous ethereally floated; a Eurodirt New York where Peter Pans from second-tier countries imitated the same from the first; a family New York of private schools and nannies; and Latin New Yorks and Jewish New Yorks and black New Yorks and theater New Yorks and gay and media and dangerous New Yorks.

When Kelch left Evanston, none of this had been clear to him. (He had first seen salt water, the mixed drink of river and harbor under the Triborough Bridge, only months before, when he came to the city to interview with the firm.) Kelch had thought that he was going to *the* New York, where everything was spangled and mingled, the butterfat skimmed off all of the Rockfords of the world—a city where straightlaced bankers from the Midwest were corrupted by B-actresses in a whirl of gin. He was unaware of the source of this idea, for the air had been sprayed far above him, so far that he couldn't see, with collective memories of Jazz Age hangovers and the Black and White Ball. At the drawn-out farewell dinner in Rockford—*You're not gonna change on us in New York.* No, Dan. *Damn, I was hoping you were*—Kelch looked blankly into space and anesthetized his impatience. In twelve hours he would be alone on a plane, and in fourteen hours he would hand in his ticket to the one New York: his offer letter from Freshler Feld. And it was a rare ticket indeed, the firm let him believe; only four people from his class in Evanston had been hired by Freshler. Kelch would later accept that maybe (however unlikely) the one New York existed, but it took him only six months to realize where he lived. He had become a member in good standing of the New York of the full intermission, the swarm of financial analysts, associates, young vice presidents of Finance, Consulting, Law, Advertising, the deracinated

e-business boys and expatriated i-business girls, a New York that
was the ladder steps and playground of a decade of aftercollege
years, the interlude allegro between white successful ruling-voting
suburbia and white successful ruling-voting suburbia. His New York
was bright, prodigal, lighthearted. As far as he could tell, it was also
the great, tidal majority over Manhattan island, too large and too
fixed to be tagged anymore with sociological interest: yuppies, *yuppies*? Yawn, yawn. Kelch's New York was not the trendsetter, but its
patronage enabled the trends. It was always in favor of modish dressing and stylish eating—this restaurant would soon be theirs—but
without the fuss, the monomania for uniqueness. It paid the taxes
and served on the juries and filled the high-rises and pledged its
blood, wattage, verve, hours to the dollarly hum of its employing
machines. It was peripherally aware of art and culture, but art and
culture were for visits from Mom. The full intermission was content
to listen to CDs from college, watch the sharper dramas and sitcoms,
see the movies—whatever was out, was on, was there. Its book-
shelves were filled with the paperbacks that its college bookstores
would not buy back, "used" stickers still yellowing on half the spines.
Occasional glimpses of the other New Yorks were appreciated and
amusing but were, by mutual consent, short and innocuous, a palate
cleanser, not a course. *Have you met Stacey's younger sister, Kelch?* And
what do you do, Stacey's younger sister? *I work at this art magazine
that you like probably never heard of.* What's it called. . . . Uh-huh. . . .
No, you're right, I never heard of it. *And what do you do?* I work
with Brian at Freshler Feld. *Oh.* Right. *Good to meet you.* Right.

Unlike Nathanson, who gave the impression of a universal command of other New Yorks, curiosity about them passed through
Kelch like a glass of water. He was comfortable and cheerful—
possessed—in the full intermission. That night, for instance, he
would have much rather hung out with Kim and Torvil, talking
about the interesting and the relevant, sports and the market and
bonus-fed apartment strategies.

It was nine o'clock, and the reservation was for eight-thirty, and the restaurant would not seat them until the whole party arrived. Marigold, normally flittering and anxious, had begun to unbind. Finally, she told the hostess to make the table for seven, and they would just see what happened if the eighth ever arrived. "You know how these types are," she whispered confidentially, overly familiar, to Kelch about the missing, although Kelch had no idea who these types even were. The group single-filed through the restaurant to a merger of tables in back; Kelch noticed the eyes following them, reading the billboard of their catwalk, assessing the degree of beauty or fashion among the seven. Marigold and Kersten were palavering in front, the two couples followed, and Kelch, carrying his soft case embranded with a Freshler conference logo, two years old, trailed at the caboose. Seeing one or two smirks in the gallery, he double-checked the tie that he was wearing that day, a good one. So fuck you.

Marigold sat Kelch at the end of the table, next to Vowels, across from the empty seat, and Kersten was placed, crushingly, at the worst possible position, at the other end of the table, on the same side. Kelch turned to Vowels, whose skin seemed drained of color by her hair of a rich black depth unimaginable in Rockford. "How's it going?"

"Oh. Fine, good."

"That's good."

"You are friends with Kersten?"

"Uh-huh."

"Kersten is such a nice person." She had rhymed the ends of the sentence. *Kersson is such a nice pear-son.*

"Sure." And Kelch would not be surprised if he didn't say anything else to her, to anyone, for the rest of the night. He was sure that he had done that at another Marigold assembly; afterward, he had even felt a small glow of accomplishment. Two days after that, he learned the potential of Kersten's deceitfulness when she reported that Marigold said that people thought that he had been totally charming that night.

He looked at his watch, nine-ten, and then at the menu, and even though he instantly reached a decision, he studied the menu longer.

"What are you going to have?" Vowels asked.

"Probably the chicken."

"Oh," she said, and Kelch thought, Jesus, I've been put in the deadwood section. He watched Elezandro-Alejandro produce some great hilarity for Marigold and Kersten, judging by their reaction. But then again, Kersten laughed at everyone's jokes, with sincerity, even his, even when they weren't jokes. Elezandro, Kelch reckoned, was the guest star tonight, but Kelch couldn't figure out how a Mexican or whatever he was could be that funny. His accent was slight, a delicate vinegar dressing compared to Vowels's. Through the corner of his eyes, Kelch took a glimpse at Vowels again; her head poked out of her shoulders snail-like; she was holding the menu myopically close to her face.

Three minutes later, Marigold squealed and sprang simultaneously: "Paulll." Her attempted sweep of a grand hostess was still wanting. She clunked into the back of Alejandro-Elezandro's chair as she rushed to the newcomer, kissed him on the cheek, and took his hands individually in each of hers. Paul Galicia was introduced around the table, and Kelch caught and did not approve of a Johann somewhere in his excessively mannerly hellos. Kelch couldn't tell if he was gay; all of the male friends of round Marigold seemed to zigzag the border between sensitive and effeminate. Paul's head was a topic sentence: his oblong, rectangular glasses were thickly bordered in blacky-emerald plastic; his hair was a competition of curls and waves; his sideburns announced their studied retrospectiveness at the bottom of his ear. He wore a stiff-cut workingman jacket. He and Kelch were roughly the same age.

"Oh my," Marigold exclaimed in mild horror as she surveyed the seats. For a moment, Kelch thought that she was going to rearrange the whole table just so Paul wasn't banished to the empty chair across from Kelch. Paul smiled gallantly and volunteered, "It's no problem. I'll just sit here on the end." He rested his hand on the back of the chair.

I'm so honored.

Marigold seemed to well up in contemplation of Paul's generosity. "Are you sure?"

"Of course." And he sat down. He tweezed the menu, holding it away from his body with a ninety-degree elbow, and after one decisive camera exposure, set the menu down, unwrapped his napkin onto his lap, and asked Kelch, "Do they have any specials tonight?" Paul's voice seemed to pass through a stiff tissue of a kazoo; it wasn't Kelch's spring water.

Although Paul's jacket did not display a gas-station patch, Kelch knew from whence its cut and fabric came. Its blank breast yearned for a hilarious oval with hilarious script of a hilarious name—Hank or Gus—from a hilarious places like Sheboygan, Wisconsin, or Rockford, Illinois. *Maybe if I ask Kersten to trade places with . . .* "Huh?"

"Do they have any specials tonight?"

"I, uh, don't know."

"Well, the lamb is great—I've had it before—although I'm not sure if I'm in the mood for it."

Thanks for letting me know, asshole. "Okay."

Paul declared obscurely, "Well, habits is habits," and wove his hands together. Kelch noticed that his thumbs, though not necessarily twiddling, were alternating in subtle thumb-wrestle pins. He asked, then, "So, Chris, what do you do?"

There was no foreplay, but Kelch did not mind; they both knew, Kelch assumed, that it was impossible for them to communicate without an initial understanding of the other's world-purpose, obtainable free of charge. "I'm at Freshler Feld," he answered with Freshler-bred humility. A firm that does not shout proves it does not need to shout.

"And that is a . . . law firm?"

As if Paul had placed a pound of disbelief on the balance scale of Kelch's forehead, Kelch's right brow sank. "No, the investment bank." He did not add aloud, You know, the fastest-growing bank in the last decade in terms of equity underwriting market share, the leading bank in terms of aftermarket performance, the number three investment bank overall (excluding retail brokerage operations), and the only one even remotely in a position to knock, over the next three years, one of the two giants out of the box.

"Sorry, of course, Freshler Feld. It's owned by a Red or a Green or an Orange?"

"Yeah, right. Orange Padaway."

Nothing.

"It's Blue, and he doesn't own it, you know. It's a public company." Kelch declared these facts calmly, not giving Paul the satisfaction of observing his tensing ire.

"Sorry about that. I must be confusing it with something else."

"And what do you do"—Kelch paused and allowed the *p* of the coming Paul to inflate his mouth into a fake grin—"Paul?"

"I'm a writer."

"What, for like a magazine or something?"

The smile across Paul's face was difficult to read; his barely turned lips included no other muscle of his face, and the stage was overwhelmed by the proscenium of his glasses. His manner was clear, however: paternal, self-satisfied, amusedly patient. "I do occasionally write some creative nonfiction."

"What does that mean, creative nonfiction?"

"You know, longer feature pieces in magazines. Post New Journalism?" Kelch didn't react. "Well, I'm sure you'd know what I'm talking about if you saw it."

"Okay." Kelch tried to steal a peripheral glance at Kersten. Marigold's eyes, waiting for his, were radically open, part signal, part plea. *I'm not going to embarrass you, so calm down.*

Paul continued, as if to himself. "Really, though, I'm concentrating on fiction."

Kelch brought his regard back to across the table. "Like books?"

Looking around the restaurant: "That would probably be more conducive to reading than toilet paper."

"Yeah, right. Toilet paper."

Nothing.

"How many have you written?" *Probably none, so you can wipe that smug look off your face.*

"How many what?"

"Books. Like have I read anything you've written?" Kelch knew he hadn't read anything that Paul had written, and he began accessing excuses just in case: thirteen-, fourteen-hour days in the office; weekends and planes and vacations of catch-up reading of trade journals, business magazines, Freshler reports; four long vacations in five years, during which he had felt a ripple to read something not related to work, although only twice had the ripple led to a last page.

Even Nathanson didn't have time to read anymore. In the full intermission, there were no choices, only priorities, only situations, and advancement.

"Unless you've snuck into my apartment, probably not."

"Well, I haven't snuck into your apartment."

Nothing.

Kelch checked the menu again to ensure that the chicken had not disappeared. From the opposite corner of the table, with an unprefaced abruptness, Marigold folded over her plate and elevated her voice: "Paul, is Chris boring you with his tales of his 'wild' days and nights on Wall Street?"

What?

Only Kersten's eyes, of all those at the table, did not then focus on him and Paul. She was looking to her left, her head conducting automated movements of surveillance. Paul leaned in to smile at Marigold. "No, no. Just chatting here." If Paul had encouraged Marigold, Kelch was sure that he would have told all these posers what he really thought of their spoiled asses. He reached across Vowels

with his opposite arm—it was too far of a stretch to be polite—
and grabbed the bread basket.

Kersten returned her attention, fully engaged, to the table. She
addressed Paul warmly. "Marigold tells me that you're a very talented writer."

"I think Marigold likes to exaggerate."

"Oh, you're just being modest," Kersten observed, exuding.
"That's great." *Kersson / such a nice pear-son.*

"Well, if you insist, I'm actually unbelievably talented."

The whole table, save Kelch, laughed, and Kelch realized that the
squeeze was on. One by one, the center filling had abandoned listening to Alejandro and had picked up the cross-currents between Kersten and Paul. Finally, Alejandro stopped talking altogether. Kelch
rubbed his underthigh; he wanted to leave, disappear—nothing good,
he understood, could come out of the present. His thigh's itch spread
to a hardball-sized irritation. He looked above Paul, to the restaurant's kitchen doors.

Marigold, ostensibly continuing the good cheer, slipped the conversation away from her cousin. She told Paul that she and Kersten
had both just finished the novel he had recommended. It had taken
Kersten three months, Kelch knew. For the first two, during the
infrequent times they sat in bed together reading, Kersten had interrupted herself by asking Kelch about their near-term plans, or his
day, or (why not?) his childhood. The last month, Kelch had done
the interrupting. Deeper into the book, then, Kersten's face would
scrunch into a pouty seriousness as she forced herself on. It made
her irresistible, and Kelch would stare at her, hoping this would
spark affection. It often did. But last week, she begged him, "Please,
I really have to finish the book." *You told me you don't even like it.*
"That's not important."

Now Kersten offered to the table, "I really liked the book." Looking at Marigold: "I mean, I thought it was really good." Marigold
sat stiffly at the edge of her chair. "But there was a lot of pretty,
um, graphic stuff, don't you think?"

She had asked the table, and the table—including Kersten—all turned to Paul.

"Well," he said, "the reviewers were also surprised by the raunchiness—is that a word, raunchiness?—in the second half of the book. But that didn't shock you, did it, Kersten?" Paul pumped his forehead, and the dark frames of his glasses hopped up and down on his nose; it was a great comic effect, obviously much used, and now successful. Marigold laughed the loudest.

Kersten answered, "I don't know if I'm shocked that easily."

"That's good to hear."

"I'm glad you think so."

"Well, you know, I always try to oblige."

"Marigold did tell me that you were really nice."

What the fuck are you talking about, Kelch thought. But he knew: nice to Kersten had a wider meaning than it had to other people; she wasn't just nice herself; she loved the word *nice*, the concept of niceness; it was a worldview, a liberating theology. Sometimes, in the company of men, nice seemed to dance over the edge to flirtation. Or maybe now she was actually flirting. As the conversation continued straight through the ordering of food and the appearance of wine, Kelch realized that he had no means of escape. He chewed expressively on another piece of bread stuffed into his cheek.

Vowels, who had managed to achieve true invisibility—not easy considering the competition from her immediate neighbors—turned to Kelch to ask a question in confidence, but the leaders had declared the table a monoculture, one conversation for all. With overdelicate respect for the shy, they halted the discussion for her. She had asked Kelch, "Did you read this book?"

Kersten uproared, then settled, covering her mouth, then laughed again, dropping her hand away. Everyone stared at her, at her errorless ivory teeth and blushed-cheek rosiness. Her face had absorbed the first sip of wine. "Chris is really an amazing person," she announced, Kelch felt, more for herself. "But he's not exactly a big reader."

Alejandro, as if racket-hit, spun his focus to the other side of the table. He politely, firmly challenged, "You must read though, right?"

"Of course I read." Kelch tried to mask his anger. "But I don't read like a lot of, whatever, fiction books."

"You mean novels, Chris."

Mumbled: "Okay, Marigold."

"What did you say?"

"I said, Okay, Marigold. You got me. Guilty. 'Novels.' "

Kelch's defense, its unsmiling change of tone, whirled a centrifugal hole in the table. No one, it seemed, knew how to respond, and Kelch almost basked in this achievement. His heart ignited apace as he thought, You snotty fat rich bitch, Marigold. Maybe you could get a man if you weren't such a critic of everyone who's not Mr. New York Culture. And you too, Kersten. You don't want to be here any more than I do. But then a feeling caught Kelch's thoughts by the wrist, twirling them around. It was an unfamiliar, uninvited feeling. He felt alone, dropped onto the flat tundra, a fleck abandoned by Kersten, yes, and by everyone—humanity. Not only alone, he felt depressed and alone, a depression in the spirit on the plains into which poured a gun-metal rain, a toxicity, despair: an obvious knowledge that life was neither good nor fair and that the dream of the weaving of human souls was a lie. It was so intensely true, though, that it was incapable of lasting for long. Kelch shuddered, to himself.

Alejandro then asked not Kelch (Kelch thought) but Kelch's suit and Kelch's fifty-dollar tie, "How can you not read novels?"

"Huh?"

Slower this time: "How can you not read novels?"

"I don't know. How can you not rob liquor stores? You just don't do it." *Do you understand that, greaseball? It's a metaphor.* He tried to look at Kersten, but she had leaned back parallel to him.

Marigold's face turned in on itself, in guilty horror, it seemed, as Paul laughed, mostly in his shoulders. She said, correcting, "Chris, you know what he means."

"Am I on trial here?" Kelch asked, in an unanticipatedly even tone, for the gravity of the situation had departed him. He felt a sudden uprush, a balloon casting off its weights, and he floated and frolicked in a painted sky. These people were not going to make him feel bad about something for which there was no reason to feel bad about. They were not his friends. They were not important. And he was right. "Listen." He marked off his points on his hand, thumb first. "A: I work a hell of a lot of hours every day. I don't know how many you all— But anyway, B: when I'm not working, I just want to relax and hang out, you know, not force myself to do something I don't want to do. And C: frankly, I don't think, in my 'value judgment,' that it's essential that a person read novels. I'm not— It's just not compelling. They have not affected my life one way or another." There, thought Kelch, suck on that.

Alejandro said, "You're joking with me," and in the same passing instant, Kersten tried to offer, "Chris is just quiet," but she aborted the final word: her excuse—the excuse—was probably not applicable now. She smiled, though; it alone often had powers. Alejandro looked around the table and was met with a few raised brows, a puff of resignation that sent a blow of Marigold's expensively softened hair ceiling-bound, and Paul's face, a blank, unreadable wall.

"Was what I said funny?" Kelch asked.

"Tell me, Chris, how do you expect to live a full life without art?"

You've got to be kidding me, Pancho. "Are we talking about art or novels?"

After a bitter-medicine swallow, Alejandro set his wineglass aside so he could close the distance to Kelch. Kelch felt Vowels stiffen beside him. Alejandro pressed, "How do you live a rich and fulfilling life without literature?"

Most of the table had never heard Kelch's laugh, and its debut was loud, unrestrained. Kelch's mouth was as wide, as impertinent as a long-tongued, horny dog's, and because the laugh's switch from baritone to soprano came late, the dismissal must have echoed even louder through the table's seven skulls. "Now you're definitely joking with me. Just think about it. How many million illiterates are there in this country? How many people in the world have never even seen a book? Billions, right? So listen: you think that all those people in Africa or India or wherever don't have fulfilling lives just because of that. That's pretty wrong, I think." Kelch censer-swung his head, *shame, shame*, and though its main purpose was to condemn Alejandro's class bias, it also pitied him for his low aptitude in the arts of disputation. Accustomed as Kelch was to the gladiator pit of Freshler Feld, he was sometimes dumbfounded by the inability of the average citizen to unsheathe the rational knife, to stab with the logical indisputable, to mock others' holes and tatters. Kelch knew that he, Kelch, wasn't even that good at arguing. He was at the Freshler mean. If Nathanson—or Wessex, what a ruthless bastard—had engaged Alejandro in this argument, this guy would have already been in tears. If they had argued against Kelch, hell, Kelch might have been in tears. Or he might have taken the other side. Who really cared?

Alejandro folded his hand. "That's unbelievable."

Kelch was gracious in victory. "Well, what can you do?"

A controlled smile spread through Paul's cheeks, minutely urging up his glasses. Kelch must have felt the thawing morning sun ray of that smile, because he turned to Paul just in time to catch it. He first regarded Paul with confusion: ready for the next round? But then, by instinct, Kelch smiled too—a half grin of amusement. Paul's words came out measured in teaspoons: "No, it's not unbelievable. It's fascinating."

Marigold coughed. Paul had not spoken softly, but the words had not fully penetrated her end of the table. "What?" she asked.

"I said, It's fascinating." Kelch upgraded his half grin a centimeter. "What he just said was fascinating. There's no other word for it."

Kelch plumped out his lower lip and nodded. *I'll take fascinating.*

Paul's smile moderated further, even from its low base, and then disappeared into the uninterpretable, a side view of a saucer. Carefully, he asked, "I'm intrigued by what you said. Do you think most people you work with feel the same way?"

Kelch shrugged. "Haven't done a survey, but I assume they do."

"Fascinating," Paul repeated the *om* of the chant. "Fascinating."

To Marigold's relief, the dinner, following Paul's pronouncement, became happily and buoyantly chaotic. Alejandro was "inexplicably obsessed" with basketball that spring, and Kersten magisterially prodded the silent couple to discuss their recent vacation, and Marigold worked with the (formerly) silent man's friend, and Paul drew a few words out of the stone of Vowels, and the monoculture of the table dissolved into variegated rows and plots, combinations and recombinations of conversations that produced a bubbling noise, a meaning-free effervescence that made all at the table feel current and immortal, infected them with the city's vain assertion that this was why you lived. The wine helped. A lot of wine helped a lot. As they lingered afterward on the sidewalk outside the restaurant, waiting for the bathroomed Vowels and Marigold, Kersten locked her arm inside the equilateral opening of Kelch's elbow, and till-death-do-us-part leaned into him. It was a mild winter, and Kelch had left his coat unzipped. Kersten blinked long to clear the fuzzy oenophilic glow. "That wasn't so bad, was it, sweetie?"

"I guess not."

"No, really, it wasn't, was it?" She seemed to be seeking confirmation that they had left the dinner admired, respected, safe, okay. As Kelch watched her, she appeared to glisten, successively, in each area of his focus, and as his eyes surveyed her face, her chin line and eyes and hair, even her weird flat-button nose, flashed perfection, a moving, transporting beauty. How lucky he was to even be near her, the flashes sighed. And he had told her that he loved her first. He should be telling her more now, he thought, telling her how he wanted to ingest everything about her, imbibe that factory of ease inside her that made her survive, flourish in this world. But instead he smiled mischievously, the boy who nipped the nearly done cookies from the oven, and said, "I didn't have as good a time as you making goo-goo eyes at Shakespeare there."

She slapped his chest with a limp-wrist *thunk* and protested, thoughtfully, "He's not even my ty—" When tipsy, Kersten sometimes misplaced her cue cards.

In a falsetto, Kelch, eyelashes fluttering, sang, "Oh, it's so graphic. You have such cool stupid glasses."

Kersten steadied her legs. "I never said anything about his— Are you *jealous*?"

That was a good question, Kelch attempted to think, but the leavening of the wine could not be suppressed. His breathing took in the windless night. "Oh, you're forgiven." And she laughed again and tried to slap his chest again, but he caught her by the wrist in a bracelet of his thumb and pointer and brought it to his mouth. His kisses then were rabbity nibbles. She giggled and tried to free her arm, and his nibbles moved up the cashmere black of her coat.

"Chris." It was Paul, two yards away. Kelch slowly let down Kersten's arm and cleared the appropriated fuzz off his tongue with his teeth. "Can I talk to you?"

For Kersten's amusement: "I don't know. Can you?"

"Alone."

The two walked fifteen feet away from the group. Paul, Kelch noticed, was serious and inexplicably sober. He began, "This is not something I normally do, but I need to ask you a favor."

"She's not for sale." Kelch smiled wide and hiccuped, tasting the sulfide repetition of the wine.

"That's really funny," Paul said but didn't smile. "Anyway, I think you could help me with a project I'm undertaking."

Kelch's smile exaggerated clownishly. "A 'fiction book'?"

Paul didn't respond directly. "I would appreciate it if you would let me interview you."

"You would?" Kelch feigned great delight and, turning to Kersten, was about to shout, Aren't you proud of me? I'm going to help Asshole write his novel. But she was conferring with the reappeared Marigold. And, indistinctly, he thought better of it too.

Paul's expression had yet to change or reveal. "Yes, I would like to interview you."

"You're losing me here."

Paul explained briefly how useful it would be to interview Kelch for research purposes. Eventually comprehending Paul's request—"I can't object to research, can I?"—Kelch gave him his business card and told him to call whenever. He reckoned Paul would forget about it; he already had.

"Could you do me a favor, though?"

"That'd be a second favor."

Nothing.

"I'm listening . . ."

"Please don't tell anyone about this."

Because of your girlfriend Marigold? Because you don't want Kersten to know you need me? Because you aren't planning on interviewing me but are going to lure me into your sex den and eat me? And then kill me? And *then* eat me. Kelch's smile was skeptical, but he said, "Okay" and returned to Kersten. From behind, he bear-grabbed her above the waist, the tops of his arms just brushing the undershelf of her breasts, and rocked her back and forth. Marigold's eyes said that they had never seen Kelch act this juvenile before. Well, Kelch was a complicated guy. He wasn't always Mr. Quiet.

"What did he want?" Kersten asked over her shoulder.

Winking at Marigold, Kelch said, "He wanted to buy you from me." Kersten giggled again. Marigold seemed even more disgusted. "But I said, Twenty bucks, buster, or no deal."

2

Scott is good looking like local weathermen are good looking, boyish athletes with defined chins, clear skin, and smiles that make their mothers proud. His straight brown hair turns sandy at the tips, and on a windy day, when it rustles, one could probably see in it the prairie land from where he comes. In other words, his good looking is a totally unremarkable good looking. The only exception is an overlapping of his two bottom front teeth.

He is not especially tall, but he seems tall. I have observed Scott at a casual dinner party. There, he was very amusing to himself and loud and inflexible in defense of his opinions, no matter how arbitrarily chosen they appeared to be. One got the feeling that his confidence emerged from his body. In high school, Scott played basketball, and he has carried forward the physical grace of a teenager who could sink a twenty-footer with his eyes closed. Yes, Scott is not overly handsome, but as in his stature he seems more handsome than he is. Although he jokes incessantly about his long workdays, which almost always, he explains, run over into work nights, his posture, his uncomplicated eyes declare that he sleeps well at night . . .

Kelch was in a vinegary mood. He had not expected Paul to call that next Tuesday; he had barely remembered the request for the interview. He apologized that he had to go out of town for a week—a premarketing trip to St. Louis, Denver, Minneapolis, Houston: breakfast, smile, lunch, smile, talk, flog, dinner, smile—and Paul bared his nerve and asked to interview him before he left. Kelch didn't have any plans the next night, but it was emasculating—bad strategy—to let Paul believe that he, Kelch, was on call. (And Paul had not been supplicating enough: Kelch wasn't asking to steal his limited free time.) No, Kelch said, and Paul huffed that it just wouldn't work then, and Kelch placed him on hold, stalled, and returned to relent. He was kind of curious. "I shuffled some stuff around, but it's still pretty inconvenient." Really, deeply, inhumanely inconvenient.

Kelch found it difficult to remember his final impression of Paul or, more relevant, Paul's final impression of him. The hangover last Saturday, a kettledrum in his head, a Sahara in his throat, had surprised him. He had expected only a ticking woodblock and arable Oklahoma scrub. The next morning, Marigold's final glare had reappeared in a half dream just before he awoke. Well, he had the right to act how he wanted: God knows, drinking was the only thing that could keep him awake around her narrow-minded friends.

Another reason for Kelch's resistance: he was tired. He was always tired. The world allowed him only a few hours of sleep at night, and no hours awake free of the horn blasts of the taxied streets, the buses' brakes, the computer humming inside his desk and his brain. It allowed him no hours free of mobile home office fax holding up his tenderized body by their rings. Even when he was with Kersten, they were bombarded by electrons, music playing or movies playing or the television playing, their fussy phones ringing, the *ank, ank, ank* of a quacking alarm clock informing them that another day was going to have to happen because the last day had disappeared. The sun waxed in the subway, waned in the office, and his six years at Freshler had passed in a snap.

As he walked into the meeting place just before nine, his mood soured further. The Irish bar in the East Village was almost empty, and it wasn't even dark and knotty and characterful. It was inexplicably large, the wood molding was newly varnished, and the scratchless mirrored signs for ales and stouts seemed to have arrived that morning from a Dublin gift shop. And Paul wasn't even there. Back in Rockford, if people agreed to meet at nine, both parties were there at eight fifty-five, but people in Rockford were not as enthusiastically self-centered as in New York, Kelch had been taught time and again, where promptness was a condemnable sign of flagging devotion to one's own person. Kelch ordered a beer. He could hear the bartender's broguish thoughts making note of his suit. Depending on how the shadows fell, she could have been either eighteen or thirty-four. Only one table was filled, by a group of underage undergraduates, for whom she was lenient and pouring.

At nine-ten, Paul came in wearing the same costume of the same ironic jacket and same proclamation glasses. He saw Kelch in the booth, slid in, and announced, preoccupied, "Technology triumphs again." *Don't you say you're sorry?* "I bought this thing"—he held it up—"a month ago, and the batteries are already shot." *Don't you even fucking say you're sorry for being late?* "And of course, I didn't bother to check it until just before I came." *And what about, Thanks for coming, prick?* "And then it was impossible to find any place open with the right batteries." Paul laid the microcassette recorder on the table and Kelch regarded it and its implications: permanence, legality, gravity, also suspicion. While continuing to fiddle and massage the recorder, Paul asked, sort of, "So what's going on?"

"This is a real happening place you picked here."

Paul looked up and noticed the bar as if for the first time. "Well, it's not too loud." He turned a few dimelike knobs on the recorder and set it on the table halfway between him and Kelch. "It's also close to my apartment."

Kelch had laid his suit coat on the booth bench next to him; he was wearing a French blue shirt—Parisian blue, Kersten had explained, more sea than sky than the other blues that constituted the rainbow in his closet—and one of his best ties, an expensive repetition of small painted peaches, another gift from Kersten. He had put both on that morning for this moment. "So," he asked, "what are we doing here again?"

"One second, and I will answer whatever . . . Testing, one, two, three. Paul. Can you say the same thing?"

"Huh?"

"Say, Testing, one, two, three, Chris."

Kelch did it, and when Paul played back the tape, they both laughed at Paul's recorded plea. Paul laughed presumably at the sharpening of his sibilants, the graduation of his nasally voice into the fully feminine; Kelch laughed at that too but as a tributary of the larger, growing ridiculousness of the whole situation. He twitched. He had to get out of there. He had to pack. Maybe something was on television. Maybe Kersten would come over. He had told her that he was eating dinner with a client that night.

"Should we begin?" Paul asked in a denial of his previous laughter.

"Hold it a second, man." Kelch lifted his palm off the table. "Are you going to"—he passed through *apologize* and *thank me*—"explain the, uh, tape recorder?"

Paul recoiled from the question, three inches, in surprise. "You don't expect me to take notes on every little thing you say, do you?" Paul pronounced *little* with a hard, hatched-tongue *t* for the syllable end and beginning.

"That's not what I'm talking about. Why do you need to do anything if this is just background research?"

"Well, I may need to retrieve our conversation in a month or, I don't know, a year, and I don't trust my memory for that long."

"So you're not planning to share this stuff with anyone?"

"Why? Are you planning to give me inside information?" For the second time, Kelch felt a sparklike twitch—a signal to leave—at the connection between the seat and his thigh. Paul backtracked. "That probably wasn't a very amusing joke for a guy like you." Like me, repeated Kelch's face, callousing with building indifference. "But seriously," Paul said, "as I'm sure I've explained to you, my project is not just a single book or article. Its ultimate goal—I'm going to sound a little pompous here—is to assemble a comprehensive, universal portrait of the city, one cutting through classes, races, genders, et cetera." *Assemble* was articulated as a special friend. "Anyway, I really need to talk to a wide variety of people, including a Wall Street person."

"A Wall Street *person*?"

"Or whatever, a banker, a financier."

Biting in his lip and guiding down, with a cupped palm, the drizzle condensed on his glass, Kelch asked as clearly as he could, "So you don't have any plans to, you know, embarrass me with this?"

"This is going into a bottom desk drawer with other tapes just like it."

"There's no special use for this."

"Just my life. But why would that be special?"

"Huh?"

"Never mind."

"Then fine." Kelch signed the contract with a large, reassuring gulp. Paul's tightfisted humor, his *Wall Street person*, irked Kelch; they seemed soaked not just in conceit but in a specific, exhibitionist conceit. After a "Not fair," Paul told Kelch that he was going to get a beer too. Kelch exhaled and felt his body sag deeper into the booth's bench, molasses into a tub. Paul stood up and gestured to Kelch that he would be right back, and Kelch thought, Aren't you going to ask me if I need one? When Paul didn't, Kelch then asked him to wait and took out his wallet slowly—he groaned with his joints, old mannish—and shuffled through the motions long enough for the inviter to insist that he was going to pay. "I'll have another one too," Kelch said and handed a five-dollar bill to Paul, who actually took it, and not only that, grimaced, Kelch was certain, to register his disappointment that Kelch wasn't paying for them both. As Paul walked to the bar, Kelch rubbed his left eye with his palm, trying to rouse himself, settle himself, clear away the disfocusing blur to the answer to Why am I here? Kersten, he knew, would absolutely adore being here now, inputting the data of her life story for some self-proclaimed artiste. But Kelch could feel what was coming: thin fingers poking into crevices, cynical, paint-stripping attempts to *understand*—it was not just Paul but everyone in New York—that were fake and unhealthy, an unnatural mutation of a child's curiosity. Kelch's life story was simple, he knew. He was born in Rockford. He now lived in New York. Paul returned, set down the beers, and took off his jacket. He was wearing a close-knitted black sweater crossed by a useless yellow stripe. He pressed the record button. "Ready?"

"What do you need to know?" Kelch's eyes were narrowing, already bored.

"Well, I always like to begin with the same question. Why do you do what you do?"

"What answer do you want—the money?" His life story had one more layer, he sometimes allowed. He was born in Rockford. He now lived in New York. Money was missing in Rockford. He now lived in New York. "Is that what I'm supposed to answer here? The money?"

Paul's forearms quickly crossed, a director cutting the scene, and after exhaling in surrender, he said, "Let's just forget this whole thing, Chris. Every little gesture of yours has made it quite clear that you don't want to be here. And if you are not going to take this seriously, then it's just a waste of my time. I'm going to make you very happy by calling it a night." He reached to the recorder to drop the curtain on the performance, but as his hand covered the recorder, Kelch's hand covered his. With no anterior intention, with mortification for being there, Kelch's hand then slid off Paul's and rested flush, ashamed against the table.

"Try again. I'll take it seriously."

It is easy to understand what he does, but it is not easy to understand why it is needed. The division name on Scott's business card is suitably imposing: equity strategy and research. The name evokes a brain trust of scientists dissecting the stock market, holing up in libraries next to reams of computer printouts, devising top secret theories of investing. Nothing could be further from the truth, at least for Scott. Equity research—Scott plays no part in the strategy function—is essentially a business of information routing and, at best, mild interpretation. As a sell-side securities analyst, Scott is responsible for a "universe" of stocks in a narrow sector of the economy. (I agreed not to divulge the sector.) Specifically, he provides investment recommendations about those stocks, the ubiquitous buy ratings and rare sell ratings quoted on cable television, and what can only be described as news about the stocks to his firm's buy-side clients: mutual funds, pension funds, hedge funds, insurance companies, and extremely wealthy individuals. The research is provided free to those clients and is a cornerstone of the customer-service strategy for all investment banks' brokerage divisions. Clients determine what bank to award their stock trades—and resulting commissions—based on a number of factors, including the quality of the research, the quality of execution by a bank's traders, the promptness of service by its brokers, and, one assumes, skybox tickets and golf outings . . .

Although seconds before Kelch had intended to take all this seriously, when he opened his mouth to fulfill his promise, he droned, uncontrolled, with the fatigue of the hundredth recital. "Um," he said, "I was always fascinated by the markets, and Freshler Feld is indisputably one of the best firms on the Street and the one that offered me the job with the highest potential." When one of the bolder, brattier candidates for a job at Freshler would ask Kelch why he should "consider joining" the department, Kelch would answer, Let me tell you how I got here. I was always fascinated by the markets . . .

"I was thinking a little more big picture."

"There is no big picture. I was twenty-one years old, and Freshler and three or four other banks came to Evanston, and I got an offer from two of them, and one was in trading and one—Freshler—was in research, and I decided I wanted to go into research because, you know, I couldn't really see myself as a trader."

Paul appeared to swallow a word in a noiseless burp. "Well, then, how about this: *what* exactly do you do on a day-to-day basis?"

"You really want to hear about this?"

"That's the purpose of this little exercise."

"All right." Kelch grabbed the two beer glasses and placed them a foot apart on the table. Distant from himself—above himself—he began. "The global economy is divided into two basic, I don't know, things." His voice had perked, to his surprise, to a gee-whiz, Kersten-ish enthusiasm. Maybe this wouldn't be so bad. Paul acknowledged this perking with a lowrise, "fascinated" smile. "A: companies who need capital. And B: investors with capital. Investment banks are somewhere in the middle." Kelch painted a road stripe down the middle of the global economy with his hand. "Fundamentally, um, origi-nally, the role of these banks was to get capital from this beer to that beer. Obviously, though, there are a lot of other services that are related to this. So if the bank here"—Kelch looked for a salt shaker or sufficient substitute to serve the role of the bank; finding nothing, he set his cellular phone on the invisible stripe—"is doing an IPO for this company, it needs to have the infrastructure, you know, like brokers and traders with contacts with these guys over here, who will obvi-ously need to trust the bank—that's the key, *trust*—before they would invest in just any offering." He catalogued, in detail, the business units that constituted the phone. "But if you're a bank with all these bro-kers, there is no way there would be enough IPOs to keep them occu-pied all day, or pay their salary. So they also work in the secondary market, you know, facilitating normal trades for their clients for com-missions—well, sometimes they're spreads but—for our purposes, just think commissions." Inhaling for the final sprint, Kelch twirled the phone on the table. "And if these clients are going to pay them an assload in commissions to do their trades, they want more service than just some broker getting tips out of *Business Week*. So all the banks have invested millions—hundreds and hundreds of millions really—into research departments, which do a few things: provide this value-added service and occasionally market offerings and generate busi-ness by generating ideas that generate trades . . ."

Three minutes of further clarification passed before Paul broke in. "I understand all that, Chris. But I don't understand exactly what *you* do. You keep on talking research, research, research. But what is 'research'? Are you sitting in a library with back issues of *Business Week?*" Paul displayed an instinct for the micro-world of pronunciation, and he paused before *Business* to convey what he thought of that word, and maybe of Kelch.

Kelch's tongue, which so often felt like a hundred-pound stick of shortening, became a butterfly wing when it came to Freshler research. Kersten had once asked him how he could be so reserved, considering the demands of his job. That's how little she knew. "No. I have a lot of sources."

"Such as?"

"Primarily the companies. But there's also stuff floating around the market."

"Like in the East River?"

With his pint glass as his prop, Kelch drank: he wasn't going to give Paul the big laugh he was expecting. But, for the record, he got the joke. "I think you're hung up on the word *research*, man. Listen: I'm not sitting in a library all day. We're talking about the real world here, not some faggoty-ass short story." No reaction from Paul. "My fundamental job is to add value, and adding value means either A: direct investment recommendations—that is, I think you should buy or sell stock X because of these reasons—or B: greater insight. You know, I see something compelling about this or that, and I know that my clients have never seen it that way before, and sharing it with them helps them think about the sector or whatever. Blue has this famous quote—quote? or saying, something like that— about maximum clarity of information: anyone can find information, anyone is able to process information, but to succeed requires two things—listen, this is great—acting forcefully with incomplete information and understanding how your competitors and clients do the same."

"That's touching, but I don't think that you're grasping my question." Matter-of-factly: "And I don't think I can phrase it any differently."

"What question?"

"What do you do? You said you don't just come up with these little 'hot tips,' so you must do something to earn your millions."

"I don't know what to— Here, let me give you an example. Tee-Fog—that's its nickname—is an absolutely compelling investment opportunity. I looked into it really deeply, its numbers, its management, and I think that it can grow over the medium term at twenty, maybe twenty-one percent on an operating basis." The undergraduates had left, and Kelch and Paul were now the only ones in the bar's tabled area. Kelch felt strangely comfortable now, enveloped by their isolation. Paul was full of himself, and Kelch reckoned that he would eventually have to show Paul who was in charge—probably by ending the interview. But the conversation was nonetheless natural to Kelch, with every point a painted bull's-eye for a punch. If not natural, at least practiced. In his first month at Freshler, Kelch was a bystander at a conference-room dinner where three older junior analysts spanked each other with comebacks. One of the analysts was a Wessex, painfully funny in his meanness, and when Kelch laughed loudly at one score, the victim, glaring, turned to Kelch and demanded, What are you laughing at, you fucking mute? Kelch stammered that he wasn't laughing at anything, which incited the other two to greater fits. Over the next month, Kelch fell in with Nathanson, Torvil, Vivitz, and Kim. It took a few weeks for an argument with his same-aged peers to wander into Kelch's territory—it happened to be basketball—and Kelch ended his own virginity by assault. At Torvil: you don't know what the fuck you're talking about—he shoots about twenty-six percent from the field. Even Torvil laughed with Kelch's ticket of admission. He was now one of Kelch's closest friends.

"Okay, so am I to understand that you have some computer program that can process these numbers better—"

"Well, I think I have a pretty deep model, but it's all arithmetic really. Adding and subtracting, multiplication . . ."

Nothing.

"Division."

His elbows knifed into the table, Paul merged his hands at neck level, and his thumbs twiddled again, competing mechanically for supremacy. "So you have this 'pretty deep model,' which can predict earnings better . . ."

"Let's hope so."

". . . but how do you come up with the data for it?"

What you are digging for, you nosy prick? "Well, from historically reported numbers and from guidance from the company."

"So when you come up with these estimates that I read about in the paper or wherever . . ."

"Huh?"

"These are from . . ."

"My models."

"And your models are . . ."

"Spreadsheets."

"And you get the numbers from . . ."

"From my model."

"But they can't all be . . ."

"I know where you're leading."

"And so . . ."

They had found a rhythm of lead-ins and lead-ons, hints and horns and rat-tat-tats. "I told you. The company guides me."

"But then how do you incorporate that . . ."

In the space to answer, Kelch slid his phone toward the edge of the table, opened it, and turned it on, checking after its health. He placed it in his pocket and stared at Paul, ready for the next question. Kelch's models, all the bits of sales data and administrative expenses, gross operating costs, were squeezable and fungible, most of all teleological: Kelch could ensure that all the top-line data credibly footed to the goal. If Mike Maggiore made it clear, in his way, that earnings for the quarter would be thirty cents per share—or more likely, that thirty-three cents seemed a *tad* aggressive—Kelch wouldn't be a jerk about it: he would make his estimate thirty cents. Mike Maggiore and the other investor-relations officers called Kelch only when the consensus was out of line—Kelch knew every day when he was out of consensus—or they answered, cautiously, when Kelch called them and asked how he was looking for the quarter. *I can't see anything now that would make me believe that the consensus will be off.* Kelch almost never called anyone at a company besides the IR guy; it was a certain bet that if the IR guy found out, he would be offended and less cooperative in the future.

"Chris?"

"Huh?"

"Are you still there?"

I have to catch a flight tomorrow. I have a lot of things to do. I'm under enormous time pressure here. "What were you asking?"

"Asking?"

"Yeah." *I have to leave.* I'm extremely busy. "What do you want to know now?"

Paul sipped his beer. "What I still don't understand is why there are all these little earnings disappointments out there if companies are 'guiding' analysts."

Kelch didn't answer right away. What was the use of killing yourself in a job if everyone in the world thought they could do it better? For how could Paul, with his glib confusion of Red, Green, Blue Padaway, even know about earnings disappointments? Those were our words, on our street. Kelch pushed his hand diagonally outward, dismissive. "It's highly technical—I don't know—just, you know, drop it." But the question: why do companies surprise the market after their own guidance? Because, Kelch knew, companies have to deliver bad news sometimes, because companies gamble that analysts can be managed, because companies are arrogant, because companies are clever, because companies like to beat estimates, because companies guide analysts to estimates too low. Because things happen. Because life is complicated. Because contracts get canceled. Because people screw up. Because modern accounting isn't adding up apples. Because modern accounting is a narrative art. Because the close of the quarter is a rush to meet promises. Because management whips harder at the seasons' turns. Because the market demands earnings growth, everywhere, in everything, even when earnings growth is the water from the rock. Kelch had once closed a bar, after a conference, with the president of an OPLL subsidiary. The president was on his fourth whiskey, and he slurred to Kelch, I'm not blaming—said, *bameing*—this on you, but I'm fed up with all you jackasses. Donahue comes up with these members, no, *numbers*, to make you people happy and then dictates them to us even though I-'m, we're'm, telling him there's no way we can meet them. Four'een percent! Does he know *any*thing about my business? My market's practically shrinking, and he's telling me four'een percent. How the hell m'I supposed to grow four'een percent. How muchmore can I shove down the pipeline? (The president clutched Kelch's wrist and locked him with his yellowing gaze.) How the hell m'I—? I'll tell you. I drink too much. Really I do. Even my wife thinks so.

Kelch didn't want to ponder Paul's question, Kelch wasn't interested in earnings disappointments, Kelch decided that he was done. "Listen: I think you ought to have a good enough idea by now—"

"Just for completeness, are there any other sources for your research?"

"I read, man, okay." Paul's eyes hovered over his glasses, which were aiming down, librarianlike. "Magazines and trade journals and that kind of thing. I also hear things on the Street, at conferences, from other companies, okay."

"Do you get a lot from magazines?"

Kelch felt the lost driver's uncanny suspicion that the lonely oak was the same one he had passed twice before. He didn't want to talk anymore. A presweat clamminess began to chill under his shirt. "You get raw data, you know, in its broadest definition, but you're not exactly going to get a sophisticated understanding of the fundamentals."

"But you get information."

"Fine."

"Now, back for a second to Tee-What's It. You get a high percentage of your information from company . . ."

"Contacts."

"From company contacts. And these are secret contacts that only—"

"Yeah, right. Secret contacts." The tendons in Kelch's neck held in his yawn. "That's illegal. The contacts"—the word struggled out—"talk to most of the other analysts at the other banks."

"And so they get the same information."

"Sure."

"But you interpret better."

"Fine."

"And that's why you're saying buy and they're saying sell on Tee-uh . . ."

Prick. "Tee-Fog. Some of them think the stock is compelling too. I mean, they're not all idiots."

"So why are you better if you have the same—"

"Relentlessly pursue the bits."

"What?" Paul asked as he sipped at his beer again.

It's why I'm better. Say that. "It's kind of, um, my philosophy, I guess."

His lower face hidden by the glass, Paul bubbled his words into his beer.

"Huh?" Kelch said.

"I said, It's not exactly the Categorical Imperative, is it?"

"Who are you talking to, man?" Kelch tried to mock Paul's idiocy by looking over his own shoulder, but he did it two seconds after the mocking intent would have been evident.

"Never mind. Go on with your philosophy."

"Well, it's not mine. I learned it from a woman I worked for."
Kelch's first apartment in New York was a fourth-floor walk-up. He
felt now as he had there, at eleven o'clock, after work, shoring up
his strength, his breaths, before the first flight of stairs. "Pursue
information relentlessly . . . track down every last possible number."
A warning of another yawn. "Not just that, but every piece of information."

"And you do this?"

"I try. I think I have much better models than many of my, um,
competitors. I think I can keep track of what's going on more thoroughly than they do."

"And you judge if you're successful at this by if your 'buys' go
up and your 'sells' go down?"

"Sure, if you want to look at it that way, you can, but the market
is a very tricky thing. Listen: it's pretty damned efficient in most
cases, and a lot of smart people get burned because, you know, the
whole market is operating in some ways on, uh, limited information.
So I'd be cautious about using recommendations as my only metric."

Kelch scratched his rib cage, displacing his tie. This wasn't the
first time he had been forced, frustratingly, to defend what he did,
of course. Before, it had usually been from Dan, his brother-in-law.
Kelch had looked up to Dan when Dan had started dating Heather
in high school. He might not have been especially popular or ath-
letic, but he was older and a little wild, in a goofball way. At pep
rallies, from the stands, he would whoop a private war cry. Even
the teachers would laugh. Nowadays Dan woodpeckered the phrase
"paper pushing" without mercy and made Kelch tight around him.
Yet, for Kelch, defending himself against Dan (even if only silently)
had never seemed as hard as now. Why didn't Paul just drop it?
Kelch played a role in the efficient distribution of capital through
the equity market. The efficient distribution of capital was the foundation of the American economy. End of story.

"Well, how do you judge then, Chris?"

"Listen: I know what you're trying to get at—you know, the old conventional wisdom that research analysts are just a bunch of monkeys who A: can't pick a stock to save their lives and B: just paraphrase company press releases and C and D. We can fill up forty fucking tapes with that. But it's not like that." *Come on, Kelch, explain.* "Okay, maybe it's like that for some guys, maybe a lot of guys, for an ass kisser like Gene Tennenberg, who happens to be rated number one in my sector—how I couldn't tell you. I mean he's guilty of A and B and C, of making a lot of noise for no purpose. But there *are* analysts like me who really add value."

"Can I be honest with you?"

Kelch: nothing.

"I don't know what you're talking about."

Like roaches animated by an overhead light, an energy enlivened, or rearranged, in Kelch. It pinged. "You know what? A guy like you would really get a kick out of talking to my buddy Nathanson." But then Kelch's fists tightened, and a ventricular knot met a swallow in his chest. Why did that come out, he wondered, like some Winnebago County farmboy? Har-de-har-har. "Because he's just as cynical about the whole process as you are. Just as wrong too. For the record." Nathanson: Kelch, you know what your problem is? *Please tell me, Adam.* You haven't figured out yet that you're a commodity; I, on the other hand, know that the differences between me and my competitors are so small as to be next to meaningless. "He insists that research is a commodity just because every analyst is handicapped by dealing with the same imperfect information."

Kelch waited for a reaction, which was late, maybe canceled. Paul eventually spoke, but his words, it seemed, bore grudges for being disturbed out of their slumber. Paul's voice expressed exasperation, impatience—inexplicably—through a modulation of rhythm, not pitch. "What does that mean, imperfect information?"

"Well, obviously every analyst and investor is dealing with the tip of the iceberg of information. With even your average mid-cap public company with, you know, four thousand employees and two hundred products or whatever, there are like a lot of things you

can't keep track of. So you're dealing—" Kelch stopped; his hand
cupped his forehead, but the outside hold could not connect to the
pumping in-brain pellet. It was a pierce sharper but smaller than a
migraine; it was clamping, like his heart. Kelch shut his eyes, which
only amplified the pain.

Paul leaned forward. "Go on."

When Kelch's mother would come home from work, she would
set down her purse (and often their dinner) and walk, silent—even
her footsteps were silent—to her room, the only one on the first
floor. She would shut the door behind her, and the door would
become a double-sided vacuum drawing in all the house's sounds,
thoughts, its movement of time. There was drama in this, although
not because of when she would come out of the room, or even how.
She would always be herself afterward, ten minutes later, and she
would always make her same entrance, smoking, in loose sweatpants,
a T-shirt. But the door, during those ten minutes, seemed a palpable
element of the air, an accident that dared you to resist your gaze.

"I just lost my . . . It's tough talking to you, because I talk about
this shit all day, and it's what, quarter to ten and I'm tired, tired of
talking about the markets, tired of even thinking about—" It came
again. A joke, maybe: "I think my brain is telling me it needs a rest."

In any interview, like in any book or any movie or any play, things
are being said and things are not being said and things are being
said by not being said. The last, primarily, is how Scott communi-
cates. He is an almost proudly unreflective person. His life seems to
operate on an assumption that what he does for a living must be
needed and beneficial or why else would he be paid so much. And
he doesn't always seem equipped to deal with the deeper matter of
life. (His favorite expression is "That's it. End of story.") At one point
during our conversation, as he tried to contemplate one of the central
paradoxes of his profession, his mind literally shut off. "I think," he
said, "my brain is telling me it needs a rest."

That central paradox was how little research there is in Wall Street research. This criticism has been around as long as research departments have. The core structural reason is that sell-side analysts cull the information about the companies they follow from a narrow band of publicly available information—information, in other words, that is available to all of the competitors in a sector and all of the clients. Theoretically, Scott could collect information from any source: journalists, industry experts, other companies in the industry. This rarely happens. Almost all the crucial information Scott uses comes from the companies themselves, and in most cases, an investor relations official whose sole purpose is to relegate, release, and stanch that information. So for one of Scott's primary functions, information routing, he is simply selling a commodity like bottled water. And there are ten other manufacturers selling identical products. And most people can drink from the tap.

In its simplest terms, Scott's job is to take the information he culls, no matter how general, transform it into a projection of a company's future financial performance, and by comparing this projection to a company's stock price, decide whether the stock is an attractive or unattractive investment. It is unclear whether Scott has enough information to do this accurately and consistently. On the one hand, he boasted to me that he "looked into [one company] really deeply, its numbers, its management," but on the other hand, he complained that he only in general has access to the "tip of the iceberg" of information. When I urged him to draw the logical conclusion that the information restrictions he works under make it difficult for him to actually look "into" a company, Scott dodged the question. "It's highly technical. I don't know—just, you know, drop it."

In a recent *New York Times Magazine* profile of the legendary seventy-eight-year-old hedge fund manager Max Nibelic, Nibelic explained that because corporate America spoon-feeds research analysts information and near-term earnings results, analysts are often caught completely off guard when companies, for whatever reason, cannot meet those projections. But what most commentators don't understand, according to Nibelic, is that this doesn't matter. Analysts accept being wrong intermittently because for the most part, outside of a few volatile industries, the system works. Corporate earnings are easily predictable, largely irrelevant as long as they are reasonably near estimates, or consistently higher than what analysts predict because companies cleverly guide them to purposely low (or, euphemistically, "conservative") estimates. This is the phenomenon of managed earnings or, as Nibelic called it, "the Kabuki theater of the Street."

The SEC has recently begun a campaign against managed earnings and the broader problems of selective disclosure. According to the SEC, providing information only to Wall Street analysts and not to the public at large is a mild form of inside information, which in theory gives Wall Street professionals an unfair advantage over individual investors. While strenuously denying any unfairness, officials at leading Wall Street firms forecast a gloomy future if the SEC institutes various rule changes to limit selective disclosure. They warn that public companies, following any new regulations, will refuse to divulge sufficient information to both firms *and* individuals. This would make the entire stock market less transparent for everyone. While there is truth on both sides, according to Nibelic, neither side appears willing to admit that the apparent foul of the current system seems to be doing very little harm. For if Wall Street analysts truly had an unfair advantage, they would use it. And they would be much better, in consequence, at making buy and sell recommendations. They are, to the contrary, famously bad at it.

This is the other classic criticism of research departments. Repeatedly, I asked Scott to explain where he, as he would say, adds value to the investing process. He agreed that he doesn't bring much new information to the market. In fact, he pooh-poohed journalists for what he saw as their subsidiary role as information gatherers. "You get raw data in its broadest definition," he argued to me, "but you're not exactly going to get a sophisticated understanding of the fundamentals." When I asked Scott if we should then judge him on whether his recommendations are accurate—whether his "buys" go up and "sells" go down—he swiftly, nervously denied the validity of that measurement.

Later, after consulting some longtime watchers of the stock market, I learned why. Numerous academic studies have proved that Wall Street analysts are consistently unable to accurately predict the movement of stock prices. In fact, in aggregate, their recommendations consistently perform worse than the market. The academic research also concludes that most analysts tend to react to changes in stock prices; they rarely anticipate and, even more rarely, cause these long-term changes. (Although they can clearly cause a stock to move significantly over a day or two.)

Scott, as far as he cared to contemplate this, dismissed the criticism in three ways. First, he implied that predicting stock prices was only one part of an analyst's job and, one would then hope, a small part. Second, he blamed the market, which is, as he put it, "a very tricky thing" and "pretty damned efficient." He is of course right to some degree: beating the stock market has been and will always be a difficult task. But maybe not surprisingly, given the fact the research departments are predicated on performing this task, however difficult, Scott didn't push too hard the argument that he fundamentally *cannot* make accurate recommendations. He relied more on a third defense: "I'm busy." Scott claimed that he (and one would assume his colleagues) cannot spend more time researching companies because of other extraordinary demands on his time. Scott's workdays usually start around seven-fifteen in the morning. Most don't end until eight or nine at night. He often works on Saturdays and Sundays. He travels a lot.

But if he's not researching companies during those seventy hours a week, what is he doing in the office all that time? For the most part, marketing: attempting to ensure that his clients receive the information that he is processing, interpreting, and routing.

Unfortunately, every one of his competitors—Scott estimates there are ten serious ones—is doing the same thing. Adding to the difficulty, the targeted clients are usually responsible for multiple areas of the stock market. A buy-side analyst might follow the whole retail sector. A sell-side analyst might focus just on department stores.

Scott thus must continually devise ways to try to break through the resulting cacophony of information. (He is aided by professionals at his firm whose sole job is to think up ingenious ways to do this.) Scott uses his firm's brokers to communicate his ideas. He writes and posts long and short reports online, including something called "notes." He mails hard copies of these same reports to clients, just in case, one supposes, their computers are turned off. He summons the furies of the information revolution to communicate via fax, voice mail, personal e-mail, mass e-mail, and a gimmick I never quite understood called "blast voice mail." He also markets the old-fashioned way: visiting his clients' offices, hosting conferences, entertaining at restaurants. Sometimes Scott's "marketing" initiatives nakedly reveal his role as an information router. He often arranges meetings between his clients and the companies whose stocks he follows, meetings that he seldom attends himself.

Of course, one wants to ask Scott, Who exactly is benefiting from all your hard work? If Wall Street research is as empirically unsuccessful as it appears to be, wouldn't it be better to try to concentrate on making it less empty rather than worrying about distributing it? But one can't ask Scott. He denies the relevance of the question to him. For the industry, possibly, for others. About one competitor, Scott admits, "I mean he's guilty of . . . making a lot of noise for no purpose." But Scott, of course, is different: "There are analysts like me who really add value."

Research analysts' concentration on selling rather than creating shouldn't perhaps be surprising in our age, whose very fabric seems so often to be marketing. When new media entrepreneurs create online content in which every article masks a product endorsement, when a movie studio spends forty million dollars saturating the airwaves for a mindless blockbuster when it could make infinitely better films for a fraction of those promotional costs, when its cousins in the music business manufacture teenage pop groups based on focus-group responses, when drug companies spend more money— two or three times more—on marketing than on research, when almost every consumer goods company has built its entire strategy around the enticement of consumers with ersatz novelty, when politicians are stage-managed by a battalion of pollsters and PR men filled with the latest marketing know-how, and when college presidents spend more time raising money than developing a vision of higher education, is it really any surprise that Wall Street, the owners and advisers and protective older brothers of all this, also devotes its little creative energy to techniques for cleverly, disruptively marketing information rather than actually creating it?

Shape without form were Eliot's hollow men. Shade without colour, paralysed force, gesture without motion . . .

· 3 ·

Even if his brain needed a rest, Kelch couldn't allow it. He slapped his hand on the table, trying to burn away the fog in Paul's ignorance and force the creaks out of his own mind. He needed to explain himself in a way that flattened resistance, and he pointed out, as forcefully as he could, for the millionth time it seemed, that a research analyst is not a research machine but spends his time banking and marketing and doing other things. He spends his time creating a virtuous circle (as they call it in the business) in which better marketing, higher rankings, more deals increased the reach of one's opinions and led to better marketing, higher rankings, more deals.

Paul mainly nodded, inscrutable, during Kelch's subsequent detailing of the pressures of marketing. His glasses weren't just an announcement of intelligence and fashionable intent; they also prevented Kelch—or anyone—from catching any testaments of conviction written by his chin or evidence of doubt in his brow. Perhaps consequently, Kelch's farmboy eagerness returned, much to his growing disgust at his inability to communicate what was good, challenging, *meaningful* about Freshler Feld. His Freshler Feld. Him. *The greatest job on earth.* Nathanson could have communicated the good with swashbuckling disputation, the parry-thrust to Paul's condescension; Veena could have done the same with her steel, unassailable logic. But as Kelch continued to outline the challenges of marketing, the conquering of new channels of information, Paul remained masterfully inert. *Why don't you fucking say something already?*

"Why?"

"Huh?" Kelch asked, disoriented. How could the sphinx have intercepted his private command?

"Why should it be so hard to get people to pay attention to you?" To Paul's credit, the question seemed to be as apathetically delivered as everything else he said. "I mean, you seem to spend an awful lot of time with your little voice blasts or whatever you call them, trying to make people listen to your wonderful investment insights."

Prick. Kelch tried to concentrate. *Prick.* "Every company"—*prick*—"needs to, um, market its products." *Prick.*

"True, but I—and I don't know that much about this area—would assume that your clients would want to hear what you think about Tee—What's it called again?"

"Tee-Fog."

"There it is. I would assume that your clients would seek out your advice. They would fight to talk to you. You wouldn't have to come up with ways to . . . It's a little . . ."

"Some do." Kelch refused to buckle to Paul's staged hesitation. "A *lot* of my clients do." Kathy Guizeta does. Miko Ahashi and Jeff Benson do. So to hell with you.

"Well, how many?"

"It depends. On Tee-Fog"—Kelch pronounced it decisively this time—"for example, more than on Allencor."

Paul's small eyes squinted. Framed by the plastic, they looked less menacing than crafty, bird's eyes of unchanging focus on the middle distance. "Thank God for relativity, right?"

"Huh?"

"Never mind."

Nothing.

"For the record," Paul then said, "I think you're missing the point."

Kelch made two fists and then loosened them, thumb-popping his knuckles in individual acts. "What would that be?"

"Why are you spending so much time coming up with those so-called strategies to break through the information overload instead of just coming up with better ideas?"

Instead of sparking with adrenaline demands for more oxygen, attention, faster blood, Kelch's heart played sudden possum. Paul, recorder, bar, room had become heavy again, drenching. Paul thought he was so clever with his recitation of the sins of research. But the Sins of Research had been looping nonstop for years now; the sins were "revealed" in every issue of the glossy business magazines, every day in the newspapers, reiterated at every opportunity by reporters and salespeople and clients and Nathanson and Torvil and Kelch himself. Even Bill Arnell knew the indictment's basic shades. So when Paul imagined himself a valiant knight, the protector of truth, slaying the dragon, how boring it was: the dragon had already—frequently—been cut and singed and pierced. Kelch was simply too exhausted to listen to it anymore: the effects of reading about one's own profession's worthlessness, pointlessness, and corruptibility tend to be minimal after the hundredth time. And what's more, the dragon was still alive.

What do you do? Huh? *What do you do?* What do *I* do? *Yes, what do you do?* Well, I breathe I eat I drink I dream I sleep I see I pee I poo I screw I do I do. *No, no, what do you* do? *Your* job. That was the first and only question they asked in the full intermission, in all New York, the only remnant of any toddler's curiosity inside the city's adult-children, their eyes all wrapped in the same gauze of ambition. And if that was the only question, then that was the only subject. No one asked Mary if she was patriotic, no one asked Jack if he was a heretic, no one asked Sam if he had a loving heart. *What do you do?* Huh? *Whatdoyoudo?* That was all they needed to know, for that was the existential truth. Whatdoyoudo? Well, that job isn't interesting. That job seems useless. That job seems *boring.* And I am better than you.

Kelch's stalled thoughts—energy—had been leaning, accumulating against the door. If Paul wanted the sins of research, Kelch would give him the damn sins of research, starting with the fattest, most unoriginal one of all. "Fine, guilty. I'm guilty of everything."

Paul's eyes connected to the tape recorder. "Guilty of what now?"

"Wherever you're leading with all this. You've obviously done your homework and are now trying to get me to admit that I'm a horrible white-collar criminal guilty of all the shit you're throwing at me."

"Are you confessing something?" Paul asked, theatrically by his standards.

"Why not, right? I'm going to just get this over with so you can return to your artist grotto and have the exact same opinion about Freshler and Wall Street that you had before. That's what you want, right? Confession—no, proof—of guilt, not a real exchange of, uh, ideas. So here goes. Listen up and listen good: we all compromise our integrity every day by conducting so-called independent research on companies that are banking clients of Freshler Feld. But, of course, you already knew that."

"Banking clients?"

His face reddening, his heart forcing his blood through a narrower pipe, Kelch shook his head in baiting disgust. "There's no need for that Orange bullshit anymore. As you know, I'm the one who has to talk to investing clients about a Freshler IPO. So how could I tell the full truth about an IPO to my clients if it's bad?

Could I really say, Sorry folks, but in my opinion this Freshler IPO sucks dick? Or, let's see, after the IPO is in the market, am I really going to say that Tee-Fog, for example, is a bad company when I know that the company generates more M&A and underwriting fees for Freshler than all the trading of the stock does? Twenty, I don't know, fifty times my salary a year. That's what you want to know, right? So just ask it already."

Nothing.

"Well, that's just a load of crap." Kelch paused. *You thought you had me there, didn't you?* But what are the sins really, smart-ass? "I'm responsible enough to know what's right and what's wrong and I don't cross the line. And just because there are multiple client relationships—this is Blue—doesn't mean that there are compromised clients. He says it, to be precise"—Kelch snapped *precise*—"complicated clients don't mean compromised clients."

Paul stared, a foreword. "Let's just slow down a bit. I think I understand part of this debate, but explain to me how you would say something bad, if you needed to, about this tea factory, for instance? Let's just say your little research methods reveal something negative. How would you communicate that—I assume the consequence would be to hurt the company's stock—without offending the company?"

"The point I'm making is that never happens." *Keep it simple.* "Because Tee-Fog isn't some fly-by-night operation. We're talking Freshler Feld here." Kelch always enjoyed holding this trump card. *Where are you at, Chris?* I'm at Freshler Feld. An impressed, plump-lipped, *Oh, okay.* He also enjoyed the inverse: ruling, to himself, about the other, Loser. "Listen: we only take the top tier of banking clients. Sure, there are bucket shops that really are just a bunch of crooks and not discriminating at all in what they take public. And there are a lot of third-tier banks—I'm not going to name names—that are notorious for propping up shitty companies with their research. And I know some guys who work, worked, with me who have done some things that aren't, let's just say, irrelevant to where you're heading with this. But listen: ninety-nine percent of good analysts work for good banks and don't need to do that."

"So you've never had to compromise once."

"Compromise. Sure. I say things differently with Allencor, for example, than with OPLL." Kelch paused to consider whether he should explain that the language of equity research had formal and informal tenses, that there was an art to covering Allencor versus OPLL, that there was an oceanic difference between *waiting for confirmation from another quarter* and *do not expect company to outperform,* that there was no need to be uncooperative when Tedeschi asked whether there would be a way to make the rating for JRSG a little more "commercial." But a torrent of words had hijacked Kelch's mind and didn't let it digress. "You know, I'm a little more polite. And maybe I will not in my written stuff say something as harshly as I would in other stuff. And of course, I'm going to give Allencor the benefit of the doubt—I shouldn't have, but that's a different story—because I'm interested in not fucking up the relationship. But that's it."

Paul's smile bent at a minimum angle, a young cattail in a gentle wind. "So, for the record, Chris, you agree that you are compromising."

"There's compromising and there's compromis*ed.* You should know this, you're a writer. We all compromi*se.* I compromised by coming here when it wasn't exactly convenient. I wouldn't call myself compromised. With a *d.*"

Paul was unusually slow in driving to the next point, and Kelch, leaning over, his eyes extra open, tilted his right ear solemnly closer to him. He immediately regretted it. "Give me a concrete example," Paul eventually said, "and I'll probably understand your heroism better."

When Kelch's mother would leave her bedroom, she would come to the dinner table and ask Kelch and Heather about their day. But to Kelch at least, it felt embarrassing, out of tune, to talk to her then, after her isolation. He would just mumble single-word sentences between large, hurrying bites. His mother would nonetheless chirp on about the personalities—she thought them personalities—who came through the office at work. It would have seemed like she was talking to herself if Heather hadn't been doing it too.

Kelch, empty, asked, "How about I get you a concrete beer instead?"

Many critics argue that analysts do not accurately predict stock price performance because their opinions are slanted by conflicts of interest. Scott, like almost all research analysts, forms supposedly independent opinions about companies that are profitable clients of his firm's investment banking division. This puts him an awkward position, especially when his firm underwrites an IPO in his sector. Scott must help his firm promote that IPO—in effect, recommend the stock—regardless of his opinion of the stock or the interests of his clients. As Scott himself described the dilemma, "How could I tell the full truth about an IPO to my clients if it's bad? Could I really say, Sorry folks, but in my opinion this . . . IPO sucks dick? Or, let's see, after the IPO is in the market, am I really going to say that [the company] is a bad company when I know that the company generates more M&A and underwriting fees for [my firm] than all the trading of the stock does? Twenty, I don't know, fifty times my salary a year."

Analysts could theoretically refuse to promote an IPO, but as is clear by the avalanche of IPOs over the past several years, this rarely happens. And even if one bank refuses an IPO, there are always other banks and other analysts ready to take on even the most dubious offerings.

The influence of banking relationships is not limited to IPOs, as Scott admits. The current generation of corporate executives is famously sensitive about the price of their stocks. This may have always been the case, but it is even more evident in this, the Age of Options, when executive compensation is almost always a direct function of a company's share price. Stories are legion on Wall Street of CEOs or CFOs attempting to bully analysts, especially young analysts like Scott, into better recommendations. Stories are also legion of companies severing or curtailing relationships with investment banks over disputes about analyst recommendations. If Scott places a "sell" rating on a company and that company ceases to do business with his firm—business that according to Scott's estimate could generate twenty-five million dollars a year—the investment bankers at Scott's firm will not, to say the least, congratulate him on his integrity and independence.

So how does Scott navigate through his Scylla and Charybdis? Through a combination, apparently, of calculated obliviousness and permanently compromised integrity. Frankly, he doesn't seem that concerned. He claims to have never personally misled investors about a stock to protect a banking relationship. (Knowingly misleading investors, Scott understands, isn't just bad business. It's a crime.) He admitted, however, to sugarcoating opinions: "saying things differently," being "a little more polite," giving banking clients "the benefit of the doubt." He nicks at the truth all the time but without ever, he insists, crossing an ill-defined line.

Again, none of this causes him to worry much. When describing the daily compromises he makes (on what is supposedly the greatest asset of a research analyst, his reputation), Scott alternates between wild self-justifications and cavalier dismissals of the importance of the question. Others do things, he admits. "Sure," he told me, "there are bucket shops that really are just a bunch of crooks and not discriminating at all in what they take public. And there are a lot of third-tier banks—I'm not going to name names—that are notorious for propping up shitty companies with their research. And I know some guys who work, worked, with me who have done some things that aren't, let's just say, irrelevant to where you're heading with this." Somehow, despite this last statement, Scott believes that his own firm is above suspicion. He summons its name like an incantatory shield to ward off any criticisms or doubt. "We," he said, "only take the top tier of banking clients." . . .

Waiting for the beer, Kelch reminded himself that he had not been condescended to so nakedly in years, excepting Hoder Leary. Paul had inexcusably crossed the boundaries of acceptable behavior. There was no reason to be here, Kelch then decided, unmuddled; if he were a more resolute, better man, he would have already walked out the door, telling Paul to find someone else to treat like a jerk. The personal tangles were stopping him from doing this, for sure, whispers from Paul to Marigold to Kersten and back to him—the *why did you agree to be interviewed if you were just going to walk out?* But something else probably stopped him too, a submerged will to victory that could not be gratified by imagined conquests. Before Kelch left, Paul must understand how off base he was. If he insisted on picking away at these tired old criticisms of research, he was never going to comprehend the first thing about how the Street really worked. Kelch now was angry.

He returned to the table. Paul was flipping or testing or changing the cassette. It was ten-fifteen, and although the bar was no fuller, its stale air was more noticeable: the bartender had turned the music louder, and it shined a strong bulb on the emptiness. Kelch handed a beer to Paul, who nodded in place of a thank you, and Kelch drank a large swallow, in anticipation. He smiled, as to a father-in-law, set his own beer down, clearing the last one's sweat off the table, and stated casually, "Well, what about you?" This was the answer, and it had come effortlessly out of his bile.

Looking up from the recorder, whose knobs he had been trying to adjust, Paul asked, his glasses now lolling on his nose's edge, "Excuse me?"

Sharper: "What about you?"

"You're going to have to be a little more specific."

"You're a writer, right?" Paul didn't move. "So all your time is spent marketing and packaging too."

"Marketing what?"

"Your books. What are they but the packaging of your ideas?"

Nothing.

"The packaging of your ideas, right?"

Paul's glasses still aimed down, but he stared straight ahead. He paused, and the stare, at Kelch, sank in. "If you really think that a painting is just a way to sell paint, I'm not sure what to say."

"I'm just talking about how you claimed that it was ridiculous for me to spend so much time communicating my ideas instead of coming up with them."

"The point being . . ."

"Well, you do the same thing."

"You sound like my father."

Kelch looked into his beer and said, as if to Kersten, "I'm sorry."

"What?"

Nothing.

"Chris, why don't we just drop the subject, or I'm going to—"

You're not going to make me feel bad anymore, asshole. Under the table line, out of Paul's view, Kelch scooped his coat by the neck and laid it on his lap. He would leave first. If that was Paul's plan too, then it would be a race to the door. "You're going to what?" he then asked, surprising himself at the deepening irritation in his tone.

"I've been a good little journalist here, but let me be honest for a second: I don't really care if you and your little buddies on Wall Street walk around this city as if you own it." Paul's delivery, in an offhand, unconscious way, reminded Kelch of a baseball pitcher— it was vindictive, blank, focused impossibly hard on remaining in control. It seemed personal. "But please don't pretend that what you're doing is anything else than what it is."

"And what would that be?"

"Chris, we've been talking for about an hour now about what you do. And one thing that is pretty clear, at least to me, is that there are no similarities between what you do and what I do."

Kelch's own attention had dulled without permission, and he now had to press harder to cut through the loaf. He felt close to losing. "I think it's weird that you believe it's impossible to consider that what I do is worthwhile."

"Correct me if I'm wrong"—Paul's head turned parallel to his shoulders to burp or swallow or yawn—"but I didn't say anything about it not being 'worthwhile,' did I?"

"You've made it clear you don't respect it."

"It has nothing to do with whether I respect it." Paul sighed. "The only thing I'm doing is reacting as any thoughtful person would to these little facts you keep on throwing out. And many of them are frankly fascinating to hear. I've suspected..."

"Facts that hit too close to home to you." Kelch nodded: the slice finally fell off the loaf, an admirably straight cut.

Paul took his glasses off to clean them on his shirt. He appeared different now; his face was in the passive voice, no Patton of a paragraph. Kelch assumed that Paul must have been getting angry too, but Paul expressed meaning through denotation, not pitch. And his eyes now were too small, without the dark framing, to discharge any meaning. "As you like to say, Chris, *listen*," Paul said, still not wearing his glasses, which unsettled Kelch, partly because it made Paul, squinty, white-pink, small-eyed, look like a newborn rat, and partly—Kelch only sensed this—because it made Paul seem shy of a nakedness and about twelve years old. "I'm not going to get in an argument with you about business and literature or whatever tenuous connections you are trying to draw."

"We're just talking here, man." Kelch flapped his hand horizontally over the table: we.

After a loud sigh of universal scope, Paul put his glasses back on. "It's fascinating. You people get everything in this city. You drive up the prices of rent, of restaurants, of movies, of— You never have to take the subway. You vacation wherever, whenever you want—"

"Yeah, whenever, right."

"You do *what*ever you want because you have the money, but it's not enough. You also want—no, *need*—to have virtue. You need to convince yourselves that you're righteous and irreplaceable and now this: creative."

"But I'm creative. I create ideas that my clients act on."

Maybe, Kelch observed, Paul's face operated on negative principles: the more angry, the more motionless, the more excited, the more inexpressive. "Thank you for proving my point. Before I started having a lot of exposure to you people, I had imagined that Wall Street types would be satisfied knowing that they made more money than, what, a thousand people in Bangladesh, and that they could buy all the trappings of wealth and success in this country." *Do you ever stop talking?* "I thought that that would be enough for anyone. But I was wrong: you people are so acquisitive"—the climax of *acquisitive* felt prepared—"that you also have to have every positive attribute too. It's fascinating: you people really do believe the hype."

"I'm not really following you, but I don't think you can honestly believe that we don't earn what we make. I mean, look at Freshler's earnings. Look at its stock price. Our shareholders aren't exactly suffering."

"Tell me, Chris, did you really think that's what I meant by deserve?" Paul demonstrated that his style could find even a lower, less engaged gear. "That really is fascinating. I have friends who are teachers making thirty thousand dollars a year. Important visual artists I know are working as waiters in *sandwich* shops for nine dollars an hour. You probably can't even imagine what's it like not making the kind of money you're making. I've learned to accept this, that I won't be able to do things in this city, eat at places, go to the theater as much as I would like . . ."

Maybe Kelch couldn't *imagine*, he thought, but he knew a few things more than Paul. He knew what it meant to have a mother gently suggest that he could wear a pair of jeans a few months longer, a few months tighter. He knew what it meant to have never seen, until he was fifteen, a movie after three in the afternoon. He knew what it meant to walk into a kitchen to see his mother, her skin powdery, her concentration drifting away into exhaustion, dropping ashes onto a tablecloth of bills. She would look up at him, smile, her face open and ready to talk—she never let him worry that everything wasn't under control—but he would slink upstairs to his own room and fantasize about getting away from that house through an orphaning or basketball or a comic-book twist of fate.

When the woman at the financial-aid office in Evanston, an aficionado of sympathy, told Ann and Kelch that through a combination of loans and work-study, Ann's share would be brought down to thirty-five hundred dollars a year, Ann looked at her son, then at the woman, then at her son again, and covered her mouth with a trembling hand of joy, just as they did on game shows.

Paul continued to recite, "And I can't help but find it fascinating that you people have now seized the cultural moment and see yourselves as some kind of modern heroes just because reporters all stand in line to blow you."

"To blow us? Where?" Kelch's joke made him feel, for a moment at least, lighter than air.

Paul sighed again. "Just tell me one last time: why do you believe you deserve all the material rewards that your job provides?"

"I don't know what you mean by deserve. Blue Padaway doesn't deserve two hundred and fifty million dollars or however much he's worth. He made it."

"And you?"

"Listen: I work seventy hours a week, at least. Eighty a lot of times. I take a lot of shit from people. Every time Joe Tedeschi orders a department-wide project, I do it. Every time someone asks me to call a client, I do it. Every time I call that client, I'm expected to report back to the sales desk, and I do it. Every time a banker wants me to give *his* client a market overview . . . I do all this bureaucratic marching-order bullshit. You can't even understand how painful it is. So you know what, I'll tell you, I'll tell anyone: I deserve every last penny I make."

"And deserve to wear hundred-dollar ties and be able to wine and dine Kersten—"

"Don't blame me, man, just because a half million bucks buys you a good piece of ass in this town." Paul's attention rushed to the tape recorder. As Kelch was about to make it clear that there was no need to even mention that this had been a joke, Paul began to laugh, uninterpretably, almost silently, in pure percussion. Kelch, inspired, surrendering, too muscle weary to measure his wins and losses anymore, leaned into the recorder. He cupped his hands around his mouth. "Sorry, honey. I didn't mean that." When Paul laughed the same again, Kelch realized that "Sorry, honey" was the first occasion that night, maybe that life, in which his timing had been right.

Paul said, "Don't worry about that."

"I didn't think I had to worry about anything."

"You don't."

Kelch said nothing in return. But eventually Paul, coughing, moved on to the next item on an agenda. "So, Chris, maybe we can talk about your background."

"What now?"

"Where you're from . . . background."

"I thought this was about, you know, Wall Street, not me."

"That's true, but I find it crucial to examine the intersection of people and institutions."

Kelch understood that *this* discussion was a losing proposition, and his tongue searched the back of his teeth, scouting for a place to hide. *I have to pack. I'm leaving for a very important trip.* He knew, from experience, that when he shared his background, he came out either aw-shucks small town, which wasn't true, or single-mother hard luck, which he didn't talk about, even to Kersten. No one needed to pity him. Well, at least for a minute there, he had felt good and loose and awake. "What do you want to know exactly?"

"For example, why did you decide to work for an investment bank in the first place? There are other activities in this world one could do. Theoretically." That was what Kersten had asked at that party when they were strangers, she was attractive, and he was country, Rockford-reared. Two minutes into their conversation: do you like it at Freshler? *Well, there're worse places to work, I guess.* (The way she had said Freshler, familiar, urbane, had been insidious, knee-weakening; her perfect-drawn lips pouted at the *sh.*) But why are you doing banking? *I know it's not that cool to admit, but I kind of think it's interesting. It's kind of exciting too.* That's like really, really refreshing, to hear you say you like your job. I think it's admirable. Everyone else here . . . Bells rang in Kelch's loins, his eyes, and he thought, Jesus, that's crazy. Then he tried to figure out if she was for real.

"Of course, I could be doing other things," Kelch granted, "and I'm not adverse to it, you know like theoretically, but I've yet to find a job that's more interesting or exciting for me at least than what I got going at Freshler."

"What about all these little tech companies?"

"I guess I'm too much of a value guy to want to work for some bubble company." And besides, they couldn't pay Kelch what he was making now. A year ago, the roulette wheel had seemed to pay off for all the players; Nathanson had sat watching, at the table's margins, bitterly declaiming, Injustice, as Ben Hsu or mediocre Matt Weiss hit their fourteen reds during those months when the game seemed rigged against the house. But now that everyone was watching the wheel, open-mouthed, drooling, it had become more erratic, and the casino's lights had dimmed.

Transposing up a half octave, Paul rewound the conversation. "Okay, but there has to be some reason you chose investment banking?"

"I can never figure out why no one ever seems satisfied with my answer to this question. If I really, really 'dig' into my motivation, it's just not— Listen: some of the guys I hung out with in college were into the whole banking-job-hunt thing, and when I was a sophomore, they started getting internships—nothing big-time, but with local brokers in Chicago or someplace—and it kind of piqued my interest." Kelch stopped, struck for a moment by how long it had been since he had talked to any of those guys. "And once I started doing the job, I enjoyed it. That's it. End of story."

Paul's face had returned to a stone wall. "I find it incredible that you are so casual about this. One would assume that in a business as supposedly all-important as yours, one would be required to make a little more structured, I don't know, serious decision."

"Who said I wasn't serious?"

"Well, you kind of fell into the job, it seems."

"*Fell* in?" Kelch drank and spoke after he swallowed. "Listen: I applied for the job and I got it. That's how the real world works, man." The metaphor was never to fall in, for there was little vertical about the life. Kelch had taken a train, a bullet express, much advertised, gleaming, modern, filled with the very best fixtures of the very best people. He had taken it because he had been invited aboard, and now, when he looked out the window, the countryside was a blur, rusty and static, an oppressive uniformity.

"Do you do it for the money?"

"You can get paid to do this?" (It was Wessex's joke.)

Nothing.

"Listen: the money doesn't hurt. But if you're asking me if I'd do it for less money, then, sure. But I'm not giving it back now because, frankly, I earn it." Kelch realized that he had already said that, maybe a few times; well, if he had, he had. It was true.

Things, it seemed to Kelch, were coming together.

Hiding behind a neutral, untoothed poker-player smile, Paul asked, "Where are you from, Chris?"

"Huh?"

"Where are you from originally?"

"Rockford, Illinois."

"Where's that?"

"In Illinois."

Paul, swallowing, moved on through the answer. "What does your family do there?"

Kelch stared ahead blankly, ground down by the inevitability of the question's appearance. Whatdoyoudo? This. Whatdoesyourdad-dydo? That. But what did his "family" do? Well, the Ghost called twice a year, visited once in six; he talked about the weather and the Cubs (Kelch liked the Sox) and asked what was the latest with Heather's kids. He had a job doing something near Phoenix, and occasionally it changed, but the few times that the Ghost tried to talk about it, Kelch had made it clear that he wasn't interested. Kelch heard his mother, somewhat incidentally, explain the why of the Ghost only once; it was addressed mainly to Heather, following, in high school, her second breakup with Dan. (Ann would hint, on two or three later occasions, of other, different reasons than the one given that day.) Ann didn't usually tell stories; when she did, you understood her reluctance. She got lost in her own expositions, missed major details, and though she calmed down for stretches in the stories' centers, she rushed the endings, rapidly smoking down— almost attacking—her cigarette, often forgetting the punch line. Yet when she told Heather about the Ghost, she took her time, didn't even smoke, remembered everything and laughed, twinkling. She and the Ghost had had so much fun so many times, she said. He was like one of those perfect little kids who knows exactly how they can get you with their smile. Even his laugh made you feel lucky. (He had lost that talent.) But if you weren't directly in front of him, even if you were just running an errand or something, he wouldn't think about you at all. You just knew it, too. (He hadn't lost that one.) The Ghost had been that way with his parents too, Ann explained. Right before they died, his parents came to Rock-ford. It was the first time in years. Relaxed as he could be, the Ghost slapped his mother on the back. *Hey, Ma.* He offered beers. *Hey, Dad.* His father was speechless. His mother seemed kind of spooked. When they left, Ann asked how anyone could survive that. The Ghost answered, "What? He's got a pension."

Kelch responded, quickly and arctic, "My stepfather is an accountant." He had not planned on answering with Bill.

"Is your father—?"

"What's that supposed to mean?" Paul, Kelch thought, might have just smiled.

"Nothing," Paul said. "I'm just asking my little questions here." He played his pianoing fingers against his mouth, waiting. Kelch, for sure, wasn't going to go on. He didn't owe this fucker anything, and he had a right to keep the facts of his life on the shelf, or in the cupboard, spine out, in any order he wanted. Paul finally resumed, "So about this Rock*ford . . .*"

Leery: "Yeah."

"How would you describe it?"

"How would I what?"

"Describe it."

What am I, a travel guide? Kelch was bored. Paul bored him. This bar bored him. Life, acutely at that moment, bored him. Because clearly Paul had run out of questions, and Kelch had run out of gasoline. With every question asked, Paul had tapped gallons from his chest. "What? It's just a place."

Scott was born and raised in a midwestern city of three-hundred-and-fifty thousand people. There are interesting connections—or more accurately, disconnections—between Scott's career and his hometown (which I will call Scottsville). According to an official at its chamber of commerce, Scottsville's economy rests on manufacturing plants—its largest employer is an assembly plant of a Big Three automaker—and, to a lesser extent, goods and services for the extensive agricultural industry surrounding the city. A few of

Scottsville's manufacturers produce parts for the aerospace industry, but one could describe the city only as an "old economy" place. With wealth transferring from the old economy to the new, it seems inevitable that places like it will continue to lose, on a relative basis, resources, wealth, jobs—in short, vitality. Over the last decade, *Money* magazine has regularly placed Scottsville at or near the bottom of its ratings of American cities for economic health and quality of life. And though the chamber of commerce official cheerily noted, "We are one of the best improved since '96," she admitted that it will be nearly impossible for Scottsville to fundamentally alter the makeup of its economy. The city is now paddling upstream.

Nearly all of Scottsville's major employers are subsidiaries of public companies headquartered out of town, out of state, or out of the country. This means that the highest-paying positions at these companies are elsewhere. The profits from Scottsville's plants are remitted elsewhere. Most ominously, the executives and investors who will determine the fate of these facilities live and work elsewhere. If the last twenty years have taught us anything, it is that these decision makers care much more about the opinions of Scott, a Wall Street analyst, than those of the people of Scottsville.

Wall Street professionals like to bandy about Joseph Schumpeter's famous characterization of capitalism as "creative destruction." It allows them, it seems, to imagine themselves as romantic poets, Napoleons, or Promethean gods. "Creative destruction" inarguably applies in certain cases, like when the computer industry knocks out the typewriter industry. Yet when you meet Scott, you begin to wonder, How can he do anything creatively? The herd mentality, the safe, consensual decisions of him and his colleagues make them seem more like foot soldiers—or drummer boys—than Napoleons. The "philosophy" guiding Scott's professional decisions, a philosophy he is proud to recite, is a cheap Cartesian bromide cloaked in the mantle of technologese about "pursuing the bits."

The dried voices of Eliot's hollow men, when they whispered

together, were quiet and meaningless as wind in dry grass. Unfortunately, as meaningless as much of equity research may be, it is hardly quiet. Never in history have research analysts, and Wall Street in general, had more power to affect the lives of nearly every person on the planet. And never have the countervailing forces to the power of capital—politicians, artists, activists, journalists, labor leaders, religious leaders—been more silent, more co-opted, more eager to please, or more, relatively speaking, impotent.

Sometimes, of course, Wall Street–prodded decisions are right, but often they are wrong. And they are rarely, if ever, creative. As Max Nibelic said regarding one aspect of this phenomenon, corporate mergers, "Every piece of evidence indicates that mergers more often destroy shareholder value than boost it. . . . But they are all the rage anyway because managements' buckets are empty when it comes to new ideas and the analysts applaud every deal."

As a result of one corporate merger, done with little clear thinking other than as a preemptive move of "consolidation," as a result of one corporate "restructuring" loudly applauded by Wall Street, one of the plants in Scottsville will probably close. (The auto plant appears particularly at risk.) And therein lies a gloomy irony. The best and brightest of the Scottsvilles of this world gravitate to the highest-paying jobs in New York or London and become a part of the system that is destroying their hometowns . . .

· 4 ·

Paul's next question popped out quickly, as if it had been long coiled. "So how did you begin dating Kersten anyway?"

Cautious, wary: "I met her at a party."

"That's funny."

"What's funny?"

"The way the world works."

"What are you talking about?"

Paul compressed his lips. "I went to school with her last boy-friend." And so had Marigold, and so had Alejandro, and so had the silent couple.

"But Kersten doesn't even know you," Kelch half-asserted, half-asked.

"I've been out of the city for a while." Paul implied a smile. "Anyway, I was just curious—"

"Well, what did you think of that guy?"

"Does it really matter?"

Kelch had never met Andrew, although Kersten would occasion-ally polish Kelch with the contrasts. Kelch was not a bully. Kelch didn't regularly imply that Kersten was uneducated. Kelch didn't make jokes about where she went to school—in fact, he hadn't even heard of it until he moved to New York—cracks about SUVs and beer funnels and rich daddies. Kelch didn't think these jokes were okay to say just because Kersten's family thought Andrew's school, their own, was the center of the world. And Kelch didn't (how shy and wicked, a dash of cayenne, she had been when she said it) have any issues in the bedroom. But Kersten, one night, early on, had also talked about how devastated—traumatized—completely stressed out—she had been after Andrew left her, after a year. She had also told Kelch, maybe not seriously, that it must have been fate that he had appeared only two months later. She and Kelch had once run into some of Andrew's friends at a party at Wessex's. The group huddled exclu-sively by a window, only occasionally bothering to glance at the rest of the room. They left after a half hour, saying good-bye only to Wessex's roommate. During most of the time they were there, Kersten stayed in the kitchenette, talking to Wessex's chubby sister, cutting up fruit, laughing loudly at the sister's dubious sarcasm. When Kelch and Kersten took a cab home, it was Kelch, unusually, who driveled pointlessly to bring some noise into the car. Later, when Kersten was brushing her teeth, she told him that they should really make a trip upstate, to Kersten's college. It was so nice in the summer.

Kelch pushed, "Come on, man." He deserved to know.

"Come on what?"

"Huh?"

"Never mind."

"You're not being fair. I'm spilling my guts into your tape—"

"Damnit—the tape." The recorder's red light had snuck off, and Paul hurriedly replaced the cassette. He inserted the previous tape into a case and stored it in his pocket, double-checking its safety with a pat.

Kelch's eyes drifted from the replacement procedure to Paul's pints, one full beer and the other half so. "Are you going to answer my question?"

"I will say this." Pause. "And only this." Pause. "You and he are very different people, and it's surprising that you would share a girlfriend."

"We're not sharing her," Kelch said, ha-ha, but after he said it, he felt uneasy. Almost every word that had come out of his mouth tonight, every dissonant joke, had seemed to move him further away from the tonic chord.

"You know what I mean."

"How different could we be?"

"Indescribably."

"More different than you and me?"

"That I couldn't tell you."

"Well, what—"

"Chris, can I ask the questions?" And Paul, without waiting for Kelch's permission, did then ask the questions. At first, Kelch was brusque, his mind occupied, stalking an opportunity to demand why Paul had brought up Andrew. But Kelch's mood loosened as Paul's questions, in Kelch's view, got sillier and stupider. It seemed that Paul was following some sort of checklist about Kelch's likes and

inclinations, the ostensible portholes into a man's essence, and Kelch
hit back the fat lobs—about movies, newspapers, fiction books,
museums (what the hell), music, politics, some stupid-ass joke about
performance art—with hard overhand smashes. For most of them,
it was "Not my thing."

The questions took about five minutes, and as Kelch answered
them, he promised himself that he would not, this time, let his
advantage go. He was sick of pushing the boulder up the hill, only
to let it roll down again. And when Paul, in a final, brief exchange
on politics, asked Kelch whether he really believed that the "current
system" was fair, Kelch laughed so loudly that he brought his fingers
under his nostrils to make sure no beer paid dividends out of his
nose. "We're not going there, are we?"

Unlike some of his peers on Wall Street, Scott did not ride an insider
family track into his current position. He is reticent about talking
about his personal background. However, an acquaintance of his told
me that Scott's father abandoned the family when Scott was quite
young. Growing up, according to the acquaintance, consisted of
many years of financial struggle for Scott, his sisters, and his working
mother. Although Scott is white and American, which certainly
didn't hurt him professionally, he is not from the WASP or Jewish
gentility we now, maybe anachronistically, associate with Wall Street
success. His rise on Wall Street is a tribute to one of its few unequivocally positive characteristics: its commitment to meritocracy.
Scott attended a Big Ten university. His firm hired him because he
impressed its representatives during on-campus interviews.

If Fitzgerald's midwesterners in *The Great Gatsby* were all "subtly
unadaptable to Eastern life," Scott is not their heir. He has proven
eminently adaptable to the dominant, frat-boy culture of Wall Street.
Scott refuses to accept any criticisms of the aggressive profit drive
and merciless strategy of his firm. He is strikingly homophobic. He

descends occasionally into low-grade racist grumbling about "reverse discrimination" on Wall Street, a notoriously lily-white industry. He is a heavy drinker. He is disrespectful to women. (When I brought up his girlfriend, Scott bragged, "Don't blame me, man, just because a half million bucks buys you a good piece of ass in this town.") He does not worry about the possible consequences of his actions on the employees of the companies he follows. He is unconcerned about the growing income gap in the country. All in all, I could locate no guideposts to his inner life, to *any* inner life, other than a vague devotion to personal happiness.

In his interests, in the way in which he discusses sophisticated topics, Scott is, for the lack of a better term, juvenile, although any innocence in tone disappears when the topic switches to money. Considering the amount of resources at his disposal and the responsibility he commands, his mental universe is astonishingly narrow. He does not read books. ("That's not exactly my thing.") He reads only the *Wall Street Journal*. He does not follow politics—"isn't exactly my thing either"—did not vote in the last election because he was "premarketing a deal," and identifies with the Republican Party, predictably, because he agrees with its "views on taxes." He does not willingly attend the theater, listen to serious music, or visit museums. ("No, save me, never if I can help it.") He watches movies frequently but primarily as a social activity, not out of any interest in the form. The only interest he does show in the nonfinancial world is in sports.

Although Scott was never an active churchgoer, he still identifies himself as a Catholic. (He claims, almost wistfully, to remember some of the Hail Mary.) Yet he holds no opinions on the character and teachings of the church or on the existence of God, except for a distaste for "boring gay-ass books about religion." Scott's education in this individualistic, secular age was individualistic and secular. The lifestyle he pursues is radically materialistic. He is a new type of man, perhaps, a man near the apex of his society who is not only uninterested in metaphysics but incapable of even contemplating metaphysics. He literally cannot believe in God. This is a long way from "God is dead." This is God is forgotten. And so is Nietzsche ...

Affectless, Paul asked, "What?"

Kelch continued, still amused by Paul's stupid question, to try, with the speed and quantity of his words, to solidify his position. He must take it, now, to the hole. "Like I told you before, no one ever handed me anything in my entire life, and I didn't have a lot of shit growing up. And so when I hear all these people whining that poor kids—" Bending over, he seemed to address the tape recorder, but his eyes were still fixed on Paul. "Not that we were on welfare or anything." Upright again: "Anyway, when I hear all this stuff about how poor kids can't get a break, I think, that's crap. I wasn't rich, and so you know what I did. I did my fucking homework, I worked my ass off in college, I did all this while holding down a job or two. And I eventually got this opportunity because I proved to Freshler that I was a hard worker and could contribute. That's the great, hidden secret of my life." As he spoke, he harmonized a rumbling, blunt bass melody of thoughts with his speech. He had long been fed up with the Pauls and Marigolds and Kerstens with their big wooded mansions, their hospitals-worth-of-doctors families, their charity-devoted mothers, always finding the time to lecture him about poor kids. What did they even know about poor kids? Kelch knew the *only* thing there was to know: they don't like being poor. Kelch's whole life, he carried an understanding around, although he had never once shared it aloud, that if his mother had made a hundred dollars less a week, if she, with all her bare nerve endings, had been one muscle less strong in the face of it all, if they had had one accident, one unplanned gust against their house, they would have been, indisputably, white trash. "And that's another thing. You should see Freshler Feld. There are a lot of black people there, and

I'm not going to say anything, but you know, I worked my ass off to get this job, and there's a lot of affirmative action and reverse discrimination in that place." Or as Nathanson said about Naomi Williamson: I'll give you three guesses how she got a job here.

Placing his barely drunk beer to the side, Paul straightened the tape recorder on the table. His voice did not modulate. "Are you kidding me right now?"

"What does that mean?"

"Because I cannot believe— First of all, I'm not even sure where this little ray of sunshine is coming from, but I cannot believe that you actually imagine that there is rampant reverse discrimination in one of the whitest industries around."

"I didn't say it was rampant. I said it happened." His jaw disconnected as he repeated the word: "*Happened*. Listen: I played basketball in high school. JV only. I wasn't NBA material, for sure, but I wasn't bad. But at one point it became clear to me that I wasn't going to get to play varsity, and almost the whole varsity team, except for like two guys, was black. A lot of them were complete ball hogs, but whatever. So you know what I did? Nothing. I moved on and did other things. I didn't whine that I was discriminated against." Kelch wondered, then, why he was talking so much.

"Let's just leave it at that." Paul's voice sank with the boredom of a fisherman's at the end of a long, biteless afternoon. With robotic stiffness, the tips of his two longest fingers began to rub his temples. He then removed his eyeglasses again, wiped them quickly in his shirt, and returned them to his face. "I want to ask a question," Paul, after a pause, announced. "A few minutes ago, you said that you did not find the Christian Right 'compelling.' Are you a Christian?"

"You're joking, right? *Chris*. I'm a Catholic."

"A good Catholic?"

"I'm good. I'm Catholic. Is that—"

"Are you practicing?"

"Listen: the last time I pondered religion was when I thought of signing up for this world religions course in college to satisfy my humanities requirement. But"—he grinned, a red carpet for the funny—"I ended up taking intro psychology, which seemed like more fun. I just don't have time for that kind of shit. We've talked about this already. I work damn hard—an incredible amount of hours in a week. Don't get me wrong, I'm not complaining. I enjoy my work. At times, immensely." *True?* Yes, true. "I find it interesting and satisfying and 'fulfilling' and all that crap, okay. But it does, you know, have its costs. When I'm done with work, I'm either tired or like frustrated over some small thing that happened in the day. And if I'm tired, I just want to go home and chill out and watch TV or hang out with Kersten or, Jesus, just go to bed. But whatever I do, there is absolutely no, and I mean *no* way I'm going to start reading some boring gay-ass book about religion or, whatever, start staring at the stars and wondering if God exists. If that's what you want to do, go ahead for all I care. It's just not going to happen with me."

Paul paused before he delivered his conclusion. "Because it wouldn't make you happy, right?"

"Huh?"

Paul took a sip of beer, and his face puckered, disgusted. Kelch couldn't figure out why Paul suddenly no longer liked beer. "It wouldn't make you happy," Paul repeated.

"Listen: the same things make me happy as everyone else: having a job I like and having fun and having enough resources to do things I want to do."

"Resources?"

"Yeah"—*duh*—"money."

Paul pursed his lips, almost imperceptibly. "Of course."

"Come on, man, don't pretend you don't care about money. It's probably the thing we have most in common in the whole world." This was right.

"Let me guess. Because we both use it."

"That's a good one, but"—Kelch aped a buzzer, the wrong answer. "That we're both really, really interested in it."

"Is that the deeper half of your philosophy?"

"Huh?"

"Never mind."

"Don't be an asshole, man," Kelch said, noting contentedly the familiarity of his tag; the conversation was finally becoming free and fun and worth his effort. His strategy, it appeared, had worked. "Let's just look at the evidence. A: you wanted to interview *me*, which means that you're interested in the financial services industry, which is all about money. And B: you're living right now in the United States of America and absolutely everyone here is interested in money. It's like the foundation of our culture." Through the Rockford weekends and nights, the college work-study, bagging groceries, trimming hedges, shelving books, Kelch had never disliked working. To him, the magical physics of work, of converting muscles, arms, back, and brain into a check twice a month, transported work, always, above itself. It was the redeemer and the reason. Sometimes, in Rockford or Evanston, he would daydream about making a lot of money, but only rarely did those dreams drift and coalesce into the concrete. More often, his daydreams diffused, like a stratus cloud, across the abstract, dreams of an idea that money, in its surfeit, would one day be unimportant, dreams of a future when he would recall sixty-dollar-a-plate crises in pleasant soft focus.

The December after his first year as an associate, Veena and Joe Tedeschi, in Tedeschi's office, told him his "number," a one hundred and five thousand dollar bonus. One check (minus taxes). Even his joints felt distant then, gelatin-moist, and in his mixture of euphoria and depletion, his heart slowed to a pacific, Buddhist beat. But the peace lasted for just a day. Not even, for twenty hours later, he sat on the sidelines as Nathanson complained about his number and Wessex needled him: it's not Freshler's fault that no one makes money on your pigs, Nathanson, it's economics. And Kelch's own pride of accomplishment was punctured and exposed. His disappointment at one-oh-five then (and at three twenty-five, two months ago) wasn't because it fell short of planned expenditures. The dresser in his apartment was already regretted, excessive. He had a car. There wasn't a damn thing Kersten didn't have. The disappointment was because he knew that a lot of mediocre VPs in the department made five, ten times that amount. And because it wasn't logical to want less money rather than more, or to want a lot less money rather than a lot more. And because he was like a stock, and if his earnings stagnated, his momentum died.

And because what other yardsticks existed?

Paul separated his pints by two feet. "I will grant you A. I am interviewing you." Generously, Kelch giggled low, not a full laugh, but not hidden. "But I do not see where you're getting B from." Paul hyperenunciated the *B*. "Yes, I'm interested in money as a concept, but I've hardly made it the central organizing principle of my life."

For the second time tonight, Kelch thought he could detect something personal in Paul's voice. Kelch lowered his nose from the trough to make himself comprehensible. "You know that's crap, don't you? If I told you right now that I knew a stock that was going to go up without any risk, I guarantee that you'd buy it."

"Those exist?"

"No, I'm being the-o-retical here. Imagine that a genie stepped out of a bottle and gave me one wish, and I wished for a tenbagger over—"

"Ten-bagger?"

"A stock that goes up ten times . . . If I shared this stock with you and gave you documented proof of the powers of the genie, I guarantee that you would back the fucking truck up." *You got him, Chris.*

"Back the—?"

"Yeah, buy it in size."

"What's the point here?"

"The point is that I want you to admit that you'd do that."

"Yes, if a long lost aunt died and left me a million dollars, I would take the money. But your little thought experiment doesn't mean anything."

"Okay. How about this: how about we get rid of the genie?" Kelch blew apart his fist, his fingers flicking out at straight lines from the knuckles: good-bye, genie. Kelch chuckled. "Let's just say that I've done my homework and really pursued the bits on a company, and I decided that a stock was undoubtedly, one hundred percent the most compelling investment opportunity I've ever seen, I bet—"

"Hold it right there." Kelch held his mouth right there, open and vaudeville. "That is something you haven't yet answered. How do you decide that a stock is a great investment opportunity?"

"I do my research. On the fundamentals."

"I know that. But I assume you research stocks that you predict are going to go up as well as ones that are going to go down. Stocks still go down, right?"

"So . . ."

"So what leads you to conclude that some are going up."

"It's actually pretty complicated, but I think that it comes down to being a contrarian." Veena had taught him this. Joe Tedeschi preached it to every new associate in Equity Strategy and Research: contrarians make money, lemmings fall over cliffs. "A contrarian is—"

"I know what a contrarian is. How do *you* use the term?"

We invented the term. Kelch swallowed at a dryness in his mouth. Explaining the market had been easier—he glanced at a wall clock—*Jesus*, two hours ago. But, then again, he felt better now than two hours ago. "Listen: the way to think about it is that the market prices most things into a stock. If you think like everyone else in the market, then you'll have nothing to work with when deciding whether a stock is fairly priced. You have to think *contrary* to the conventional wisdom. Get it: contrarian."

Nothing.

"It's a really useful concept in its way," Kelch offered, friendly and upbeat. "Blue Padaway says . . . I can't remember, but what I was saying was that I always try to make my decisions from a contrarian point of view. After I pursue the bits. To find the compelling opportunities." Kelch burped into his blown-out cheeks. *Where was I?* I was setting him right.

"But if everyone—"

"Hey, man, I know what you're doing." This was true, although Kelch could find no irrefutable clues on Paul, who, it appeared to Kelch, was still tasting a lingering bitterness of his beer. "You're avoiding answering the question. If I gave you a stock that was a ninety-nine percent sure thing—like Tee-Fog a year ago, but we'll keep away from names for now—you'd invest in it."

"I would have to know what the company does, and I would need to make sure that I felt right about it."

"That's bullshit," Kelch said, spiking after the touchdown with a heavy tipple and then placing his empty glass aside to distance his arguments from the irrelevant presence of alcohol. "It goes against human nature."

"Maybe human nature as you people understand it."

"No." *Come on.* Make this clear. "Anyone. Human beings want security, right? And what is security but money. So what you said is bullshit."

"Personally, I don't feel comfortable investing—"

"That's bullshit."

"Are you going to let me finish?"

"Come on. Do you own any stocks?" Nothing. "In some trust fund somewhere?" Nothing. "Do your parents own any stocks or even mutual funds that you benefit from in any way whatsoever?" Paul did not move. "If any of those are true then what you said is bullshit." Kelch plinked the word again: "*Bull*shit."

"I would hope that not everyone believes that it's 'bullshit' to temper some natural instincts for financial security with some concern about how one obtains it, or to disagree with you and your little cronies on Wall Street who believe that making money is the only thing any sensible person can possibly be interested in, and that any person who is not obsessively trying to make money must be a mental defective."

"You see"—and Kelch did see, himself, as he said it. It was that clear. "That's the thing that I keep on hearing from you, and it just proves my point."

Scott identifies himself as a contrarian, one who truly understands that "the market prices most things into a stock" and that a stock's price reflects the net effect of the conventional wisdom of all the players in the market. According to the contrarian philosophy, the only people who can thus beat the market are those who understand where the conventional wisdom is wrong or incomplete and make decisions contrary to it. This makes sense. And thus probably every person on Wall Street thinks of himself as a contrarian. But the data indicate that few are. After our meetings, I examined Scott's stock recommendations and earnings estimates. (This information is easily obtainable.) Of the three stocks Scott recommends, two of them were also recommended by seven of his twelve rival analysts. His third recommendation, one he referred to with special pride, was recommended by eleven out of fourteen analysts. Only one analyst had placed a "sell" rating on any of the three stocks. And Scott's estimates of quarterly earnings rarely differed by more than a penny from those of any of his competitors.

This surprised me. I had assumed, from observing him in all his narrowness and inflexibility, that Scott was a below-average analyst. But this is not true. The most respected Wall Street poll ranked him the fifth-best analyst in his industry sector. This, I have been told, is a real accomplishment for someone his age.

If Scott then really is an above-average analyst, if his competitors, colleagues, and clients share or even aspire to his inadequate approach to the market, if they are also unable to devote sufficient time to individual stock analysis, shouldn't they all have a tendency to be more wrong than right? Thinking about the market this way, it is not difficult to understand why stocks are so often wildly mispriced. If a stock is twenty dollars on Monday and fifteen dollars on Tuesday after a minor shortfall in earnings—not an uncommon occurrence these days—then the market either overvalued the stock on Monday or undervalued it on Tuesday. But the market isn't a supernatural entity. It is people. It is Scott.

Which brings us to a root question: if the Scotts of the world are doing a poor job of setting the prices of individual stocks, could they be wrong on all stocks? This of course would result in an unjustified bear market or, in what many say we are experiencing right now, a bubble. After getting to know Scott, I don't understand any better how market bubbles form and I can't offer any more reasoned arguments why or when bubbles burst, but I do believe now, more than ever, at a gut level, that a bubble exists.

What is frustrating isn't that the Scotts have caused the apparent bubble, or that Scott is so blithe about the bubble, but the fact that a bubble means that the market is not efficient. Wall Street defenders rest all their claims of social utility and brush aside every criticism of their actions on the idea that the stock market is the necessary, beneficial mechanism for the efficient distribution of capital. The efficient distribution of capital, in turn, is an absolute good with immeasurable benefits: the longest bull market, lowest unemployment, strongest growth. Sorry about the closed factory in Scottsville, folks, but the market, our shareholders, insist that we must cut costs and the market knows how capital should be used. But what if, as the bubble implies, the market is collectively, grossly inefficient? How do you make it up to a thousand people laid off because of a rash decision to please an intellectually lazy analyst like Scott?

And therein lies another sad irony. Possibly the only beneficiaries of that inefficient distribution of capital are the people there, supposedly, to ensure its efficient distribution . . .

Don't get me off track, Kelch thought. I know what I'm saying. I know why this makes sense. "Listen: you keep on expecting me—

all your questions expect me—to be the living, breathing justification of Wall Street."

Nothing.

"But that's not what I am. I have a very specific job." Kelch burped deeply under his sternum and then tapped it quiet. He felt the beer slosh through his arteries more merrily than he had expected. "And I do it—I've told you this a few times—pretty fucking well. I don't know why you want to make more out of it than that."

Paul was a glacier of superior silence.

"Listen: if I was making thirty-five thousand dollars a year, we wouldn't be here right now." *That's it, goddamnit.*

"Is that true?"

"Of course it is. You're only interested in me because you read about how much we make on the Street. But if we were doing the exact same thing but making the same money as some guy on an assembly line, you wouldn't care a lick." *Care a lick?* Where did that come from?

Paul's eyes, half-closing, seemed to narrow in premeditation. His lips sealed themselves tightly against the formation of a snarl. The involved effort was apparent in his nostrils—pulsing—and his words sounded as angry, as involved, as his could be. "What is your point?"

"That it's just 'fascinating' that I get all this grief from people because I earn a decent salary. Listen: I told you, I wasn't born rich. Frankly, I'm not rich now. By any standards of this city, for sure. Don't get me wrong, I do all right, and, just for the record, my family wasn't on welfare or anything. But my father—" *Stop pushing me about that, you prick.* "I've worked since I was twelve years old, every day during the summer, after school. During college— It was ridiculous— My sister didn't even go— Listen: I've made sacrifices. I couldn't play basketball anymore because I had to get a job." Kelch's strong leg, his right, began to bob; telegraph taps from his foot communicated up to his lap. "And I think that it's funny that when I finally start making some real money for the first time in my life, everyone jumps on my case."

"You are—"

Kelch held a finger up to shush, to stab the air, to demand temperance. "*Listen* just a second, okay. You've been talking nonstop for two hours." Kelch looked to his right, at a table being filled with different undergraduates. "Let's stop being theoretical, okay. My sister's—my sister Heather's—husband, Dan, was from the same 'class' or whatever—social class, not high school class—as we were. But he partied just a little more in high school, maybe he is a little naturally, I don't know, slower, and his dad—*whoa*. Anyway, he only went to community college for like a week until he quit and took a job at this company that makes parts *for parts* for industrial equipment. Now, let's say, me"—Kelch pointed his locked-straight thumb back at himself—"I partied a little bit more in high school, or let's just say I fucked up one class, maybe that's all it would have taken, one class, and I would have never gotten into Evanston. That would have been *it* for me. You got it? End of story about being here right now. No one would have given me a second chance." Kelch's weaker leg joined his right as the Morse code resounded, more insistent, in longer, faster sentences. "And let's say in Evanston if I drank more or didn't care about my grades or again if I screwed up just one class—overslept a final, let's say, and gotten a D or maybe even a C. If that had happened, Freshler never would have hired me. Do you understand that? Those guys, *we*, aren't a goddamned charity." The legs' messages clarified their potency, their anticipation. "But that didn't happen. I didn't screw up, because I didn't *let* myself screw up. And because of that, I didn't end up working next to Dan. But if I had, you would have written me off like him." Kelch switched to a different, poorly executed voice, a white man imitating a black comic imitating a white man: "We shouldn't judge the ol' fellow. He's just a hard worker who hasn't gotten the breaks." Kelch's normal voice returned. "And you wouldn't care what I thought or read or anything." Kelch pushed his palms down on his knees, now jerking upward, erratically giddy. "And so it is about the money. It's all about the money. You don't give a damn what Dan thinks. But that could have been me."

Paul's eyes tightened further under his glasses. His mouth remained shut.

"Answer this: are you one of those pretentious New York assholes who gets your kicks out of making fun of working-class guys?"

Nothing.

"Are you, with your coat there, the kind of person who laughs when some guy walks into some fancy New York restaurant and you can see that he's wearing a shitty two-dollar tie or his wife is kind of cheap looking or, my God, he's drinking beer out of the bottle? Are you the kind of guy who then makes a snide little crack to your fucking boyfriend about Jersey trash or?"

Paul's lips began to open, but they held together, a quarter-inch apart.

The bouncing in Kelch's legs amplified, ungoverned. "Are you one of those jackasses that, uh, when you go into a deli and the guy's a little slow in ringing you up, you say to no one in particular"—the comic voice—"'I'm really happy that I don't have anything better to do today?'"

Nothing.

"Are you a hypocrite—that's it, a hypocrite?" Kelch's left leg hit under the table and shifted the topside glasses an inch in unison. "If you're not—and I'm absolutely, fascinatingly sure that you're not— then you can't judge people differently, and you can't apply some *progressive* tax scale like the goddamn IRS on goodness, or whatever, 'morality.' You know, like the rich have to be 'better' at a higher percentage of their income. Listen: if you're not a hypocrite, then you only have two choices. I'm either a perfectly decent, hard-working, just-trying-to-do-my-best kind of guy or I'm not. I can't be some perfectly decent hardworking guy, but, you know *but*, am horrible only because I work at Freshler Feld and take the salary that the company has decided to pay me instead of working at a plant in Rockford and taking the salary that that company could pay me. And, and, *and* I'm so goddamn horrible only because I was able to get a job at Freshler Feld and make this kind of money because—God forgive me—I couldn't afford to waste the hundred thousand dollars that you have to pay nowadays in this fucked-up country for a college degree."

Without premeditation, Kelch's whole frame popped up. Two-thirds standing, he towered over Paul and looked down on him from a judge's raised bench. Paul glanced up: his face was still neutral and still silent, still an impenetrable white globe. "And just for the record, asshole," Kelch added, "I'm never going to be poor again."

Scott's success seems sadly emblematic of an American form of decadence. All the traditional signs of decadence are now present on Wall Street (and its dependents): a moral and spiritual emptiness, a smugness, a shallowness, an underlying fragility, an elevation of mediocrity, a frivolity of life. But this, remember, is an American decadence. It is optimistic, not fatalistic. And it is not limited to an artistic or aristocratic minority. The quantity of decadents, like our cars and our land itself, is large and oversized. We live in a democracy: anyone who is sufficiently clever, and is willing to work hard, is welcome to join the fun.

The decadence is peculiarly American for another reason. It is not primarily a decadence of sensuality, although gluttonous materialism clearly plays a role. It is, rather, a decadence marked by business and, most notably, money itself. Our cultural forebears, the Puritans, lived within a triangular worldview of God and stern morality and hard work—hard work as manifested in capitalist enterprise. When a society such as that, no matter how filtered it has been through other cultures and generations, turns decadent, when the pillars of God and morality snap and disappear, it is not surprising that the one straight side of the triangle remaining, the money side, mutates into a circle and encloses the society with some facsimile of a worldview. Perhaps this is the unanticipated prize or our national "triumph," when *peace* and *prosperity* are stapled together on their way out of our mouths. With no more struggles, the heroes of national struggle—Olympic athletes and astronauts, generals and scientists—are replaced by heroes of wealth and corporate bureaucrats like Scott . . .

It was a bliss Kelch felt as he settled again into the bench—an eruption of glee from every cell of his body as they transformed themselves into light and joy; a bliss not only that he had *won*, match point, that he had beaten Paul into submission and silence, that he had planted his flag with the last inarguable word, but a bliss that Paul had asked to be here in the first place, had interviewed *him*. It wasn't a sexual bliss that Kelch felt, for a sexual bliss always consumes, is always imperfect, stained with the next moment, with *it's over*. This bliss could have lasted forever. It was why marbled victories have wings. It was the bliss of being unequivocally, victoriously, divinely right.

For all Scott's bonhomie, he is living a markedly one-dimensional, one-track, one-note life. Stubbornly comfortable in his skin, he shows no concern for anyone or anything not directly capable of adding to his material well-being or personal happiness. He is, in the literal sense of the word, pathetic.

But what happens to Scott if the bubble breaks? What happens to all the Scotts, these hollow men, these stuffed men, their head-pieces filled with straw, if a deflated market someday can no longer support their half-million-dollar salaries or more, if the jobs into which they have invested their entire identities, from which they mine all their virtue, crumble? It is difficult to think about, not because of its economic unfeasibility—it is in fact very feasible—but because of the implications this could have for us all. Maybe the only thing more disturbing than a society where Scott is on top is a society where thousands, hundreds of thousands, of Scotts are angry and embittered and suddenly unemployed. So maybe we should hope and pray that Eliot was right, about the whimper not the bang, when he told us seventy-five years ago that this is how the world ends. This is how the world ends.

It was a bliss of almost embarrassing depths. He didn't believe it, and it wasn't true, and he wouldn't have expressed it aloud, but he could find no evidence to dispute a sensation that this was the happiest he had ever been in his life. Like work, like chemically converting your will and brain into dollars, into a currency of power, the interview had converted all his inchoate, unspoken, subdermal suspicions into a truth, glory, an achievement—a bliss. Bliss was a binomial bit, the one to the zero of despair.

BOOK THREE

· 1 ·

He spied as she leaned against the headboard. The comforter covered only her ankles, and she was examining a puddle of loose, gentle babyskin around her navel. Her breasts, always at odds, peeked farther in different directions as her back slid down the headboard's smooth-sanded grille. Unhurried, Kersten looked to the door, and Kelch took a step back. He knew she could hear the silence: the conversation with the Ghost had been over for a minute.

The first time Kelch had seen the khaki frame and headboard in the room—and the matching bow-curved, two-column dresser—the charade had depressed him. He had become accustomed to the frame since then, but he occasionally resensed, as now, that the room was unfairly adult.

He held his breath as Kersten, inexpressive, looked at the door's three-inch opening. With the slaps of a blind man, experimental and misdirected, she reached for the edge of the comforter and pulled it higher. She wetted her lips, and her mouth opened.

Not yet, Kelch thought. I'm not ready.

Kersten didn't call out his name.

If the Ghost knows, Kelch concluded, then everyone knows, because the Ghost doesn't know me at all. The Ghost, in fact, had made it his life's one goal not to know him. Everything he had done—done at least since Kelch was five—had been done with that poorly concealed purpose. And if the Ghost knows, everyone knows. And Kersten—*a good piece of ass in this town*—knows. Why else would she have brought up Paul Galicia at dinner? But why hadn't she accused Kelch already—directly—accused him of humiliating her, exposing her, hurting her? But the bit, pursue the bit, remember the bit: the Ghost knows. And if the Ghost reads that long-winded magazine, then everyone must read it because the Ghost, chuckling off the world with his indiscriminate laugh track, was hardly the magazine's natural target.

How do you measure betrayal—that was the mass-stuff forming Kelch's state. How do you incorporate a Judas kiss into a physiological calm? How do you summon the conviction, the reaction, the proper scale of revenge, of hysteria, passion, violence, the right quart can (or tablespoon) of total consumption, of rage? You can't, maybe, can't run a marathon if you can't run a mile, can't convert your awareness of a betrayal, awareness that you have a new chemical experience labeled A: betrayal and B: danger, into the old antibodies that your body has always produced: disappointment, apathy, inertia, jealousy, disgust. Kelch had read the article last night on the shuttle from Boston, and the incomprehensibility of the words, the impossibility of life as lived had pretzeled his interior, cast him into nausea, but the reaction was quickly, almost immediately over. The anger had been subsumed into exhaustion—a lit tissue, up-snowing charcoal flakes—and his face had become fevered, not feverish. He had moved through the article with growing, sinking disbelief. It didn't make any sense. After he had finished, his fibers and wires—not his veins, not his marrow, nothing identifiable in an anatomy textbook—were fully cooked; they accepted the notion of consequence; they just wanted to fast-forward to the end. Kelch was sitting on the aisle, and once the plane landed, he remained fixed to his seat. The man next to him, also dressed in blue suit, blue shirt, cleared his throat twice, trying both times to prod Kelch forward. Finally, he muttered to Kelch to excuse him. Kelch rolled the magazine into a tight iron rod and rammed it into the seat pocket. He went straight home, into an impotent sleep.

Kersten forced out a cough, maybe testing her voice.

Kelch felt a hand, a fist, punching from the inside of his chest, landing with the same expanding beat as his pulse. The punches were concentrated, but they were also comprehensive: they implicated every inch of his inner chest wall, delineating his cavity, that accused hollowness, with the methodical, transforming pressure of a potter birthing a bowl, damp gray clay. Kelch placed his palm against his breast, and his hand felt its double as the in-chest fist accelerated its eager search with insistent, global thrusts. *Can she hear this?* He looked through the door again; Kersten was pulling the comforter up even farther. The punching grew louder, impatient, too loud (he concluded) just to be his heart. The punching, it seemed, intended to push clear through his chest. He had become modern healthy eating, skinless and boneless, but there used to be a skin between his heart and the grim city air, a skin ensuring his privacy, his dignity. There used to be Rockford; there used to be I'm not a pussy, not Jewish, not a millionaire's son. I'm midwestern unpretentious. I'm loyal to my roots. But how could the Ghost's hand, then, reach clear out of the receiver and jab straight through him? *Aren't you Scott?* Go to hell. *But you're Scott, right?* Shut up. *Okay, but you're Scott.*

He pushed open the door gradually. He could tell that she had not been looking in his direction: her head had swiveled toward him as if he were only coming from the other side of the room. Kelch stood in the doorway, stripped of all but his underwear.

"Who was that?"

"What?"

"Who was that on the phone?"

After listening to his own heavy pause, Kelch answered, "It was Johann."

Upbeat: "He really is annoying, isn't he?"

"Yeah, sure. . . . He had a question about Tee-Fog." Kelch sat on the bed and parked his back parallel to hers, his legs paraplegically limp above the comforter. Had she been listening, he wondered again. How loudly did I yell at the Ghost—loudly, too loudly, no, not loudly, quietly. She couldn't have heard anything unless . . . "It's going to be an interesting day tomorrow. To see how the stock moves."

Nothing.

"You know, whether there's another shoe to drop."

"Chris . . ."

"Yeah?"

"Everything's all right, right?"

She gazed into the faraway as Kelch repeated, to himself, her words. This was the second time tonight she had asked that. "No," Kelch said, unexpectedly clear and unmumbled, and Kersten's strings tensed, he could feel, beside him. When she got scared, her fear was like the stem of a wineglass, breakable by an unkind thought. "I mean, look at what happened today. A: my marquee stock blows up. And B:" What is B? You always need a B. "B: the bankers start pressuring me to prop up the pig like I'm for sale or something. I wouldn't particularly call that all right."

"I want you to know that you can tell me anything."

Kelch struggled to untangle his legs from the comforter and sheets; they submitted, eventually, undercover. "I don't have anything to tell you."

"Okay, but don't feel like you have to hold it in."

He looked away from her, at his side table, for a magazine, a book, a handgun, anything. "Just drop it already."

He didn't expect it, but perhaps he should have. She squeezed shut her eyes, brought two tight—but cutely out-of-character—fists up near her chin, and cried, siren-pitched, "Stop fucking yelling at me. Stop it. Stop it. Just stop it. Stop it now." Two months into their relationship, in a horsewhipped, consuming push to initiate coverage on JRSG, Kelch had lived at his desk for eight days in a row. (When Kelch excused himself with a late night at the office, the identity of the other woman was never in doubt. It was the office itself.) On Thursday afternoon, the report delivered to production ahead of schedule, a voice mail left for Tedeschi to herald the accomplishment, Kelch, light as a milkweed's spoor, invited Kersten to dinner anywhere she wanted. She spat back, "Why don't you go to dinner with your fucking job." Kelch laughed, of course, but then she decompressed, an inverse gasp. *Chris, this is not a joke.* I just never—*I need to know if you're serious about this.* About dinner? *Chris, I can't—I can't—I can't do this again.* Do what? *I'm going to be twenty-seven in two months.* I'm—I'm—I'm. (He was confused.) And he heard her, over the phone, begin to cry petitely, at first in short triple bursts, then in opened-up, coughish bawls, longer and louder. Kelch tried to understand what was happening. I'm sorry, Kersten, just tell me what you want me to do? *You aren't going to fucking do this to me.* Do what? *I need you to care.* I care, I care. *I need to know that we're in this together.* In what? *Damnit, don't you understand?* I'm trying. *Don't you understand that I'm the nicest and most caring person you're ever going to meet?*

When Kersten brought him to Connecticut the first time (for the whole night, he tried never to full-mouth smile because his two crossover teeth, he was aware, clashed with the cherry wood, the tartan prints, the highboy and silver set from Our American Ancestors, the Oriental rugs and hunter green carpeting, the smell of the clean wool and perfect folds of sweater drawers, the knowledge of lemon duster and professional help), he sat at the dinner table and ate enthusiastically; he was thus only able to listen. It was obvious to him that Dr. and Mrs. Henry's understanding of each other was saturated, exclusive. They corrected each other in amused voices. They exchanged we-know-what-that-means with not-this-again-honey. It was also obvious that Kersten shined here, effortlessly, with a certain magic, as the centerpiece of the palace and the silken product of Our Love; she shined even more than she did over her own group of friends from college; she shined noticeably more than she did alone with Kelch.

Kelch had met the Henrys on five subsequent occasions, and he suspected that they still thought him slow. The second time, Mrs. Henry was visibly compensating. The third time, visibly reproached.

"Calm down, Kersten. Okay, just calm down." *I can't deal with this tonight.* "I'm sorry." He looked it too, panda-bear.

"You really are the cutest thing, aren't you," Kersten announced, the previous outburst disavowed—more, denied—in an enthusiastic return to her natural state. She turned to him, cupping her palm over his far temple, letting him feel her hand's cool touch cure him or take, the gesture implied, his temperature. But he didn't want this; he didn't want her smothering sympathy; he didn't want her on his side—he didn't want to have a side. Her hand seemed to be bringing all that the night was trying to bury—a double-active mind, a plugged fever, a loneliness—up to his skin's surface, in a scorching blush. But there was another stream of instinct now, of relief, of a willingness to try anything. Following that, he closed his eyes, bit over his lip, and circled his neck around a ball joint, bringing her hand along on the revolutions. Perhaps this was all he needed now: sleep, a sweet, flowing, vacant sleep, where nightmares could not catch him. He had never had nightmares before. He adjusted to her in his shut-eyed darkness, his lips meeting hers, and they eased down the headboard into the pillows. Her return kisses were silent, and as he (startling himself) raised his leg doglike to untwist his body through the sheets, she placed both palms on his chest. "Sweetie, hold on a second." *What now.* "Everything's okay, right?"

Kelch rolled back prone, stared at the ceiling, and exhaled loudly.

"Chris?"

"What?" He had knocked the word, intentionally roughly, off the shelf.

"You didn't answer me."

"I was just thinking. Is that okay?"

"About what, sweetie?" From the periphery, he could see her hand rise, self-consciously hesitant, to contemplate his face again, but she set it down without contact.

"About Tee-Fog. What else do you want me to think about?"

Nothing.

Kelch had been ready, in general, to declaim the injustice of Tee-Fog, to analyze the fundamentals of Tee-Fog, to explain why *I give up* was *the* dumbest thing he had ever done in his life, but Kersten wouldn't care. No one cared. Her back high on the headboard again, she looked straight ahead; her face was cryptic and, from his lower vantage point, skewed by a cubist bias. She offered, Kelch supposed, what she guessed he wanted: "Maybe we should just go to bed." Jerkily, without pausing to anticipate the darkness, he flipped off the lamp. After two minutes of unlit silence, a quiet less interrupted than hardened by the high squeak of a cab's tires attacking the street below, by the segregated sirens of East Harlem, by a jet engine faint in its solitude, Kersten said tentatively, "Oh, I don't think I ever got a chance to tell you." Kelch closed his eyes and opened them again. "Marigold e-mailed me. Paul Galicia, who you did meet, just published a piece about Wall Street."

Kelch considered his possibilities: goddamnit, I'm trying to sleep; or (loudly) I told you I don't fucking know who Paul Galicia is; or Why is Marigold such a troublemaker; or Yes, I think I know that piece, it's the one that's about to ruin my life. He said instead, "I'll check it out." If he was so casual about checking it out, obviously it wasn't him.

"Okay." He heard her turn away from him.

The fist in his chest seemed less interested then in surveying his hollow than in making noise for noise's sake, alerting Kersten to its presence. Kelch understood that if it had had the power, the fist would have yelled, There is nothing here, or yelled, Pay attention, or yelled with a spelunker's distant echo, Why, Kersten, aren't you in here with me? Kelch didn't know the answer to the last question; he knew, in fact, only opposite clues: that she wanted nothing more than to be in there; that he, intellectually, wanted her there too.

Kelch knew the clichés—Kersten still probably believed in them—of the son in the triangle of single mother and sister. Who grows up to be sensitive. Who grows up comfortable with women. Who *loves* women, because he has known them all his life. Maybe, at ten or eleven or twelve, Kelch had been on that path, pulling fewer pigtails than average, never making loud jokes about precocious breasts. But by the time he entered high school, the clichés disgusted him, to the core. He refused to be a jerk who confided his crushes to his sister, or shared a beer with his super-cool mom, or invited her to visit him in New York for ten straight days so that they could spend real time together again. He had wanted nothing more than to get out of Rockford, away from their logic of rings and gaps and confessions, away from the senses of humor that always seemed out of tune. He needed to be in a world of men, where truth was facts, and so he worked at it, worked for it. He had never been abnormally mean to his sister and mother—Dan and Bill appeared, almost too conveniently, when Kelch might have needed to break more violently away—but whenever they had tried to smother him, attempted in their subtle ways to make him one of the girls, he had slithered out, and away. He was never sure if they were his enemies or his friends.

After a minute, Kelch heard a breath sneak out of Kersten only to hear her snatch it back. He needed to ask, achingly, What are you after? He needed her to tell him, but he couldn't ask her directly. He needed to learn it through osmosis, and he continued his night watch. He knew that she could feel his eyes.

"Why did you ask that?"

"What?" Her voice was pouty, put-upon.

The dark-night space between their mouths was a robbing ground for highwaymen, armed with obscurity. "Why did you ask me about Paul Galicia?"

He could tell that she was propping her head higher on the pillow. "I don't know anymore."

Kelch felt the soft rustle of the sheets and wondered if she was positioning her hand to touch him again—he might have wanted her to—but it was her pedicured foot, her toes in-curled, that rubbed against his shin. He froze, unsure if her touch was considered. Listen, he then thought, trying to concentrate on anything else. *Stop touching me.* This is not a fantasy, this is not happening to someone else— fifteen rows and a movie screen do not separate you from the action. If they know, it's over. Do you understand *that?* This is about your life—your existence—being over. You'll never be able to live down the embarrassment—embarrassment, hell, you're an idiot according to that article, a hypocrite, a *racist,* a fucking homophobe. It doesn't matter if it's true or not, don't you see? "It's not me" is not a bit. No, it is a bit, but it's N/A: Asian sales as percentage of PKW's total is N/A, not applicable. The company has no Asian operations. . . . What *are* the applicable bits? The Ghost knows. Kersten's acting like she knows. Then everyone knows. And everyone thinks that you're an idiot and a fraud and a loser. Freshler Feld won't just brush this whole thing aside. You compromised its reputation, and for what? Because you wanted to be liked by that asshole Galicia?

This is panic, Kelch then felt, unarticulated. Panic was not screaming and sweat. It was not insanity. Panic was a heart throwing its shoulder against a chest wall, trying frantically to escape, a brown rat out of burlap; panic was a fatty wax sealing the eyes tight; it was the lungs constricting, imploding, insisting on not breathing; it was the whole body agreeing, resigning, crying not to breathe, not to see, not to move, not to exist because maybe it would be better if you were dead. Panic was your body preparing you, escorting you, limp, to the deep closet of being dead.

Tinny, delicate: "Chris, I—" Her foot stopped rubbing against his shin.

I love you, I love you, I need to love you, just please let me love you without doubts, without logic, without conditions, without knowing that it isn't true.

Her foot felt like a corpse's, cold and porcelain. "Chris, I don't know . . ."

This is panic, Kelch felt again. *I* am panicking. Kelch had felt

panic before, to be sure, but it was always a specific panic, vertigi-
nous, of the job, of the Street. It was the panic of OPLL's divisional
president, of how m'I suppose to grow fourteen percent. It was the
rational panic of facing the drop: there was never a reason fortified
enough why Tee-Fog or Allencor couldn't be ten dollars instead of
twenty, why the shares in his personal account couldn't all tumble and
scream, why Freshler Feld, Inc., couldn't employ three thousand people instead of twelve. The stomach of the firm, hungry for bodies, now
exploded at twelve thousand because the market—the profits—bore
it, but the market was a force. It did not have opinions on whether
Freshler Feld should be its current size or smaller, profitable or not.
The market didn't care like the sky doesn't care; the atmosphere has
no feelings; it is uncontainable, immaterial, a metaphysics, like them
all, whose only proof is its churches and priests. And because the market couldn't care, even in theory, it didn't care if Kelch had a job in a
year, if he could pay his twenty-three-hundred-dollar rent, if he had
just stayed in Rockford and rotted. But that panic was always filed
away—for the solid, like Kelch, filed for months—because the market wasn't just an atmosphere, it was also, as Blue said of Freshler, a
community. People wouldn't let the market collapse without a reason,
and there were only reasons, vested powerful trillion-dollar reasons,
for the market's evermore ascent. Unite the clout of Freshler and its
competitors, of every investor and pension holder on the globe, and
you ought to be able to own the sky.

That panic was different from the panic now. Now was a torturer
and his torturee, perhaps claustrophobic, clearly anaerobic. Now was
a panic of pain, of suffocation, of castration, not fright.

"Chris, please talk to me. I didn't mean to—" She skipped ahead,
nearly panted; her voice splintered into high notes. Then it held
itself. "I didn't mean to upset you."

He wasn't listening.

"Chris, are you awake?"

They know, he thought. They know, he knew.

"Say something. Please."

I don't want to talk.

She lifted his near-side arm and inserted her head into the crevice. She placed her hands at his ribs' southern border and laid the side of her face against his chest's edge, an Indian calculating the buffalo. The plains-sweeping herd must have been deafening, but she kept her ear stamped to his chest. He shuddered—the ripples' headwaters were under her pressed cheek—and packed his eyes tight. He heard a sound, and at first he feared that it was his own, but it was Kersten's whimpers muffled by his chest—animal whimpers, owlish, stuttering *who*s. He didn't move.

I'm panicking. Help me.

Her flushed palm moved downward on his naked chest—he squinted open his eyes—and her hands planed around him, sealing her nestled shoulder closer into him. He could think only—he could feel—enemy or friend. It was a choice and a question and a clarity of an icicle dropped onto his back. *I'm panicking. Help me.*

"Chris?"

I'm panicking. Help me.

"Chris?"

I'm panicking. Help me.

"Do you love me? You know . . . really?"

"I-I-I told you I did."

"I know," she admitted in a baby voice, which grew up, in a phrase, to a toddler's false innocence. "I just needed to hear you say it."

· 2 ·

Usually, Kelch evinced a half-aware, over-posed preen when he walked into Veena's office. He could just stop by; few others could. He tried now consciously, in a dialogue with his feet, to achieve the usual walk, but the ground was still unsettled after her five-thirty summons. When Kelch had served directly under Veena, talking with her (outside of receiving orders or reporting back) had been limited to infrequent instruction on career, market, or sector and more infrequent reflections on her achievements. Although he had held on to these lessons, and they had built up, his walls swelling with new layers of paint, he always left her office reminded that as good a junior as he might have been (and he suspected he had been the best), he still, in her judgment, lived far below her white-towered room.

As Kelch stood in front of a guest chair in her office, his legs stiffened for a moment to let him know that he could, if he wanted to, if he was brave, tell Veena that he couldn't spare the time to be here, that there was nothing to know, that he had to leave thousands of voice mails, that nothing had happened. That morning, in the first seeping of the newborn day, he had believed the final story. He had even been allowed to believe it as he assembled the evidence of the uselessness of sleep—his bones seemed to have collected more weariness in the night. He believed it until he watched Kersten sleeping, her face a snowdrift of smoothly rounded peace. It sickened him, and Galicia and Hoder and Buchalter and Nathanson all returned, not in a rush of acute pangs but in a building adaptation of his body to its new weight and burdens, to the idea that his life would go on, as long as it went, with this heaviness, this power-lessness, atop it. When Kersten finally awoke, she and Kelch bumped into each other around their bathroom tasks, skin bristling, a train traveler's awkward passthrough. She tried a few times to start a sunny morning, but he showered and dried and dressed uttering only grunts and hums.

Kelch could tell that Veena, on the phone, was talking about BPN, and by the impatient benevolence delivered in her regular clip—pecking, humorless—he could tell that she was talking to a B-grade client. He also suspected that she was not looking at him now but through him, to his cork-brown, anxious heart. "Look it here, John, the fundamentals remain outstanding. Obviously. . . .

Obviously. . . . I do not foresee that in any way materially affecting the company." Kelch gazed out of Veena's double-wide window, corner-arched like all of them in the Freshler building, and he adjusted his angle two inches to win a view of the harbor. That view was skyscraper-interrupted and shaded, but the yardwide clearing, in window inches, to the harbor's cheerless tanker-spotted blue became, by its corporate consequence, brilliant, Caribbean. Looking at her computer, Veena ignored the client buzzing out of the receiver. She then willed him into compliance: "I told you that the shares had significant upside. Just because— Yes, it is a compelling price here, though obviously less compelling..." Half of Veena's office, if walled, could have housed a content million-dollar vice president, but half instead contained an abbreviated sitting room, a brooch of her rank. Except for attendees of the monthly sector analyst meeting, almost no one ever sat on the two improbably curved chairs or on the modern understuffed couch. A chrome-and-glass cocktail table supported fanned copies of Veena's research reports, her signature "Trends" pieces in particular, and two end tables were lucite gardens, mini-skylines of spiking plastic plaques, commemorating Freshler deals—IPOs, spin-offs, buybacks, tracking stocks— in Veena's sector. She claimed credit for most of them. "Is that it? Obviously..." At the end point again of Veena's stare, Kelch thought—feared—that he was serving as a surrogate for her disgust. Although her eyes were direct, immense, she was a lawn jockey, small and dark and stiff.

"I will send to you what I can send to you. . . . Look it here, John, I will transfer you to one of my assistants, who can take care of this." She placed him on hold and walked to the doorway. "Mandy—Peter—Nathaniel," she addressed a mob gathered under a palace balcony, letting them sort out the trivia of who would obey. "Pick up seven-six seven-two and handle it please." Veena's freestanding desk was arthropodal; its legs parabolically, concavely transported the wiring to the topside's electronics. She kept most of her paper files in the cabinets in the hallway—the office's unclutter

was expensive and proud—but some papers were locked in a low
lateral cabinet under her window. Two frames were ever present on
the cabinet; the smaller one contained a picture of her two sons,
Something-esh and Something-eev. A colleague had once told Kelch
that the boys, now in their early teens, were both prodigies,
although she had said this mostly from a feeling, it seemed, that
Veena's sons could be nothing else. In six years, after two early
mistakes, Kelch had never asked about them, and he often suspected
that Veena displayed their picture only to dispel the subterranean
rumor that she wasn't oriented to marry or breed. (In that case, -esh
and -eev didn't do a particularly effective job.) The other frame, a
few inches larger, housed the internally famous "Murderers' Row"
cover from *Forbes*, in which Veena glared from the center of the six
intentionally severe, black-suited Freshler analysts. Although Equity
Strategy and Research had expanded, gained in power, broadened
its reputation in the ten years since the cover had appeared, that
picture still represented the apogee of the golden era, when analysts
in the firm (and on the Street) arose one morning and realized that
they had ascended from the trainers' room of support services to the
dollar-showered ball field of Wall Street power. The market had
learned what they could do to a stock.

Kelch had understood that his morning suspicion of a cleaner,
better reality was wrong, at least doubtful, but the day had pro-
gressed and passed with nothing particular happening. He had, of
course, talked about Tee-Fog with clients, even referred to *I give up*
with a few of them, and thus maybe this was the bargain, his stomach had deduced, the *one* load that someone, in the night, had chosen for him. If that was it, it was fine. He could deal with it.
Remember, Kelch thought, Veena had said, "I need to talk to you
about yesterday." Tee-Fog had happened yesterday.

As Veena sat down again, Kelch glanced at the gargoyle diamond
guarding her left hand. "That was John Tuvich at Monroe." Her
accent retained traces of high-caste Indian, British engineering, but
she packed and dispatched her words so quickly that she allowed

no time for dallying vowels or imperial sibilants. She talked like the Freshler building: efficient, tastefully coordinated, technocratically cosmopolitan.

"Oh yeah, that's what I figured."

"He's an idiot."

Kelch would have called Tuvich an idiot too, but he would have said it because Tuvich, the last time they spoke, hadn't found it necessary to acknowledge that Kelch had left him a voice mail every week for a year. "That's what, you know, I always, um—" If you spoke slowly or contortedly enough, Kelch knew, Veena would save you from demonstrating any inclination to garrulity.

"Hold on, please." She picked up the receiver. (She had declared headsets tacky.) Kelch watched disappointment alight on her eyes— disappointments to her always seemed related to the world's ingratitude—as she connected to a voice mail. Was she embarrassed that she had kept him waiting for only five minutes?

Disowning the attempted call, Veena returned to Kelch. "Tuvich asked me to send him my model." She made a sound, a brief stomach-born scoff, began to rifle through some messages on her desk, and then looked up, her mouth sour and restless. "What a motherfucker."

Tell me why I'm here.

"How have the numbers been this Q?"

Why are you asking me this? You said, you *promised*, that this was about yesterday. "OPLL, uh, beat consensus by a couple of cents."

Nothing.

"But I don't think there's a lot of interest."

"Right."

"And Allencor tomorrow, um—"

Distractedly, Veena pulled the phone toward her—"Excuse me, I must return a call"—and dialed, but she was dead-ended into a voice mailbox again. She discharged the phone and called out to her secretary, or Kelch's replacement, or her new associate, or the insolent universe, "Someone get me Tom Eddington please." Eddington was an A-list client—he managed a dedicated sector fund—and Kelch's tongue had bungled and ballooned, completely failed, the ten times that they had spoken over the last three years. With Kelch, Eddington would always begin, "Veena told me you would know . . ."

Kelch recognized something novel in the jerky inconsistency of Veena's movements, and he thought, obliquely, that maybe he wasn't here about Tee-Fog. But everything that day had been about Tee-Fog. Every hour that had passed had seemed to confirm, at least made him feel, that reading the article on the plane—in the air?—flying?—had been a cheap hallucination. But then again, if this was about Tee-Fog, they would be talking about Tee-Fog. Veena would have reflexively—guiltlessly—speared him, gutted him, and hung him in the smoker the first second he entered her office, with one of her favorite lines: *unacceptable* or her maddeningly unjust *typical*, prefaced always by a deep-chilling pause.

Veena's words seemed to rubberneck at their own accident at the exit of her mouth, a mouth as adverse to small talk as it was to long sentences and hints of a fairer sex. "How's it going otherwise, Christopher?" She sucked in her lips, and they close-danced around her teeth.

"Well, I decided not to downgrade Tee-Fog."

"What happened there?"

Huh? "It got whacked, you must—"

"Right." She stood up, but as she kept her chair maximally elevated, her head was only a foot higher than when she sat. She returned to the doorway, and the noises of the huddled cubicles outside her office—the keyboard clatter, the gossip about downgrades and blowups, even the telephones—seemed to switch off in an extrasensory perception of her presence. Kelch had developed that sense too. Veena glared at her servants' quarters, and, her words pouncing, she demanded from her secretary, "Are you getting me Tom Eddington please?" Her secretary, new and nervous (they were always new and nervous), rushed out the excuse that his secretary was trying to locate him now.

Veena sat down again. "So what is happening with you?" He stared back; his mouth was open, befuddled, moronic; he blamed it on her: she never repeated herself. Her next comment reasserted this. "Obviously, earnings are keeping you busy."

"I was saying, you know..." Kelch watched his feet, for a moment, as they crossed under the desk's shadow. He then looked at her. "OPLL reported and—"

"How did the numbers come out there?"

She was breaking him up, he felt, atomically, sending his head through a centrifugal spinner. *Listen*: tell me I'm fired or tell me I'm hired or tell me I'm tired—God, I'm tired—but don't sit there like I'm the one torturing you. I didn't do anything wrong.

Kelch just wanted everything to end, for something to cut open the knot of ambiguity or maybe to allow him to hide under ambiguity's blanket. Whichever way, he was willing now to cede the plan of action to Veena. She could tell the market—the world—whatever she wanted. Every CEO in the sector knew that if Veena Gupta, one of the two remaining at Freshler from the old Murderers' Row, put a sell on your stock, you could kiss your gains for the year good-bye.

"Christopher?"

"Huh?"

"You were saying something please."

"About Tee-Fog?"

"How could I possibly have any idea?"

"I mean, *yesterday*"—you asked me here to talk about yesterday—"with Buchalter, I had a conversation about, you know, and he thought that—" *Don't make me...*

"Robert Buchalter is a motherfucker."

Kelch blinked his eyes to bask, in that one stingy moment, in a cozier world. He smiled then because he knew that Veena had dropped her remark out of distracted habit, not significance, smiled because he had heard that ruling on Buchalter so often that it was home. Buchalter and Veena were an old couple, irascible, loving, and corporately married, Buchalter always bewailing that Veena was trying to kill *his* banking business, Veena always complaining that vain, bald Buchalter, the whore of whores of Freshler Feld, was on a personal mission to destroy her reputation. Neither of them believed it—or they believed it but didn't care—and their dances usually ended cheek-to-cheek with victory over the other firms in securing the big IPOs and assembling their cities of lucite plaques. They batted .350, and all the while they remained comfortable and proud that on his side he wasn't being bullied by any research analyst and on her side that she had stood up to the corrupting, intellectually dishonest bankers. Kelch also smiled because of *motherfucker*: Veena always used it to great effect. When addressing new Freshler sales-people just of out business school or young analysts congregated to absorb her wisdom or B-minus clients who were dumb enough to quote a rival to her, she would declare with an unflappably straight face, "What do I say? I say, Mr. Lynch is a motherfucker." Kelch would then watch the word suck inattention and noise—all noise—out of the room.

When Kelch returned to Rockford, he would inevitably compare his mother to Veena, and Ann Arnell, glandularly untidy in her recent comfort, never matched up well. She would have been inca-pable of holding a Buchalter in line or even existing in the same thought. Kelch was grateful to Veena, not Ann, for Veena had made him indispensable to the firm, had taught him to be tough, to be fearsome, to check life against the bits. She had enabled him to make four-hundred-and-fifty-thousand and expect that number to be just a pit stop on his near-term race to double, triple the amount. His mother, when you added up the columns, had only held him back. So had Evanston, probably: they had educated him so poorly that he had had no idea of what he would receive from the oppor-tunity to absorb, by contact, Veena's every word and principle. Always, those three years that he had worked for her, he had wanted to do even more, wanted to be, in a way, the third -esh or -eev in that photographed bower. That daydream's logic, to itself, wasn't looped: Kelch had been her corporate son, and look at what it had brought him. If he had been her real son, then everything would have been better still. The market would have come naturally, and he wouldn't have tied himself up in doubts of when to upgrade, when to play it safe. If he had been Veena's son, he would have kicked his legs up on the Henrys' dinner table, not sat knees-together in unease. If he had been Veena's son, he would have made Nathanson feel like a jerk when Nathanson had never heard of some composer. If he had been Veena's son, he would have been compelling, and the world—Johann—would have been compelled. And if he had been Veena's son, he would have never felt guilty about wanting to get away from his mother and his sister, about being revolted by even distant hints of "us against the world." If he had been Veena's son, it would have been a businesslike arrangement. And it would have been perfect.

Kelch leaned closer to Veena and confided, "Well, I think Hoder Leary might have called Buchalter about—"

"Don't worry about Hoder Leary." A few times on the morning call, Veena had deferred to Kelch. Other times, documented, she had told him that she appreciated how he listened: every other idiot on the Street never shut up.

Kelch waded deeper: "I don't think he likes me. Um, ever since I picked up coverage." *Say, Hoder Leary's a motherfucker.* Say it. Please.

"Obviously." And she, binary, flipped her attention to the phone. Kelch looked on as she dialed eight digits. (Eddington worked in Boston.) "For crying out loud," she said, hanging up the phone, and marched to her door again. Her movements, like her hair, were no-nonsense but not cheaply achieved. "Mandy," she shouted, only her volume altering, "are you trying to get me Tom Eddington or are you just going to sit there all day?" Kelch could feel, in sympathy, Mandy's unseen cowers; Veena had probably caught her once with nothing to do. Behind her desk again, Veena glanced through a draft of a report. "Do you have anything to tell me, Christopher?"

"You called, I mean, you know . . ." *Slow down . . .* "Well, there was something that happened on the conference call that I think you might have—"

"Obviously, I know what happened with Hoder Leary."

"Well, I guess— I wonder if you thought what I did was justified?"

"Look it here, you have been working at this firm long enough to understand the behavior that I and Freshler Feld expect of you. Behavior on that conference call—" She hesitated. "It is not worth our time to sit here and talk about proper behavior. Unfortunately, your behavior was typical." *Stop saying that.* Veena had spat it whenever Kelch made a mistake. It was always aberrantly imprecise. "But this in no way—" She stopped and offered a stationary, nostrilly glare. "Why did you do it?"

"What?"

"Why did you do it?" Her *it* shook like a small cymbal. "You don't imagine that I encouraged you to that sort of behavior."

In six years, the only thing I've ever tried to do was please you.

Kelch swallowed and his thought pulled at his lips, nausea's marker, but he resisted, keeping his face neutral. Remember: Tee-Fog. "I mean, it just happened. I didn't exactly plan it."

"Didn't you?"

"Of course not."

"Of course?" Veena asked, apparently genuinely curious. She preferred, Kelch knew, direct examinations, questions with the answers already known. "I think that— Hold on." She swiveled her chair and looked in the top drawer of the file cabinet behind her. This was not Veena: even when AXZ blew up—Kelch had run into her office, breathless, pink-skinned, fearful and excited that he was delivering world-historical news—she had decided before he got there, in a snap, to ride the stock back up the U. She swiveled back her chair, empty-handed. "Sorry, continue please."

Sorry? "I don't know what you want to know. I mean, I'd be happy to start—"

Her regard, normally so clear in its intention and unapproachably aloof, was ambiguous, glitchy.

"I mean, when I did it, I did it without really thinking."

"That's intelligent."

"I mean, not really without thinking, you know, but I looked at the bits—"

"The what?"

"The bits, pursue the bits."

"Right."

"So, I mean, I looked at the bits, and I thought that—"

"Get on with it."

Kelch pinched his nose before he jumped in. "Hoder was just being a total asshole to me." The water enveloped him, the private silence of a birth canal. "I thought that—"

"*I* thought that I told you that I'm not interested in Hoder Leary." She crossed her arms over her chest and scooted her chair back six inches; her lack of interest in Hoder Leary, Kelch thought, was not said as an indication of interest in anything else. He thought that he could have even been right.

He had been a perfect junior to her, he knew, had stayed in that damned cubicle outside her office until ten, eleven o'clock every night for three years. As a matter of course, as a spreadsheet's appendage, he had lost whole months that he could never recover— not that, now rewarded, he wanted to—and he had canceled that weekend in Las Vegas, the date with that Danielle, Final Four tickets, for Christ's sake. And nowadays, he wasn't even able to think about other things for weeks on end. He had done it all to please her because they had been a team, the number-one-rated Murderers' Row team. There wasn't a day that went by, in his own office, when he didn't think, explicitly, "What would Veena do?" For all that dedication, for all that love, she owed him, in a way. All he demanded was for her to understand how good a boy he had been, to understand that he had found, with her, who he wanted to be.

He asked her in the right voice, earnest and grade-school, "Am I in trouble?"

"That isn't my concern, frankly," she answered, not seeming to address him directly. Her neck pulled her face skin into a tight wall against the barbarians.

And he thought, This is going to Blue.

Veena continued: "You are how old?"

"Huh?"

"You are how old please?"

"Twenty-eight."

"And you are what now?"

"What?"

Breaking apart each word: "Are you still an associate?"

You know exactly what I am. Your recommendation probably got me promoted. "A VP."

"Look it here, Christopher, if you are a vice president at Freshler Feld and twenty-eight years old, then I do not think it's appropriate for you to start whining to senior analysts, 'Am I in trouble.' If you are, then get out of it."

He did whine then, but soft, irresolute: "Do you know?"

"What"—a pause—"are you talking about now?"

Candidly: "I don't know."

Her phone rang, and she rolled her chair sideways to talk to her secretary through the door. She called out, loudly and vindictive, "Is that Eddington?"

Mandy approached the office and smiled queasily. "It's just someone who needs the latest 'Trends.' "

"Then why are you interrupting us please."

Jesus, Veena, can't you be a human being to me once? She had only rarely been this bad. *Can't you just tell me, off the record, why I'm here? Can't you see that I've been nothing but a good boy all these years?*

She returned her focus to Kelch. "Do we have anything more?"

"Huh?"

"I asked, do we have anything more to discuss?"

"How would I—I mean, how would I know?"

"Look it here, Christopher, it is not clear to me what you are after or why it is suddenly my responsibility. Obviously, I am not in the least bit interested."

"But—"

"I consider my part in this matter closed," she addressed the other presence again.

"Yes, but—"

She returned to her phone and dialed. As she was waiting for it to connect, she covered the mouthpiece. "I need to make this call."

"Yes, but—"

"That means that you need to leave my office please."

But we're not through.

She hung up the phone, at first misreplacing the receiver, then forcing it onto its rest. She walked to her doorway. "Mandy, are you still trying to get Tom Eddington?" She returned aside her desk, and her eyes, no longer ambivalent, asked him what in God's name he was still doing here. He stood up and looked down at her, down a tunnel of his near foot height advantage, a tunnel wall of his ears plugged and his ears hammering, of his brain blurring into a televised static fixed onto canvas. He let his face plead. Avoiding his crowding body, she moved to her chair and awkwardly grabbed the phone.

Like everyone, Kelch usually hurried around the floor's perimeter; no one ran, but almost everyone accepted that a fifty-dollar or five-hundred-dollar hour demanded a certain public speed, and they had all downloaded an electronic idea of pace. Kelch's face—it was slack, almost stupid—publicly wondered if his current walk, in its contrast, as slow and exaggerated as Armstrong's on the moon, was revealing everything to the cubicled masses. He almost, for relief, wanted it to. The outside, city side, of the floor contained managing directors' and vice presidents' offices; each inhabitant of those offices ruled over a feudal village on the inside, shaft side: a village of secretaries' low-walled cubes and junior analysts' higher pens and associates' sunless cells. Although Kelch's office should have been near Veena's—their industry sectors abutted—her expanding village had forced him to the other side of the floor. At Freshler, as on the whole Street during the boom, even the most highly self-appraised had difficulty complaining about their paychecks, so the firm dispensed excess vassals, "for competitive reasons," as yet one more luring perk. When Kelch had worked with Veena, they were a team of two; now she commanded two junior analysts and a private associate. The work, of course, had expanded to meet the larger teams; the firm was now a family with ten children, not two: more stomachs meant more pressure meant more work for all.

Kelch's steps sped up to normal as he tried to convince himself that the day's story—of Tee-Fog slowly thawing into an anecdote— a drunk-driving close call—was still intact. Veena had not done anything to shake the reality of that morning, or more precisely the second reality of that morning, of his being more tired than hurt, of an article—a what?—unmentioned, intangible, only rumored to be. *It hadn't happened.* It didn't exist. Logically, if it had happened, if people knew, if he was involved, he would be living in another reality. And today couldn't be. There would have been pain, and panic, and confrontation. Kelch wasn't trying to delude himself, he understood; he was just recognizing the situation: it had been two days, and everything today was less.

When Kelch had downgraded Allencor, over a year ago—he had upgraded it again six months later—the stock had already fallen twenty percent over two days. When he had made the announcement of his downgrade, the clients—the salespeople—his scarlet conscience—were dismissive, smirky, eye-rolling. But no one but him knew why he had done it. They didn't know that he had stared at his choices, at the chessboard scenarios, for hours, in a shallow pond's glistening mirror. He had realized at that moment—maybe he had always known—that there was nothing, no practiced skills,

no inarguable absolutes, no divine light, that could dispel the inde-
terminacy. When he realized this, he felt, in a sense, a freedom, a
self-granted lightness of not being able to hug the hard pole, of the
semipotence of man. He felt peaceful, only in a sense again, as he
stared at his narrow pond reflection even closer, for there was nothing to do. He fell into the pond, nose-led—he had been leaning
too far—but he didn't sink. He turned a full revolution, and on the
dry ground again, he stood up, ready.

Now approaching Joe Tedeschi's corner office, his feet stuttered
in disagreement over whether to race past it or circle back, longcut-
ting through the elevator throughway. But he noticed that Tedeschi's door was closed, and he knew that that meant that Tedeschi
was in a meeting, or out of the office (or being filmed), and Kelch's
braver, faster foot won the debate. Hurrying past the office, he
ordered himself to look straight ahead. In the guest seat, the occu-
pant's collar merged smoothly with the nape's hair tapered out of
its kinks. Kelch waited, by instinct, to explode or surrender or even
consider what—whom—he had just seen until he rounded the corner. Ten yards on the other side of the corner, he was greeted by
the smile of Julie What's-Her-Name, Roger Trosen's secretary, with
whom he had flirted at the Christmas party.

"Hi, Chris." He stopped and rested his hands on the low cubicle
divider and glanced back at the corner. She asked, "How are you?"

"Uh, fine. How are—" Say it: how are *you*.

She soaked him in a flood of her smile. Her complexion was
bumpy, raw chicken. "Roger's on vacation, so it's been pretty quiet."
That seemed to explain everything.

"That's good, right?"

"Uh-huh." Kelch couldn't remember much about her from the
party, other than the clumsy way she had repeatedly made Kelch
understand that "working for Roger isn't what I really want to do
long term," and his private response that he didn't really care. She
was thickly built but compensated with a comely chest; the final
attribute had been the motivation for his earlier, innocent attention.

Her purse was open on her desk, and she seemed to be midway through cataloguing its contents. A small bottle of perfume was at the edge of the material lineup—the same perfume that one of the girls from Evanston had favored—and Kelch remembered her ill-advisedly wide aromatic reach. He couldn't smell it now. She must have been warned off of it.

"I bet you've been swamped with earnings, right?"

He glanced again at Tedeschi's corner and then at the corkboard behind Julie's desk; on it, she exhibited a pet lover's calendar and three greeting cards, thumbtacked half open. "Yeah, I've been swamped."

"Roger just *hated* to be away this week, but it's his niece's wedding."

"Okay."

"It's in *Australia,*" she said, not as if the country was far away but as if the country were hardly imaginable.

"Huh."

"It's not really *his* niece, but his wife's, and so he was—"

"Hey, Julie." She looked up, expectantly. "I got to—" The "go" was never to be added, and Kelch began to move down the hall. He turned around once but didn't see anyone—didn't even take in Julie again—and decided to go to his office and finish it all there, or strangle the life out of that asshole and get the hell out of this horrible, dirty place for good. He looked over his shoulder, resolved for it to be the last time. As the body appeared, pants first, Kelch turned fully around. His quickening heart and involuntary scowl arranged by themselves, it seemed, to lead a charge back down the hall, to knock the prick down and smash out every one of his teeth. He could see the other's gait readjusting for his presence, but he couldn't yet see the software running in the other's eyes: surprise or anger or preparation. Kelch stopped. Had Tedeschi noticed him through the window? Had Veena alerted them both?

Nathanson neared. "Hello, Belch."

"What the fuck were you doing in Tedeschi's office?"

"A hello would be nice."

"I said, what the fuck were you doing in Tedeschi's—"

Before Kelch could reach *office* again, Nathanson delivered his counterpunch: "Since when do I need your permission to talk to anyone?"

"Come off it, Nathanson, you sneaky—" Both he and Nathanson, freeze-tagged, watched a junior analyst pass, a guy to whom Kelch had once, after having mistaken him for David Kim, overexplained the reasons for doing so. "I can't even believe that—"

"Kelch."

"What?"

"I'm not going to argue with you here." So they single-filed, suspended, into Nathanson's office on the floor below. Following Kelch inside, Nathanson shut the door, closely supervising the latch click. Leaving Kelch standing, he sat at his desk, and Kelch, inertially intent on stalking about, was reminded how small the inside offices were. Freshler kept them tight to remind the inhabitants, by the crush, that the outside world was pounding and in charge and watching through the whole-wall windows. Kelch's stalking knees bumped into Nathanson's guest chairs. Full-gripped, awkward and rough, he pushed them under the desk. He could barely stand to look at Nathanson—threats and blames and hateful obscenities were all rioting at the back of his mouth into a stalled, silent tornado. Nathanson, indisputably, was wrapped up in all this.

He looked at Kelch, ostensibly bored. "I'm waiting."

Through clenched teeth: "What the fuck were you doing in Tedeschi's office?"

"First, you really have to do something about your repetition problem. Second, it's none of your business." Kelch froze with his back against Nathanson's expressionist poster; Kelch had put nothing on his own wall. "Third, I was talking to him about Joel."

"Joel? What does, what does, what—" What does that word even mean: Joel?

"Einstadt."

"What, are you suddenly—? Is he working for you now?"

"Have you gone insane?"

"Yeah, right— It's just that—I was not informed that I. Joseph Tedeschi suddenly had so much time on his hands that anytime some jackass wanted to shoot the breeze about his friends, he was welcome to walk right in."

Nathanson shifted his attention to his computer and, owning now Kelch's stare, started to click and read. Kelch knew that waiting e-mail to the addicted at the firm was as resistible as an open safe to a thief. That may not have been Nathanson's reason now. "What do you want me to say, Christina? That's what we were talking about."

Kelch, still fixed on Nathanson, pulled out the chair rudely and sat down. He thought, for a moment, of what Nathanson was seeing now, on him. If Kelch's face had been playing his heart's true show, it would have been blurry-eyed, unshaven, water-stained red rock, the twenty-fourth hour of a frantic, rageful day. Kelch leaned over the desk, his hands beneath it, to see himself better in Nathanson's presence. He heard Nathanson's fingers lift off the keyboard, but Nathanson did not turn to him. Kelch, throat scratching, asked, "Do you know?"

He did not even turn away from the screen. "Know what?"

Both elbows now on the desk, Kelch's posture abandoned its youth, and he became the OPLL sub-president, persecuted, confessing, drinking, drunk. Kelch, when alone with Nathanson, didn't argue much: it never seemed worth the struggle. "I don't know."

Nathanson looked at the hall through his window and then concentrated on some papers on his desk. Half-engaged: "Are you in trouble or something?"

"Why would you ask me that?"

"Look at you, you accost me in the floor, scaring that fat Chinese kid—"

"Korean."

"—then you come in here, pacing around my office like a caged rat and then start bombarding me with questions as if I'm being paid to psychoanalyze you."

For dignity, Kelch determined to straighten himself, but as he began to speak, a coup overthrew his bones, and he dripped like a dead wind sock in the chair. A feeling, unopposed, descended through him then, a poured lead rain beginning at his skulltop, a rain that was his first understanding—in body, not mind—that a million people would receive that magazine in their million mailboxes. Millions more would look at its cover on a newsstand shelf. They existed, those people: most of them had already put their real popping eyes to real printed paper, and their misapprehension, then, existed too. Even the eventual truth could never erase that experience. This realization didn't linger as a sting: it insinuated itself, dust and spit, into Kelch's lungs, a million particles, one each for the million people who now thought that every suit on the train was Scott. He felt a throat's gritty warning of a coming cold, but it was spread, thickly, sea-salt through his cavity. Kelch asked again, the urgency drained, "Why were you in Tedeschi's office?"

Kelch knew that Nathanson neither stammered nor shunned eye contact in the arguments that were his life. When confronted, he spoke more forcefully to the arguer, the client, the loser (future tense). Looking at Kelch, in an examining way, Nathanson answered, "I told you." Kelch squinted at Nathanson's examination.

Kelch's new face, perhaps, wasn't the face he felt, a face of haggard weariness. For Nathanson, Kelch distantly suspected, was examining him for Scott's face, or the Scott skin over his face, trying to complete a connect-it puzzle. Kelch said, "That's crap."

Nathanson turned his palms out, head high, being arrested. "Clearly you know better than I do what I was doing in his office."

"Maybe I do."

"That makes a lot of sense."

Leaning his head back, Kelch concentrated on the beige of the ceiling's uniform matte tiles. "Fuck you, okay." Kelch thought he could see, through his eyes' bottoms, Nathanson smile.

"Tell me, Chris, why is it so excruciatingly difficult for you to believe that I was talking about Joel? That is still unclear to me."

"Because Tedeschi doesn't talk about new associates with people with no relation businesswise to them. It's literally inconceivable." Kelch sat up. *Literally inconceivable* had taken his last ounce of life to summon.

"You mean that it is literally (your word) impossible to *conceive* that Tedeschi and I were talking about Einstadt?"

"Just shut up, okay." Nathanson did. "Listen, Adam." Abruptly, he forgot what he wanted him to listen to. "I, uh, I just want to know what you were doing in Tedeschi's office. It concerns me."

"It doesn't concern you one tiny ounce."

Is that what I even . . . "It does."

"Why would it in any way concern you?"

Kelch felt weak, hungover. "Because it was about *me*."

"No, it wasn't." For Nathanson, Kelch knew, the facts of the argument were facts of the world.

"A*dam*."

The lights of the office, hidden upcast tubes built into the cabinet tops, shifted (or Nathanson shifted) to highlight a sharp-featured outrageousness. A dull glare bounced off Nathanson's teeth, which seemed to have multiplied in his too open mouth. "Jesus, Kelch, when did you become such a whiny little girl?"

"You know, Nathanson, as far as I'm concerned—" Kelch stopped. He wondered what was happening as far as he was concerned. And was he really a whiny little girl? Nathanson's features had not subsided; his cheekbones, his chinline played even louder, more wry. He was a poor winner. And so: "We're not even friends anymore."

Nathanson's mouth hid into itself, in exaggerated nonplus. "We're not friends anymore? What are you, six years old?" He quickly licked his lips, preparing, it appeared, for a longer riff. "Are you going to have your mommy call my mommy and cancel our play date—"

"Just shut up already."

"*I'm* supposed to shut up?"

"Yes."

"After you say something as asinine as that. I mean, I won't even go into whether we ever really were . . . I'm still trying to figure out what that's even supposed to mean."

Kersten had once asked Kelch who was his best friend. Kelch hadn't answered the question. "A: if we were friends, you wouldn't pull this shit on me. So B: we're not friends."

"So following your logic, if we *were* friends—"

"Just shut up, okay."

"Is this how you resolve things on the Great Plains? I always thought it was with shotguns at the barn dance."

Kelch looked through the window: he had to get out of there; he had to go home and talk to Kersten—no, anyone but Kersten— or, Jesus, where was he even going to go? Everywhere now, after now, felt less safe. "Is all this funny to you?"

"Is what funny?"

"All my problems. You know, if you came to me with a problem, I wouldn't be like you're being now."

Nathanson stowed his keyboard nearer his monitor. "If you want to discuss something, let's do it. But do not—I repeat—*do not* stop me in the hall, accuse me of something about which you have no idea, about which you couldn't even *begin* to have an idea since, one, it's none of your business and, two, you weren't even there. Don't stop me in the hall, wrongly accuse me of something, and then start whining like a four-year-old. I would be happy to discuss any and all of your problems, Kelch—I've known you long enough to know you have plenty of them—but I will do so only if you don't try to push some secret agenda. Got it?"

"Forget it."

"What?"

I can't breathe.

Nathanson pulled out his keyboard again and began to tap away, casually.

3

On his own floor now, Kelch lowered his eyes against contact, and as he slinked toward his office, his left hand guided him, grazing the cabinets. He had walked out of Nathanson's office slowly, without theater. He had thought about adding a parting shot—"you'll regret this" was the first one to come forward—but he didn't in the end, sure that Nathanson, smiling like a card deck's joker, jubilant and hateful, wouldn't care. He entered his own office and noticed, only partly concerned, that it was the one thing in his life lately that smelled as it should. Like nothing. When his nose had ceased to function, yesterday or the day before, its membranes hadn't swollen; it hadn't become mucus clogged; it had simply chosen not to work.

And as he sat in his chair, his back perfectly cared for in every dimple and knoll, his feet softening into the carpet with his knees at maximum comfort, he realized that this chair too was the one thing in his life lately that acted as it should. This chair, this office, this *job* were him, were real, had happened, had proof. They were bits. A thought presented itself to Kelch that he was now supposed to inventory who knew, who didn't know, what's to know, the whole home guard. But he didn't have to do that, he then decided, because no one knew, because nothing had happened, because he wasn't letting anything happen, because it was an undeniable, hardest-diamond bit that if anything had happened, it would have happened by now, two days later. And it would have happened if that article, big-picture, net-net, had anything to do with him. Scott was a composite or fiction or slander, but he wasn't truth. This chair was truth.

Even the Ghost's call had been so inexplicable that it existed now as a distant sensation, a dream of a childhood Kelch could not remember. He refused to acknowledge it.

Kelch nodded amicably to his computer. OPLL's earnings release was on the screen. Switched on, more awake, Kelch began typing the bullet points for tomorrow's note. It was a matter of will. He was strong enough to fasten himself to his responsibility. *Although OPLL's 1Q results were above expectations, we do not see any compelling need* . . . Three hours earlier, OPLL had reported eight cents per share versus his estimated six, but it wasn't a reverse situation of Tee-Fog. Give him a week and his sell would be vindicated again. (He had actually rated the stock a hold, but his clients all understood his intent.)

Johann shuffle-footed into Kelch's office, theoretically too absorbed by the papers in his hand to look up. When Kelch had returned from Nathanson's office, he had ignored Johann waiting upright in his cube, the same notes in hand.

After a glimpse, deniable by its brevity, Kelch resumed typing. *We are also not totally convinced that the company has addressed all the issues that management has stated needs addressing* . . . Johann coughed conspicuously, but Kelch glued his attention to the OPLL note more tightly, understanding as he typed that behind him was momentum, the concept, the quarterly high tide that cleared away the castles of civilizations past. Allencor had been the sick pig of the barnyard for two quarters. *We have no faith*, Kelch had written, *that management will be able to achieve the margin growth plan highlighted at its annual meeting*. Six months later, faith had been restored in a big-tent conversion; neither fire nor brimstone had been needed to compel belief; it only took forty-one cents, instead of thirty-eight. And so, the corollary was becoming clear, if Kelch continued to beat estimates, then the potholes in his performance, this stupid Paul Galicia thing, the abstraction of Scott—Tee-Fog, too—would disappear. Kelch understood in his fingers' fluid, horse-gallop rhythm that he would march over the article in the exact same way that Tee-Fog would march over its earnings disappointment: by performing better in an explosion of diligence and energy. He would meet or beat all expectations. The Street claimed that its memory was long and severe, but its memory was short and precise: if Tee-Fog reported strong results in three months, yesterday would be forgiven; if it did it again in six months, yesterday would be forgotten, not just morally forgotten but actually, collectively forgotten.

The old-hand senior analysts regularly joked that the analysts Kelch's age were babies of the boom, helium infants of an idyllic age. Mirthful and loud, the old hands described for the children an imperfect future when salaries would no longer rise seventy-five percent per year, when analysts wouldn't assume that they could, with a wand, double their number at a rival firm, when research departments would not thrive on the self-pumping logic that competition demanded everlasting expansion, costs be damned. But even the old hands, who thought themselves leathery and hunched, were fresh faced. Only the ancients, hardly any of them active anymore, had ever experienced a real bear market, a bear market when you could smell the fish-gut brine of stagnant money, when firms were entombed and people were canned, when strategists not only predicted but believed that stocks would depreciate for the foreseeable now. The ancients scoffed at the old hands' belief that they had endured bear markets over the last twenty years. They hadn't: there had only been a bull market in five acts, and the old hands were like a fortunate family that congratulated itself on surviving Grandma's death or Bobby's rejection from Yale—all supposed proofs that the family was just as resilient as those hardluck families who were drug addicted or criminal justiced, bankrupt or unhinged. The old hands rewrote a struggling past to justify an evolved present.

Kelch and Nathanson and Kim and the rest couldn't dream of a bear market, just as they couldn't dream in Spanish. Yes, they thought of the bull ending; they even accepted, intellectually, the bubble over their heads. But its bursting was a black hole, a murky theory of the labs, a spectacled scientist saying, Boo.

(But on those mornings when the Dow dropped three hundred, everyone was the same age, the same thought. Analysts and juniors would gather around a shared quote screen, mesmerized by the minuses, the red. Occasionally somebody would clear his throat, always there would be morbid jokes, and people would leave the screens silently, with sheepish drunk grins, as if they had accidentally walked in on someone in a bathroom stall. Later at their desks, they would struggle to concentrate on work.)

Kelch typed more enthusiastically, allowing his fingers to make the explicit argument of the note and the higher argument that he *could* swim through the unpleasantness. Thirty seconds passed, and Kelch had still not acknowledged Johann, who was a statue of abidance, reading his notes. Kelch typed even faster, throwing glissandos off a piano, knowing that faster work meant faster days meant faster months meant faster forgetting meant faster peace and a faster return to what the world *knew* he was: Chris Kelch, a hard worker, Chris Kelch, a good analyst, Chris Kelch, a good boyfriend, who just wanted a good, happy life. And who would not have to be angry or defensive anymore. The stockroom sentences and modular phrases of his opinion on OPLL were filtering, without thought, from his storeroom to the screen. There was the usual recap of the results, the usual doubts raised euphemistically about management targets, the usual hand-me-down, nearby phrases snapped together agreeably by kit, and as his fingers waltzed into the last paragraph, a pleasant warmth, like from the rumored outdoors, told him that he still had it, that this was why Freshler paid him four fifty. Johann cleared his throat. I'm not listening, Kelch thought as Johann said, "I was looking at the OPLL results, and I believe that this situation may present us with an interesting trading opportunity."

"Good thinking, Johann."

"Yes, I thought that—"

"Too bad for you that *I'm* writing the note." It was this easy.

"I was assuming that you were doing that. However, I think if we look—"

"You know what they say about assuming, don't you?" Kelch, returning to the note, didn't repeat what they said about assuming.

"Nevertheless, I think we might be premature in—"

"Premature?"

Taking a half step back, meeting the wall, Johann lowered his hands to his sides. "Yes, I—"

"How old are you, Johann?"

"Pardon me?"

"How *old* are you?"

Nothing.

"Is that a difficult question to answer?"

Johann answered, cold, "Twenty-two."

"And how long have you been working for me?"

"How long have I—? You know as well as—"

"Did I ask you if I knew, or did I ask you how long you've been working for me?"

Swallowing: "Over nine months."

Kelch felt great, as if he had just passed a tollbooth into a clear ownable road. "Listen: you want to know what I think is premature? A twenty-two-year-old with a grand total of nine months of experience sitting there and correcting me on how I do my job."

"I didn't think I was 'correcting' you." Johann's body didn't slump, but it appeared to shift its weight, relaxing, to his lower gut. "I merely suggested that perhaps—"

"And I'm sug*gest*ing that you not butt into things you don't know anything about."

"I assumed—pardon me, I thought—that after you asked me to write the Tee-Fog note that I would have, going forward, a larger role in the note-writing process."

Don't throw Tee-Fog in my face. "Well, whatever, you were wrong."

Johann repeated Kelch's "whatever."

"Yes, Joanne, whatever. Whatever you believe is less important than whatever I say." Kelch smiled, but when he looked again at his OPLL note, its expository magic had been pin-poked. He stood up, pretending to need something in his high cabinets, intentionally advertising the height of a man who wasn't a pale, soft-cheeked, North-stock doll molded into a monotonous blank. He turned, and with one hand gripping the rounded corner of the desk, announced, "I'm really starting to have questions about you."

Johann's look, in response, could have meant disbelief, alarm, denial, but it was too controlled on its surface to even allude to its intention. "*You* are having questions?"

"Jesus Christ, stop whining." Kelch wondered then if he could fire Johann. But Freshler Feld didn't work that way, he knew. As much as Tedeschi propagandized entrepreneurship as the department's core value, there were committees, secret rules, lawyers' briefs that the firm would require before Kelch could excise Johann from his life. But Johann's disrespect alone was a legitimate reason for dismissal. Getting fired would be a good lesson for him too: a lesson in how you treat people, in how, when you come into a company like Freshler Feld, you must abandon all the pride your parents took in you, all the A's your boarding school awarded you, all the college-dean pep talks about how you, personally, were a leader of tomorrow. You were a leader of nothing, as a low man at Freshler Feld, not your life, not your time, not your opinions.

Even when dumbfounded, Johann was not dumb. "I think that I am going to go back to my desk."

"Like I'm really fucking scared of you. Jesus, man, you don't know how thin ice—how thin the ice is you're on." Johann's normal expression, smarmy and unhandsome, was hardening. Kelch was done with him. "Excuse me, I have to make a call."

"A call?"

"I wasn't aware that I needed your permission to make a telephone call." Johann didn't move. Kelch began to dial, but he had no one in mind to call, and so he pressed the matter. "Should I put this on speakerphone so you can sit here and listen?" From habit— he had pressed the keys in a single motion—the digits of the Rockford area code spelled out on the telephone's screen. He held his headset over his head, a helmet before the game, and glared until Johann, who appeared prepared to never leave, finally left. The numbers on the screen had erased in the interim. Kelch let the headset fall back onto the desk.

As he sat there, staring at Johann's impression stamped on the air, a feeling—a strong one, almost a knowledge—grew that he, Kelch, had actually been sitting in this chair, this blankly, for days. That feeling may have been a strategy, future-projected. For he wasn't feeling discomfort, the gravelly lungs from the million readers; he wasn't feeling panic either, if panic meant constriction, the dark bedroom, the closing in. He just felt dull and damp, worn nervous, like his mother over her tablecloth of bills.

In two days, *nothing* had happened, and if he could just sit there forever, he then thought, he would be content. He could freeze the market, freeze himself, stop reporting quarterly growth, stop caring about quarterly growth, stop being part of the machine that chewed up everything for fourteen percent.

It was only a shot glass of pity that Kelch felt then, but it was explicit and enough. For it was no exaggeration—it was a bit as irreducible as a sand grain, as immovable as the headquarters' frame—that none of this was fair. He wasn't particularly angry about the unfairness: he was too drained. It was the same type of drained as when he left the office near midnight, or when he waited, a long trip over, at a closing airport for a delayed black car home. It was an encompassing lassitude that was the reward of his life, of his unfulfilling sleep, of the unsleeping demands. It was like an unrelenting down week in his personal account. The feeling tipped as it always did—immediately—and Kelch's half-closed eyes closed onto the other half.

He woke from the narcoleptic allusion to the ringing of the phone. Kelch was less startled by the name on the screen than by the time displayed next to it. He had been gone—thinking? sleeping?—for forty-five minutes. That was a good start. The cord tangled itself around his wrists as he hurried to answer it on the third ring. Throat-caught: "Hello?"

"Chris, Pamela." Pamela McGruder had awarded herself, through

her ten-year service as Joe Tedeschi's secretary, the status and aloof-
ness of a single-named celebrity.

"Um, what's up?" What's up: he had never, he was certain, said
that before.

"Five o'clock tomorrow afternoon, Joe needs to see you." As an
appendage of Tedeschi's calendar, Pamela counted and apportioned
her seconds; any small talk was to be regarded by its receiver as a
luxury and a gift.

Nothing.

"Hello?"

"Let's see." Kelch consulted his computered schedule and began
thinking, on the very topmost layer of thought, out loud: "I have a
company reporting earlier and, um, I may have to meet with a client
at one and—"

"Hold a second thank you." The phrase was a single word, dispensed automatically. And Kelch did hold everything: his thoughts,
his reaction. "Hello?"

"Yes."

"Re: five o'clock tomorrow?"

"I guess, I mean . . ."

"I will call you if his schedule changes." And with a click, she
moved on.

Kelch knew that he would have to call Kersten sometime that day.
It was already nearly seven, and they hadn't yet spoken. This was
unusual—why hadn't she called him?—for they always talked at
least once a day to establish when Freshler Feld would allow them
to see each other next. For a time, they had e-mailed each other
from their work desks, but Kersten's gooey partings (*XOXO—K* or
a lowercase *me*) made Kelch squirm. He had told her that Freshler
was starting to crack down on personal computer use.

He focused rigidly on the task at hand. If he called her cellular
phone, she would immediately pick up. If he called her at work,

she might still be there. "Hi, it's me." He left her a message, relieved, at home. "Um, I have to work late tonight." He knew he sounded stupid, see-through, but he let his wheels creak further down the slope. It wasn't a lie: he always had plenty enough to do. "Because OPLL, that pig I'm always talking to you about, surprised its 1Q." *You don't understand what's going to happen to me tomorrow.* "Um, where . . . It's nothing bad like Tee-Fog, but anyway, I have to write, um, a long note about it and so I don't think I'm going to get home till ten or eleven or so and then I think I'm just going to crash." *Because Tedeschi doesn't talk about new associates with people with no relation businesswise to them.* "Hello? Oh, sorry, I, uh, anyway, give me a call here if you want"— he shut his eyes, leaping off the quarry's rim—"though I may not be able to talk."

It was unclear to Kelch how he had convinced himself out of his office. He stared at the television in his apartment—now, for once, not on—and at his muddy-laked likeness in it. It was ten o'clock. His eyelids seemed a conductor, and his body followed the orders for a slower, diffusive movement. His neck contoured around his couch's back pillow, and his arms faded to his sides.

This was what he wanted to be: alone. People could not talk to you, accuse you, know you when you were alone. It was the best state of man. Alone, you could decide what had happened or not. Alone, you could construct your own time of truck-sized seconds, traffic-jammed. For if time did not move, it could not bring what's next.

The first morning Kelch had awoken in this apartment, his pride had surprised him. His bedroom, granted, might be smaller than his bedroom in Rockford, one of three cluttered bird's nests in a warped, splintered, paper-hatted cube, designed, so it seemed, by a child architect, her blueprints, her blocks. But this apartment—that small bedroom—was his, or at least his to rent, and he didn't have to share it with any acquaintances from Evanston or colleagues from Freshler. A cookie-colored entertainment center was the western wall of the living room. His couch obediently faced the black, back-connected bricks of TV, VCR, DVD, cable box, CD changer, amplifier, speakers. Kelch stored his slight collection of CDs—the discs were mainly new, the tastes long ago acquired—and his expanding movie collection (all watched once) in the center's crown. On the bottom glassed-in shelf, dust collected over college finance textbooks and finance memoirs, two paperback thrillers, a few management easy reads, and the gift books, one celebrating the anniversary of Allencor, another (*High on Ohio*) TFRW's home state. On top of the entertainment center, Kelch displayed, tastefully he thought, six commemorative mugs, each marking, in order, Chicago's basketball championships.

Sitting on the couch, Kelch occupied himself temporarily by memory-measuring the distance between his hands and the five remote controls collected on the end table. He didn't permit himself to think about Tedeschi. As he leaned toward the table, his right shoulder, brushing the armrest, led his whole body in recline. He was tired, but it wasn't exactly a sleepy tired; it was more, or also, a muscular tired, a tired of a drone bee swarm-lost in the conifers, uncommanded and exhausted, with no place to go. He might be so tired that he would have trouble falling asleep. Or this sleep could be the one to bring his dream of snow-blanketing—erasing—recent history.

He closed his eyes.

He was sure the phone didn't ring, and he wasn't holding a phone. Nevertheless, the conversation was occurring, and Kelch was already asking a question. Where are you?

Where was I?

No, where are you now, Kelch repeated as he had originally, he thought, asked. The vista's black was not uniform; a sooty sunrise rose from the east, casting a yellow in an upper corner of the dark gray slate.

You should know. What does that mean? You called me, buddy. No, I didn't. Sure you did.

The Ghost's voice was almost the same as it was last night: an airy, light-fried fritter, tobacco-stained to a lower hum than Kelch's. The midwestern golly-gee seemed exaggerated, manmade.

Talk to me, Scott. Huh? Talk to me, Scott? What? Talk to me, Scott. Are you drunk?

Did he get drunk? Had his escape (expulsion?) happened because he was a drinker—or had he been a puncher, a cheater, or just a noncontributor, a drive-through depositor of genes? He was a runner, of course—that was History's official judgment—but he had more floated away than run. Kelch had brought no pictures of him to New York, and he couldn't be sure, if they were ever to meet again, whether he would still be able to identify him, the grin fixed in dumb joy, amnesiac good cheer drooling from his lips.

Where are you? Where was I? *No*, where are you calling me from? You called me, Scott. Stop fucking calling me Scott. Come on, buddy, it's something to be proud of. Huh? You sound like a pretty successful guy to me. Did you even read the article? It seems like I'm the only one who did, buddy. Then how can you say that? Because you probably make more in a year than I make in a decade. So? Well, that's nothing to sneeze at, buddy. That's how you judge? That's how we judge.

There must be a body, Kelch understood, or at least a cassette player connected to that voice; there must be carbon holding together the hydrogen, not just sound waves, ripples in the ether.

Just so you know, Scott, I always thought about you. No, you didn't. I did. You've never even said you always thought of me—not even now. I'm sure I have, buddy. Listen: you've never even apologized to me. When was I supposed to apologize? You have seen me even if you don't mind missing five years here and there. Hey, buddy, easy on the anger; when I was lucky enough to catch up with you, I didn't want to start crying about water under the bridge. *Water under the bridge?* What else would you call it?

A laugh when there are no bodies, only sounds ricocheting in false stereo, does not erupt. It exists, almost only a theory, and serves a role, like a taped foot marker on a stage.

By the way, where are you? Where was I? No, where are you calling me from now? But you called me.

I'm not done, asshole. What? Don't you understand, I'm not done, I'm half built. Re*lax*, Scott, you're fine. Have you ever seen me with Kersten? I'm sure you got no problem with girls. Oh, yeah, I'm real special about making them feel wanted and all that crap, but I don't know what I'm aiming for. Well, buddy, that's a question man has been wrestling with— No, listen: it's your fault; you made me this way: here are the lyrics, sing the song, but I'm not going to tell you the tune.

Why did you do it? Do what, Scott? Come on. Well, I wasn't happy. You weren't *happy*? Sure, I figured that there was no reason to be unhappy the rest of my life.

A thin strip of other-side light seeped into Kelch to remind him of his arms and legs, his webbed numb fingers, and to whisper that this was a world, not every world.

You know, Scott, I have to give credit to your mother. You do. No, listen to me for a sec: I have to give her credit for raising you two. I said, You do. Just hear me out: I never would have thought that ol' Annie could have held it together so well, but I don't think you—you, in particular—could have turned out any better. What about me?

This Bill wasn't much of a father figure— Huh? A father figure. Why in the hell would you say that? We're talking facts here, buddy. What? Facts.

The facts, asshole, are that there weren't any father figures. You want to hear what there were? You wanna hear? There was Coach Huckle. He couldn't have been nicer, more fatherly to me in eighth grade, looking out for my best interests. *You Catholic? I'm Catholic too, and I appreciate the efforts of the Church in the educational area, but I'm also an American and I think as Americans we got to learn to live together with all creeds and colors in the public education system.* Especially on his basketball team. Then, when I didn't become the great white hope—didn't grow that much taller, never got that much quicker—

this goddamn father figure of yours checked out. When I finally quit altogether, you know what he said? *Good decision for a smart kid like you. You're not like some of the other types here who don't have any option but the basketball—*

There you go, buddy.

Jerry Selin, Finance and Investments 102, was a real father figure when me and four other jerks would stay after class to hear his stories about the bears who called the '87 crash or some ex-colleague managing a billion-dollar fund. We thought that was really something back then. He always wore a suit and recommended articles and took our questions seriously, and he told me twice in semiprivate that I probably had the right kind of head for finance. And he believed in it, you see, like Blue Padaway: the greatest job in the world. You know what happened when I returned my senior year to ask him advice on getting a job. This fucking father figure of yours asked me, Which year did you take my class again?

That's what I'm talking about, Scott, father figures. Aren't you listening to me? You must have had others like them who helped your mother and me raise you.

There were no fathers period, asshole. Just hypocrites and self-absorbed, self-serving, self-righteous, self-worshiping jerks who blew their whole wad fighting with their parents so they could wear blue jeans and listen to the Beatles and be what? Fucking "happy" right? And what did they have, *you* have, left for me: nothing. And what happens then? I'm Scott.

Exactly. Huh? I mean, you're Scott—you're making half a million dollars a year. You don't understand. But I do: congratulations, I'm proud of you, buddy.

Kelch had fallen deeper into a black as leather skinsmooth as the couch. The other-side sunrise had diluted to a gloss.

But where are you? When? Where are you now?

Here I am.

This is about Kersten, isn't it? You're wrong, asshole. You can't fool people here, Scott. Stop it—you don't know anything about

me. Here we go again. . . . You've made it your life's one goal not
to know me. Are you through, buddy? You have no right to even
pretend that you know me. She makes you a man, doesn't she?
What? She makes you feel like you're not just a stockbroker. I'm
not a stockbroker, you fucking prick. Well, you're Scott, Scott. Shut
up. That's how I see it.

This isn't about Kersten.

Then what, buddy?

This is about the analog.

—It was four fifty-nine and Kelch, his eyes grainy, caked, and suddenly open, saw the digital pins of the VCR turn to five o'clock. Five
o'clock: shit goddamnit: Tedeschi. He had missed the appointment,
and so it was over, and he could just unpack his résumé and pack up
his files. He bounded off the office chair—no, it was his couch—and
reached down to his tie, the same one he had been wearing yesterday.
His shirt and undershirt were cling-wrapped around him. Kelch confirmed his wallet in his pocket, but where were his keys? If he got a
cab and, shit, rush hour, but if he called Pamela McGruder and—
Quickly, he swung open the window—it opened vertically, forty
degrees maximum—and looked out. Usually, by craning his neck, he
could sense the traffic on the avenue, although not as well through
April's advancing leaves. But the sky, he noticed, was still dark, dark
stretching toward brightening, and the street, unhurried, had yet to
rise for its coffee, its paper, its electronic day.

· **4** ·

But then it was the other five o'clock, or more accurately, five-
twenty, and although Tedeschi was still on the phone, he waved
Kelch into his office. Inside, Kelch was to wait longer, but Tedeschi,
by admitting him inside, had at least recognized, sideways, his right

to attend the meeting to which he had been summoned. Kelch sat in the same chair that Nathanson had used yesterday, and he cupped his knees in his hands, a good attentive schoolboy, as Tedeschi masturbated his voice into the telephone. That morning, three blue chips had reported at the fair-to-middling end of consensus, and Tedeschi was beating someone—it must have been a reporter; the lecture proceeded uninterrupted—with the frying-pan hard truth that Tedeschi's bull market was in no way in jeopardy. He looked straight at Kelch, but any natural impulse to gesture for patience or to wink, eye-roll, sigh in confederacy was suppressed, or never born. Kelch was a stained-glass window, blessed to witness Tedeschi's incalculably precious time.

Like almost all the young analysts in the department, Kelch knew everything about Irving Joseph Tedeschi, although everything did not extend to the answer about his name. Nathanson, on authority from the senior analyst he used to work for, claimed that before Tedeschi started appearing on television, he was known in Freshler, as everywhere, as Irv. Yet when Freshler Feld, to its competitors' consternation, became the most visible beneficiary of the boom, when it joined the head table of the Street, when it skipped through the meadows collecting, as if it were lilies, thirty percent annual earnings growth every quarter, when Blue's strategic focus on U.S. equities, technology banking, and trading systems was hailed by the business monthlies as an act of pure, unparalleled genius, Tedeschi became the public face of the firm's narcissistic optimism. And when the cable networks, the nightly news, the financial pages began to invent oracles and assign halos, Tedeschi's candidacy was strong. His election was sealed when the deadlined producers and reporters, the unmanned cameras, understood that Tedeschi was, if not exactly cooperative, at least obliging. According to Nathanson, only when the cameras appeared did Irv start to parade around as I. Joseph Tedeschi. He probably, Nathanson joked, paid an image consultant sixty thousand dollars for the name: I, Joseph, the seer, see seven years of feast, O Pharaoh, followed by seven years of famine. Tedeschi never mentioned the famine.

Wessex, however, would howl that Nathanson was as wrong as wrong could be. On the authority of a trader on the listed desk, he insisted that Tedeschi had always been Joe to his friends, to his family, and had always done his best to keep Irving attic-locked. This, almost inevitably, goaded everyone to call him Irv behind his back or, for those who could get away with it, to his face. A lot of people used to be able to get away with it, Wessex would add, sighing, nostalgic for a time before his. Before Tedeschi became the department's director and strategist, he covered the conglomerates.

Kelch once asked Veena to break the deadlock.

Stop bothering me with your nonsense.

Three months after Kelch joined Freshler, his mother called him to ask if he knew Tedeschi and to register her opinion that "Joe seemed very distinguished looking." Kelch supposed that, on television, Tedeschi looked fine, maybe distinguished: his face was unwasteful; his still-grayless-at-fifty-four hair was disciplined, full, and burnished—no, sir, not a toupee; and his signature tortoiseshell-frame glasses, ten years past their stylish peak for everyone else, worked. Tedeschi's charcoal or deep navy suits shielded a corporate, not human, body, mysterious and imposing, gold bars stored in its vault. He allowed cameramen to film him in only one particular chair near his window and only above his nipple line. Purposely, one assumed, for at his nipple line, his body began to expand in every direction like a Christmas tree. It did not expand to debilitating dimensions, and its heft may have been, in isolation, no more than average sized, but it seemed bigger, maybe, because of his small hands, small feet, small coconut-sized head—even small, sweet-corn teeth. Tedeschi was not Humpty-Dumpty, but he was badly proportioned, newborn-baby proportioned, and his shape, more than his size, conspired against his bought attempts to match vanity of form to vanity of mind. Even if Tedeschi's ties cost a hundred and fifty dollars apiece, they always seemed too long or too short. His pants' cuffs always brushed his Italian-shod heels. Most problematic, when Tedeschi sat down, his rump readjusted itself upward and nudged his shirt out of his pants. The rocking finished the job. Tedeschi did not rock his torso violently from the waist; he kept it in motion, a slow pendulum in winding need. He stopped rocking when he talked; he began again when he listened—or prepared to talk again, which, to him, was the same thing. When Tedeschi stood up, he automatically tucked his shirttail back into his pants. But sometimes, when he needed to make an emergency call on the market, or an emergency call on the bathroom, he forgot to tuck, and he would rush through the Freshler cubicle range, a triangle of sail flapping behind him.

(Tedeschi's rocking was hardly the most memorable quirk of the Freshler aristocracy. The head of Real Estate Principal Transactions, during late-night in-office meetings, took off his button-down and worked in his undershirt; a star trader smashed phones so often that the firm assigned him two desks so that the repairmen wouldn't interrupt him when the carcasses were removed; so many senior bankers suffered from chronic back pain and conducted meetings, supposedly, lying on the floor that Kelch no longer paid attention when a new name was added to the list.)

When Kelch read a quote in the *Journal* from chatty Maura Kearney, ranked one below him in the sector, or, occasionally, Gene Tennenberg—they were also on TV sometimes—he reminded himself that the respected analysts at Freshler and other bulge-bracket firms looked down on those who tanned in the media sun-lamps. An analyst *was* his opinion; an analyst was paid for his insight. To give it away free, to the housewives and day traders, was a disservice to your clients. More to the point, talking to a reporter strongly implied that you had a lot of spare time on your hands—a glaring sign of professional infantilism.

But the Street did not direct any of its usual sneers for the overly quoted at Tedeschi. Along with two or three others, I. Joseph was the official voice of the bull market. Unlike the oracles who were known for their reasonableness—by temporarily catching a bearish flu, they earned reputations as thoughtful, even intellectual—or the oracles who coined broad, sound-bite themes for the bull market— the Popeye Expansion, Cherry Tree Growth—Tedeschi never wavered from his faith or, particularly, colored in broad pictures for admirers of the aesthetics of the boom. Nor was he like Veena: she stated truth confidently and expected to be heeded. Tedeschi, rather, argued, overbearingly, carpet bombing. Reporters had come to understand that you didn't ask him for a comment, you asked him for a response; you didn't ask him to appear, you asked him to debate. His mind was formidable, encyclopedic, and his strategy was to hit you on the nose with an encyclopedia. If a reporter asked him if weakness in the PC sector, for instance, was endangering the overall market, he would cite sales figures by manufacturer, remind the reporter, with a wave of his tiny hand, of the doomsayers during the PC slump four years ago, link the facts to overall IT capital expenditures, and conclude that the expansion was not in danger. He dismissed people who cited "anachronistic" valuation models. He questioned bears' underlying data. He also, unaccountably, referred to the chairman of the Fed by his first name. All this was tremendously effective. In a few of the more slippery moments of the boom, when the house of cards was teetering at the base, Tedeschi's word had steadied the market. If he was always in danger of singing his lullaby against the nightmares of bubbles and deflation once too often, the analysts in the department appreciated him—the whole Street, in fact, appreciated him—because his reputation was dying for their sins.

Almost three minutes after Kelch entered the office, Tedeschi hung up the phone and rocked twice, farther forward than normal. Kelch worried that this might be a calisthenic preparation for attack, but Tedeschi, it became clear, was simply trying to get out of his chair. Surrendering, he pointed to the door. "Please shut that, Chris." When Kelch returned to the chair, Tedeschi had stood up somehow and was paging through one of the fifteen or so two-foot-high stacks of paper rising, vestigial columns of a Greek ruin, on his long wallbound file cabinet. Next to his name, Tedeschi's filing system was the second great mystery of Freshler research. He didn't, everyone knew, let Pamela McGruder touch his papers, nor allow the cleaning crew to dust the cabinet. Some assumed that Tedeschi's quick-retrieval mind had established a complementary retrieval system for his papers. Others concluded, daringly, that he really was a slob. Tedeschi toddled back to his desk and searched through two of the six shorter, foot-high stacks at his desk's borders. His lips were moving noiselessly, somewhere between self-moistening and mumbling.

When Kelch had realized twelve hours before that it wasn't twelve hours ahead, he had decided to go to work as soon as he could get ready. (This wasn't the first time that this had happened. At least one Sunday a month, Kelch's heart would seize up as an alarm clock appeared behind his eyes, scolding without sounding. Sometimes he would already be in the shower before he realized that Monday was tomorrow.) Kelch hadn't, of course, woken up as he had two days ago, with the joyful, passing feeling of new birth, but when he woke up today, bolted by electricity, he accepted the rush of activity, even confused activity, as perhaps a better plan to keep from dwelling. This shouldn't be difficult, he knew. Kelch had done well his whole life by focusing on the future, on personal progress, on the steady accretion to the good life of the tasks at hand.

He had reached the Freshler building at six-fifteen, pampering himself with a cab ride. (The subways that early hung heavy with coercion and defeat.) When the elevator dropped him foggy-headed onto the thirty-eighth floor, he shyly nodded to the analysts and juniors already there—it was earnings season—but the other morning-banished souls barely paused to notice him. They too seemed to understand the double importance of work that morning, of moving on, of paving over. As the day advanced and no one looked at him funny except Johann, who always did, and as he found himself able to concentrate on PKW's earnings, on Allencor's upcoming numbers, he decided that it was over. All yesterday's surliness with Kersten and Nathanson had been unnecessary. All the stuff that didn't make sense, like Veena (partly) and the Ghost, were clearly the outlying data points that would get rounded away by statistics. He didn't even bother to count them: this was the third day after, and nothing had happened. The article's phrases, its accusations—its existence—fluttered distant and harmless beyond memory, the lyrics of last summer's pop songs. And a final thing: if anything did happen, what did he care? What was he supposed to have done wrong?

Of course, his evolved strategy wasn't perfect. The approach of the Tedeschi meeting occasionally pierced his mosquito net—it was the first time he had ever been summoned under unclear circumstances—and he had lost his breath at those pierces and had to gasp harder, constricting, for the next ones. But the net had, every time, repaired itself quickly before the worries could become anything more than an irritation of uncertainty. Every person he met in the hall who benignly ignored him as usual and every half hour that passed without incident overwhelmed him with evidence that the meeting with Tedeschi was about Tee-Fog, his private screw-up. And maybe it wasn't even a screw-up: at lunch with a newish client (Kelch had been the happiest he had been in ages, or at least since the weekend), the client, a humorless woman, had agreed that Hoder had deserved *I give up*.

Still standing, Tedeschi thumbed through another stack of papers on the side of the desk closest to Kelch. With his left hand levering up the stack, his right hand paused as it found the pea in the mattress. In a single motion, he laid it on the desk, square to Kelch. It spanked loudly as it landed, the other pages following in instant echo. "Explain this."

His breath held, Kelch asked, "Explain what?"

Tedeschi had still not sat down, and he opened the magazine

dramatically, but to the article's second page. His stumpy hand attached to the page, and he turned it to the beginning of the article. "Okay. Explain that."

Kelch stared at the title, "The Hollow Man," and began to read, curious as to what this was. *With a word, he can destroy millions. Even a tone, a temperance of zeal* . . . Kelch could have sworn to have never seen this sentence, that cover, before. He lifted his eyes from the page before his mind had agreed to stop reading, and he caught a film of his own reflection inside Tedeschi's tortoiseshell frames. "Um." Kelch felt the zero Kelvin at the unnamable past at the universe edge. "Explain what?"

Tedeschi's left eyebrow sank nearer its corresponding eye, and his lips disappeared inward. He was either angry, crippled to deformity, or having a wonderful time. He nodded at the magazine. "Explain that." He began to rock.

"I mean—I don't even—I'm not sure what you're asking me."

"Explain that."

"Like, um, what am I supposed to—"

Tedeschi's rocking stopped. "Explain that article."

There was a simple answer, the sticky melting wet coat on the ice cream of life's problems: that isn't you. Kelch had finally been feeling good; he had *decided* that nothing would happen. "It's, uh, difficult to explain." He squinted at the page. "Because I've never seen this magazine before." His body was delayed, unresponsive to the ignition.

Tedeschi smacked his lips. Recapping for the benefit of all involved: "You just said *never*."

"I mean, of course I've seen the magazine in general, but you know, I don't read it."

"So you've never heard of Paul Galicia?" Nathanson or Wessex would have pretended that their minds were too filled with profundities to remember Galicia's name. Tedeschi, clearly, knew that his mind was too profound to forget it.

"I mean, why—I mean, how would I—" Kelch's mouth was fully

open, and Tedeschi resumed rocking across single degrees, a tuning fork's hum. Kelch brought the magazine nearer to him and closed it to the cover. "How would I, uh, know anything about this?" Opening the magazine to the reproving page, Kelch recognized the cliché: the cornered defendant in a prime-time courtroom, right before the last commercial break.

"You do know about the article, I presume."

"What?"

"You do know about the article, I presume."

"I think my girlfriend mentioned something about it." The words he had now were water cupped in a fingers' slotted bowl, colorless, tasteless, fleetingly a shape.

"Your girlfriend?"

"Uh-huh."

A statement: "Your girlfriend."

"Um, because you see, she may, I'm not sure about this, may have a friend, a cousin I don't know, in common with this Galicia guy." Kelch laid his right hand on the magazine's margins, and its after-tremors shivered with the page.

"A cousin in common?"

What am I doing with my life?

Again: "A cousin in common?"

"I don't know."

"You don't know."

"Maybe it's someone else"—he stopped and waited for, maybe hoped for, the implosion—"who writes for the magazine."

"Right. Someone else." Six months earlier, nearly everyone in the department under thirty had watched, with a chatty cruise-ship conviviality, a videotape of Tedeschi debating a regional bank's bearish strategist. The bear, his hair combed over a balding scalp, had stated offhandedly that market valuations were at the very high end of the traditional range. Tedeschi began his assault without delay. *And bull markets end because of what?* His victim, who was sitting in the studio next to the host, tried to answer, but Tedeschi, whose head, satellite delivered, hovered on the screen between them, asked again, *And bull markets end because of what?* That's not what I was— *Bull markets end because of what?* For any number of reasons. *No, not for any number of reasons. Bull markets end because of what?* This continued for two more minutes, until the bear, his pundit's light makeup beginning to blotch and grease, defended himself with the wrong punch: I have no idea why bull markets end, just let me . . . He heard his own words—the host leaned back in his chair, grinning, allied (as always) with the winner—and the screen switched to Tedeschi's brain made flesh. For three seconds, his face was a Rushmore of carved dignity. A smile then built itself, tier on tier, into the thundering crescendo of *ridiculous.* A pair of junior analysts showed the tape six times in a conference room during the dinner hour. In the session Kelch attended, he laughed louder than anyone else.

"I would think, Chris, that you would want to ask me why I was talking to *you* about this article."

"Huh?" Kelch felt starched.

"I would imagine if, as you say, you have never seen the article that you would want to know why I was even mentioning it to you."

I've never done anything to you. Just let me— "That's what I was asking because I'm sure it doesn't have anything to do with us or anything."

"*Us?* Now, that's a different line altogether. Why are you so sure, Chris?"

"Huh?"

"Your contention that the article has nothing to do with 'us' implies some knowledge of its contents. But if you haven't read it, as (again) you claim, then you wouldn't know that, would you?" Kelch's tongue was a brick, and he stared at the magazine, still open to the incriminating pages. He didn't even bother to answer. Is the caught fly relevant to the spider's web-weaving? Does jar-sealed air know about the properties of glass? He felt a pulse in his stomach, injecting a sickness.

Tedeschi, merciful in his victory, granted, "Equity Strategy and

Research." *I'm very tired. I have to lie down. I have to dig a hole and die.*
Tedeschi repeated himself: "Equity Strategy and Research."

"What?"

"The article mentioned quite casually in the seventh sentence,
Equity Strategy and Research. Those words exactly." The change in
the department's name had stirred a collective, quiet moan when
the firm had adopted it five years ago. The other banks called their
departments Equity Research or Investment Research, and the dis-
senters at Freshler had complained that Equity Strategy and
Research placed research as an afterthought, as if the global department was Tedeschi and his three hundred elves. It was bad enough
that Tedeschi, uniquely on the Street, was both strategist and
department head.

Kelch's mind was skim milk, stripped of the butterfat that
retained thoughts, flavor, a gravity. If he had paid for the hole, why
couldn't he just dig it and die? He didn't want to be brave; he
wanted a world with no need for bravery. He had declared, goddamnit, that nothing had happened. "I didn't, you know, uh, read
the article, so I guess . . ."

Tedeschi had stopped rocking. "Of course."

"No, so I just . . . I don't know."

"Of course." Tedeschi assumed a practiced calm. His voice was
somewhat high, like a clarinet, edged with Brooklyn. But because
he spoke with granite confidence, knowing that market indices trem-
bled when his throat twitched, his voice, however objectively inel-
egant its accent and pitch, flowed, emphasized the right beat in every
sentence. He was accustomed, Kelch knew, to resignations, turf battles, soft blackmailing for bigger numbers.

Kelch threw a long pass, too tired to drive up the field, too many
points behind. "I don't know anything about this."

A self-savored pause, and then: "Please stop insulting me."

"Huh?"

"Please stop insulting me."

Tedeschi undoubtedly read about the sins of research every day;

it was sold in bulk, a dollar a pail. So why's he picking on me, Kelch thought, still staggering. But this thought seemed to thicken a growing suspicion that this was a real experience he was having, not just a sensory one of sounds and grunts and indigestive reactions.

Tedeschi leaned over the desk, and his manicured fingertips reached to retrieve the magazine. His hand was an inch from it when he abandoned the mission. He sat back. "Since you clearly haven't read this article, let me summarize it for you."

Kelch took a seemingly endless blink. *I don't know what I'm—*

"Someone in this department decided to speak to a writer for this magazine. And this writer proceeded to attack this department. Are you following me so far?"

Kelch nodded.

"Are you following me so far?"

Kelch thought that he had nodded. "Uh-huh."

"And in this article"—Tedeschi's voice smoothed around its authoritative molding—"attacking this department, there were a number of quite vicious comments about me." *What are you—?* "And I find it ridiculous that if someone had something to complain about, he would use *this* as his forum." Tedeschi began to rock again, gently, somnolent.

"I don't think anyone would do that."

"You're going to have to speak up."

Kelch swallowed. "I don't think anyone would do that."

"Don't try to kiss my ass here," Tedeschi ordered, and again, he was standing. He looked at the magazine, jerked forward as if to snatch it, but then moved to a stack on his long wallbound file cabinet. He allowed the stack to lean against his chest and quickly drilled through the pages, examining only the corners. He muttered as each buried page disappointed in turn. The action, to Kelch, was too loud to allow in any thoughts. Tedeschi roughly pushed the stack up; the top page fell off and skirted down another pile. He walked to the other side of his office, where a coffee table in a

sitting area, an area the same size as Veena's (though more tradi-
tionally furnished), held five more stacks, comically unstable Dag-
wood sandwiches of Freshler reports, corporate annual reports,
compensation reports, file folders, manila envelopes, ink-bleary magazine pages with articles of interest, articles about him. As he moved
to the table, he tucked in his shirttail, missing the right half.

"Oh, to hell with it." He returned to his desk, his face sour. Sitting
and adjusting himself like a beach chair onto the sand—he was the
chair—he said, "Chris, let me ask you something." Kelch had to
consciously close his mouth. "You kids are not treated poorly in this
department, are you?"

"Huh?"

"I, the firm, we pay you a lot of money to work here, correct?"
Kelch nodded.

"Four hundred and fifty thousand last year, correct?" Kelch felt a
small shock of seriousness, of incitement, perhaps thrown off by his
salary, now mentioned and involved. His mind had tipped into clarity, almost, and he understood at once that he had been acting
inexcusably weak. For he had done nothing wrong, and even if
something was happening now, he didn't have to accept it. Anyway,
Tedeschi had no right to accuse him of being overpaid. Everyone
had read *that* article: "The Ten-Million-Dollar Bull," and that was
two years ago. Tedeschi continued: "And what did I tell you in your
last review?"

You told me my number. "You told me, um—" How could anyone
be asked to access memories when the hard drive was occupied?
"You said that you were happy that I was ranked fifth and that you
expected me to improve my ranking year over year, but that the
meeting wasn't, you know, to set specific targets." Kelch almost
smiled after his complete sentence. Tedeschi's rocking started anew,
and his eyes locked on Kelch.

"That's exactly what I told you, Chris. But I'm beginning to
doubt my judgment. It seems to me that you and Mr. Kim and Mr.

Torvil and your supposed friend Mr. Nathanson do not realize how easy you have it. I've never given you the one-or-done speech, have I? Ranked-or-spanked?" Kelch had heard about ranked-or-spanked but had assumed that it was apocryphal. If an analyst failed to win, place, or show in the coming year's polls, the threat supposedly went, Tedeschi would cut his bonus from the previous year. "Did I ever give you ranked-or-spanked?"

You know you didn't because you haven't given it to anyone. Because if you fire me, what are you going to do, pay Tennenberg three million—four million—to cover my sector? Come on. You would have to pay more than me for Arnold the Sixth.

"If I have been nothing but generous to you kids, why am I now being treated like a clown?" Kelch, at the edge of a forming confidence, tried to respond, but treasonous thoughts are difficult to sustain, press forward, in a general's chambers. Kelch's throat was a tight sandpaper tube.

Tedeschi's arm bolted straight forward, as if cannon-shot; it brought his turnip-shaped body with it. Kelch flinched—Tedeschi's punching me, stabbing me—but realized then that Tedeschi was only reaching for the magazine. Holding it by its spine, Tedeschi shook it, and a folded piece of paper fell onto his lap. His brow nodded aha, and he brought the paper closer to him for inspection. Kelch could see the type through the sheet, bullet points atop, thicker blocking below. He knew immediately what it was. Kelch: Scott, Rockford: Scottsville, father: father. But who would go to the trouble? "This is what I'm talking about," Tedeschi said as his eyes inputted the data, " 'a philosophy he is proud to recite, is a cheap Cartesian bromide cloaked in the mantle of technologese about "pursuing the bits." ' "

Kelch: nothing.

"Do you see what I mean?"

"What?" Kelch asked, as if interrupted.

"These attacks on my reputation."

That's not even about you. That's not even about me. Kelch's throat tightened further. "I don't think that's an attack, um, on your—"

"Why would you think that?"

"I don't know anything. But I'm just saying that it doesn't sound to me, um, like an attack on you—"

"What does it sound like then?"

I did it. Is that what you want to hear? *It was me?*

"What does it sound like then?" On television, or when lecturing the massed department, Tedeschi's hair was immovable, his sweat remained secret, he was the bull market's consort. His heft, however, was a contradictory subtext, a reminder of bodies past—not just his body, but the research analyst's public body—and the stigmas of bookworm, of herd-prone, of second-rate. The hair, the stability, his inconsistently fine-detailed face always won the perceptual battle, on television at least, over his mismatched body. But now his temples began to oil, his face pinked, and when he spoke, his mouth opened cavernously. Kelch noticed, maybe for the first time, Tedeschi's gray baby teeth. Kelch had still not answered him. "What does it sound like then?"

"I don't know."

Tedeschi began to rock while declaiming, each forward pitch ready at any moment to tumble into a somersault. He usually rocked only while listening. "You understand that I don't appreciate this."

Nothing.

"I work damn hard to benefit this department, to manage it effectively, to bring credit to its reputation, to encourage everyone here to succeed and to prosper. And"—the rocking paused temporarily forward—"I will not be made into a laughingstock by a bunch of underappreciative junior analysts."

A vice presid—

Tedeschi paused, waiting perhaps for his rocking to generate more energy. "Do you understand me? I am not going to be treated like this."

Nothing made sense, but strangely, nothing hurt. If this was it, he could accept it, incorporate it, straightforwardly. "I—"

"This is unacceptable." Tedeschi slowed down the chair as he tried to stand up, but the countermotion, or an adhesive connection between the leather and his soft-clay rear, clumsied his movement. While decelerating, he had picked up the magazine with demonstrative intentions, but his throw against the desk was an infant's first: the arm hadn't acquired the instincts of the arc. It was ugly. Finally, standing: "I am one of the great contrarians on the Street, Chris, do you understand that?"

Nothing.

"Do you understand that?"

"I—"

"The record is clear that no one else has called this market as consistently I have. Time and again, people who have neither the *guts* nor the will nor the courage of their convictions to be in this business have tried to pressure me or have argued with me that the expansion was over. *I* proved that they were wrong. Do you understand what I'm telling you?"

Kelch smiled a too broad idiot's smile.

"Is something funny?"

Tedeschi was the Street: his opinions had been a proxy, a gospel, a reassurance for the majority. Tedeschi was a contrarian because only contrarians, the Street's singular dictionary proclaimed, were ever right. Tedeschi was a modern hero—forward!—calling for the boom to continue, year after year, as valuations rose, as sense evaporated. Tedeschi was a company man: Freshler Feld needed the boom to continue to feed its growing, insatiable brood. Tedeschi was a genius: his brain was an immeasurable computer, his tongue a silver salmon, gliding upstream through the current as if it were air. Tedeschi was a condiment: adding flavor to the market, but stuck between the bread.

"I said, Is something funny?"

"No, I—" *I was just thinking of*— Mumbled: "Something else." As if he were a four-year-old, anesthetized by a television's cartoon shapes, Kelch's eyes took charge again, riding his mind.

"You were what of something else? Let me tell you something: I have just about had my fill lately with you bull-market brats who believe that you run this firm. I'm tired of putting my heart and soul into this department only to have you betray me. You and your good friend Adam"—he sneered, dishonor among thieves—"who thinks that just because he does a few favors for me I'm going to spend all my time managing his franchise."

Nathanson, mentioned twice.

"I don't ask for thank-yous from you kids. But I do demand respect. And I will tell you something else." Tedeschi, as a rule, delivered thoughts in tidy bow-wrapped paragraphs; he had never needed addenda before. "One of these days—maybe soon—this market is going to turn, and the hiring environment will not be so indiscriminate, and I'm going to have a few things to say to some people who have gotten a little too accustomed to walking in here and *demanding* things from me. It's going to give me great pleasure to rid myself of some of the dregs in this department who have crossed the line once too often." The heat of the monologue had dyed Tedeschi's face a worn-brick red. His hair, at the temples, now shined. Tedeschi had aggressively expanded the department over the last three years by early promoting, internal transferring, luring analysts from rivals with two by twos (two million, two years), two by threes, four by twos—the whole lumberyard, guaranteed. "Tell me, Chris, why did you write that article?"

Treasonous thoughts, in general, are impossible before the general when the silver stars on his breast hypnotize with a gleam. Kelch had tried to remind himself that he had *decided* nothing would happen, and that hadn't worked. He had tried to insist that what had happened was hard to decide, and that hadn't worked. Now, he gave up, allowed the world—how things happen—to exist on its own terms. At least for the moment. Because he only wanted the proper reaction—a write-down, maybe, a restructuring—that would cause the minimum amount of disruption.

"How could you think that no one would see through this? Do you think that I—we—are that stupid?"

Paul had e-mailed Kelch a month ago. *Chris, I have decided to use some of the content from our discussion for a different project. As a result, you are going to be quoted in a magazine article. Of course, you will not be named in the article, and I absolutely guarantee that your anonymity will be fully protected. You're going to be just one of my sources. For some fact checkers, however, I need you to reply to this message to confirm that you did meet with me and that I did record our conversation.* Paul's name, his conspicuous glasses, Kelch's own slatternly agreement to meet with him that night had mostly been scrubbed from Kelch's memory. He had become a remembered impression, not a remembered fact, a restaurant at which you cannot recall what you ate but can recall that it was bad. Kelch didn't consciously decide not to respond to his message; he let it rot electronically in the box. Two weeks later, Paul sent him another. *Chris, we cannot print the article unless you reply that you did meet with me and that I did record the conversation.* When that message came in, Kelch stared long at it, at its sentence's shape, and then with a playful click of the mouse, a thick grin on his face, he deleted it. Two days after that: *Chris, this is really unacceptable behavior on your part. Maybe you have a legitimate excuse, but this article is very important to me and my career, and your failure to cooperate could jeopardize its publication. Please confirm that you did meet with me and that I did record our conversation.*

I met with you, Kelch typed. *A tape recorder was there.* He then sent the message with no regards, no small talk, proud of not sincerely signing his name. His terseness, he thought, would communicate to Paul what he really thought of him.

Then, last Thursday, a final message came, with no regards, no small talk, proud of not sincerely signing a name. *The article's done. It will be out Monday.*

Kelch deleted the message immediately, almost before, it seemed, he finished reading it. It was junk, stray bits.

Tedeschi leaned his meat-patty hands against the desk, his fingers spread for balance. "Why are you just sitting there? Don't you have anything to say?"

Frozen, Kelch stared at Tedeschi, looked into his semireflecting glasses, at his dark, mud-colored eyes. This man—his reputation was clear—did not have a temper. The department had its hotheads, its bullies like Les Wethel who squeezed tears out of their secretaries, but Tedeschi's caricature was calmly confident like the market itself, a smooth golden Buddha atop a mountain of facts. Kelch thought, Why can't I just go back to work—neither of us wants to be doing this. With his eyes, with his earnestness, Kelch tried to transmit this—that he was still loyal, still hardworking, still eager to dedicate his long days, his blood, to the department, to the number one ranking, to attractive valuations, to the greater glory of Freshler Feld. But Tedeschi was not moved. "I-I-I I'm not sure what to say."

"You're not sure what to say?"

If he could just return to his own office, he then thought, he could show Tedeschi all that he had done today, all that he had done in six years of crammed, restless hours. Work could work. Allencor was reporting about now, and Kelch could prove to Tedeschi that his estimates were (almost certainly) penny on. And PKW had reported earlier, and Kelch had left messages with the twelve key clients who owned it.

"You know what bothers me most about this article?"

This was all he ever wanted to be in his entire life.

"That this Paul Galicia would quote Max Nibelic of all people attacking *this* department"—Tedeschi pointed down, near his lap— "strikes me as such shoddy journalism as to make the whole effort risible." Tedeschi was rocking again in a self-soothing, bedtime path. His tone calmed to match it. "I've been listening to journalists quote Nibelic for twenty-five years, and none of them ever seem to mention the tiny fact that this crackpot has missed two of the greatest bull markets in American history." Tedeschi leaned his head to the right and softly tugged his ear. He was being pensive. "I'm not sure what I'm going to do yet about this, Chris, about you. It's not the article that disappoints me. It's the betrayal behind it."

What the hell did Tedeschi know about betrayal?

Pamela McGruder knocked and opened the door in unison; she inserted her head in the gap. She was wearing a black spring-weight sweater under two thin necklaces; she was, in a matronly, fussy way, put-together. "It's Frank." She glanced at Kelch, adding for his benefit, "Teppner." Teppner was the head of North American investment banking.

Tedeschi asked, quarter-smirking, "What does my friend Mr. Teppner want?"

"He just said to tell you"—Pamela looked at her notepad— " 'high comedy.' "

Tedeschi's laugh seemed to be more from a recognition of humor than as a reaction to it. "Tell Teppner that I'll get back to him." Pamela nodded. "And tell him I'm with the comedian right now."

As Pamela shut the door again—the shutting was expertly silent—Tedeschi leaned, his arms crossed, toward the desk. He rested his head into his chest, now inflated to meet the challenge. At first his voice quivered; then it bellowed. "That's exactly the treatment I'm not going to tolerate anymore. Do you hear me, you fucking brat?"

Kelch whirred, a hobbyist's small motor, the battery weak and dying. He tried to catch his breath, release his breath, remind himself of a breath, of oxygen needs. A thought then escaped, not out of his mouth but out of his brain, squeaking like the pulled lip of an untied balloon. *I'm not Scott.* He only had minutes, a second, to prove this. Everything was ending too soon.

"Do you hear me? I will not sit here and have Frank Teppner and Alice Tazoré, damnit, and Blue make a fool of me because of some moronic junior analyst in my department."

I didn't do—

"How do you excuse yourself?"

"I'm not Scott."

"Not who?"

"I'm not Scott. This article"—Kelch pointed at it, lying on the desk, its cover bent broken underneath it—"has nothing to do with me. I-I-I——" He was the one who had been betrayed. "I don't even know this Paul Galicia." Tedeschi began rocking. "I don't know what to say because, because I'm still trying to figure out even why I'm even here." And his thoughts compressed with the moment, with the shutting door and the lost opportunities. I've given the best years of my life to this firm and I call stocks like I see them and I make my clients money and I make the bankers happy. Every day, I put my words, my reputation, out there for Pressure Hell. Don't throw me away.

Tedeschi's chair stopped. He inhaled, as if preparing to strike down a mortal with a thunderbolt command. But he exhaled, brought his chair still, and uttered in an unexpected voice, skeptical but pacific, "You are telling me, right now, that this article has nothing to do with you?" He was, it was obvious, through arguing.

"This has nothing to do with me."

"If you are lying to me right now, I will personally see to it—" Tedeschi stopped, smiled ambiguously. "Well, I don't think I have to spell out what I could do. I told Blue how *I* wanted to handle it, and he overruled me. We used to have an expression"—he paused again—"an expression on Emmons Avenue: fish or cut bait."

"I-I-I don't know."

To himself, almost: "If he wants to let a bunch of lawyers and PR consultants run this department, I'll be happy to retire. Frankly, I'm getting a little sick of it all anyway."

Kelch said something. Tedeschi, interrupted, asked, "What?"

Kelch repeated it. "What am I supposed to do now?"

Disgusted: "Why don't you go ask Blue."

5

Dan, Kelch's brother-in-law, let no facts of what Kelch did at Freshler Feld penetrate his hard-shell brain; nonetheless, Kelch's career to him was a great cosmic joke. *I'm explaining to a guy at work what you do, and he keeps telling me to get the facts straight.* (As he aged, Dan's voice slippered into its birthright, the voice of his fathers, *the* melding into *da,* and *into* end, the *hell with you*s and *you bet*s becoming sentence glue.) Dan, I told you, I am the official opinion of Freshler Feld on a universe of stocks. *Hear that, Heath'? Not only does he live in New York, he runs the whole universe.* Not the whole universe, Dan, a universe of eleven stocks. *So, you don't run the universe, you are the universe.* You're not even listening to me—*I'll start listening when you knock off all this universe crap. Am I right, Heath'?*

Dan's easy humor was unregulated, mean, and not even remotely funny. Yet Kelch missed it, its fatalism, its buffoonery, its shrugging off its own inconsistencies. Nathanson and Wessex were funny, actually, but their jokes began in the ego; their observations stung, had cant to reveal. Dan's jokes were drool, a constant varnish on his chin. It irritated Kelch to imagine that he could be jealous of him. But he was. Yes, the punch clock must have been unforgiving to Dan, and yes, it must have been a daily torture to watch the Rockford newscast's frontline dispatches of expansions, closings, layoffs, lockouts, battles over three percent raises, and yes, consumer debt to him was a real thing, not just an economic index. But Dan's life was his own. This, Kelch believed, was indisputable. Dan had lovingly greeted the growing medicine ball torturing his belt; he treated a football sweatshirt as sufficient attire for every situation save Easter church; his hair was stringy, cut by chance, ridged permanently from his hat. He drank Coke at breakfast and let Brandon sneak a long sip before school. Work for Dan was us versus them and the us's worked, but the thems always had to worry about crap. Dan was lucky, Kelch was certain: he never had to smile into a telephone; he never had to frost a stale cake of a spreadsheet with false precision; he never had to congratulate Hoder Leary for a great quarter on an in-line quarter or grin stupidly as Hoder lectured him on management élan. Dan *knew* that nobody was any better than him, than anyone. And only an asshole would think he was.

Heather: Chris, just because we don't make your kind of money doesn't mean we need your charity. *What's charity? They're Christmas presents.* Well, it makes Dan feel weird. *Why would it make him—?* I don't know why, but just because we don't make a hundred and fifty thousand dollars a year— *Is that how much you think I make?* Whatever, a hundred thousand dollars a year. Just because . . .

Dan was the road evaded and the road home, a nightmare, a white flag, an exile's cracked mirror; he was irresistible, a fantasy of release, a climb back into the cold, dried pupa, now powdery, maybe gone, but maybe faintly warm.

Kelch's office door was closed. Inside, staring at the computer screen, at the tickers closed and resting, at Tee-Fog a half point above its Tuesday fall, he felt his brain stem shudder. He drew down his face's skin with a roaming, scraping hand. The hand stopped, its heel against his mouth, and he blew his cheeks against the hand seal until they popped in flatulent defeat. And then he froze, froze like an insomniac silencing his rustling sheets, knowing that tomorrow and tomorrow's tomorrow will only make his anxieties more feral and alive. Kelch held his breath and clamped shut his eyes, and a new shudder moved from his hardened jaw to his neck to his fingertips. The shudder was a jackhammer, trembling through his tendons, through his shut-off eyes, engulfing with a silent thump on thump the gagged thoughts at the lightless bottom of Kelch's appearing cracks, thoughts of what was going to happen, of what it meant to ask Blue, of not smelling, of the Ghost and the analog and Kersten and stockbrokers, of changing and accepting and understanding what had just occurred in Tedeschi's office. No. No. *No.*

Nothing was going to happen. He wasn't Scott. He couldn't allow—
It couldn't happen.

Then he yelled it, *Fuck*, and he tried to yell it again, but it tangled
a knot in his mouth. The sound that finally came forth—a birth
pain, maybe a growl—was loud and jungle and carried a death.
Trying to repeat the word wonder of the *fuck*, he attempted to yell
it once more, but again he only groaned; his breaths were heavy
and emptying; his chest expanded to the snap-back edge and collapsed into itself in exhaustion. Then his thoughts cleared up. *Why
did you have to do this to me, Kersten?* You with your damned cousin
and your boyfriend Galicia, and if it weren't for you, none of this
would have happened. I'll tell you, friend or enemy—*I* betrayed
him? He's betraying me after all I've done for him. He can underpay
me, pay me a quarter of what they pay Tennenberg for the same
shithole job, and Tennenberg does one deal in three years and I
do *six*, and I barely pass four hundred and that jerk makes at least
two million, and you're telling me that I'm the one doing the betraying. . . . But I will betray him if that's what he wants. I'll tell the
whole Street what a fraud he is, how he sits there with all those
stacks of paper and couldn't tell me anything about shit, and how
he's a broken record with his *the expansion will continue, the ex-paaan-
sion will continue*. Why do bull markets end? I'll tell you why they
end. They end because the frauds pumping them up are revealed for
what they are. Everyone's going to know it too, because he deserves
it—I'll, I'll, I'll *expose* him.

Kelch, his brow meeting his chin in pug-faced anger, looked
around his office, for a guidebook on exposés, for further fuel for
his justice. He found it in the telephone.

I'll call that guy from the *Journal*—No, I'll call Galicia. That's
brilliant, brill-fucking-yent. I'll call him and tell him exactly what
he wants to hear, give him the biggest scoop of his—*his*—pathetic
life. Don't waste your important career on vice presidents anymore,
jackass. Here's a real story: the great I. Joseph Tedeschi has stopped
thinking about the markets because he wants to rub his fat ass in

being the big bull, Mr. Bullish, Mr. Bullshit. That's exactly what I'm going to do, Irv. You want to know why? Because the world is changing, and we're going to take over soon and make a new kind of firm where there's not all this damned politics, where if you walk the walk, you can talk the talk, and if you play, they pay, and where worthless old skeletons from 1975 with their out-of-date views are not, *not* going to boss us around anymore. Read the damn papers: there's a revolution out there, and you're going to get hanged.

Kelch's teeth hurt, inside out, as if the enamel were nerve endings, and his lips were ice. His teeth walled in his thoughts, but one word breached them: *kill.*

You hear that? Are you listening to me? I'm going to go in there and kill your rocking ass. You want to know why? Because, because, because it's not *fair.* You bring us into this good-for-nothing firm and throw a couple of measly dollars at us like we're goddamned animals who will do anything for a buck and then when something so stupid it doesn't even make a difference to anything happens, a bunch of half-truths and just crap, you just wait for that to happen so that you can fire us. And then you can replace us with pricks coming out of some loser MBA program who will work a thousand hours a week for one twenty-five because they're idiots, who can't even tell a P/E from-from-from the hole in their ass. (Kelch nodded vigorously as he jumped with a horse's elegant line over a potential stumble.) Well, I got a surprise for you. If you think I'm expendable, well, fuck you, just try to replace me. I don't see a lot of other guys my age at number five—so go ahead and try to meet your stupid budget or whatever you're trying to do—fine by me—but there'll be a little shock waiting for you when the polls come out and I'm number one for some other firm.

And know what else I'm going to do? I'm going to sue your ass for unfair dismissal. How would that look on the front page of the *Journal*? Your buddy Teppner would really have something to call "high comedy."

None of this has anything to do with me. If you had just seen that, you would have been safe. But you're not safe anymore. If I'm going down, I'm taking this whole firm with me.

All right, Paul, let's get it on.

The headset had found its way onto Kelch, and he adjusted the microphone and turned to dial, but he couldn't remember Paul's number—he didn't know the number—he had never called him. He stared ahead, emptied, as these facts plexus-pinched him one after the next, and with both hands he swatted off the headset, which crashed into the monitor. The monitor yawned. Kelch picked up the headset and threw it awkwardly, rudely against the monitor, but the flat screen again didn't blink. The closed-market quotes rested deeply, confident and exact, their snores singing their infallibility: the market was always right. The throw had ricocheted off the monitor, and the headset had landed, draped, over Kelch's arm. He grabbed the whip handle of the cord and lashed the headset against the monitor, again and again, his arm hammering a final nail, his mind filled only with sensations—colors—with rage, with hate, with swelling inadequacy: the headset and monitor, afragrant conspirators, plugged sisters, hugged each time they met. It was like throwing droplets of rainwater against a brick wall, it was stabbing your enemy with a green bean, and Kelch's head dropped into his chest, which was rising, retreating, rising heavily. He glared at the gloating flat-screen monitor. He seized its by its flanks, and he cast it into the sea.

The monitor's cord, like a dog leash, jerked the monitor back, and it dropped six-o'clock onto one of Kelch's guest chairs. One corner caught the chair. Kelch jumped up from his seat and hurried around his desk. As he stood over it, a trembling in his neck spread over his chest, and he saw himself kicking the monitor back into silicon and plastic and wires. But as he stopped to allow his breathing to return from a near wheeze, he plowed his hands through his hair and held them at the back of his head. He then squatted down to cradle the fallen monitor. He inspected its abused face: the upper-lefthand corner had cracked, baseball-size, and the pixels beneath it were a sickly miscolor, an unripe banana green. The rest of the monitor, however,

was unharmed. Kelch looked out his window expecting to see gawk-
ers gathered in the hall. Then he set the monitor on his desk, and his
thoughts swirled for peace: he could just tell Torres that it had fallen
when he was arranging stuff on his desk. Torres didn't ask a lot of
questions. He hadn't even asked why Kelch had needed that new keyboard. So if Torres was around, Kelch would ask him for a spare—he
would tell him that he absolutely needed a new one tonight, for a
project—and Torres would have to give it to him. And everything
would be all right. Because if he started fresh, from right now, all
this—Hoder, Kersten, Tedeschi, go-ask-Blue—would disappear. It
was easier that way. It was essential that way. There were no other
options. Kelch opened his office door and moved into the wider
hall. (From his cubicle, Johann turned to grin at him, but Kelch,
speeding past, did not process his look.) Torres was margined on
the fortieth floor, and Kelch figured that IT guys like him must stay
at least until seven because Jesus—

Joel Einstadt was waiting in front of the elevators. "How's it
going, Chris?"

None of his friends in the department called him Chris. "Huh?"

"How's it going?"

"It's going great." Did he say that, Kelch wondered about himself,
because he always said that. Did he always say that? He listened to
his breathing, which was still loud and clipped. It was embarrassing,
and he held it in.

"That's good."

"Where are you heading?" Kelch asked in a rushed mumble. Einstadt was the same height as Kelch and roughly the same build,
maybe thinner. His dark hair was short and clean, matted protec-
tively over his scalp. Whiskers from that morning had begun to
revive, and once-boyish dimples on his face had prematurely drawn
down his jaw, deepening into parentheses. All this notwithstanding,
he was the opposite of strung out: his incongruous, glass-blue eyes
proved that his life was still more forward than backward. He was
a nice guy, almost beautiful.

"I'm going downstairs for coffee."

"You know, they, uh, have coffee in the pantry for free." Kelch let out his breath.

"They have something in the pantry for free. I'm not sure that you could call it coffee."

Kelch stared at Einstadt. "Did Nathanson tell you that?"

"Did Nathanson tell me what?"

"That the coffee was bad?"

"Believe it or not, I discovered that fact all on my own." Einstadt was volleying politely, it seemed, letting Kelch jog for his return but making him feel the resistance of contest. Kelch smiled, considered laughing out of politeness, but his well was dry-hole and shut. The elevator arrived, and they rode down it together. As Kelch realized the direction, his temples throbbed, draining his face. *Why can't I just be still?*

In the Freshler lobby, Einstadt asked, "Where are you off to?"

"Um, I got on the wrong elevator. I, uh, I was going up."

Einstadt's face didn't comment. "Well, I'll see you later then." Kelch looked at him again, and Einstadt's raised eyebrows waited tolerantly. "Is everything all right?"

"Huh?"

"I don't know— I don't want to— But you look a little pale, and . . ." He pointed, finger circling, to Kelch's right hip, and Kelch, corkscrewing, looked at and reached to it at the same time. His shirttail was untucked, Tedeschi-style.

"No, everything's fine," Kelch, tucking, declared with enough conviction left over for belief.

"Well, then, see you later." Einstadt turned formally to the doors. He took five steps before Kelch asked him to wait.

Kelch came to this bar infrequently and always for the same reason: a birthday drink, a so-long, good-to-get-to-know-you drink for someone that he didn't like or didn't get to know, always with a group obliged to acknowledge the existence of a long-term temporary secretary or an unpopular junior analyst. The closest bar to the Freshler building, it was as narrow as a rail car and kitchenbright. It had no theme—not even Irish—no ambitions, no sense of boom or bust, a few regular drunks, and its reason-to-be niche after the four o'clock bell when the smaller-firm specialists, floor brokers, clerks from the Exchange stopped in for a beer or a shot and some gossip before heading out on the rails, in daylight, to the near suburbs, to Queens. The traders mainly cleared out by half past five, and by six-fifteen, when Kelch and Einstadt arrived, only a handful of the immovables, the home-fearing, remained. One woman, her face beneath a cascade of eyeshadow and rouge, flypapered compliments from a half-conscious suitor with a cackling, encouraging *Oh, shut up*, again and again, her accent a New York limbo between Catholic races, between outer boroughs.

Einstadt had stammered when Kelch had asked him to go somewhere to talk—he had said that he needed to finish a section of a report he was working on—but Kelch had requested only a half hour, which disallowed any stinginess, even from an acquaintance. Kelch walked Einstadt to the bar before any conditions could be set. After a low-key joke about the coffee here, Einstadt ordered a diet soda, and Kelch paid for it and his beer and escorted Einstadt to a navel-high table. There, Einstadt wiped off the stool, rubbed the transferred shine between his fingers and thumb, and shrugging what-the-hell, sat down.

Kelch sniffed at his beer; it tasted, in the back of his throat, tinny. "Um, so how's it going at Freshler so far?" He wondered then, acutely, why he was here.

Einstadt set down his politely sipped soda. "What?"

"How do you like it at the firm so far?"

"Well, I can't complain, although I never guessed how frustrating it would be trying to initiate when valuations flop around so much."

Deeply: "Yeah." And a lumpish silence sat on them both.

Placing aside his beer, now a third empty, Kelch rushed head-on against the silence: "Not that I don't care, but I didn't really want to talk to you about, uh, that."

Einstadt layered an "Oh, really" into tickled laughter. Kelch thought, If you're going to make fun of me, I'll just skip this whole damned thing, but Einstadt then broadcast, closed-toothed, a smile through his dimples and his backlit sapphire eyes. "Sorry," he said. "I'm here to listen."

"Well then listen." Einstadt's eyes dulled and his dimples filled. "Sorry, just listen: what I wanted to tell you is this. I mean, this is what I brought you here to say." Kelch had not yet revealed to himself any plans for this drink, for Einstadt. He felt unsettled, of course—the engine knocking after the keys had been removed—and he couldn't quite rouse himself to analyze the length and bits and reactions of the last hour, because the movement from Tedeschi to his office to his rage to here—to here?—was beyond his ability to deliberate. But it seemed, strangely, that the inconceivability of being in this bar—this bar?—confirmed the inconceivability of the last hour, the last three days, his life's unwelcome turn. He didn't want any of this. Why couldn't it just go away? But at least one thing now was for certain, Kelch thought: the idea that nothing had happened was no longer exactly true. He had just told Einstadt that he had brought him here to say something. Then say it, jackass. He drew in a breath. "That is, um, you know, I don't know why I'm telling you this versus telling someone else this, seeing that I don't really know you, but you're here, I guess. So anyway, you know that article, the one by this Paul Galicia, the one I'm sure everyone on the whole Street is talking about, well, that was me. I mean, it wasn't me, but it was me who the guy Paul Galicia thinks it was."

Nothing.

"I don't mean it wasn't me who talked to him. It was. It's just that the guy, this guy Galicia got so many things wrong in the article that this 'Scott' or whatever he's called doesn't resemble me in any way—I mean, how many sisters do I have?" He got that wrong, didn't he? "Anyway, the point is—what I'm trying to admit is—and I'll admit it, there's nothing to be ashamed about—is that I did talk to this Galicia guy and that he does think that it was me that he wrote about." After the admission, Kelch paused, but he felt no different, felt no liberating limb-looseness of an airport after a long flight, felt no lonely sun ray on an autumn beach. His body slumped, shoulders dropping, torso curved in.

Kelch processed Einstadt's expression. "You knew, didn't you?" Einstadt shrugged. "Who told you, Nathanson?"

"Well, I can't say. I mean, people were talking about it and—"

"So the whole Street does know."

"Well, the people I heard talking about it all seemed to know you pretty well. I don't see how anyone could figure out that it was you or would *want* to, frankly, unless—"

"Listen: people have their ways. Don't forget that for *one* second as long as you're in this business."

"I've been working in this business for a while."

"Huh?"

"Before I went to business school."

Stop bragging, prick.

"But I interrupted you," Einstadt half-apologized. "Go on."

"I don't even know what else to say. I mean, it's like A: I'm this victim, and B: everyone's giving me shit about everything now—and I mean *every*one—and C: I don't even know what I did wrong. No, I do know: I didn't do anything wrong, and that's what pisses me off. That all these people are all worked up over this." He drank a serious swallow. "That's not it. What's it is— Listen: it's all just so damned random and, and, and *weird*." As his voice squealed its tires on the last word, Kelch's downcast eyes strained harder, aimed at the table, as if Dan were looking down at him, shaming, from a Rockford troposphere of Rockford mores. "And it's not like I don't

accept consequences." His head rose. Einstadt nodded—or was nodding—and his eyes declared, independently of his silence, their sympathy. "Listen: I'm not a fucking crybaby. I just want to do my job."
And he wanted to stop talking, forever.

"I don't think—"

"Listen: I'm not going to start whining, but I've been treated like
shit by the whole world lately, and I'm tired of it."

"It seems tough, um, that you find yourself in this pickle, and I
can see how that's not an enviable—" The woman at the bar threw
her head back, howling even louder, her only way to express heightened excitement through the expressive limits of her *Oh, shut up.*
Barely rotating his torso, Einstadt peeked over his shoulder. He
turned back to Kelch. "She's been in a pickle a long time herself."

"Yeah right, a pickle jar."

Nothing.

"You know, a pickle jar of liquor."

Einstadt's smile seemed unconvinced. The guy had no sense of
humor, Kelch thought, just like his, Kelch's, mother. Kelch's body,
a paper bag of chestnuts, rested unevenly in the chair, and he finished the beer, save a teaspoon of backwash, in a final gulp. "I'm
tired of arguing with people about all this shit when they don't even
know what happened. I mean, doesn't anyone in the whole world
want to hear *my* side of the story? Or can anyone in this fucked-up
country just say anything about anyone and the whole world takes
his word for it."

"Well, time and chance happeneth to—"

"I mean, listen: why does the whole world have to gang up on
me? Am I such an evil guy all of the sudden that everyone feels like
they got a right to accuse me of shit I didn't even do? I'm no
different than anyone else in this fucking firm—in a lot of ways,
I'm better—and I don't see why they have to make me a poster boy
for *their* problems." His voice reset itself. "I'm an okay guy, right?"

"Sure."

"I don't try to hurt people?"

Shifting in his seat, as if he had seashells in his pocket, Einstadt hummed his accord.

"So does it make any sense whatsoever that every single person I know has taken this opportunity to jump down my neck like I killed someone, or that Freshler Feld can think of no greater problem for its management to deal with than trying to get me to quit or whatever the hell they're trying to do? Listen: I'm not a crybaby . . ." At both iterations of *crybaby*, Kelch swallowed at *cry*, for his ducts, on instruction, stretched, ready for the challenge. His eyes didn't wet, he was sure, but they were becoming increasingly untrustworthy. "But I didn't *do* anything." Leaning closer to the table, Kelch waited for Einstadt's ruling, the Dear Joel advice column response promised, from the first, by his eyes. When Einstadt said nothing, Kelch asked, pleading, "What should I do?"

"Do about what?" Einstadt rushed his answer, dispelling any suspicions that he had been inattentive, wandering.

"About *this*. About having my name slandered and my whole life ruined?"

"Seriously, I don't think that your whole life is . . . But, um, I guess, if it were me, I would ignore it and keep on working and assume that eventually it would go away if my performance remained strong."

"Exactly," Kelch blurted out, in enthusiasm. He slapped the empty glass back and forth between his hands. "You're so right about that. That's what you're supposed to do, what they *teach* you to do." But then he looked down again, a sad puppy. "But it doesn't work if the shitty-ass firm you're working for is suddenly so hungry to make an example out of someone, to put someone on a, I don't know, on a pedestal— No, not a pedestal, to put me in those lock things with the hands and . . ." Before he could move his arms into a full explanatory charade, Einstadt supplied *pillory*. "Yeah, when they're so eager to put me in the pillory to warn all you young guys that they won't let me do what's right."

Einstadt looked at his watch and, with his watched hand, cuffed his other wrist as though wrench-tightening a nut. He then grabbed the edges of his stool and backed away from the table ten inches. "Then I would just tell them."

"Tell them what?"

"Go to whoever is deciding, I guess, your fate, and list the reasons that you're not what this article has depicted you as being."

"Just go in and say, A, B, C, D, I'm not this, I'm not that?"

"That's a possibility."

"*Why?* It should be *obvious* to them."

"Well, obviously it isn't."

"You want to me *write* it out?"

"*I* don't want—" Einstadt swallowed the rest of the sentence. "That's one way, I suppose."

"I could— Listen: it's not that complicated, the differences, I mean. This guy Scott is, well, fine, he looks like me, or he is me, or I don't know. I mean he got the physical description fine in his asshole way, but anyway, I'm not a racist, and I'm not a 'homophobe' or whatever, and I definitely don't disrespect women." Kelch lost his place. What exactly had Paul written? When Kelch had read the article, he hadn't been able to concentrate on the details, or maybe he had just rushed past the details, starving for the switchback, the star turn of the crucial *however* that never came. "And I'm not over-paid by any fair standard, and I'm not hollow or shallow"—he said *shollow*—"or whatever he's talking about. You would honestly think from the article that I'm Hitler or something."

Einstadt reached for his soda, not hurried but accelerating.

"You know, the stupidest thing about all this is that everyone, I bet, probably doesn't care about that stuff but is so worked up about how this guy supposedly 'exposed' Freshler Feld." Kelch, unusually, quoted with rabbit fingers. "But he didn't, and I shouldn't have to explain this to Tedeschi. This guy Galicia writes like he's a big expert on the Street, but I *know* him: he doesn't know the first thing about it. So it's just so out of control because if you read that article as your only source of information on research departments, you would think that all research analysts were just a bunch of overpaid whores, who spend all their day fudging their ratings so they can jerk off banking clients, and who, even if they *wanted* to pick a stock fairly, couldn't do it because they're too busy with stupid-ass marketing bullshit to add value—" Although Einstadt was visibly trying to repress it, his smile won. It was wider than Kelch had ever seen it and revealed two rows of perfectly set teeth. Kelch bit in his own lower lip, without intention, and stared at his fingernails. Then, without looking up, he smiled begrudgingly too. "Okay, the prick's right about some things." And they both laughed.

As Einstadt laughed again, shaking his head to a private encore, Kelch reached for his beer. The glass was almost empty, and he inserted, it seemed, his whole face into it. His tongue exited downward and mopped the glass's side. The interior was sealed and inodorous, and Kelch breathed in harder through his nose, railing against the glass-seal, trying to vacuum a smell, any smell, out of the tightfisted aquarium. A drop, a dewdrop, of beer drew into his nose.

Kelch set the glass down, coughing, snorting. He held both hands over his face, and he leaned his sharpened elbows against the table. And through the teepee door of his hands, he said it. Einstadt asked for clarification, and Kelch said it again, but even more quietly, indirected, a prayer rising smokelike into the cathedral's dome. The world was more abscess than access; the dark behind the curtain was a projection of the unlit mystery beneath the floor.

But this—*this*—was really happening.

"I can't hear what you're . . ." Einstadt pressed.

Kelch slid his hands off his face. He said it again: "It's me, isn't it?"

"What?"

"It's me. Scott, he's me." Kelch interrupted Einstadt as he was about to respond. "Listen: I don't mean he's me totally, but I mean, professionally, that's what I do, that's what we all do. And so why wouldn't I be Scott?"

"Chris, everyone knows that analysts aren't perfect, but I think most people would be surprised—"

Kelch didn't know why Einstadt was talking. "Just listen, okay: obviously, I'm so mad because he got it right. I mean, aren't we all paid a ridiculous amount of money?"

"I think you're missing the point—"

Kelch slammed his voice against Einstadt's obstinacy. "I'm not missing any fucking point, okay. Listen: I don't know if I'm him or he's me, or whatever—I'm not going down that road anymore—but I do know two things. A: obviously there is some truth in that article"—*why didn't I figure that out before*—"and B . . ." Einstadt's fingers stood athwart his lips, like scissors shears. Kelch tried to continue, "I don't even know what B is. No, I do. B is, I'm a bubble."

"And that means . . ."

"What do you think it means? It means, I'm a bubble. I'm valued—overvalued—I don't know, by irrational exuberance. You know exactly what it means."

Einstadt placed his hands on his arched lower back. "I'm not sure you really believe that."

Kelch considered. "Of course I believe it. I'm a bubble." *That's exactly it.* His loosening chest, he then suspected, was the better feeling he had sought.

"I know it's fun, maybe even healthy, to beat yourself up, but it isn't going to help—"

"Do you think I'm doing this because it's *fun*? Do you think that I'm the kind of guy who beats myself up? Where do you get off even— You don't even *know* me."

With both hands on the stool, Einstadt backed up farther, a clear, afriendly threat of departure, but his eyes were still as empathetically blue, still as cursed: how could they ever be angry?

"I'm sorry," Kelch said in a puff. "But I don't see how you can prove to me that I'm not a bubble."

"How are you more of a bubble than anyone else?"

"Exactly." Kelch hit the table in emphasis. "Everyone on the Street is a bubble." Bubble: its shape inside its letters, its lifetime a moment of transience and beauty; it is an amoeba, transparent, like truth. "I'm just the unlucky asshole who got pricked."

Einstadt laughed. "That's fine, Chris, and I'll grant you that we're probably paid more than we're worth compared to a schoolteacher or some guy who has to work in a coal mine, but—"

"Exactly. Those people work hard. We don't work hard. We just put up with crap."

"None of that, though, is really all that relevant to your original question."

"Which is?"

"What you should do now."

"It's obvious what I should do now. I should go tell all these people to fuck off and find something better to do with my life."

"Come on . . ."

"No, listen: this is *bull*shit, and I don't have to be a part of it anymore." *Kersten, that stuff about a piece of ass was just stupid.* I said it, it was a joke, and I apologize. But it wasn't me. No, it was me. But there is a new me now.

"What are you going to do then?"

Do meant work, and work meant him, and him would be better defined, self-defined, a blossom of authenticity. The blossom was vague now, a bud, carnation-colored, but Kelch could sense it: it existed. "That's not the point, man."

Einstadt's eyelids descended over his pupils, most of the way, precluding any mixed messages from his eyes. "Chris, I really have to get back to the office."

Kelch looked past Einstadt. The woman at the bar was kneeling, wobblingly, on her stool, her head near the liquor well, either as an invitation to be spanked or in an unstealthy attempt to steal liquor. Her suitor's leer at her defenseless pumpkin indicated his suspicion of the former. Kelch looked at Einstadt. The bar was beginning to feel contagious, making everyone suspect that they were a loser. "Do whatever you want. I just want you to know that it's pretty obvious what I have to do now."

"I just don't think it's that cut and—"

"Listen: I've seen a little more of the Street than you have, and I can tell you—"

"How old do you think I am?"

"Huh?"

"No offense, but you keep talking to me like I'm a twenty-one-year-old kid." Einstadt had been in the department for two months; he was, Kelch had assumed, culturally if not actually a junior analyst. "For your information, I'm the same age as the rest of you. And just so you also know, I looked very hard at what else is out there, professionally speaking, when I left business school, and it's clear to me that you have a pretty sweet position at Freshler."

"But what's the use of having a position if you're a bubble?"

"Well, for financial security—"

"If you can't get up in the morning and respect who—"

"Because it's interesting—"

"Then you're nothing, you're worthless—"

"Because it's challenging—"

"And I don't want to be—"

"Because . . ." When Einstadt gave Kelch the finger, Kelch clamped down the last of his own wide-elbowed words, which had been knocking aside, he thought, Einstadt's arguments. When Einstadt gave him the finger, Kelch decided to storm out of the bar, letting Einstadt know how he insisted on being treated, but Kelch, his heart still calculating its vengeance, then realized that Einstadt was holding up the next-digit neighbor. With his other hand, Einstadt was pointing to the platinum band.

"Oh" was all Kelch said.

"I mean, from what I hear, you're pretty serious about your girlfriend." *You don't know her. This isn't about her.* "So I assume that you have to put these things into—"

"Man, if you're stuck, you're stuck." It hit Kelch then: he wasn't stuck. He could be whatever he wanted in the world. He could have whomever he wanted by his side. Kelch's whole hands, finlike, aimed at Einstadt's ring. "But *I* don't have to sit here and have people laugh at me. Not for all the financial security in the world."

"Chris, I don't think—"

"Listen: something is either bullshit or it's not bullshit. And all this stuff here, the damned securities industry"—said in a highbrow, overdelicate mock—"is bullshit." Kelch bent his neck back radically and tried to coax the glass's condensation down his throat. "I mean, some stupid nineteen-year-old college kid who day-trades instead of going to class, that's bullshit. For everyone to pat him on the back on how clever he is, that's bullshit. And for him to make an assload of money doing it, that's even more bullshit. And for some second-year associate in investment banking to be making, I don't know, two hundred and fifty thousand dollars a year to put together pitch books or whatever—not even that, to oversee a bunch of junior analysts putting them together—I mean, *come on*. That's a fifty-thousand-dollar-a-year job. It's called being a clerk. It's just bullshit, the whole world we're in. And if you have to do it because you're married, well then I feel sorry for you. But I don't. I am—I was—a completely overpaid jackass wasting money on bullshit, being paid a salary that I don't even need—or want. But that's not important anymore. Because— Listen: I can do something with my life where I can— I ought to be able to find—I am—" A suction just under Kelch's breastbone pulled his skin tight, and his pectorals were nudged inward, pursuing. It was the in-chest fist, and it had grabbed a handful of Kelch's subdermal fat and was trying, so it felt, to pull it through his body, to turn him inside out. It was Kelch's duty to resist. "I . . ." He rested his forehead high on the heel of his hand, and his fingers gripped his skull, as if testing a cantaloupe. "I . . . I'm not going to live like this anymore."

Kelch noticed Einstadt's sand-colored hand shyly making its way across the table, a day mouse out of the hole, but the hand retreated in recognition, apparently, of its inappropriate end. "Chris, if I can help . . ."

When you drive into Rockford from the interstate, the city's outer edge is fresh and clogged and all abloom. This is the city's good face, leaning sunward, for the world. Chain managers doubtless swagger when they regard the neighborhood they created, a land for giants, its electronics stores as big as ice rinks, its hardware stores as big as high schools, its everything-marts as big as skyscrapers reclining on the ground. Every year, the rich store-soil spreads farther outward. That is the only direction possible, for the marts hit infertile land in the other direction, at the old outer edge, whose covered malls are without anchors and whose strip malls pray to hang on to their deep-discount stores. Supermarkets are window-boarded, parking lots are empty, the mall survivors seem half-stocked, and liquor is sold where men used to buy pants. Tanning salons are everywhere. All this in the boom. Only thirty years ago, the mid-ring's malls and white-brick professional buildings poured champagne in victory over inconvenient, no-parking, stonework downtown. And downtown, twice-beaten downtown, is now a ghost land at midday, workdays, weekends; its factories, its offices have almost all moved to deep country. A few stores cycle through its streets to capture tax breaks, to defy business sense, but the landlords no longer bother to throw the For Rent signs away. So where those dapper Rockford working men used to buy suits, there is now municipal spackling for the city's punched heart—community centers, outplacement centers, centers for the arts.

"No, you don't understand," Kelch said, finally. He removed his hand from his forehead and examined his fingers. Worn-out, auto-convincing: "This is a good thing, don't you see? This is the best thing that has ever happened to me."

6

After Einstadt left, Kelch stayed, moderately startling himself with the decision to do so, apologizing to Einstadt that he needed another beer. *No, go ahead, thanks for hearing me out.* I don't think I actually helped— *Don't worry about it.* Kelch finished his second beer, determinedly and alone and mostly bored, and returned to the Freshler building, swinging his arms, a morning browser waiting for the stores to open. He did feel fine then: he knew that it was the right decision to leave the firm, leave that world, start anew where he was appreciated and priced right. He felt more than fine; he felt liberated from three days of torture and nonsense. People weren't made to go through things like that. Everything was settled.

Kelch reckoned that he should call Kersten right away and whisk her off to some small hotel on the New England coast and spend an entire week making love. But he felt an equal—maybe stronger— desire to disappear from Kersten forever, never calling her or dealing with her crap again. Yet the decision on Kersten—if it was even that—didn't seem difficult now; the answers would come, as his thoughts now were, like an unrushed brook, tinkling and lyrical. Even at his desk again, listening to a message telling him that Blue and Chuck Livin would be able to meet with him at seven A.M tomorrow as Joe Tedeschi had proposed, Kelch's thoughts were surprisingly spare and dim and disconnected, stars in the city sky, postcoital. How exactly, he asked himself, does one choose no bullshit? Or, more precisely, what are the mechanics involved in leaving the gilt strangle of Freshler Feld? Should he write a letter to Tedeschi, to Blue, call a press conference (Galicia, front row)? Should he sneak out under the cover of darkness, his office emptied of every file and paper clip, or should he leave the scene of the crime untouched, his indentation on his chair still warm? His forefinger traced the monitor's cracks, tentacles spinning out of a bull's-eye, and he fixed his eyes on the upper-lefthand tickers, his once dear universe now skewed and discolored. Right before the close, Allencor had fallen a point and a half, but Allencor, Kelch told himself, would no longer be an extra taste bud on his tongue, its daily performance tugging at his being. He was stripping himself of all those extraneous senses, those false fronts, and returning to what he was: just an ordinary guy who knows that there are more important things in this world than work and money and analyst rankings.

Four months ago, Buchalter had arranged a meeting between himself, Kelch, and Allencor's CEO on how Allencor could regain investor interest and trust after its earnings disappointment. Kelch had done most of the talking—he had prepared four critical points—and the CEO had taken occasional notes. When the meeting ended, the CEO told Kelch that it had been very, very helpful—two *verys*—and as Kelch and Buchalter left the CEO's office, Buchalter gave Kelch a wink. That feeling then, Kelch knew, was the kind of great that he could feel now, and it was the kind of great that he would feel again when he was finally freed of the bullshit, of this stupid job and this horrible business.

Swiveling in his chair, Kelch noticed, oddly pleased, how clean he was going to leave his office; the architects would give him an award for not sullying their next-century crispness with artwork or snapshots, for not delaying employee 25525's workstation replacement by 25526. There was nothing portable, nothing personal in view except, sitting modestly atop his cabinet, a dozen fruit-sized lucite tombstones commemorating deals. He clearly wasn't going to take those, although he had clasped the first one with a trophy winner's confused delight in the pleasure of the material itself. Kelch opened his junk drawer, where a disappointing treasure greeted him: a toothbrush and a deodorant stick, a birthday card from three years ago, delivery menus, to-all memos, and last year's rankings. Except for a few high-end pens that he had received from the companies in his universe, Kelch wanted nothing, he realized, from this place.

But as good as Kelch felt from his shoulders up, his legs felt swollen and girdled, heavy in pool water. They were lazy, indeterminate. They were not going to instigate anything just then.

Johann knocked on the open door and entered simultaneously. Staring at Kelch, he halted inside the doorway. Kelch wanted to stop time, regard his own face in a mirror, look for transformations. Johann fake-coughed. "I'm sorry if I'm interrupting, but I noticed that you were not in your office during the Allencor conference call, and I wanted to update you in case you did, in fact, miss it."

Kelch exhaled through every blowhole, emptied his body of air. "Sit down, Johann."

"Thank you." Johann smiled for a photographer, for a family picture, for a family he hated. "I am still not certain why Allencor closed down a point and a half, seeing that the numbers were in line with consensus. They reported—"

"They?"

"*It.*" Johann smiled the same again. "Allencor, specifically Renald, said—"

Could he, Kelch wondered, in a deep breath, simply walk out of the office, out of Freshler Feld and Johann's crap, into a sun-setting harbor, leaving no forwarding address, forgoing his last pay, letting the firm dangle in the wind. Could he, he wondered, tell Johann exactly what he was. "I don't care what Renald said, Joe-Hann."

"What?"

"I said, I don't care what Renald said, Joe-Hann."

"That is really funny, the way you say my name like that all the time."

"Cut it out, man. Just cut it out. Listen: we're not going to have to see each other anymore, so there's no need to get your last digs in, okay?"

"Why is that?"

"Because I'm leaving the firm."

Nothing.

"I said, I'm *leaving* the firm."

"Have you been let go?"

Kelch's chair suddenly straightened as if it shared a nervous system with his spine. "Why would you think I was 'let go'? Who even calls it—I mean, what would make you even—" Johann was poker-faced, Galicia-faced; he didn't respond. "I'm not an idiot, Johann. I know exactly why you think they would let me go, but let me clear one thing up: you have no fucking idea what you're talking about. That article had nothing—that article *has* nothing to do with me leaving."

"So what is going to happen to your sector?"

"How should I know what's going to happen to my sector?" When Kelch was a junior analyst, he also used to dream the Twenty-fifth Amendment daydream about what would happen to Veena's sector if she quit, died, was hired away. Tedeschi, Kelch fantasized, would of course have bestowed it upon him, already famous, heeded, and number one. And Kelch would have taken the ball and run. "I'm going and that's all you need to know."

"Why, may I ask?"

Why? "Because this firm is bullshit."

"Bullshit?" Johann crossed his legs and cupped his knee in his dovetailed hands. He had repeated the word as if its pastoral first half were gingerbread quaint.

"Yes, the firm—the whole research business—is just crap, Johann. And I'm not going to spend my life flogging shitty IPOs for the bankers or yelling about a bunch of stocks to salespeople who don't want to hear about them anyway. I'm sick and tired of the voice mails and the marketing. And I'm sick and tired of taking orders from Tedeschi and filling out stupid forms. I've got better things to do."

"Such as?"

"Don't be a prick, okay?"

"Perhaps I didn't phrase the question"—puckering—"perfectly, but I was only wondering what you plan to do now."

"That's none of your business."

"So I take it then that you do not have your next opportunity"—he broke the word into a thousand spiked syllables—"lined up. Or are you just unable to disclose it now?"

"I don't want to talk about this with you, Johann."

"I was just asking a question. There's no need to resent me."

"*Resent* you?"

"I just wanted to know where you were going?"

Kelch had decided—his new decision—that he would let nothing in the back of his mind or pulling at his ribs reverse his direction: he was feeling great. But as he and Johann faced off, an absence flashed in his intestines, the absence of Freshler, the absence of what-doyoudo, and you, and you. The absence was ineffable—metaphysical?—but it was not the loss of God; it was the absence at the core of clean science, of the universe at pinpoint, and it was sown into the seams of his chest. His stomach convulsed—his brain was off—unsure of the intruder, unaware if it was native. He burped quietly to let out the gas of a scream, but it only inflamed the absence. Through gritted teeth, Kelch said the only words that could escape: "You're fired."

Johann grinned uneasily, as if he had missed the joke. "Excuse me?"

"You're fired, Johann. I, um— When I gave notice to Tedeschi, he asked me what he should do with you, and I told him that I would, um, fire you before I left."

A grin overstayed on his face. "That's not true."

"Who the fuck are you to tell me what's true and what's not true?"

"I know it's not true."

With rising confidence that he and Tedeschi had had this conversation, Kelch said, "Do you honestly believe that I don't have the authority to fire you or that I don't—wouldn't—want to do it?"

"But I talked to Weller last week about a trans—"

"A what?"

"A transfer."

"So you were sneaking behind my back?"

"As you would say, 'listen': clearly we do not get along, and I thought that it would be better for both of us if I worked for a different analyst."

How could a generation pass in a half decade? He and Nathanson and Torvil and the rest had been ambitious, for sure, but they had grown up loyal and patient, had absorbed the lessons of ladder climbing, of American hard work. But the bull market, the pretender revolution of youth and age, had spoiled useless the junior analysts coming up behind them. There was frantic demand in the market for college bright-boys with economics degrees, and the juniors now came into the firm scoffing at low rungs, inapplicable steps in the new era. A baby's first year sets the mold of its life, and the babies like Johann had been given everything at birth. "Were you trying to sink me?"

Johann sat on the edge of his chair, as if to leave. He appeared unaffected. "I think we should continue this discussion with other individuals present."

"You do, do you? I don't think you really get the picture here. You're fired."

"I find that difficult to believe."

"Why?"

"Well, I would think someone other than you would need to dismiss me, considering your, how should I phrase this, recent notoriety."

Kelch looked at his headset, but it rested sadly on his desk in a broken-limb crumple, and anyway, who could he call right now, who in fact could prove that he had the right to fire Johann? More so, who could actually do it in thirty-five seconds? No one, but Tedeschi, or Weller—yes, Weller. Inspired, Kelch rotated his punched-pixel monitor so that Johann could witness his own execution. He began typing. *As I talked about with Joe Tedeschi, I do not think Johann Hausen is working out at the firm, and he told me to contact you about firing*—Kelch reconsidered the casualness of the last words, backspaced, and, his fingers step-dancing, changed them to *procedures for dismissal.* Johann was still; he was watching, acting, Kelch was sure, as if he were calling a bluff. *Considering some recent examples of gross insubordination*—that may have been going too far, but Kelch forced himself on—*I think we should try to begin whatever procedures are necessary as soon as possible.* He addressed the e-mail to Weller, the department's chief operating officer, and his narrowing eyes delivered the message to Johann: who's bluffing now? He sent the message, and a brief shiver was overwhelmed by relief and giddiness and adrenaline, the suicide tying the rope knot.

Johann, ashen, stuttered, "I-I-I can't believe you did that."

"Well, believe it."

"But why?" Johann did not ask the question in his normal voice, whose every pause, whose very syntax, usually tried to add a score of years to his age. He asked it schoolboy.

"Because I can, Johann."

"I— There is no way that that is— I— There is no way that what you did is legal. It's not— There are rules about these kind of things."

"What? Are you going to call your daddy's lawyer?"

"You cannot— What are you talking about?"

"He's not going to bail you out of this."

"But I didn't do anything."

"You've been cruising for this since the first day you worked here."

"I am— This is intolerable."

"Trust me, Johann, net-net, this is probably the best thing that has ever happened to you in your life." Kelch set free a laugh. He felt generous, merciful, balloon light, and a little drunk. He would let nothing disturb him now, not Johann's crack about "recent notoriety," not that message about Blue, because what he had told Johann was the truest bit he knew: this was the best thing that had ever happened in either of their lives. They wouldn't have to deal with each other, with anything anymore.

A jet stream blew Kelch, almost uninterrupted, into Nathanson's office, and he didn't bother to knock as he swung gaily around the door frame, like around a lamppost in a musical. He shut the door behind him. "Okay, Nathanson, let's get this over with."

"Can't you see I'm on the phone?" Nathanson spat, covering his headset's mouthpiece with his hand. Kelch couldn't recall if Nathanson had been sitting that way—crouched, shoulders in, machinating—when he came into the office.

"I don't care. We're going to have this out right now."

Nathanson spun his chair away from Kelch, garbled something into the phone, and set it down. "That was an important client, asshole."

"I said we're going to have this out right now." Kelch's heart was no longer beating a mournful, church-bell plod; it was beating music, the feel of music, a bypass into mood, and Kelch was riding a vital bop rhythm that had brought him from strength to strength, as Veena would say. His mood celebrated its inverse: he was not reiterating a buy on Tee-Fog because Buchalter had pressured him to do so; he was not shaving numbers off a model to sneak his estimates into consensus. He was being a Dan, stripping off the nonsense and skipping naked through the glen.

"At least sit down." Nathanson's feature-filled face contorted. "You're making me nervous hovering over me all the time."

Kelch complied. His mission was still coalescing, but it was clear that he needed to demonstrate to Nathanson that everything was perfect and natural and good. "I just have two things to say to you, Nathanson, and then I'm going to leave. A: you're not going to be seeing me around here anymore. And B . . . Never mind."

"What?"

"I changed my mind. I can do that now because I'm through arguing with you and everyone else here about the color of paint on the wall."

"We both know what this is about, Christine. So you should probably be a little more subtle with your displacement."

When he was talking—through talking—with Johann, Kelch

had seen Johann, for the first time, as an exaggeration of Nathanson, or maybe a Nathanson in training. "You are a small miserable guy, Adam." Kelch stopped; that didn't seem the best way to begin sharing his new, deeper appreciation for life. But he continued anyway. "You and everyone here are so proud of yourselves and your salaries and your 'power,' and you, particularly you, couldn't even imagine"—he stretched *imagine,* taffylike—"working for a company that actually makes something, and you complain about every minor administrative inconvenience as if you're not being paid enough to put up with ten times the crap. And what's more, what's more is that you actually believe that if the world were fair, you'd be making three million a year. That's the problem with you, Adam: your fucked-up belief that you always deserve more." As Nathanson glared at him, Kelch prayed for a smoother ribbon of words and more moisture for his throat. "But it's all a scam, don't you see? If Freshler Feld didn't exist, the other banks would pick up the slack without anyone noticing a thing. I mean, do we really do anything so unique—or even that difficult—in an IPO that we deserve seven percent of the gross? We're in the least price competitive industry in the world. But you don't care because you're so much 'smarter' than everyone else, right? Smarter than all those idiot companies who need to go public or whatever, or all those idiots out there buying mutual funds or, God forbid, putting their 401(k) money in equities. And so you *deserve* more than everyone else and deserve to eat hundred-dollar dinners like it was nothing and to never be bored or inconvenienced. This whole thing's like a tax by arrogant New York pricks on the rest of the country because you all think you're the smartest people around."

Kelch expected—now needed—Nathanson to interrupt him, or even for Nathanson's eyes to demand an estimated time of conclusion, but Nathanson continued to offer nothing but a medical, dissecting glare. "But you know what, that's not even my point. . . . My point is that you're such an argumentative jerk and that being such a contrarian fucker is going to come back to haunt you because it's all linked together, you see . . ." As Kelch turned the sharp rhetorical corner, he couldn't see the links himself, but he sped up, assuming that if it was a tight fit, it would be better to take it fast. "This business and being 'smart' and you being such a miserable prick." He paused and then, *Yes*. "That's it, you see, listen: if you don't take every opportunity in the day to try and prove how smart you are or how much smarter you are than everyone else, then you might actually start doubting that you're so smart, and if you're not as smart as you think, so *deserving* because you're smart, then you don't deserve any of this, right? Because the only reason you claim, you can claim, that you're *entitled* to all the money and benefits is that this is a 'meritocracy' and because you're smart, you have all the merit."

Nathanson clapped in slow time, his hands hitting each other in the sweet spot, resonating; Kelch understood that Nathanson's clap was borrowed, sneering, from the movies. "That was a very moving speech, Martin Luther King. Probably the most words that ever came out of your mouth at one time, too. I was worried that you weren't going to be able to tie it all together at the end, but no, you managed even that."

"Don't be a prick."

"*I'm* not supposed to be a prick? You're the one who decided at seven"—Nathanson checked his watch—"seven-eighteen on a Thursday night to delineate all my faults—"

"I'm just telling it like it is once in my life."

"I'm just a little confused, Kelch. You never before felt the need to express your theories about the deep sociopathologies of the securities industry. But now when everyone in the firm thinks you're a jackass because of that article, you—what, coincidentally?—change your mind on everything you've done for six years. It's a little transparent, isn't it?"

"It doesn't matter to me what you think."

Nathanson rotated his chair toward his computer and began to type. Only one eye, only briefly, glanced back at Kelch. "You know what, Kelch, thanks for stopping by."

Kelch gulped at his dry throat. "That's all you have to say to me?"

"I've told you a million times that I'd be more than happy to talk to you about whatever problems you had or have. I know I may be a 'small mis-ra-ble guy,' but I think I've been helpful once or twice in your life." The referents had been visible the whole time, just under the iced surface of Kelch's memory. "But if you came in here just to insult me, I don't think I'm required to sit here and listen."

No one could hurt him, Kelch thought. He had shed his false skins; his armor was authenticity. "You really can't help being a prick, can you, Nathanson? Well, just so you know, Tedeschi didn't do anything to me, so your little plan was ruined."

Nathanson shook his head, disappointed. "Do you honestly think I have anything to do with any of this?"

"Listen, Adam: I know what you did, but I don't care anymore. Because, you see, I've accepted that I'm Scott so it doesn't—"

"You're kidding, right?"

"Why would I be kidding?" Chris Kelch now told it like it was, and carefully, confessional, he told it. "Net-net, I admit the article wasn't that far off."

"Please, Kelch, if I was ever nice to you for a single second in your entire life, pay me back now by admitting that you're joking."

"What, Adam? You argue all the time that the sell side is on its way to total extinction as the buy side consolidates. I never believed you before, but maybe when people put things on paper, it makes things clearer. That this is all bullshit."

"I don't know what you're quoting as to what I may or may not have said, but I just want to confirm that you hand-on-the-Bible believe that everything you have been doing for six years is 'bullshit.'"

"Yes."

"That all the salespeople, the clients, the bankers, my God, could do their job without you because what you do is bullshit? That in six years, you've never done anything productive for—and I can barely believe this number—a half million dollars a year?"

The theater in Kelch's chest threatened to perform again. *Half million dollars* was sharp pointed, refluxing; even worse, it was material. There existed the panic of absence—the panic heightened by the din of the soul's own babbling—and there existed the panic of presence, of the puzzle's conclusion bringing its own end. He could not confront the half million dollars or even think about the half million dollars, nor of whose side or what side. By choice now, he didn't remember the way she would look up to him, into him sometimes, her eyes besotted, figuratively, literally, like the time outside the restaurant, the night they met Paul. "I'm not even talking about the criticisms of research. I'm saying that I'm Scott, you know, the person." He wondered, briefly, if he had switched things around.

"Did you even read the article?"

"Huh?"

"The fact that you're saying what you're saying seems so totally absurd to me that I can't believe that you actually read it."

"Why would you say that?" Kelch had more eaten the article than read it, devoured the words' intention—and on the airplane from Boston, the words' hot pins had pricked his eyes, popped his ears with white noise. Kelch could still feel the memory of that reaction, but he had recast it, in his recent mood, as the physiological response of confronting one's true self.

"Because if you actually read it, there would be absolutely no way that you could sit here smiling about being the subject of what is indisputably a character assassination."

"That's not what it is at all."

Nathanson pushed his chair back, and his head disappeared under his desk. Kelch heard a zipper open, and Nathanson then jack-in-the-boxed up, rising above his point of descent. His tight crab-apple cheeks had reddened at their tips. He laid the magazine, its cover crinkled, on the desk and opened it. Kelch noticed pen scratches around two or three passages; Nathanson famously claimed that he never needed to take notes. "Do I need to do this?"

"Do what?"

"Prove to you that this article is nothing to be proud of."

"I didn't say that I was proud of anything. I just said that I wasn't going to hide from it anymore." This was all very clear.

Nathanson shouted, his voice pinched, "You should hide from it. Because this, this, this isn't even you." From their locked eyes, it appeared that neither of them knew if Nathanson had barked this because he believed it, because of their friendship, or because to hold one's head high as a contrarian demanded a total commitment to disagreement, even when it was inopportune. Nathanson did not hint at a likely reason. Instead, he mumbled, "Never mind," and began the prosecution. "You don't mind 'so much power rests in someone so average'?"

I'm not going to play this game, you prick.

"Or well, the physical description: 'totally unremarkable good looking.' I mean, how— Actually, I always thought you were at least moderately unremarkable good looking." They both smiled lightly, an agreed time-out, and Nathanson inhaled before resuming the case. "Okay, here: 'almost proudly unreflective,' or this: 'his mind literally shut off.' None of this offends you?"

Those are just words.

"Or this, the whole T. S. Eliot thing. What a pretentious fuck. Does he really think he's profound just 'cause he's got a Bartlett's? Or here: 'calculated obliviousness and' . . . Or . . . Wait, no, that isn't about Scott." He flipped forward four pages and backed up one. "Here it is. 'Scott was born and raised . . .' This is the part where the asshole does his tremendous job of protecting your anonymity by revealing every known fact about your life." Kelch didn't smile again: his inaction was a shield against Nathanson's seduction. "Here we go. 'He is strikingly homophobic.' 'He descends occasionally into low-grade racist grumbling about "reverse discrimination." ' And this one, I don't even know where he got this from: 'He is a heavy drinker.' And the great one: 'He is disrespectful to women.' I'm sure Kersten loved that line."

Don't talk about Kersten. I don't want to talk about Kersten.

"I mean, none of this bothers you? Or here: 'I could locate no guideposts to his inner life, to *any* inner life, other than a vague devotion to personal happiness.' With italics even on *any*." Nathanson read from the next page. "Or what about here, where he lists all your juvenile qualities. That you have no interest in books or politics or, right, 'metaphysics.' What a pompous fuck." Looking up from the magazine: "You're telling me that none of these descriptions strike you as things that, maybe just a little, tiny bit, one should not be eager to claim as one's identifying characteristics."

I don't care what's in that magazine. I don't care about stupid words anymore, about talking, twisting, reading. Kelch felt as if he were on a dock, watching, powerless and disconnected, workers untying a boat—his mood—everything being good and fine and settled—so that it could leave without him. He couldn't change his mind again.

"Are you awake there, Kelch? Or are you just going to— Wait, here he says you're *not* a below-average analyst. Maybe that's why you've forgiven him." He turned to the final page. "Or here, the overwritten conclusion—"

Kelch put a stop to Nathanson's performance. "None of that matters because I've lost a lot of illusions."

"Alottova—a lot of illusions? Where are you *getting* this stuff, Kelch?"

"Adam, I'm comfortable now with who I am." This was what he should have said from the beginning. It was bad strategy to bait Nathanson.

"You're comfortable—let me paraphrase the article for you— you're comfortable being a totally reprehensible, lobotomized, computerized corporate bureaucrat with a dead soul—a *functionary* who doesn't read, doesn't think, doesn't care about anything but making money and serving your masters and being 'happy'?"

"But that's not me."

"You just said, and I quote"—Nathanson had been edging into a scream, but he backtracked—"and I quote, 'Adam, I'm comfortable now with who I am.'"

"So?"

"How do you reconcile your sudden comfort with who you are with a *description* of who you are that sums up your entire person as 'pathetic'?"

"Because I've changed."

"Since I saw you this afternoon, asshole?"

"Let me finish, okay. I realized that this job has taken its toll on me and that I'm a bubble, and that if this job isn't good for me, it's bad."

"So the world's that simple, huh? I cannot believe that I hadn't figured it out before."

Kelch's heart moved up one gear. "I don't know anything about the world, but I know that I'm at peace with myself now."

Nathanson's feature-jammed face transformed into a set table; his eyes, his mouth, his head were all round circles, dinner plates. "Kelch, I've worked with you, I've hung out with you, I've been friendly with you for six years now. And I never imagined that crap like 'I'm at peace with myself' could have ever, *ever* come out of your mouth." He paused. "So what are you going to do now, mahatma?"

"I can do anything I want." It was true: if he was free, free was he.

"No, you can't. You have to do something to pay the rent. Are you, after your big speech, going to go back to Rockwell and take a job on some line that pays, what, four hundred and fifty thousand dollars less than you're making now? You might have to make adjustments to your lifestyle, pal. Just a few small ones."

Kelch spoke slowly. He had sandbagged the levy against leaks into the binary. "That's not important anymore because whatever I decide to do won't be unfair and bullshit like this place."

"'Unfair' and 'bullshit'?" Nathanson read back the two words missed in the dictation's first pass.

"Just forget it."

Nathanson had sat erect again in his chair, and his voice now returned to a simmer. "Do you have any idea what kind of jobs are out there, Kelch?"

"Do you?"

"I thank God every day that I haven't had to work outside finance. Working here is intolerable enough. But clearly this firm has pumped you up with such an inflated sense of your own worth that even when you accuse it of sins unequaled in the history of mankind, you still think you're Superman."

"Listen—"

"No, you listen to me. I guarantee—and I have never been more sure of anything in my entire life—that if you walk out of here, you're going to wake up tomorrow and realize that you've made the biggest mistake of your life."

Kelch refused to be lassoed by Nathanson's verbal ropes, to find his newly acquired mood stitched and constricted into a jacket too small. There would be no regrets because regrets meant the old mood, that cast-aside world. He said—the best defense—"I think you're taking this personally because you saw things in that article that were true about you."

"About me?"

"Yes." Kelch's grin was sponsored by his ease of delivery, and his body remembered, explicitly, the escalator of defeating Paul, every second's elevation granting a higher virtue. "The reason you're so upset is that while I accept that I'm Scott, you can't accept that you're him too."

Nathanson, it seemed, was tiring. "Okay."

"What does that mean?"

"It means I'm trying not to have to tell you again that you're a fucking idiot. That article has to do with one person and one person only—you."

Why couldn't they just stop, Kelch thought. Why did everyone have to dip their fingertips in the critic's acid fingerbowl to explore, to expose, to poke into one another's weaknesses? Every day in the department, every analyst shouted that he had had enough, that no amount of money was worth the aggravation. Kelch was the only one brave enough to do something about it. He tried to communicate this: "You don't know what you're talking about."

"I'm through." Nathanson's left hand chopped in an old man's ancestral dismissal. He turned to the computer screen and switched programs, letting the new application absorb him. "Good-bye, Kelch. As they say in your part of the world, So long, been good to know you."

Kelch smiled. *My* part of the world? Nathanson's ignorances were all connected. Manhattan island, in the real country, was a pimple, not a nose. "I've never seen you give up so easily before."

Nathanson didn't turn to Kelch. "Good-bye."

Kelch backed up his chair and balanced his hands on the armrest, as on a pommel horse. But before he lifted himself, he concluded, "It's just a little disappointing seeing you, you know, so unlike yourself."

Nathanson swung his head sharply at Kelch. Kelch watched a scowl, on a large screen, in close focus, twist itself around the explosion of words: "I'm trying to spare your feelings, you idiot. I'm trying to avoid telling you that the reason everyone at this firm thinks you're an asshole is because Scott, whom you are suddenly so proud to be, is such a one-dimensional empty loser that it's difficult to even read about him without being painfully embarrassed for you. I don't think you understand any of this. And do you want to know why? Because the article is right. You really are pathetic."

Kelch was dancing along a cliff edge, in frolic, with speed and bounce, his stomach a churning tank of gasoline. The feeling wasn't—couldn't be—unease or heartsickness or fear: he had made a brave decision. "That's just crap and you know it."

Nathanson, shifting his chair loudly, focused again on his computer. "You know what? I'm through with you. Have a nice time at the ashram."

"I bet what you're the most disappointed about is that because I don't care anymore I ruined whatever plans you and Tedeschi were cooking up."

Nathanson exhaled loudly. "What new fantasy of yours are you talking about now?"

"Your little conspiracy with Tedeschi when I caught you in his office."

Yelling, livid: "I was *defending* you, you dumb fucker. Tedeschi asked me what I thought, and I told him—and God how I wish I hadn't—that I was sure that the article would not affect your performance. I told him—and what a jackass I was—that I thought it would all probably wash away in a month or two. And this"—he held up one finger—"is the fucking thanks I get."

"You can never be wrong, can you?"

"Get out." As Nathanson stood up, his chair was hurled back, crashing against his cabinets. His unbent arm pointed to the door. "Get out of my office now."

Kelch stood up too. He offered Nathanson a generous final handshake, one granting that the six years were over but they weren't all a waste. He had come from Evanston without close friends.

Nathanson didn't move.

"You're not even going to shake my hand?"

"Get the hell out of here now."

Kelch's walk back to his office was more parole than death row, and he thought of Dan. Or, he talked to Dan. *Did you hear that guy, Dan?* Yeah, I thought you were filled with shit, but he really takes the cake. *Now you know what I put up with for six years.* I told Heath' that I thought you were goddamned nuts for ever living there and hanging out with those stuck-up losers. *Well, don't worry, it's over now.*

Kelch's smile was real but only eye-shown, and he congratulated himself airily for the pain he would never have to experience again. He would never have to write a maintenance note filled with nothing about a nothing quarter just so his clients wouldn't think he was asleep. He would never have to sit in a room as some aggressive fund manager grilled him about Tee-Fog or Allencor as if he ran the company himself. He would never have to work all day Saturday, all day Sunday, to put out some statistical because it looked good when Tedeschi counted total pages for the year. He would never have to daydream that Buchalter might single him out at a closing dinner (again) for being "essential" to some stupid deal, and he would never have to hear cynical salespeople tittering at a recommendation because it was a Freshler deal. His list of nevers was literally infinite, skyspace; the daily compromises—the phrase appeared, but not its source—were the molecules of his existence, and he could no more count them than count his blood. To shed all those compromises was not a reconstruction, a new carburetor, new tires, but new threads on every bolt, new coke in the steel. Kelch's favorite nevers were right there in the department: never biting his tongue again before Veena, never arguing with Nathanson. Nathanson was smart, Kelch allowed, but he was farsighted by his big brain. For Scott was Kelch, yes, but a former condition of Kelch, of *Chris*. How could Kelch in that condition have read books or studied music or art or anything like that? How could he have followed politics—how could he have worried about God? Those hobbies take time, take energy, and Freshler Feld was a jealous force, trading jewels for joules, leaving its gears exhausted. The firm was at fault, but now that he was severing his cord, he would be able to begin again. This was a brave decision.

I tell you, Dan, it's good to be getting out of this place. Maybe now you can get a real job. *I was thinking the same thing.* If you want, I'll ask some people around here. *You bet.* Hey, you're finally talking normal again.

As Kelch sat, he realized that this was the bookend: he had swiveled the same playful way three years ago when the office became his. He decided now to pocket the best pens—they were his, after all—but he was not, just yet, ready to stand. Maybe he needed a cake, a conference-room farewell, to prove that he was free to go: great to know you, best of luck, keep in touch. Maybe it was Nathanson; Kelch was sure that he, Kelch, had won the last word, but he couldn't swear to it; the conversation had bunched at the end. He wasn't, improbably, angry at Nathanson now, or even that interested in him. Everything Nathanson had said was off track. The article—Scott—wasn't all that hard to understand. Kelch wasn't a one-dimensional loser. He didn't have very, very serious problems. He only had opportunities. It was clear that— It was clear— It—

Kelch froze in his chair; he couldn't hear his heart, hear if he had a heart; he couldn't even hear the chatter of the cubicle range. He listened for an outside echo, a breeze, but none ever pierced Freshler's inner architecture.

What the fuck am I doing with my life?

In Rockford, at this time, in the summers, in Kelch's yellow-haired boyhood, his dinner would have long been over—at six, the pizza or macaroni was already on the table; at six-fifteen, it was gone—and Kelch would have been in a neighbor's driveway or in the schoolyard for two more hours of playtime. And in his boy's own truth, he knew then that those gifts of temperate summer dusk meant that he would live forever.

"Hi, it's me."

"Christopher, what a nice surprise." Kelch could feel her suddenly brighten through the phone. The day had been made memorable by his call. Since she had married Bill, her face had smoothed and puffed; even her teeth seemed cleaner. Heather hypothesized that she had gotten meatier because she had never eaten right when Heather and Chris were kids. Kelch thought it was because nowadays, at least occasionally, she tried to stop smoking. "Are you still there?"

"Yeah, sorry."

"I was thinking of calling you, but I didn't want to bother you at work." He heard her lighter's spinning click. "It's not so important, I know, but I talked to Father Graham, and he is much calmer than he was on Tuesday. The Wulle Trust is still up significantly for the year, and he is confident that Tee-Fog is going to re-bounce."

"That's really wonderful."

"It is sort of wonderful, isn't it?" She paused, it seemed, to check her notes. "Anyway, so how's everything there?"

Nothing.

"Christopher, is there something wrong with the connection? I can't hardly hear you." She said this rapidly, as if on a pay phone, running out of change.

"There's nothing wrong with the connection."

"You should see the weather here. Rockford may not be much when you live in New York, but you'd have a hard time finding a place with a nicer spring."

"Mom."

"Yes."

"I'm quitting Freshler Feld."

Nothing.

"Are you still there?"

"Oh, uh— Oh, I just needed to catch my breath."

He heard her catch it with a long drag, and he was astonished, again, that this woman had anything to do with him. She must have been nonmaterial, his birth a one-time item.

This conversation had a single goal of a single sentence. Kelch knew it already, of course, but he just wanted her—anyone really, but disappointingly, there were no alternatives—to say it. "Today's my last day here."

"Did you get . . . Oh God, is there something wrong?" Her voice wasn't exactly curious; it seemed staticky, searching for the right station of words.

"No, I'm just tired of it, okay."

"But, oh, um, but you always told me how much you loved it."

Had he told her that? Had he loved it? Or had he just been blinded by the six figures, by the suits, by seeing his name immortalized in the *Journal*, by his sham cool superiority over everyone in Rockford, even more satisfying because he never let it show. But this wasn't the topic. And he used to feel great. "That's history, okay. And I sure in the hell never loved it." He looked under his desk, then behind his chair; he had forgotten, it felt, to pack something in his case.

"Oh."

"That's all you can say?"

"What is that, I didn't—"

"All you can say is, Oh."

"Well, it just seems so sudden, I mean, nothing *bad*"—she drew out the word, lambish—"has happened to you . . ."

"Only good things have ever happened to me in my whole life."

"I know that but . . ."

Nothing.

"Chris?"

"Yes."

"Well, what are you going to do for, uh, a living?"

"What does that have to do with anything?"

"A person has to work, right?"

Yes, he thought, I have to work, but I also have to live, I also have to accept that God or whoever didn't put me on this earth so I could make halfhearted recommendations about stupid-ass stocks. Kelch had once been proud of what he had done in his life, of his conquest, in his small way, of New York. And he recognized now that there was no option of going back to Rockford, of putting up with this every day, of being suffocated and smothered by her interest, by her stupid ideal of a closer son, by her understanding everything he said, in poor translation, at sixty percent. He hated her just then. He just needed one sentence, damnit, and then he could get off the phone.

"Are you still there, Chris?"

"I find it hard to believe that you can't be more supportive."

"Oh, but, oh—I've, I've been supportive of you every day—"

Why couldn't she just yell back? Why couldn't they ever break through their brick wall of nervous chitchat, of empty calories? "Yeah, until I want to stop organizing my whole life around making money."

"I only asked for . . . I only asked you why, oh, you were quitting. It, you know, it's a big decision, and I'm your mother, and I am just *interested* in your life and . . . I am not . . . I am not"—repeated, apparently, for herself—"judging you."

Nothing.

"Have you talked this over with Kersten or with Joe Tedeschi?"

"That"—*Joe*—"just proves that you don't know anything about me."

"Christopher, where is this coming from?" He could hear her fumbling through her purse to find another cigarette. She never left a pack out in the open; that, she claimed, only encouraged her to smoke. "I mean, have *I* done something—?"

"This has nothing to do with you 'doing' something. This has to do with a curious fact that your attitude is A: one thing when I'm a big Wall Street hotshot and B: another thing when I want to do something that's not about money." Kelch listened for her response, but he could hear only an obscure rattle, a low arthritic clapping of phone against ear. He also thought he could hear Bill calling from another room. "Are you listening to me?"

"Oh God, I still don't understand."

His voice leaped higher. "Stop saying that. What's not to understand? My whole life I've been doing things because other people told me to or to please other people or to impress other people, and I've finally decided that I'm only going to do things for myself from now on. I'm not doing anything for you or for Heather or for fu— Joe Tedeschi."

"Fine."

"No, listen: I'm sick of it. I'm sick of being told what to do."

"Fine," she pleaded again.

"*Listen*: I'm starting over from square one, and I'm going to do things for the right reason, and I'm never going to do anything again because you want me to." He had made a decision. He had a right to its rewards.

The phone soft-rattled again, a paper wind chime. "What have I ever wanted you to do?"

"Just forget it, okay. I don't want to talk about it anymore."

"Christopher, this is all so— I mean, I don't know." She stopped, inhaled. "I want you to know that I really do support you, however you want to make a living."

"That's exactly the crap I'm talking about, Mom. Why do I have to do anything for a living? Why can't I just live the way I want to live?" He reclined his chair and stretched his legs to their limit.

The purse opened again in the background. "That's fine, Christopher. Okay, um, no one doesn't want you to live the way you want to live."

"Don't agree with me just to agree with me."

"What do you want me to do?" She repeated the question inch by inch, as if hoping a long-roped bucket would reach the bottom of a well: "What do you want me to do?"

Nothing.

"Hello?"

"I want you to tell me that you approve?"

"Oh God. I've approved of everything you've ever done in your entire life."

Nothing.

"I swear, there is something wrong with this goddamned—this telephone. I can't hardly hear anything you say."

Kelch didn't notice his mother's change of tone. "So this is a good decision?"

"Whatever you want to do I believe is a good decision."

"But you're not saying that because, you know. You're saying that because you honestly think I'm doing the right thing?"

Her change of tone was canceled. "Of course."

Nothing was met by nothing, and Kelch rushed his departing words. His headset removed, his eyes shut, he pinched his nose high at the bridge. He diagnosed his mood: was this victory again? He had done everything that he had to do. Now he should be able to stand. Eyes open, he scooped his head forward, encouraging, it appeared, a flooded motor to start by bringing his ear closer to the engine's failing purr. Come on, come on. His neck whinnied up, urging his mood to rev, the mood that had once sounded the trumpets—great pulsing in his arteries—as he stood over Paul.

Why, he asked himself, did he have to get his mother to approve? In his entire life he had never agreed with anything she had said. For eighteen years—even before he could talk, probably—he could think of no better plan than getting out of Rockford (and no surer ticket than hard work). And so why had he needed that single goal, that single sentence from her, of all people?

Why hadn't he called Kersten?

Nauseated, he looked at the phone. A chill, as from a draft, spread under his skin. *A half million dollars*—who cared if she was offended? He cared if she was offended. He wanted her to be, obviously, or he would have called her by now. Kelch became lost, then, in enemy or friend, in loving her first or not loving her at all, in calling her to explain, for comfort, for agreement, or in running away from her, from *them*, from the stifling insistence on talking all the time, on sharing, on dwelling in the illogical slop of feelings. Why did it have to be so impossible?

But it wasn't, maybe. Maybe the answer was simple: if he was going to live his life differently now, then that's what he had to do.

Or maybe the practical concerns would decide. She would start crying if they talked about the half million dollars. She would insist that he tell her that he loved her again. She would repeat in her baby voice, I just needed to hear you say it. How could he stand it: stand to beg *her* for forgiveness—that was coming—when she, damnit, should have been begging him. It was her fault. He would have never hooked up with Paul if it wasn't for her, and so she deserved all the blame—or maybe the credit, because his life was going to be better. No, she deserved blame, because he would have found this out in his own damn time. Kelch on his own had discovered that life was not funny. He on his own had discovered that it could never be absurd. And so it was unimaginable to sit in a room and ask her for understanding and patience, to gulp in preface one last time before he assured her that he loved her. It made him sick to even consider it.

The thoughts multiprocessed through his mind, at light speed, but his mind was a riot, too much humanity, unstably at odds.

The Ghost must have had evidence.

It *was* a matter of evidence. The feeling now, when he was finally going to leave, was a matter of evidence, and not loving her was a matter of evidence, and knowing what was right was a matter of evidence. This required total commitment. This demanded cutting all ties. Only *afterward* would he be able to erupt from a bubble's womb, pushing up against a translucent rainbow, bathing for an instant in the soap-film skin, and emerge to dry in the stirring air of the world to come.

But she wanted nothing more than to love him. And if he couldn't—

He put on the headset, dialed most of her number, and posed in the mirror of the cracked monitor. The sensation now was clear. Christopher Kelch wouldn't wait for a feeling to descend upon him from some god who had never done anything for him; he would make his own freedom again, make himself happy and whole. In the world to come, Christopher Kelch would love from a position of strength, would love whom he loved with complete abandon, would be loved in return straight in the eyes. He would speak only from his sincerest heart, would not compromise for money, would not confuse money for success. In the world to come, Christopher Kelch would serve truth in his actions, and truth would fill him and own him and enbliss him and conquer every blood cell, every doubt, and redden every unbinary gray.

Insert a quarter here, for the world to come.

7

Kelch had been on this floor once before and had been surprised, that time, by the hush, an outdoor-loud quiet of muffled telephones and secretaries' efficient dispensation. The hush now was different: the peripheral noise had been stored away. The other time Kelch had been on Fifty-two—at Freshler, Fifty-two was a proper noun, a people-place-power, a Pentagon, a White House—he had delivered a preliminary report from Veena for a committee on gender diversity, which she, genderless in her own mind, had headed complainingly. That visit had been in the afternoon; it was now seven in the morning.

For the last two nights, Kelch hadn't slept well and hadn't slept long, nine hours at most in total. The compounding debt interest was now demanding its due.

Each office on this side of the floor was guarded by at least two desks, unprotected by cubicle walls. Four secretaries were already at their posts. Carpet to ceiling, true with the oak paneling, stainless steel arch shapes repeated themselves along the wide hallway like a foreshortened colonnade of a minimalist Arab bazaar. With everyone at Freshler, Kelch was an amateur geologist of office space, and another time, he would have noted that the conspicuous fallow on the hall side of the desks could have housed ten associates. But now he noted nothing. His inside was a Rockford winter, empty streeted, a frozen flat plain. His skin felt heavy.

Blue's secretary led Kelch past the boardroom, past the offices of Freshler's general counsel, CFO, and COO, until she reached Blue's corner. (The other side of Fifty-two barracked most of the big four's special assistants and the rump of the general counsel's staff—Blue's bodyguard kept close against liability and risk.) Three secretaries' desks, arranged in an L, stood beside Blue's closed door. There was no glass in it or on the connected arch-stamped wall: regardless of Blue's populist touch, he was not to be democratically observed.

Kelch did not see the man coming out of a door on the far side of the arch until the man was upon him. "Chris . . . Chuck Livin, Blue's chief of staff."

As Kelch watched his own hand rise to meet Livin's, a loud, meant-for-private yawn waved over his own responding "Hey." Kelch didn't think to excuse the yawn. He didn't think to stop to say, It's a little early for this, or It was a long, horrible night. He didn't consider confessing that this whole scene, to him, was not happening in a reality he could attest to. His fatigue, his surrender, his mistakes, the inertia not to come, another inertia overwhelming the first, the piercing judging silence of the cab driver that morning, all of it had clogged his ears and relegated every action to behind a linen drape.

Livin answered Kelch's yawn with an "Okay," the first syllable ladled up. He seemed to Kelch (vaguely) too handsome for that hour: his shirt's cuffs were in step with his coat's, his tie's knot was catalogue-perfect, his eyes and hair were unaccountably alert.

None of this was Kelch's idea. He only wanted to rest, lower his trail-weary saddle onto one of the two unfilled secretary's chairs, lay his beaten forehead onto his crossed arms, and sleep the deserved sleep of the damned.

You look exhausted, sweetie . . .

What—wh-what are you trying to say . . .

Look at me, fucking shit. Look at me . . .

I told you, I wouldn't—

Livin said, "Blue's just finishing up a conference call with Freshler Tanashi"—the firm's Japanese joint venture.

Kelch, as he answered, dimly recognized that he was being the straight man. "Now?"

"It's a twenty-four-hour job"—Livin smiled with a politician's facile intimacy—"in a twenty-four-hour world."

Gazing down at one of the unoccupied desks, Kelch rubbed his fingers against its light wooden top. He held open his eyes, consciously, as his tongue—it felt huge—stammered, "You know, I don't exactly know what, um...But I can save you the trouble because, you know—" Another yawn, full-bodied.

"Chris, we wouldn't meet with you if we didn't want to meet with you." And Livin smiled again, this time more cursory, more polite. Kelch nodded, dog-scratching the back of his hair. The secretary said something quickly to Livin in a private frequency. "Great," he replied, and with his open palm facing upward like a maître d's, he guided Kelch into Blue's office. Before he shut the door, he delivered, underbreath, further instructions to the secretary.

The office was not as movie-set as Kelch had imagined. (He had seen pictures of it before but blurry, as a background.) Yes, the wall of windows revealed a wide view of the harbor, its sight lines flying over the old financial district like a bird over the scrub, and yes, the square footage was probably three or four times Tedeschi's, but the office felt like a furniture showroom displaying the latest samples for the office-home of the future. (The future, it appeared, would be Californian.) On the walls, under the ceiling, the designers had installed accentuating arches two feet high. The room was separated into four quarters, all well coordinated in tawny wood and Freshler green. In the front left quarter of the office, eight seats waited erect around a glass table polished to a mirror. Behind the dining room set stood a living room set, a long off-white leather couch and two boxy, low leather chairs. Blue's painter's-pallet-shaped desk, its legs camouflaged by angles and light, floated, it seemed, over the entire back right quarter of the office. Two matching computer screens, flat and oversized, guarded the desk's far sideline. And in the front right quarter of the office, finger-thin seven-foot-wide shelves—shafts of tasteful yellow light built in—rose to the ceiling from a yard up. On them, exotic gifts from the foreign offices, deal plaques from Blue's youth, and awards for his exemplary citizenship asked politely to be observed. Below them was a counter, a sink, a squat silver refrigerator.

Kelch watched Blue walk back to his desk and sit down, holding a plate, and Kelch then noticed Freshler's standard meeting breakfast spread on the counter: the pulpy orange juice, the trio of leaning obelisk coffee pots, and pastries, muffins, bagels, and famed Freshler fruit (always in season, regardless of the season). "Help yourself to something to eat, Christopher." It sounded too casual to be an order. "Chuck will probably try to steer you to a doughnut, but there's some fruit there too. The oat muffins are exceptional." Livin didn't take any food on his way to the couch.

Kelch's legs were elms, his shoes, the unearthed topsides of deep-buried roots. His ability—his need—to run was canceled out by Blue's presence.

"If you're not going to eat, though, you might as well sit down." The head of Freshler Feld gestured to the chair, the only one in front of his desk, placed strangely left of center, as if a valet had precisely stagehanded the room for this meeting. Kelch, embarrassed to have to think to move, finally walked to the chair. Livin sat on the couch behind him. Blue could thus see both of them, staggered, in inverse perspective. Kelch had seen enough Mafia movies to know that Livin was sitting in the shooter's seat.

"Have you done much business with the Japanese, Christopher?" Kelch opened his mouth; he could answer that question. The firm had once sent him to market his universe to Japanese institutional investors; a not small minority of them had slept through his presentations; he had not been invited back. But Blue didn't wait for Kelch's stuck tongue. "Good people. Smart businesspeople. But tough to deal with." So sayeth the Lord, his forefinger emphasizing the triple point.

Kelch had meant to say, "I'm sure," but he suspected that he only grunted, if that. He was a twisted-about boxer, embracing the reassuring, warm tingle of the new punch.

"Have you been following this Tanashi mess in the papers?" Kelch had never heard of the Tanashi mess, but he grunted again, this time more possibly affirmative. He watched Blue's face subtly compress, but he couldn't even begin to decode its meaning: a smile, a chew—a sign to Livin? Blue touched a napkin to the corners of his mouth, folded the napkin twice, set it on the plate, and moved both to the side. Shifting slightly to his left, he picked up a neatly squared folder, the only loose item other than the plate on the bare runway of his desk. Kelch, saving his energy, didn't even bother to be surprised. Blue skimmed the contents of the folder's lead document, three pages, closely typed. He shut the file and placed it on the opposite side of the plate. He then interlaced his fingers at the center point of the cleared rectangle in front of him. "The Tanashi situation is interesting, but I only have twenty-five minutes to discuss our matter, and that obviously takes priority. After we talk, Chuck"—a schoolteacher's pause—"if we determine that it's necessary, can go over some of the finer points. He'll finally be able to put his law degree to use." Blue smiled, mostly in his eyes. Kelch forgot to. "I understand that you may find it unusual that I have taken a personal interest in this matter. However, I thought that I could administrate"—his mouth embodied *administrate*, his tone administrated *administrate*—"this issue much more effectively than the other proposed solutions." He smiled again, as an ending, not a beginning. "Considering your signed nondisclosure agreement, possible future action by either party, your whole issue has, or may yet have, the potential to cause unnecessary headaches for all involved. Freshler Feld is too busy of an organization for a sideshow like this. Is this all clear so far?"

"I-I-I." The stuttering seemed also a call for the lost. I. I. I.

"Yes or no?"

"Yes, but I—" Kelch cloudily imagined that he could administrate this issue in twenty-five seconds, not twenty-five minutes, by telling Blue that he had already quit, practically speaking. He didn't do it, not because he didn't think of the idea but because the idea rose in his throat, not in his mind. He had made so many decisions that there was no room to even consider another. In fact, he could only think now that the Blue Padaway here looked exactly like Blue Padaway. No worry lines or packed bags or anxious creases hid under his eyes; he was not shorter than you thought; a finger was not mysteriously missing; his shirttail did not live, like Tedeschi's, by its own rules. Kelch had seen Blue in the cafeteria twenty or so times over his six years—one time Blue had invited himself to a table two buttresses away from Kelch's. On three occasions, Kelch had received a famous Blue convocation, once to Kelch's group of new junior analysts, once to new associates, and once to newly minted VPs. (Someone in each audience had asked, Why are you called Blue? Each time, he had answered, with perfect timing, Have you ever been called Harold?)

Kelch had even been this close to Blue before—given the desk's breadth, maybe even closer—when Blue visited Forty-five to congratulate Hoder Leary as Hoder watched Tee-Fog's first trade cross on Freshler's systems. But Kelch would have assumed—again, if he could have assumed—that Blue, in his own private office, would have been different, looked different, removed of his wizard's ten-story mask. Kelch would have been wrong. Blue was fifty-six, but here, as always, he looked six years younger—the CEO's perfect age. He was oat muffins, never doughnuts: trim, beige-skinned (but not exactly tan), with a runner's black plastic watch, all confirming that he was energetic, vibrant, like the reinvigorated Freshler Feld under his command. But the fine gray strokes through his temple's hair, his long serious nose (uncurved, unethnic), his grown-up eyes reminded one that Freshler Feld had long been a player on the Street. Like Livin, Blue was wearing his suit coat, unusual at Freshler for internal meetings. And like Livin, each thread on Blue's clothing was accounted for, each stitch made for him. (Even Livin seemed made for him.)

Blue leaned forward, waiting for Kelch to finish. "You think you can what?"

"I mean, I'm not—"

"Not what?"

"Going to sue the firm or anything—"

Livin cleared his throat loudly from the shooter's seat. Blue raised his hand, a traffic sign, its heel remaining fixed to the desk. "Christopher, I cannot emphasize enough that this is not the place to discuss that. Again, Chuck and the people involved in this issue from our side will be happy to meet with anyone on your side after this meeting. But if we are going to handle this my way, as I have proposed over considerable objections, then you are going to have to be patient." Kelch nodded unclearly. "Great. I think, with that, my preliminaries are through. Do you have any other questions before I continue?"

Having questions required having thoughts, occupying space. But Kelch had no access to his interior: it had been rendered silent by a frosted opaque shell around him, a shell bulky and light like styrofoam but dense enough to filter out whatever it was that made the daily pings of existence make sense. "Huh?"

"Hold on a moment. Chuck, can you please get one of the women to come in here and clean up this mess." As Blue pointed to the landfill beside him—a clean plate, a folded napkin—his upper lip curled in minor revolted contemplation of the filth. Livin said that he would do it himself—clean it up himself—and as he brushed past Kelch with Blue's dirty plate, he betrayed no opinion of his task. "Thanks, Chuck. . . . Now, Christopher, what I want to talk to you about is, first, Freshler Feld as a community and, after that, your situation."

Kersten, I don't know what you know or what you don't know, but I've been thinking a lot about things lately . . . When he had called her, she had said that she would of course meet him at his apartment, and she was waiting for him on the street, the handle of a plastic bag gripped two-handed, when he arrived. At that sight, he called the whole thing off. She was innocent and beautiful and ignorant—and nice. But when she got on her tiptoes to kiss him, her eyelashes practically fluttering, her smile wide and somehow grotesque, he backed away slightly, cringing. Their lips barely brushed, and Kelch steeled himself. She had brought dinner and they were then on the couch, and as Kelch's chopsticks, overworking, indented a salmon roll, the makes-no-sense utensil, the rawfuckingfish (as Dan called it, one word), the furniture in the apartment, her little-girl exclamation that the restaurant was amazing, everything in his closing-in life agreed that the momentum was undeniable. She was to blame, and if he didn't get out of it now, how could he ever reclaim being right? She asked, seemingly more interested in the food, What does that mean? *It means that I've realized that what I do is*—there was a sensuousness, a taste, as he said it—*bullshit.* Full-mouthed: okay. *It's like—I've been thinking—that my whole life is like a bubble. A: I don't do anything interesting or, you know, useful. And B: I can be so much more.* Kersten had set her chopsticks down on the plate—she had made them use plates—and held the dish on her lap with both hands to keep it from flying to the ceiling. *Every fucking day of—sorry—every day of my life is nothing but cell phones and e-mails and whisper numbers and voice mail— If I have to leave another voice mail, I'm going to go nuts.* I know your job stresses you out sometimes, but that's what I'm—*Just let me talk, okay. It's not just my job. It's everything about my life.* Chris, she said, with the first trembles, high-pitched. *Everything.*

"Christopher, I've been proud of what the firm has been able to accomplish over the last eight years. I've been with Freshler Feld for two decades, and, obviously, I've been proud of it every day. But I think it would be fair to say that Freshler Feld eight years ago was not in the same competitive position as Freshler Feld today." Eight years ago, a New York tabloid had winked, "Gendel Out, Gentile In." Blue was the first un-Semitic chief. (Gendel had been forced out after the Lancaster County mess.) "To be honest, though, the prime factor that has enabled our recent success is the same factor that has been the dominant trait of Freshler Feld for eighty years: community." These words were familiar to Kelch in their exterior shape, in their repeated stamp on annual reports and employee minds, but as Blue plugged them straight into Kelch's consciousness, Kelch found them uniquely, originally compelling. "Let's be frank, Christopher. What separates Freshler Feld from other financial services firms? Are our systems more advanced? Maybe. Is our organization more streamlined? Not particularly. Are our business processes more developed? Debatable. Are our *people* smarter or harder working? Well, on the margin, probably, but there are a lot of very good people working in the financial services industry who are not lucky enough to work for a firm like Freshler Feld. So what is it? It's our *culture*, and our culture is based on the concept of *community*. Those online boys are only picking up on this now. Let me tell you something. At some of the other firms in the industry, the professionals are remarkably fractious and self-absorbed. Is this because they are somehow worse"—Blue held his mouth around the *s*—"people? Of course not. It's because the cultures of their firms encourage that argumentative mean-spiritedness. The culture of our firm encourages the opposite, or so I hope: a sense of community, the sense that you, for example, can pick up the phone and call a fellow analyst in Tokyo or a senior banker right here in New York and expect him or her to help you. More so, be eager to help you because they know that you are equally dedicated to the firm's success and that you are calling them for corporate, not personal, gain."

True, Blue's light touch was irresistible, and Kelch believed Blue's words because Blue believed those words—Kelch had seen enough to know that Freshler was quite possibly the best place to work on the Street—but Kelch's mind was still waking, or forming, or healing, or dissolving a syrupy fog of morning.

"It requires constant diligence to foster a culture of community, Christopher. One way I do it is by empowering all my coll— Is there something you want to say, Chuck?" Blue's brow, for a moment, bent hard into itself. "Then I will continue." Pause pressed; press play. "One way I do it is by empowering my colleagues and continuously demonstrating my trust in them. I also make an extraordinary effort to get to know the young professionals at the firm. I also take a personal interest in any action by anyone at Freshler Feld that does, or has the potential to do, serious damage to our sense of community." He waited for two seconds. "Christopher, you did not just damage your own professional reputation in talking to this magazine. You damaged the fabric of this firm. Is that damage irreparable? Probably not. Nevertheless, it is my job to make sure that the firm's hard-won culture of community is not damaged at all. Ever." He leaned slightly forward and recited the next sentence. "A firm's culture, I like to say, is like a sheet of ice: stable but fragile."

Kelch nodded.

"I am not going to insist on an answer as to why you chose to cooperate with"—Blue brought back the file and opened it—"Paul Galicia. That, frankly, was your decision. But I hope that you will understand why we must take actions, including this meeting, to ensure that this article does not do any more damage to the firm's resources—and the culture of community is just that, an invaluable resource—than it already has the potential to do." Kelch listened to his own breathing; each exhale was copying itself in heartbeats. "It contained some awfully vicious things about the firm."

Livin's voice washed over Kelch's back. "He claimed . . ."

"What are you referring to? Oh there, yes: 'He claimed to have never personally misled investors about a stock to protect a banking relationship.' Actually, Chuck," Blue noted, as if thinking aloud, "that's more your area. Let's see. . . . Here: 'Scott refuses to accept any criticisms of the aggressive profit drive and merciless strategy of his firm.' *That* is the type of characterization, in fact, this 'merciless strategy' garbage, that I object to, Scott." The room became more clear-edged, alive. Kelch now could account for all his senses and hear Blue over the whole audible range. "Is our firm in any way merciless or unacceptably aggressive? Of course not. To the contrary, our work is consistently *beneficial* to our clients, helping them to achieve all their objectives in the capital markets. Isn't that actually closer to the truth?"

"I-I-I."

"Yes?"

"I mean, yes, I guess."

Kelch did not speculate for whom Blue meant his subsequent "Hmm." Blue placed the closed folder to his side.

Although Kelch had read the words of the article, they had never passed into a memory of real life lived. They were false; then they were true; that was enough. Blue's recital now was an abstraction of an abstraction, a fun-house mirror where *it wasn't me* and *it was me* became laughing, rope-skipping, clothes-matching twins. Last night, Kelch had promised himself that it would be better in the morning.

Blue rose and rolled his chair back under his desk. He paused to pick a piece of lint off the chair (or so the action implied; Kelch couldn't see any lint). With his back to Kelch, he took four paces to the window and stared out over the crowns of the lesser skyscrapers, into the harbor's faint painted backdrop. His hands were clasped behind him; the stance, it was clear, was reflection. "Your situation reminds me of a similar situation that happened to me four years ago—"

Livin: "Three."

"Three and a half or so years ago, I was profiled in the *Times* Sunday magazine. And while the reporter was generally, I suppose, fair"—Kelch had read the article (everyone had read the article), and the reporter was fawning, acolytic—"she did take her shot by ridiculing my speech to the new junior analysts." The writer's shot was a BB. Who wouldn't, she asked, think that a job at Freshler Feld was "the greatest job in the world" if one was powerful, universally admired, good looking, and exorbitantly compensated? "You know how I decided to respond to the attack? I turned it around. I embraced it." Kelch knew this too: a CEO is a small-town mayor, a colonial high commissioner. "I decided that if I was going to be made fun of for offhandedly referring to a job at Freshler Feld— not just my job, by the way—as the greatest job in the world, then I would no longer refer to it offhandedly. I would make it the centerpiece of my convocations to new hires and promotes. For I do genuinely believe that a career in finance, and at Freshler Feld in particular, is the greatest job in the world. Just consider it: the culture of community, intellect, merit, and drive; the opportunity to

analyze, advise, and influence companies, economies, and govern-
ments at the highest levels; the ability to provide capital for corporate growth *and* capital appreciation for investors; the daily,
diverse, sometimes daunting challenges offering you the chance to
test your mettle every single day. The global opportunities our industry now avails to young people just out of college or business school
are truly incredible compared to those when I began in the business.
To be on a first-name basis with the CEO of a Fortune 500 company. To facilitate a billion-dollar block trade. I'm jealous of you
young people."

Kelch's buried pulses revived. *I know this. I've heard this. I know.*
He tried to resist looking over his shoulder at Livin. Failing, turning,
his held breath popped quietly free. Livin was reading one of the
magazines from Blue's coffee table, and Kelch waited for Livin's eyes
to rise to meet his—Blue was still lecturing the harbor—but Livin
remained casually absorbed in his reading. Kelch then whiplashed
his head over his other shoulder, and as a migraine warning hinted
behind his brow, he searched for the other person who must have
been audiencing for Blue, from another shooter's seat. This was
going to end badly: he didn't want to be here anymore. "Is there
anything more interesting than to see how these cycles turn?" Blue
continued as he returned to his desk. "Fifteen years ago, everyone
wanted to be an arbitrageur and the press was obsessed with the
evils of arbitrage. Five years ago, it was derivatives. Now, it's equity
research." He pulled out his seat, and after leaning over to dust it
off with a hand-broom sweep, he sat down, his face fixed again on
Kelch's, his eyes lowering only briefly to inspect his hand for transferred dirt. "But let's look at the facts a second. Chuck?" Kelch
followed Blue's eyes. Livin nodded, uncaught. "Good. I have a few
more minutes. . . . I began my career in corporate finance, of course.
But do you know where I, knowing what I now know about the
industry, would perhaps choose to work if I could start my career
over again . . . ? Equity research. Absolutely." *Please. I don't want to
hear about it anymore.* I don't care if you're going to take my job

yourself. "Because what could possibly be more exciting than to be the keystone in the efficient distribution of equity capital?"

Nothing.

"That's right. Nothing. You worked for Veena Gupta for three years, correct?"

From high chest, heart-attack country: "Uh-huh."

"And now you are one of the most highly respected voices on your industry sector in the world. With little formal training, with only your intellect and merit and drive, with your quantitative and qualitative capacities to judge strategies and people and markets, and of course with the Freshler Feld community behind you, you have built an enviable personal franchise. What an experience you've had, earning the trust of your clients"—*please, it was me*—"winning the confidence of the companies you cover"—*I confess, I betrayed*—"seeing your heart broken by a stock one day and your predictions vindicated the next. That's not even taking into account the secondary benefits. The global travel. The rewards from mentoring young people into the business. The compensation." Blue didn't wink, but the left side of his face curved up, winkishly. "We work very hard in this industry, and I don't think anyone could fairly accuse us of not earning our compensation, but it would be silly not to admit that a lot of people in this country work hard and don't get four hundred and fifty thousand dollars in total comp. But do you know what I consider the most enviable benefit of being a research analyst? The freedom. When I ran San Francisco"—Blue had conquered northern California and the Pacific Northwest for the firm—"some of the younger professionals in the investment-banking division expressed what we thought of then as impatience about their more structured career trajectories. They all wished—they still wish—to have had more latitude and *al*titude and input into the business. They were, frankly, somewhat jealous of you research analysts." If Blue weren't Blue—if he were David Kim, for instance— Kelch could have argued the opposite case, on the bits, but Blue's vision, coming from Blue, was a naked woman, overwhelming and irrefutable. Kelch couldn't listen to this now. He had rid himself of much, in triumph. "You analysts have a freedom in your career management, in your opinions, in how you choose to market your franchise, that one would be hard-pressed"—*I'm hard-pressed*—"to find elsewhere in the financial services industry, or any industry for that matter."

Kelch's body was an asystolic tomb, its ticktock canceled. The in-chest fist, it seemed, had turned on itself. Other fists had joined in, concentric nesting dolls: a fist clutched the in-chest through his porous skin—he could feel the penetration—and the in-chest clutched his heart, whose own heart fingers squeezed his last min-nowlike droplets of blood.

You wasted a year of my life. How can you say it was a waste? *I can say it because it's true, you fucking fucker.* Calm down, Kersten, just calm down, okay. *Calm down? How dare— I should have just listened to everyone when they told me that you were going to be a waste.* Huh? *Everyone told me that you were too-too—* Too what? *Too everything: too quiet and too boring and too immature and too one-dimensional and too-too—too Wall Street.* Who told you that, Marigold? *Marigold and my brothers and, I don't know, and everyone. And they didn't even have to tell me. I already—* She screamed, a train-whistle scream, and her eyelids crushed together, sealing themselves for erasure, as she clenched her hands into tiny thumping mallets. She yelled again, *How dare you.* She paused and added, *You shit.* I got your point, he said. You can stop being melodramatic. (He thought, People can hear you through the walls.) *Melodramatic? You lied to me for a year and you accuse me of being melodramatic.* See, Kersten, that is exactly what I was talking about, that we're just different kinds of—(he realized as he began that he had lifted the wrong foot, but he took the step anyway)—different kinds of people. *That's not what you said at all. You said that this was about you. You said that it was about changing your life so you wouldn't be a "bubble"*—she spat the word, viperous—*or whatever you think you are. You said it had nothing to do with me . . .* Hey, Kersten, we tried, I mean, listen—*Why don't you just keep your mouth fucking shut like it usually is. . . . I tried to ignore—change—I don't know, but* *everyone's right: you can't change anyone.* She paused later, in the eye of her anger. *I don't ask for much, do I? I'm not unreasonable in thinking* *that I have a lot to give someone? I'm not crazy in thinking that I'm a good* *and caring person and that I could make a really nice life with someone?* No, this has nothing to do— Her palms, parallel, began moving up and down, Japanese, wildly. *Stop saying that. Stop it. Stop it. Stop it.* *Twice in one year, damnit. You hear me, twice in one year. So. Do. Not.* *Tell. Me. This. Isn't. About. Me. Because it's about me or it's about an* *entire city where every man thinks he can dismiss you like you're his god-* *damned secretary and, and, and where every man is so fu-fucking blind that* *they have no idea what they have right in front of their face and who, who,* *who—how dare you—waits a year to reveal their true colors.* He listened closely to the last phrase, seemed to hear it in clearer isolation. He asked, What did you say? *Reveal your true colors, you fucking jerk.* Is this about the article? *What article?*

In the world to come, he had thought, sincerity and love would be the air's floral smell, and truth would be the quark of every atom. In the world to come, he had thought, Chris Kelch would finally be Chris Kelch: free and filled and whole and good and home and home and home.

Blue quietly brought the file nearer to him. He opened it, and his attention detached itself from Kelch for a blink. "Much of the misinformation in this article is easily refutable. Seriously, how often do we read about the corruption of research analysts?"

Nothing.

"Yes?"

Kelch barely heard anything as armies in both ears tried to reinforce the barricades with wax: the clogging, the exhaustion, the blur was making its return. "Um, often."

"Exactly," Blue continued, unmindful. "We hear about it too often. The public discussion of this issue is tremendously unfair. We have done study after study of our buy-side client needs. Do you know what every single study says? Our clients want *more* research, better research, more analysts. They want so much more that we have to limit our research product to protect our own margins. There are simply too many shares, too many competitive pressures, and too much uncertainty for an asset manager to run even a small-sized portfolio nowadays without leaning heavily on the insight and information provided by the sell side. Do you think our clients would pay us the commissions they do, rewarding us explicitly for the quality of our research, if they didn't find sell-side research irreplaceable? Of course not. Just talk to your colleagues at Freshler Feld Asset Management. They'll echo everything I'm saying."

Stop already, Kelch thought, the thought crippled, hunchbacked by his missing sleep, by last night's taste in his deserted mouth.

"Now, as far as the supposed conflicts of interest of research departments, we both know the answer to that charge. For what is the most noticeable impact of participation in the investment banking process on your average analyst? It makes him or her a better analyst by giving him deep exposure to a company's management and allowing him to interface with some of the world's leading M&A experts. And, to be frank, without a robust banking business, a firm could not afford the most insightful analysts, who gravitate to the firms that can meet their compensation expectations. Of course, any good research analyst is sensitive to the commercial implications of his or her ratings, but complicated clients don't mean compromised clients. Decent analysts are sensitive to management reaction—I've tried innumerable times to impress this on the boys at the SEC—whether *or not* a company is an investment banking client of the firm. All we ask of our analysts is that they be respectful to corporate leaders who are all very accomplished and are all sincerely trying their best to create shareholder value. I do not see how our critics can expect us to erect an arch between capital sources and capital needs without using our world-class experts to ensure that everyone is treated fairly. As you know, Scott, America has the most open, efficient, and healthy capital markets in the world. How could we enjoy those markets if we, collectively, were intellectually lazy or dishonest or even in any way inefficient in processing and distributing information?" Blue leaned back in the chair, his hands flat against his desk; he spoke to the rows behind Kelch, keeping Kelch in the line of grace. "Have you ever studied up close inefficient capital markets? They break your heart. Bad businesses thrive. Good businesses are stillborn. Cronyism reigns. And *no one* wins. Investors, over the long term, don't make money. And worthy companies' cost of capital is exorbitant, hindering their ability to compete in the global marketplace. One could make a strong argument that our country's efficient, broad-based markets are our most important comparative advantage. And who are the key players—the intellectual capital, if you will—in our system, which is the envy of the world? Research analysts, of course." Blue glanced at Livin before continuing his sermon, selling justification by faith. "I've been in this business when research departments were smaller and less sophisticated. No one can tell me that the system is less fair today."

Kelch had to disagree; he could disagree: he was running into the countryside, and disagreement demanded only that he keep his head straight. But, breaking, he turned around and looked back at Blue. Twelve hours ago, it had all been so clear, that he was right, that the article was good, that Blue was ... That Blue was ... Kelch *had* to disagree. His knees began to bounce, buoys in a wave storm.

"Net-net, of course, the greatest beneficiaries of the capital markets in this country have been the investors. You may not know what it's like out there, but for a working family to know that its retirement savings will allow it, unexpectedly, to buy a boat, a small vacation home, or even a golden anniversary cruise, or for that family to know that its son or daughter's college fund has appreciated enough so that the son or daughter will be able to attend the schools that we all profited from—those are tangible, wonderful dreams coming true. For real people. What other industry can say that they make dreams come true? And not just the dreams of the so-called upper classes: half the country has direct exposure to the equity market, and the other half certainly benefits from it in diverse ways.

You should talk to some of them, the middle-class working American families out there, and ask them what they think of the stock market. I guarantee that you will never have any doubts about what we do here again. You should especially talk to the more sophisticated individual investors who know how the sell side helps—in many ways, enables—their asset managers to provide capital appreciation. These people are *extremely* grateful for what we do here. We've done studies about this. It's true."

It's true, okay. It's done, okay. It's over, it's fine, I'm Scott. Just let me up.

"People ask me all the time, Do I find my job fulfilling? You probably find that a funny question, but I enjoy being asked that because then I can respond, Every moment of the day. Because, without any glory, we in this industry lay the foundation for the economy to prosper and grow, for entrepreneurs to see their businesses take flight and their hard work rewarded, for investors to accomplish their lifetime financial goals."

She was standing at the window, facing outside, a cloud over the potted violet she had bought (and taken care of). He had tried, once, to put his hands on her shoulders. He had half-intended his gesture to be reassurance, as friends, that everything without him would be fine; the other half had been a test of her fixedness, a rocking of a refrigerator to see if it would move. She was not to be reassured, and she would not move. Hissed: *don't . . . touch . . . me.* He went to the other side of the room, continuing to stand at first, but when she remained a temple's column, her eyes staring into the yellow black of the street's ambient-lit midnight, her fingertips caressing a violet petal, surprisingly gently, Kelch sat down and waited and watched. She was never going to leave. And her resigned shoulders said that she was never again going to talk or plead or shout or cry. After five minutes—they seemed like five hours—Kelch rose from the couch and asked her once more if he could do anything. Nothing. He asked her if she wanted to be alone. Nothing. She just stood there, locked, reminding, accusing with her tearless silence. He wanted to say, Let's communicate, or something like that, to restart time, but he watched, not speaking, his throat constricted, as she plucked off a petal and let it drop to the floor. Are you sure, he asked stupidly, that I can't do anything? He knew that they both knew the only answer to that question, one supplied before thought, from an unconscious pool: haven't you done enough already?

Well, then I'm going to— Where could he go? It was his apartment. *Then I'm just*—

And he decided to hide out in his bedroom. He had been calm with Kersten because he had to be: the conversation didn't make sense any other way. But that strategic calm seemed to have soaked into his bloodstream. There were still no machine-gun heartbeats, no scratching, frenzied ideas, no second thoughts. He shut the door behind him and listened for her to leave, to break out in unstoppable wails, to smash his television against the floor. But, lying like a wooden plank on his bed, his shoes still on, listening so hard that sounds were invented, he heard nothing, for minutes, then for a half hour. Finally, he heard steps and the apartment door unlocking, opening, closing, without the hysterics of a slam. He held his breath, unsure, and cautiously opened the bedroom door, anticipating an ambush. She was not there, it appeared, and he gingerly verified this in the bathroom, behind the curtains, under the couch, in the cupboards. He searched for her ghost, or her mark, an impression of revenge, repercussions, punishment, an end. She had dropped a few more violets to the floor. He moved—really only motioned—toward them to clean them up, but his reflection was caught by the window, defenseless against a sniper snare from below. He sat on his couch instead and turned on the TV. As he flipped from station to station, the sound muted, the images soothing and boundless in their fluid disappearance and revolution, he asked himself, finally, what he thought about all of this.

He was alone.

Mission accomplished.

But a half million dollars—it had never come up.

Kelch shut his eyes and held on to his breath. He knew that if he exhaled, the carbon dioxide wouldn't come out as relief but as smog, as shaking—as collapse. He had said it first. She had been the first. He must have meant something then. He hadn't meant anything now. It had been momentum, dirty, stupid— What more did he want out of life— She was the nicest and most caring person he was ever— Kelch opened his eyes and stared harder at the TV, overruling any muscles in his face, preempting any shudders. He knew then, or at least sensed then, that the only heroism he had— had ever had—was the heroism not to break.

"And so," Blue continued, "I wonder if the only *real* criticism they have, then, is that a research analyst is not omniscient. But does anyone who knows our industry really expect that an analyst operating only with the limited, publicly available information at his or her disposal will be able, every time, to recognize minute changes in the financial performance of a company when company management with *all* the data is unable to do so? It's a minor miracle that analysts are ever— What?" Kelch felt Livin standing up behind him. Blue answered Livin's unspoken prompt. "Okay, Chuck." Turning to Kelch: "So I hope that helps put the issues in clearer perspective for you. . . . Just to summarize: first, Freshler Feld's culture of community is the key to our success; second, our culture of community must be protected and nurtured; and third, it would be difficult to dispute that this community—what we do here at Freshler Feld—is truly a wonderful, beneficial, *worthy* way to spend a life." He stood up smoothly—no Tedeschi rocking—and offered his hand. "I'm glad we could have this discussion."

Kelch's first attempt to stand, by will and levitation, failed. He pushed his hands on the armrest to try again. This couldn't be over. It didn't make any sense, and he was done, in this life, with things that didn't make sense.

Blue watched him rise, inexpressive. "Chuck will see you out. Thanks again."

It came out, word on top of word, in one mouthful. "But what's going to happen to me?"

Blue's head rose ten degrees. He pressed his finger to his temple. "Good question. I thought I had made it clear."

Kelch's face, on the borderland between smiling and sick, hung open for an answer.

"Well, Jim Frederic's office"—the general counsel's office—"has some documents that they will need you to sign to protect the firm in case of further action, but frankly I can't foresee those documents ever really coming into play."

"Um . . . but . . ."

Livin, holding the Kelch file in front of his belt, stepped closer. "Nothing's happening to you, Chris. Blue wanted to do it this way."

You can't do this. I've *quit.*

Blue smiled and shook his head, sheepish at his own forgetfulness. "Right, right. I've glanced at your reviews, Chris. I've looked at the analyst poll results. In a very short time, you have established a remarkable career at Freshler Feld, which means to me that you are a remarkable person." Kelch swallowed. "I don't think that Freshler Feld can afford to lose you, especially in this hiring environment. Hoder Leary understands this too." Blue altered his tone slightly, a precise sanding and shaving, as if being recorded. "Now I have as much respect for Joe Tedeschi as any person in this firm—Chuck has heard me say that a thousand times—and I think that you would be hard-pressed to find anyone who has contributed more to Freshler Feld's success over the last twenty years. Nonetheless, Joe doesn't always prefer to take the easiest, and in this case the most pleasant, route out of situations. But there are still advantages to being the chief." He raised his eyebrows, mainly to Livin.

"But I—"

With the file in his lead hand, Livin pointed to the door. "Chris, Blue has an important meeting scheduled to begin in three minutes. We can continue this outside."

"Thanks for stopping by," Blue said again. "I always enjoy the opportunity to talk to the young professionals at the firm." Livin continued to point to the door, and with his other arm near but not touching Kelch's back, he steered him forward. When they reached the door, Kelch rotated slightly for a final look at Blue. Already on the phone, Blue had moved the closed file to the far side of his desk.

Livin shut the door behind them. Fifty-two had awakened more while they were in Blue's office. Another of Blue's secretaries had reported for duty, as had others' assistants, now warming up the floor. Kelch noticed Freshler's CFO standing in a doorway, apparently delivering the first instructions of the morning. Livin absorbed in his own rhythm the faster-percolating energy of the rising day. "Judy," he addressed the recently arrived secretary. "Can you let Henry Kwan know that the meeting will begin, miracle of miracles, on schedule." And to the other secretary, almost immediately, he said, "Carol, can you escort Mr. Kelch back to the lobby." Livin regarded the file in his hand, made a visible mental note, and put his arm out to Kelch's side to clear room, ostensibly, for his path to his office. Kelch watched him take three steps.

Livin turned around abruptly. "I almost forgot." He was busy, busy, busy. "Carol will show you to the lobby, but before you go, let's make sure we're all on the same page."

Kelch heard Blue's commandments, echoing. But the heroism of living could create a fill and a mass. Hollowness—right?—was only a word. Kelch couldn't lose again. He had made a decision. He had *done* things. Once, for a moment, he had felt good, unassaulted. At six-fifteen, when he was a boy, there were two more hours of summer daylight, of playtime, of immortality. *Hello, Miko. Hello, Mark. Hello, Steven. Hello, Rob.*

"Someone from Jim Frederic's office will speak to you about the documents that Blue mentioned. Probably this afternoon. Standard stuff. All off the shelf."

Ten months ago, in Kathy Guizeta's office, Kelch had spread his model across her desk and explained how Tee-Fog's effective tax rate would not increase for the next two years. She was hung up on the idea that this would affect only the company's cash flow. Kelch leaned in closer and, slowly, fatherly, guided her to understand how, in this case, it would affect both the cash flow and income statement. Eventually, on the third pass, she looked up, nodding—their heads were now only two feet apart—and her eyes, chestnut-colored, gleamed in appreciation. *Oh, now I get it. That's really interesting.* Kathy's blouse was fashionably open at her neck. She smelled like peaches.

Livin held the folder by its spine, and it nodded, matching his emphasis. "It's probably best if you direct any follow-up questions to the person who contacts you. However, if absolutely necessary, you can give me a call."

Hello, Kathy. Hello, Leigh. Hello, Erik. Hello, Carl. This is Chris Kelch at Freshler Feld. Three things strike me about Allencor's 1Q. A and B and C.

Transferring the file from his right hand to his left, Livin fist-cracked his knuckles and offered his hand to Kelch in departure. "It always amazes me how, in the little things, the man always does what's right."

Hello, Sanjat. Hello, Frank. Hello, Kersten. Hello, Scott.

Kelch didn't notice the hand to shake it until it was too late, and Livin brought it back to his side, clenching and opening it again, apparently encouraging its circulation. "So look for those documents. And thanks again for stopping by." He walked to his office. At his doorway, he turned around again and smiled, closed-lipped, at Kelch.

Kelch was frozen. This was all he had ever wanted to be.

Livin said, "That was harmless, right?" and then disappeared, shutting the door most of the way.

Time was knotted, the ends perhaps staring at each other; at the center of every machine lies the vacuum that is faith. Maybe this was the world to come. Or maybe it was just the happiness of the concussion, a workaday sensation compared to a knockout's dumb bliss.

Listen:

Carol had moved around her desk and was waiting three steps away from Kelch, in the direction of the lobby. She was in her early thirties, shruggingly attractive; her hair was bottle-blonded, her figure neat, and her olive eyes in the false office light suggested gray. She led with an open-palmed hand, as Livin had done, and smiled. "Shall we?" she asked, almost as if she were asking him to dance.